LIGHTNESS
FALLING

LIGHTNESS SAGA

BOOK 2

STACEY MARIE BROWN

Copyright © 2017 Stacey Marie Brown
All rights reserved.
Cover by Dane at Ebook Launch (https://ebooklaunch.com/ebook-cover-design/)
Developmental Editor Jordan Rosenfeld (http://jordanrosenfeld.net)
Edited by Hollie (www.hollietheeditor.com)

ALSO BY STACEY MARIE BROWN

Darkness of Light
(Darkness Series #1)

Fire in the Darkness
(Darkness Series #2)

Beast in the Darkness
(An Elighan Dragen Novelette)

Dwellers of Darkness
(Darkness Series #3)

Blood Beyond Darkness
(Darkness Series #4)

West
(A Darkness Series Novel)

City in Embers
(Collector Series #1)

The Barrier Between
(Collector Series #2)

Across the Divide
(Collector Series #3)

From Burning Ashes
(Collector Series #4)

The Crown of Light
(Lightness Saga #1)

Crown of Light

To my readers:

Meet me around the corner in back for the next one.

Love,

Your dealer

ONE

Red eyes glowed through the darkness. Patchwork faces opened their mouths, displaying bloodied daggered teeth. Shrill roars cried out into the icy night while mist billowed from their lips. Hundreds of monsters lined up at the edge of the forest, growling and shrieking with war cries and stomping their feet in a terrifying beat.

Fear sat on my chest like barbells, pressing my feet into the earth. *Strighoul.*

Two stood in front of me, one whose broken front teeth gave his ghoulish appearance an even more alarming cast. He settled a step behind the other and bounced on his toes like he wanted to inch forward and take the lead. I knew the man in charge. He had been close to tasting my flesh once before.

Hovek.

Still dressed in a faux fur vest with a worn long-sleeved shirt, Bermuda shorts, and cowboy boots, he took the role of leader with a smug grin.

"Come out, come out," Hovek taunted, his red irises burning right through me. He snapped his fingers at the toothless strighoul. "This one may not give us much power, but we will enjoy her just the same."

It took me a moment to see Toothless was gripping a person. Her stout but short frame stumbled forward as he yanked her in front of him. A gasp caught in my throat.

"Marguerite!" I screamed and lurched toward the woman. Her silvering hair was neatly styled, and her normal smock was replaced with a flowery dress, long coat, and small-heeled shoes. Her Sunday outfit.

Stuck deep in the mud, I couldn't budge to move near the woman we had all grown to love like a grandmother.

Her face was set in an angry line, and her eyes glared up defiantly at the strighoul.

"If you harm her in any way." A deep voice rang out behind me, and I twisted to look. "I will personally see every one of you gutted, drawn, and burned alive."

Tall, broad, and sexy, with jet-black hair, olive skin, and eyes black as night, Lars took a step toward the border of his property. Rimmon and Goran were right behind him. Normally his irises were an intense yellow-green color, which could pierce you with a glance, and have you on your knees groveling. The dark pits meant we were well past that. Fury pumped off the Unseelie King, choking the air with his magic. Lars was protective of his own, and we all knew how special

Marguerite was to him, the one human he truly let get to know his heart. She had been with him since her childhood and had become the foundation of his home.

"You shouldn't let your things run free then." Hovek took her from Toothless, pulling her into him. "All alone on the bus. Poor lamb."

"*¡Pinche idiota!*" Marguerite barked at Hovek, wiggling in his grip, looking more pissed than scared.

"Don't we have a feisty señorita here?" Hovek's lips split in an unnatural smile. "She will be like a fiesta in my mouth. Crack her open like a piñata." Hovek leaned over, his gray slimy tongue trailed up the side of her face, his gaze still on Lars. Marguerite fought against him, but it only put a bigger smile on Hovek's face.

"I warned you…" Lars growled, his eyes creasing, and the skin of his face paled as his toes bumped against the property line. Goran and Rimmon stepped forward ready to protect their King if he crossed the boundary. I knew all of Lars's men were there, hidden somewhere in the darkness, getting ready to protect their ruler.

"No," Hovek growled. "I'm here to warn *you*!" He pulled Marguerite into him. His long nails dug into her throat, and his hand squeezed down. Lars froze, seeing pain flinch across Marguerite's face. "Our current benefactor has a message. You back off, call home that dark dweller, or we…" Hovek eyed down the line of strighoul, waiting on his word. "You will get a fight, one even the almighty king can't stop."

"There isn't anything I cannot fight," Lars growled. "No one challenges my power."

"Oh, really?" Hovek let out a chuckle, the other strighoul joining him in a sinister chorus that chilled my bones. "We almost breached your walls last time. This time, now that I am leader, we have the magic to do it. We walk away if you agree to the terms, if not…you will be on the menu too. And how I have dreamed about tasting you."

Lars's face remained impassive. "Let her go."

"Nope, we get one parting gift. We don't work for free." Hovek's nails dug deeper, slicing Marguerite's neck. Trickles of blood pooled on her pretty dress.

Shards of terror pushed up through my inners like nettles, their stingers embedding deep in my lungs. I needed to stop this.

"Wake. Turn light on." A squawk came from a tree near me, whipping my head around. "Free from dream or all is lost. You can stop."

"Grimmel!" I exclaimed, spotting the black raven sitting on a limb, his head tilted. Wake? This was a dream? It felt so real. I glanced around again, realizing no one seemed to notice or acknowledge my presence.

Wake up, Kennedy! This is not real. Wake up, now! I screamed in my head. Nothing. If anything, I felt the vision cling on tighter, brushing the cool wind against my cheek.

"Help me. What do I do?"

"Told you."

"I can't wake up."

"Then lost in the land of dreams forever."

"Grimmel, please."

"Light has the power to shine, but keeps locked in a chest."

If I could ever figure out what the damn bird was talking about, I'm sure I'd have the answers to the great mysteries of life, but his words were as much an enigma as he was.

"Grimmel. Help Queen," he said.

"Yes, please help."

"Listen." He slanted his head the opposite way, his wings flapping. "Receive." Then he took off flying into the night, squawking loudly.

Hovek let out a wail, breaking my attention away from Grimmel. Hovek's mouth opened like a shark's. Hundreds of glistening needles dove down into Marguerite's neck. She screamed as he tore into her flesh. With a waggle of his head, he ripped her throat from her neck, and her body crumbled to the ground in a heap. Her eyes went wide and vacant. This expression hit me so deep all I could feel was bile rising in my throat.

Ian's image flashed before me first, then Jared's face enveloped the body, his head cranking toward me, lips parting, and blood dribbling down his chin. His eyes went white with death. "You'll always be mine..."

A scream drew up from my lungs, but Hovek's bellow stopped it.

"Now!" Hovek turned my gaze from Jared's grotesque expression to his. Gore slid from Hovek's teeth as he shouted at his troops.

Like a branch snapping, the tension splintered into pieces, bringing everyone to life. The strighoul leaped forward, their teeth clanking together in anticipation. Fireballs of green and red flew in the air like fireworks and rained down on the protective shield, tearing at its surface. Lars had been attacked only months after the war, but the shields had held and were able to fight them off. This time, the magic sizzled through the armor around the compound, shredding it like paper, the power burning away the so-called unbreakable fortress.

Lars, Goran, and Rimmon barreled across the boundary while Lars's other men leaped from the darkness with thunderous cries. The sound of bodies and weapons smashing into each other pounded my ears with a sharp tune, like a badly played cello or bagpipes.

Raindrops of magic ripped through the protected field, landing on my skin with a painful sizzle. A hiccup of fear shut my eyes briefly, and panic rose up the back of my throat. The vision touched me, breaking the third wall. I was no longer an observer; I was falling deeper and deeper in.

Kennedy, focus. You need to get out of here. Distress swirled my brain, and I fell to my knees, feeling the gush of the soft mud. A scream billowed up. *Anchor. I need an anchor.*

His face flashed into my head, but I quickly shoved it out. *No. I needed to find a way out.* I rocked back on my knees.

> 1.) This is not real.
> 2.) This is not real.
> 3.) This is not real.

The problem was it felt just as real as anything else. I could smell the pine-scented perfume of the forest and the musky damp dirt. I could hear the thudding of bodies in death. I could feel magic crackling over my skin.

My body shook as I gazed on Marguerite lying before me. Her eyes were open and dead, blood pooling from her mouth.

"Save me," her mouth moved.

I scrambled back, my head hitting a tree with a crack. Pain zoomed up my spine, knocking me flat on my back, blinking through the sharp sting. I stared at the sky as it burst to life with color. Half the shield had already torn away.

A black object circled above me. It took a moment to realize it was Grimmel, circling overhead like a vulture waiting for the final breath of its next meal.

I closed my eyes, the noise reducing down to only his continuous screeching. I focused on him, which allowed my body to soar up and glide along with his wings, the squawking growing louder till it pierced my eardrum.

Flash.

TWO

I shot up as a scream tore past my lips. My bones rattled with fear, and my heart pounded in my chest. The room around me was dark with only moonlight streaming through the curtain. A black raven zoomed past the window, shrieking a few times before it flew off into the night.

Was I still in a vision? Was this real? Images slid through my mind and choked the air from my throat. Sweat trailed down my brow. My visions had come less frequently since the war, but when I did have one, the recovery was horrendous. Each time it took me longer than the last to center myself.

"Majesty?" A man burst through the door, his huge blue eyes lighting up where his dark skin blended with the night. He held a raised sword. "What's wrong?"

All I saw was a weapon. *Threat*. With primal instinct, I scrambled out of the bed and sprinted for the glass doors leading outside.

"Majesty," the man yelled as I tore through the doors. "Sturt, she's heading out the back."

Ten steps out the door a huge red-headed man stepped around, his hands held out like he was trying to corner a wild animal.

Trapped.

Panic lathered in my veins like soap, bubbling and expanding. Something deep inside tickled my throat wanting to protect me, and words I didn't understand spoke in my ear. But in my gut I sensed their significance.

Attack. Kill.

Horror flushed through a part of my brain. *I don't hurt people*.

I bit down on my lip and kicked back, turning the other way when a woman came around the corner, blocking my escape.

Terror seized me, and I whirled seeing them approach me from all different angles. I had been here before. Surrounded. Strighoul. Warehouse. Death.

The unfamiliar terms continued to twitch at my throat, desperate to be uttered. The tangy flavor of blood slid over my taste buds as my teeth dug deeper into my lip, trying to hold the spell back. What was wrong with me? Where was this coming from? The malevolence churning in my stomach scared me as much as the people encircling me. I could no longer understand what was real or a dream. Visions no longer kept their distance. They were as real as my everyday life. They could touch me, hurt me...

"Majesty, it's us," the woman said. I was familiar with her dark chocolate skin, her violet eyes, and her black hair pulled back in a braid. Still, dread coursed through me, flowing out my pores in streaming sweat.

They all took another step forward, closing in on me. *No.* My heart fluttered against my chest, and stole more of my air. Fright clawed through my ribs, stretching out, spurring my legs to run. The person by the door had left a gap for me to get back inside, and I took it. Sprinting past him, I darted into the room, going for a door at the far wall.

I swung the door open, my brain registering it was a closet. A massive one but a dead end. I clawed through the hanging clothes, the garments shielding me from view and giving me a false sense of safety. I hit a corner and flipped around and pressed my back to it. I curled in a ball, my limbs trembling. I tucked my head down and rocked. My mouth moved, uttering, "Is it real?" over and over, needing an anchor.

The floor resonated with the sound of boots pounding into the room.

"Lea, go get Torin," a man with a Scottish accent said.

"The one night off he's given himself in months. He's going to be so furious with himself," the woman replied.

"He always is anyway." Another guy snorted, sounding like the first one who ran into my room.

My room? Was this mine?

The woman retreated while the rest kept guard. Tiny specks of understanding nipped at my conscious, but distress kept me locked in a ball, chanting. I needed something to moor me to reality.

A few minutes later, the thumping of feet echoed from down the hall, and a man ran into the room, along with the woman they had called Lea, and a tall brunette woman, her hair pulled back in a long ponytail.

"What's going on? What's wrong?" The moment the man spoke, I felt a dash of calm brush my shoulders, and the blackness inside dissolved. I knew that voice. I peeked out through the clothes.

Tall, broad, with piercing blue eyes and dark hair pulled back with a tie. He was gorgeous, but they all were here. Recognition flickered through my head.

"She woke up screaming. Rowlands came running in thinking she was being attacked. She freaked out and ran. She's been rocking in the corner, chanting his name over and over."

"*His* name?" Blue Eyes asked.

"The dweller's."

The dark-haired man frowned, rubbing his head. "Okay, I got it from here. Get back to your posts." The men and women nodded and headed out of the room. He clearly was the leader. Could he help me?

I knew I had to do something. Images itched at the back of my mind, wanting to tell me something. Fear and grief punctured my nerves like porcupine quills. Something horrible was going to happen.

"Georgia?" The guy grabbed the brunette's arm, the one he ran in with. "Update Thara when she returns from her errand. I'd like to see her and Castien first thing in the morning."

Castien. Thara. Another flood of awareness circled around those names. They both made me feel safe, warm, connected.

The girl nodded and slipped out of the room, shutting the door.

He turned to me. My eyes tracked him as he slowly moved to me.

"My lady?" His voice sounded calm and smooth. "Do you know where you are?"

I stayed quiet.

He walked up to me, squatting down. My back pressed against the wall.

"Are you all right, my lady?" he asked, his gaze rolling over me.

My lady. Yes, that felt familiar.

"Another vision?" He reached out to touch me, and I jerked back. Anchor. I needed my anchor though I couldn't recall what that was.

"Are you real?" I whispered.

"Yes. This is all real," he replied.

My head spun, more and more beads of understanding setting in.

What do you hear? A voice spoke in my head.

"I hear my pulse pounding in my chest." I rubbed my temple, tugging on my ear.

What do you smell? The deep voice came again.

"I smell leather and flowery shoe deodorizer." I took a deep breath, my heartbeat slowing.

What do you feel?

"I feel the soft rug between my toes." With one last long exhale, my brain clicked out of feral mode, cascading me back to reality.

My closet.

My castle.

Torin.

Vision.

"Oh god!" Breath tripped up in my throat, and I leaped up. "Lars! Marguerite!"

"Whoa." Torin grabbed me. "Slow down and tell me what's going on."

"What day is it?" I remembered Marguerite got Sundays off to visit her family, and she always wore her Sunday dress.

"It's Sunday."

It was dark, so was it either late Sunday or early Sunday morning? My brain couldn't remember.

"It's almost ten at night, my lady."

Right. I went to bed early with a headache.

"I need to talk to Lars." I tried to push past him, but he held me in place. "Let me go! They're going to be attacked by strighoul. Marguerite is going to be killed. I need to stop it!" If I remembered correctly, she usually returned to the compound around eleven after an evening dinner with a cousin.

"Sturt!" Torin whirled around, yelling. The tall ginger-haired man came instantly into the room. Now that I was in full capacity again, I knew his face. He was one of my personal guards.

"What?" Sturt burst in the room and looked around, ready for something to jump at him.

"Get word to Lars there is going to be an attack tonight on his compound. Marguerite is in danger."

Sturt's eyes whittled down in confusion. "What?"

"Don't question me. Go now!" Torin yelled. Sturt swiveled around and ran.

Shoving from Torin's grip, I followed, running to where we kept the private phone to Lars, which was more of a walkie-talkie. The fall of barriers between the Otherworld and Earth had destroyed a lot of technology. Some earth-made devices couldn't handle the abundance of magic thickening the air now and they fizzled out. Lars was a leader in developing new magic-resistant products like cars, airplanes, and phones.

Sturt was already speaking with Lars's new assistant. Since Rez's departure, Lars had gone through assistants like he did designer suits. Some lasted a day, some almost a week. This one had only been there a few days.

"I'm sorry, what do you want me to relay to the King?" The woman's voice sounded annoyed.

"You're going to be attacked," Sturt growled into the device.

"This compound is impenetrable. I highly doubt we have anything to worry about," her snooty tone clipped.

"Lady, if you don't hand me over to the King—"

I reached up, grabbing it from Sturt.

"Listen to me, this is the Queen. Get me Lars. Now!"

"Maj-Majesty. I apologize. If I had known—"

"I don't care! Lars. Now." I strangled the device, wishing it was the girl's neck.

The walkie-talkie went silent. I began to fidget as I waited for her to reach Lars. Would I be too late once again? Could I change what I saw, or was I always cursed to see what was coming and not prevent it?

The phone crackled. "Ms. Johnson?" Lars's familiar voice spoke over the airwaves. "What is wrong?"

"Lars, send someone to retrieve Marguerite. Now," I demanded. Lars was not one to be told what to do, but he also knew not to question a woman who could see the future.

"Goran!" I heard him shout. A bustling of feet came over the airwaves. "Get Marguerite. She's at Russell's. She likes to take the number ten bus back."

"Yes, sir," Goran replied. A door slammed.

"Lars?" I pushed the side button. "Get men to sweep the outer forest. Strighoul are going to attack the compound soon. Whatever magic they have, they are able to get through this time."

Lars bellowed for Rimmon, relaying what I told him to his frontline of defense. Rimmon was the size and build of a house. He never said, but I suspected he was half giant or ogre.

"Anything else, Ms. Johnson?" Lars's voice was brusque, but in complete control.

"*Don't* let them get Marguerite." I put a hand to my chest, which ached at the "memory" of her dead eyes in my vision. We had lost too many already. I really think Marguerite would tip us over, and for sure it would Lars. His clear love and respect for her were beyond reproach. Ember and Marguerite were the only two I knew who had the power to challenge Lars and get away with it.

"I won't let them get her," he replied firmly. "I'm indebted to you for this warning. I must go." With that the walkie-talkie shut off.

I hated not being there, not knowing if they would get Marguerite safely, or if I failed again. I stood there, the device clenched to my chest, the bones in my fingers aching at the pressure of my grip.

"My lady, there is nothing you can do now." Torin stepped up, prying the phone from my hands. Taking away my only tie to the King, my legs began to move. I paced across the room, twisting my hands until pain darted up my arms. I felt desperate and frantic to know what was going on. To be able to change at least one vision. I had no idea why Marguerite would take a bus, but I doubted it was because Lars wanted her to. She was one of the few he couldn't dominate. If she insisted she wanted to take the bus, she would.

"I will send some men over," Torin said softly, hooking the phone back in place. "They will report immediately what is going on."

"Thank you." I nodded, and my gaze went to his. I was so grateful for Torin. He seemed to know without a word what I needed.

"Order the troops stationed closest to the King's property to assist." Torin nodded to Sturt; the Scottish guard bowed and hurried out of the room.

"Majesty." Torin placed his hands gently on my shoulders, leading me out of the room and back down the hallway. He moved close to me, his tall muscular built comforting me with his nearness. He was also trying to block me from watching eyes. It was still early but as soon as people spotted their Queen running down the hallway in a T-shirt and underwear they clustered together, whispering in hushed tones.

I held my head high, ignoring the stares as Torin led me back to my rooms. Aneira, the former queen, had been off-her-rocker crazy, but I was the one who had them gossiping like a bad game of telephone. Fae had never liked Druids, but one who was also a powerful seer made them even more uncomfortable.

Lea and Rowlands were waiting at the door when we returned. It was their night to guard the crazy Queen. I liked them but didn't fully trust them yet like I did Torin, Castien, and Thara. They bowed when I passed, as Torin took me all the way into my chamber. After a year, I still hadn't bonded with this room. It felt foreign and impersonal.

I patrolled the door, not able to relax as we waited for word. Every second tripled in time. Even though it was Torin's night off, he still carried his walkie-talkie, ready to be called upon at a moment's notice.

A crackle came over the airwaves, making me jump, my heart in my throat. "Sir? This is Cyren, captain of the fourteenth."

"Report."

"Everything is clear. The strighoul had run off by the time we got there."

Air I didn't know I was holding flew out of my lungs.

"Whatever they were planning, the King's men stopped it. But the magic the strighoul were going to use to attack was powerful and strange. I never felt it before."

Strange?

"What about Marguerite?" I stepped forward, my hand plastered against my throat.

"The human woman? Any word on her?" Torin asked Cyren.

"Yes, I saw Goran taking her into the house. She was unharmed."

My legs bowed, and I leaned into the bed, weak with relief. *Thank goodness she's okay.* Joy filled my chest. *I stopped it.* I actually prevented a vision from happening for once.

"Thank you, Cyren. Head back to your post."

"Yes, sir." Torin clicked off the device and silence filled the room.

"You did it, my lady. You prevented the attack."

All the tension I'd been holding flowed out with a sob. I slid off the bed to the ground. My back rocked into the bed as I let go. I cried with relief because I had saved Marguerite's life, but it also let in a deeper grief: I hadn't been able to save my family, or Ian, or Jared.

Torin sat next to me and wrapped me in his arms. The warmth of him soothed my tense muscles, and I curled into his chest. He held me till the tears subsided, his hand rubbing my back in circles. Over the last year, he had become my friend, confidant, and security blanket. Being Queen was lonely and frightening. His support had become my lifeline, keeping me from drowning under the weight of my position. I didn't know what I'd do if he wasn't here.

I sighed, snuggling farther into his protective embrace. He tightened his hold, his chin tucking over my head. "Thank you," I whispered, pulling back just enough to peer up at him. Torin's blue eyes stared down, his eyes searching mine. We were so close, our mouths only inches apart. My heart squeezed, and I struggled to swallow. His eyes dipped down to my lips causing heat to flame up my neck into my cheeks. His fingers gripped my back tighter, his head leaning slightly toward me.

Holy nerf herder. Was Torin going to kiss me? Emotions I couldn't decipher thundered over me like a tidal wave. "I'm sorry." I jerked back, looking away, fear gripping my lungs in a vise. "You had a night off, and I ruined it."

"Don't ever apologize, my lady." His words were soft, intimate, spiking my heart to thump harder. "Not for that and not for earlier."

Earlier? Right. Another "episode." Now that I knew everything was all right with Marguerite and Lars, my previous breakdown came flooding back with the darkness I had felt inside. I could no longer recall the spell wanting to break free, disappearing as mysteriously as it came. I shoved it away, centering on what I did understand. "They must think I am a freak." I tapped my head on my knees.

"No. Unique maybe. They've never dealt with many Druids before. But we're all adjusting. And so are you, my lady."

"Adjusting?" I snorted. "Is that what this is? This place still doesn't feel like home. Not sure it ever will." Since I moved in, I tried to get rid of anything reminding me of Aneira, which was hard because this castle and pretty much everything in it represented her. I had no time to meet with someone to go over major renovations with my time spent on making sure my kingdom wasn't attacked or falling apart.

It had been fourteen months since my coronation as Queen, when Luuk had threatened us with an uprising. Luuk was a noble fae and very powerful, controlling half the European Seelie under Aneira. He had terrorized me at my coronation, claiming he would bring my reign to a quick end. His warning echoed daily in my head, not letting me forget. His face, because of his albinism, was also hard to forget. His threats hadn't happened overnight or in some big declaration of war. No, he was making his mark in smaller attacks: violence bombings at markets in Europe frequented by pro-Queen communities, or violence in places in America that promoted me as leader.

Was he behind tonight? Would Luuk go as low as hiring strighoul? Aneira had done it. Luuk was just as devious and crooked. I guess he would follow in her footsteps. And like all terrorists, he hid behind others actually doing the dirty work. He was excellent at taking claim for something then disappearing for months. The attacks were becoming more frequent, with more people joining the cause, and so far we had very few leads on him. Daily, I went round and round for hours only to end with nothing more than what we came to the table with. It was grueling and aggravating.

Torin's hand brushed mine, and I let him lace our fingers together. "I'm sorry you have to suffer those visions. It tears me apart how much they hurt you."

My head fell on his shoulder, taking solace in him. His friendship meant the world to me. I trusted only a core group here, but I went to Torin for everything. As my First Knight, we spent so much time together it was inevitable we would grow close.

I loved our time together and looked forward to spending the day with him. But I didn't know how I felt beyond that. He had given me plenty of signs he wanted more but didn't push. At first his feelings seemed to stem from gratitude because I gave him back his title, pride, and reason for being. The darkness in him altered after he became First Knight again, and he stared at me like I was his sun, beaming down on him, giving him life.

Then after nights and days of us talking and laughing, his stare grew hungrier, looking at me a bit different. I couldn't deny there were many times I thought about crossing that line. I had feelings for him, but I didn't know if they simply came from me being grateful to him. Besides the numerous times he already saved my life from attacks out on the street, he had given me laughter and comfort when I thought I could never feel happiness again due to so many things: Jared's and Owen's deaths, finding out my family had perished in the war, becoming a Queen who many hated...losing *him*...

"You better get some sleep." Torin squeezed my hand, getting to his feet. "You have an early morning tomorrow."

I sighed. At eight I was talking budgets, at ten a meeting about sending more men over to Europe to track Luuk's militia, and noon was about how to deal with the growing racial problem between fae and humans.

"Yeah. Sleep would be good." I nodded. He tugged me up, his fingers still intertwined in mine. I remained jittery from the vision and Marguerite's rescue, but the adrenaline slowly ebbed from me. Hopefully I would crash.

"Sleep well, my lady." He faced me, his frame towering over mine.

"Thank you again, Torin, for everything." I looked up at him.

He didn't step away, his body close to mine, tension beating in the space between us like a drum. The dark room shrouded us, creating a bubble of just him and me. "Always, my lady," he whispered. His gaze dropped again to my mouth.

This time I knew he was going to kiss me. I felt his form lean down a hair, freezing me in place. I wasn't sure if the terror I felt was because we were going to cross the line or if I wasn't ready. He inched closer, heat from his lips emanating against mine.

An image of blazing green eyes fired through my head like an arrow, wrenching my heart. My legs shot back, away from Torin, air sucking through my teeth. Awkward silence dripped like rain from the ceiling, drenching the room.

"Uh." I stared at Torin's chin, not able to meet his eyes. "I better get some sleep. Don't want to fall asleep in my meetings."

Hurt flicked so fast through Torin's face I wasn't sure if I saw it. He looked down, clearing his throat. "I will have a large coffee waiting for you first thing." He bowed his head, turning for the door. "Good night, my lady."

"Night." A rush of guilt tumbled around in my stomach at the sight of his deflated shoulders.

After what had happened between him and Ember, her choosing Eli instead of Torin, the last thing in the world I wanted to do was cause him pain. He was an amazing man, and I absolutely adored him. The more time we spent together, the more I realized we were alike: studying, lists, memorizing facts, always being prepared. We both reveled in order and precision. Granted, we wouldn't be an exceptionally impulsive couple, but we were certainly compatible. So what was my problem? What was stopping me?

I flopped on the bed, burying my head in my comforter. I could lie to myself all I wanted, but I knew what was blocking me. Or *who* caused me to skitter away from Torin like a mouse.

Torin didn't bring it up, but he knew I chanted *his* name when I was having one of my "episodes." Humiliating. I hadn't known I was doing it at first. His voice also filled my head at those terrifying moments, asking me the three questions, calming me down. The man who haunted my dreams and heart.

It had been sixteen months since he walked away from me in the tunnel. My coronation was the last time I'd seen him, and it had been so brief I still questioned if my mind made him up.

Overhearing conversations at the dweller ranch when I visited, I knew he was around, but none of the dwellers spoke of him to me, nor did I have the guts to ask. People in the castle liked to gossip, and I had heard he was making his way through every woman's bed he encountered. Even my employees.

Sneaking into the kitchen one night to get a snack, I walked in on two of the staff giggling and comparing notes over their "mind-blowing" encounter with the dweller. I almost vomited. Whirling around, I ran out of the room. *He can sleep with anyone he wants. I don't care.* But no matter what I told myself, nothing eased the deep ache in my heart, like fire irons branding lines across my chest. He was perfectly fine without me. Happy and back to his old ways.

I wasn't.

The memory of that night looped in my head, torturing me relentlessly. The cruel things I had said. The pain was so deep over Jared; I wanted someone else to hurt like I did. To feel the mercilessness of my agony. It was selfish and malicious because Lorcan was hurting just as much if not more over the loss of Jared. Not an hour went by I didn't internally flog myself for causing him more agony.

"Ken—"

"Shut up, there is nothing you can say. Nothing will make this right. We were selfish and cruel, and Jared is dead because of our actions. We. Killed. Him. What we did, I hate myself for it, for making such a huge mistake. I will never forgive myself...and I will never forgive you."

"You don't think I feel as guilty? That I'm not devastated? But what we did? It was not wrong or a mistake. I'm in love with you, Kennedy."

Those words haunted me, tormented me. I wanted to go into my memory and change what I said next. Have a different outcome.

"Remember when you said if you truly believed I wanted nothing to do with you, you'd walk away? Do you believe me now?"

"Yes," he murmured and turned away, striding out of the tunnel.

And out of my life. Forever.

~~~~

I still believed what I said to him. We caused nothing but pain and death to those around us. It was for the best. It would have never lasted anyway, but it didn't take away from the persistent yearning in my soul. I was constantly restless, never sitting too long, itching to move and find something to help. I roamed over this entire castle and grounds daily, never fulfilling the emptiness.

At first I had thought Jared haunted me, never letting me find peace. But I knew Jared was too good, too sweet, to ever wish me grief. Even when he was dying, he told me he loved me, knowing I had been with Lorcan. I ripped out his heart and set it on fire in front of him, and he still forgave me.

Only one person would take glee in torturing me, crushing me in his hand. I pulled my head up, staring out the doors to the moonlight glistening off the lake below. He was somewhere out there, screwing a woman and pounding a nail into my heart, not letting me move on.

"Damn you, Lorcan Dragen."

THREE

For the sixth time in a minute, I shifted in my chair, twisting a strand of long brown hair around my finger, tugging on it till my head ached. Taking deep breaths I tried to maintain my levelheaded exterior. But if one more cabinet member made another passive-aggressive remark right now about the way I was leading, I was going to scream.

The meetings had dragged on this morning with none actually coming to a conclusion anyone liked. The politics of this part of the job were awful. But this discussion, the problem with the hatred between races, was by far the most dreadful. All the people in my cabinet were fae, except me. They tended to be more understanding when fae attacked humans since they felt it was the fae's nature. But if it was the reverse? Then we needed to step in. Punish them.

Hypocrisy at its finest. This was when I wished I could get rid of them all and start over to make things a little more impartial. Just because I was Queen didn't mean I was fully in charge. I had the final say, but it took a lot of people to run a kingdom and put in the tiny fine print before I signed on the dotted line.

"It should have never gotten this far!" Kavan, a short noble with dark curly hair, deep tanned skin, and light violet eyes, stood and slammed his first on the table. "We need to show we are in control!"

"And how do you suggest we do that?" I crossed my legs, letting my hand fall from my hair. "I have my bounty hunters out handling what they can, but it is not easy to know when and where flare-ups will hit."

My bounty hunters were Ember and Eli. They had moved back to the dweller ranch after a near-death incident with West, another dark dweller, but they were barely ever home. Unfortunately, I had to keep sending them off to deal with outbreaks of fae or human attacks on each other. They were in Japan this week, dealing with a flare-up of Yokai, malevolent demons, who were assaulting the human locals.

"We attack first! We kill. They need to fear us, or they will keep acting out. Humans…and fae…" he added quickly. "Both need to know their place." He pinched his shoulders back.

"Attack who? Where?" I folded my hands on my lap, trying to keep from losing my temper. "We can't even pinpoint Luuk and where he will attack next."

"We need tougher laws. Random searches."

I leaned forward, trying to keep my mouth from dropping open. "Are you suggesting, Kavan, we stop and search people, arbitrarily?" Did they not learn from Earth's mistakes? Racial profiling was a nightmare that did not bring justice. It only separated the groups more, filling them with even more hatred and resentment.

"Yes."

My head snapped back to Torin, my jaw clenching.

It was subtle, but Torin had learned my signs. In a blink he took a step forward. "I am sorry to interrupt, but her Majesty is already late for her next appointment." He swiveled my chair for me to rise.

"Yes, I apologize. We will have to continue this another time." Maybe in a few years...or never.

Torin rushed me out of the room before they could even respond, his hand on my lower back. Thara waited outside and moved with us, bookending me as we walked down the hallway.

"Thank you," I muttered to him.

"I knew if I didn't get you out you would hex him or something." Torin grinned down at me.

"Can I do that?"

"Quite frowned upon, my lady." He rubbed my shoulder.

"So that's a soft no? Room for negotiation?" I peered up at him. A soft smile tugged on his mouth, his eyes roaming over me with amusement. But the humor flickered like a light switch when our eyes met, desire rolling through his like a storm. My head snapped forward, and I took a deep breath. "I need to get out of here."

"We can go to the gardens or take a walk in the forest if you want?" Torin offered.

"No. I need to get out of here completely. I feel like a rat in a cage. Just once today I need to feel I'm not a fraud, that I am doing something good." I tugged down my glasses and rubbed the space between my eyes. "I want to head to that children's center."

"The visit is scheduled for tomorrow, your grace," Thara replied next to me. Her long hair was swept up into a high ponytail, brushing her back as she swung her head. "You know you can't simply make unscheduled stops now."

"Why not?" I glanced back and forth between the two. "Isn't it better if it's spontaneous? Less threat, right?"

"Also less protection." Torin frowned.

"Just wait one more day," Thara encouraged. "Our meeting is all set for tomorrow at three."

The walls closed in on me, and the need to wander, to find whatever was missing in my heart, agitated my limbs.

"Please, if I don't get out of here…" I shook my hands out, itchy with pent-up frustration. I also needed to practice my magic soon; it was getting prickly under my skin. With all the business parts of my new job, I had little time and even fewer people to work with me on my magic. It had taken a backseat to all the other stuff, and it didn't like it at all.

Torin stared at me for a while, then sighed. "All right. I will have the first string in place in twenty minutes."

"What?" Thara exclaimed. "Torin, you know how dangerous it is. We should stick to the schedule."

"It is not our place to tell the Queen what to do. If she wants something, it is our job to make it work." He arched his eyebrow, an amused grin twitching his lips, like this was some inside joke passing between them. "Got it, soldier?"

"Got it. *Sir.*" She half rolled her eyes, but a smile hinted on her mouth.

"Good." He nudged her arm with a familiarity only close friends displayed. They had been best friends for centuries. At first Thara had been very formal around me, but she had eased a lot, and I knew Torin had a lot to do with it. It was quite obvious she was in love with him. I saw it when he wasn't looking at her, the way she grinned privately or gazed at him.

I hated to cause turmoil between the two. Thara would walk over glass if he asked her to, but Torin did not seem to return her feelings. I had no idea why. The woman was so stunning it was hard to look at her. She was also faithful to a fault when it came to him. But Ember had been his "fate," or so he thought, and he never gave Thara a chance. When life with Ember didn't pan out, he was lost until he turned his affections to me. Too bad. Torin and Thara would be beautiful together.

"Your grace." Thara bowed, stepping back. "I need to go prepare the vehicles and inform the gate." She turned on her heel, heading quickly down the hall.

"You are so blind, Torin." I shook my head, watching her outline disappear down the corridor.

"No. I'm not." His tone made me swing around to look at him. His expression was open, his eyes steady on me. "I see exactly what's in front of me."

I gulped, my cheeks suddenly hot. I glanced away, pretending I didn't understand his meaning.

"I'm gonna go grab my coat." I cleared my throat. "And let Olivia know I'm leaving." Olivia, my secretary and a fox-shifter from Lily's skulk, helped me survive most days. I think she loved lists more than I did.

"Let me, my lady."

"No. You need to go do your job, which is not retrieving my coat, and I will meet you out front in ten minutes."

Torin bowed; his blue eyes never left mine until he turned down the hall, already barking orders to my security team.

I exhaled and relaxed the moment he disappeared. My nerves were all jumbled and confused. When he said things in a more personal tone, I didn't know how to handle it. I had never been the girl guys wanted, not in my human life anyway. And even if things had changed since joining the fae world, I still thought of myself as the nerdy high school girl with little to no experience with the opposite sex.

Jared would forever be my sweet first love. We fooled around, but fear and naiveté kept it pretty innocent. Then Lorcan shattered all my walls when he came into my life. I'd pushed past all my self-induced boundaries, found a passion underneath I never knew I was capable of. But that moment in time was like a bubble. Another life. Another Kennedy. One I could never be again.

Torin was all new territory. As the previous First Knight under Aneira, he'd been treated as a sex slave for decades. He was Aneira's plaything, but in the most demented sexual way.

This was another reason I stepped back from his apparent desire. I cared for Torin deeply, and I didn't entirely trust his affection for me wasn't a habit borne of his role. I wanted to be loved but not because it came with the job.

~~~~~

Peering out the window, I saw the two large reinvented craftsman houses connected to create the new children's home. It had been open for a few weeks and construction was still wrapping up on one of the houses.

Torin hopped out of the car then ran to the other side. He waited until my guards were in position before opening the door. He took my hand and helped me out of the car. I actually didn't care for the pomp and circumstance, but he was a stickler for all the old school rules. And as Queen, especially one under threat, I had to do a lot of things I wasn't necessarily comfortable with.

Stepping out, I glanced at the vexed sky. The clouds were dark and shoving at each other until one got hurt and started to cry. It was late February, and daylight in the Pacific Northwest already crept for the horizon.

"Olivia called ahead to give them notice." Castien was already on point to my left. His presence was like taking a happy pill no matter my mood. He was an extension of Ryan. I was so glad when he agreed to come work for me. When we first met him in the castle, we thought he had worked for the former Queen, but really he had been working undercover for Lars. He was the reason we survived our days as Aneira's captives, and when he and Ryan fell in love.

Torin positioned himself on my right while Thara stayed ahead of us. A few of the security team moved into their five-star design around me. Because I was breaking rules and visiting a day early, I only had a quarter of my usual guards. I still felt as though I had a parade constantly marching about me. I could do nothing truly in secret when riding around in a security detail of six or seven cars black as night, bullet and magic proofed. It was hard to stay under the radar.

I remember as a little girl telling my mom I wanted to be president someday. In a strange way it came true. Be careful what you wish for, right? If only I'd known what the reality of that wish would entail.

We moved up the steps. Thara reached the door the same moment it opened. A tall, slender-boned girl smiled brightly at me. With her cornflower-blue eyes sparkling, long wavy blonde hair reaching her waist, together with high cheekbones, she looked to be in her late teens or early twenties. Her face was so beautiful I almost mistook her for fae, but I had no doubt she was fully human as fae auras possess colors that humans can't even imagine.

"Majesty." She dipped in a shallow curtsy, her voice and hand trembling. "We are so honored you are here."

"Thank you." I touched my chest lightly. "This is an extremely important cause to me. One that is particularly close to my heart." Everyone knew my story: I had been adopted and raised by humans, kept safe from Aneira's grasp. Now along with my biological parents, they were dead, leaving me an orphan.

"Please, come in." She stepped back and allowed us to enter. The front half of the first floor had been gutted and redesigned into a homey but efficient welcome area and social space full of toys, books, games, a sofa, and a warm blaze in the fireplace.

"Wow." I scanned the space, genuinely liking the setup. I immediately felt relaxed and comfortable. Smells of sugar cookies, honey, and fire laced the air. I could see why terrified children coming in here would be calmed.

"We've been working hard to get it open quickly since Lars gave us the place."

Another woman came up behind the blonde. She was a little taller than me, athletic, but curvy in all the places I envied. Heart-shaped face, huge green eyes, and long brown hair. She was stunning, but not in that supermodel sort of way. She was prettier because she was natural and comfortable in her own skin. A glow dusted her cheeks, her hand rubbing absently over her baby bump. I decided she was fae, but something was different and special about her I couldn't put my finger on. I instantly liked her. She had a no-nonsense, don't-mess-with-me vibe. A darkness in her aura told me she had lived and seen terrible things but held an abundance of love.

"Welcome to Honey House." She held out her hand. "I'm Zoey Daniels."

I reached out, my eyes catching two markings on her palm. They weren't tattoos, but scars cut into her hand. The top scar was like the symbol for pi, but curved at the ends. The bottom one looked like a lowercase cursive R. The files in the back of my head fluttered, trying to retrieve from where I recognized them. No clear memory of how or why I knew those symbols came to me. But my gut twanged with warning, like they were negative and alive, telling me not to touch them.

Before I could pull back, Zoey's hand slipped into mine. The moment our skin touched, a jolt of electricity zapped up my arm, my vision stolen from me. I still felt her hand in mine, like the images were shooting from her arm.

Flash.

I stood on a street, but the houses and buildings were nondescript, a backdrop to who stood yards away from me. Her pupils dilated, hair blowing back in the wind, her arms out wide, fists closed. A huge lump laid at her feet as greed and power pumped off her, slapping at my skin.

Zoey.

But my seer sensed this was not the Zoey I had just met. It was her face, but merely a shell. Twisted darkness filled her like a Cadbury egg, thick and gooey.

"Zoey?" I took a step, realizing the lump at her feet was a body. A massive bearded man with tattoos, braids, and an axe strapped to his back. He looked like a Norse god or Viking. Blood trickled out of his mouth and nose.

Was he dead? Did she kill him?

Zoey opened her palms, the markings on her one hand ignited with light. "Zoey is not here anymore. She's been a bad girl. Now it's *my* time."

Flash.

I gasped, stumbling to the side. The image happened

so fast awareness of those around me never left, the vision already dissolving from memory. I jerked my hand back, but the feeling of evil still lingered in my soul.

"Are you all right?" Zoey curled her hand, cupping it with her other, like she knew the source of my distress. I could no longer remember what I saw, but I still felt it. Evil. Power.

"Majesty?" Torin stepped up, his hand touching my arm.

"Yes." I forced a smile, shaking my head. "I'm fine." An awkwardness hung in the air, and I pressed on trying to cover it up. "I'm sorry, I missed your name?" I said to the blonde.

"Annabeth, Majesty," the girl said softly.

"She's my partner and the reason we were able to get most of this done in time." Zoey glanced down at her stomach with adoration but sighed in frustration. She was the kind who carried it in front, like she had swallowed a small ball. She must have been about seven or eight months.

"Please call me Kennedy." I waved my arm. "You guys have dealt with Lars, which probably makes us instant allies."

They both laughed, but something flickered through Zoey's eyes. I couldn't know for sure, but I felt she had more history with Lars than I was led to believe.

"Let us take you on a tour of the place." Zoey turned to me. "We are still getting on our feet and one wing is under construction, but we already have fifteen kids here. Fae and human. Some children with special needs."

Zoey and Annabeth showed me around, going over how things were run and how the labs, which Lars also helped fund, were set up to find cures for children with diseases and disabilities. They told me how their first Honey House in South America was flourishing.

I spent several hours coloring, playing games, and talking to the children who resided there, falling in love with each child in minutes. They all seemed happy. For some it was the first time they had their own bed and constant meals. They felt safe and loved. Of course, most still dreamed about a family adopting them, but a majority of the older ones felt they had found home. This was their family.

My heart overflowed, and a couple times I had to hold back the tears. This was exactly what I wanted to do more of. To feel like I was helping and improving the world. By the time I headed to the front door, I was so impressed I offered to support them in whatever way they needed.

"Thank you, Kennedy," Zoey said as she led me toward the exit. "You don't know how much this means to us. To the kids."

A loud crash toward the back of the house made me jump. My team reacted instantly, reaching for their weapons.

Squeaks, jabbering, and more bangs continued to flood through the walls.

"Uh...Zoey?" Annabeth popped her head out of a door I knew from my tour was the kitchen. "We have a little crisis..."

"Don't tell me." Zoey glanced at the ceiling.

"Yeah, he kind of found where you hide the jar of honey. The big jar. It's tipped over... Now he's hanging off the cupboard handle by his cape."

Zoey palmed her face, shaking her head. "Get him down. I'll be right there."

Annabeth nodded, smiled at me, and dipped back into the kitchen.

Zoey breathed in and looked back at me. "Sorry."

"One of the kids?" I grinned.

"You could say that." Her lip quirked up. "No, actually the kids are much better behaved."

"I'll let you go deal with it. I just wanted to thank you again for letting me stop by. This is amazing, Zoey, what you are doing here, what you've created."

"Thank you. And thank you for coming." She went to reach for my hand and stopped, placing it on her growing belly instead, dipping into a stiff curtsy.

I smiled, lowering my head in respect to her. I was envious of her, of the life she had. If I weren't Queen, I would like to be doing this kind of work.

Torin escorted me to the door and steered me out. As he closed the door, Zoey yelled from inside, "Sprig! I swear, I'm going to let those bears eat your brains this time."

I had no idea what she was talking about, but the way she said it revealed the deep love in her voice.

FOUR

We made our way down the steps in formation, sprinkles of rain falling from the sky. I hit the cement path and stopped cold with the sensation of bugs crawling over my skin, scurrying around like someone turned on very bright lights. My head shot around, trying to find the source of my itchy nerves.

"What, my lady?" Torin stiffened next to me, picking up on my reaction, his gaze darting around.

"I don't know, but something is off." My spine quaked with a chill.

Torin didn't second-guess or hesitate, rushing me faster to the car. A whoosh hissed through the air, metal bounced off the cement, rolling under the car.

"Bomb!" Torin bellowed. Twisting, he leaped for me right as an explosion went off under the car, breaking across my eardrums. We both flew back, his body cocooning me as we hit the lawn.

Time skewed my brain so I could not take in what was going on. The shrill sounds of a large metal object smashed onto the ground, scraping across the concrete. Peeking out, I watched the car tip on its side and slide toward us. I slammed my eyes shut, gritting my teeth, waiting for the impact. But the squealing of metal skidded to a stop.

I lifted my lids, looking into Torin's wide blue ones. We both twisted to see the vehicle merely inches from us, smoke billowing out from the undercarriage, but otherwise fully intact.

Shouts came from different areas. They were calling "Queen" over and over.

"Are you all right?" Torin cupped my face, concern deep in his face.

"Ye-ye-ah." I nodded, though my voice shook. It took him a moment, his eyes running over me intensely, before he scooted back off me, tugging out his gun. "Stay down, my lady."

Fae used to battle only with swords, arrows, clubs, and sticks, partial to the old world, in which taking down an enemy took talent and training and the best man actually did win. Any idiot could kill with a gun. But since the walls had fallen, things were changing. The fae used guns more frequently now.

"Torin?" Thara rushed around the car, panic lashing through his name.

"Yeah, we're fine." He kept low, meeting her.

"Thank the gods." Her hand reached out for him, briefly inspected the cuts over his back and face. He tugged her hand away, squeezing it to let her know he was okay. He huddled us at the rear of the car.

"Castien?" he called into his ear device. "Castien, do you copy?"

A frown pulled Torin's mouth down, and I knew he was not getting a response.

No. Please say nothing happened to Castien.

Screaming from inside the Honey House drew my attention to the building, faces of children lined the windows upstairs, looking out with horror. Fear welled up inside me. Dark. Consuming. Wanting to attack the threat to these children. There was nothing I wouldn't do to protect the kids. Nothing. It felt like a thundercloud rolling in my stomach. It was the same sensation I felt the night before—the desire to kill whoever might hurt us.

Druids were not killers. We healed. Protected. But the rush up my legs, pushing me to stand, was not from the light. It would destroy if it had to. A pregnant woman and children were in that house. The blast was meant for me, but they were in the crossfire. What if they got hurt because of me? I stepped forward, fury luring me out to find the culprits.

"Majesty! Get down!" Torin screamed, right as a bullet buzzed past my ear, startling me out of my trance. Torin grabbed for me, yanking me down next to him. "Are you insane? We are under attack!"

I jostled my head. What the hell? Was I insane? What had come over me?

More bullets bounced off the car that shielded us.

"Did you see any of the assailants?" Torin asked Thara.

She shook her head, swallowing. "No. I didn't see anything."

"Shit. We are supposed to be the best of the best and here we are acting like amateurs. Totally unprepared for this," Torin spit back at Thara, but he sounded more as if he were berating himself.

"Castien?" Torin called into his device again. His scowl deepened, and I felt sick. "Sturt, Lea, Rowlands, Vander, Georgia, your status?"

I could hear the responses coming from his ear device.

"Sturt here," a deep Scottish accent responded. "I'm in front of the first car with Rowlands."

"Vander and Georgia here," a woman spoke. "We're behind the third car. The attack is coming from southeast, near the intersection."

"Lea? Castien?" Torin barked their names, and more gunfire pinged off the car by our heads.

My lungs tightened. The only reason they didn't respond was because they couldn't. I gripped my stomach. Not only was Castien one of my friends, but I cherished him beyond belief for how happy he made Ryan. They were soulmates, their love shining through all the devastation Ryan had gone through. Castien had brought him back to life. Literally. If he died protecting me because I asked him to be one of my elite guards, I would never forgive myself.

Hearing Zoey's voice, I glanced at the second floor. She ushered the kids away from the window, yelling for them to follow Annabeth. She then looked down, finding me.

I had known her for a few hours, but what I saw in her face reminded me of Ember. Fierce and ready to join. More than that, it was almost like she was begging me to say yes, to let her join the fight, like something under her skin itched to be released. But I could only think of the baby she carried and the children inside the house. She wouldn't just be risking her own life. I shook my head. "No," I mouthed. "Protect them."

Her lips pinched together before she nodded and slipped away from view. I breathed a sigh of relief, knowing they would be all right.

"Get the Queen to the front car," Sturt spoke into Torin's ear, the buzz carrying to me. "We'll cover you."

"Okay. Listen for my count," Torin replied, getting his feet underneath him. He hurried me to the front of the car. "Thara, I'll go out first." He glanced back at her.

"No, Tor—" With one daggered look from him, her mouth clipped shut.

"We are the Queen's shield; we stay tight. We protect her no matter what," he continued. "My lady, you stay directly behind us. All the way to the car."

"Okay." Would I ever get used to letting people put their lives on the line for me? No. But I understood it was a requirement of the job.

"In three," he spoke into the mic. "Three. Two. One." He leaped up, his gun raised, shots flooding at him with ear-piercing pops. Thara darted up next to him, a scowl trenching her mouth and eyes. She was excellent at keeping her aura colors hidden from me, but I saw a flare of black and crimson before she went to grays again.

"Now," Torin hollered at me. I jumped up and moved behind them. As a unit we started to move, slugs ripping through the air. I heard Torin swear several times, but I couldn't see what it was about.

"Ahh!" Thara yelped, leaning to the side. "Leg. Hit," she said to Torin, but she didn't even falter, keeping pace with him. The slight gap between her and Torin let me see what had upset Torin. My stomach buckled, coiling with acid.

Two bodies lay in the street. Blood covered them from head to toe. It was so thick no recognizable features could be seen. My hand went to my mouth, a strangled cry breaking free. Victims of the bomb. But I knew who they were.

"Castien!" I screamed, shoving through Thara and Torin.

"My lady. No!" Torin's voice bellowed from behind me, but I couldn't stop. The need to get to Castien and Lea drilled my legs into the pavement. I fell to my knees, hearing the gunshots in my ears, but my focus blocked out anything but Castien gasping for air, his body shuddering with each intake.

He was dying. "Oh my god." I bent over, taking his head in my lap. "Castien…"

Blood spurted from his mouth, his lips parting to speak. "Tell Ryan…" He coughed.

"No." I cut him off. "Whatever it is. *You* will tell him." Sobs thickened my throat. I was aware of figures moving around me, weapons firing, defending me from assault. But I blocked out everything. Castien's life was my only concern. Swallowing back the tears, I tried to speak, but sobs clogged my throat.

His life was in my hands, and it depended on me speaking clearly. I dispelled the gunk in my throat and started again, shoving out the words with weight. Red liquid gushed over my hands as I placed them over his internal organs I could see through the gashes. I lowered my lashes, the healing chant spewing from me.

A sharp zing of pain sliced at my arm, breaking my enchantment. I slumped to the side with a cry. As I gazed down, my arm oozed blood, a bullet burrowing to a stop inside my flesh.

Arms slipped from behind, pulling me up and away from Castien. "No!" I thrashed against the hold, curling back down for my friend. "He needs me. I will not leave him!"

"And I will not lose you too," Torin snarled in my ear. "Your life is always first. And Castien would be the first to agree with me."

"I. Don't. Care!" Torin had no idea the desperation I felt, the need to make sure Castien lived. It completely overshadowed my own life.

He spoke sharply into my ear. "Okay, if you don't care about yourself, think of the others you just put into harm's way by coming out here. They could all die...to protect you."

I went still at the thought. I had put them all in danger, and because it was Castien, I hadn't even thought about the others coming to defend me. I glanced around, seeing my service team surrounding me, most of them bleeding from multiple bullet wounds, not one looking to move until I did. Their dedication and strength floored me. But when I peered down at Castien, my soul wanted to break apart.

"Please, Torin."

I was sure he would ignore my plea, but instead he shoved me behind him, toward the first car.

"Go! I'll get him." Torin waved me on. "Go!"

Without hesitation, I ran for the car, diving into the backseat. This one didn't have the protection like the other one, but it was upright and ready to roll.

The longest minute of my life ticked by before Torin was back with Castien in his arms. He shoved him in next to me before climbing into the driver's seat. The wheels squealed as he punched the gas, bolting us forward. Gunfire rang off the trunk, and I ducked my head below the seat.

"What about everyone else?" I peeked up, glancing backward.

"They are heading for the third car."

"Lea?"

Through the rearview mirror, Torin's lips twisted, turning white. "She's dead."

Tears built up behind my lids, choking me. I nodded, staring down at Castien, his head in my lap. His breath was steadier from the little I was able to heal him, but not enough to make me feel we were in the clear.

The chant started off steady, my magic filling him. But like a leaking bathtub, my energy seeped out quickly, the buzz of my adrenaline tipping over the top and nose-diving down.

The throb in my arm pounded like a heartbeat, one that had just run a marathon. Pain sliced up my nerves, and twisted out what was left of my strength until my speech slurred. My head dropped forward onto Castien, blackness licking at the edges of my sight.

"Majesty," Torin called back to me, sounding like he was in a well. "Stay with me, okay?

I tried to pry my lashes open, but nothing happened. The stinging discomfort in my arm made me welcome the darkness more.

Sleep, my body commanded. And I listened.

FIVE

I awoke to the familiarity of my own room. The electric blue lake and green mountains capped with snow were like a painting through my doors. Yellows and oranges reflected off the clouds, telling me a new day had begun.

I sat with a start. *Morning?* Had I slept almost an entire day?

A throb of pain cut across my arm, and I glanced down at the gauze wrapping it tightly. Healing it hadn't even crossed my mind, not when Castien needed all my energy.

Oh. God. Castien.

I flung the covers off, my bare feet padding across the floor. I barreled through my door, heading toward the infirmary, vaguely aware I was dressed only in a flimsy nightgown. Not something I would ever dress myself in. My favorite sleep attire was a *Firefly* T-shirt I got at Comic-Con years ago. Much of my personal staff was horrified by what I wore, thinking the Queen should be dressed like royalty in bed too. Nope. Never going to happen. Not conscious anyway.

"Majesty! Where do you think you are going?" Hazel bounded out of the chair outside my door. She stood at my height but was thick and stocky with silvering hair and a stern face that liked to frown at me a lot. She was my attendant, sort of like a lady-in-waiting. She had been in this role for centuries and did her job well, but she was not the German, cookie-making grandma she appeared to be. The woman had to be old even by fae standards, but she was plucky. I think she could out wrestle and outrun me if I tried to slip past her.

"I need to check on Castien."

"You most certainly will not." She pointed back to my room. "You need to rest."

"I'm good. All rested."

"March it back there, missy. You will go nowhere dressed like this." She continued to wave me back to the room. "Highly inappropriate for a *Queen* to be seen like that in public."

I was pretty sure she didn't like me, or the fact I was Queen, but I would never get rid of her. She was like an institution in the castle. No one could recall a time she was not in it.

"I have to see if he is okay."

"You can after you are properly dressed." She'd given up pointing where she wanted me to go. Her hand turned me back into my room.

"Scandal follows you enough, Majesty. I don't think they need another picture of you running around in your underwear."

Another one. Right. The press did get lucky that one night I freaked out after a vision and ran straight out of the gates before my guards could catch me. It happened a few days after my coronation, dressed only in my *Firefly* T-shirt and tiny boy-shorts. Nice to wake to that on the front page. The reporters were a lot more vigilant now trying for more pictures.

Dressing myself in whatever was within grabbing distance, I flew out the door, not letting Hazel block me this time, and sprinted for the section of the castle containing the infirmary. Thara was on guard outside my waiting room, but she let me go, jogging after me without a word, seeming to understand exactly where I was headed.

Thara, Castien, and Torin were my core sentinels, the ones I trusted with my life. Torin ran my security unit. But those three were in on my every move and decision I made, so they could better protect me. And I considered them friends.

My knee-length boots hit the floor as I bolted to Castien. My subjects did double takes as I passed, their mouths agape at their Queen running like a flailing ostrich.

"Your grace?" A green-haired healer stood up, curtsying as I ran to the front desk. "We weren't expecting you."

"Castien? Where is he?" I sucked in gulps of air. Damn, I was out of shape. Torin had started basic training with me a couple weeks ago, saying I needed to at least know how to defend myself. I was not the best student although I had been enjoying the drills more after my meeting with the noble committee. I didn't like being bad at things, but I'd never excelled at exercise. PE was always my lowest grade.

"Room six." She pointed toward the back.

"Thank you," I replied and rushed in that direction with Thara silently on my tail. I got to the door and stopped, my hand on the knob. Anxiety and guilt lumped in my stomach.

"I'll wait for you here, Majesty." Thara's voice drew my head up to her.

She was tall, five ten, with long, dark brown hair and light caramel skin. Her Native American heritage dominated her proud face and almond-shaped eyes. She was breathtaking. Always regal and stoic and a little cold and serious, she didn't sugarcoat things, which I respected. As Queen, even when I knew they hated me, I got a lot of ass-kissers. I appreciated her upfront attitude.

Her particular talent was to *see* people's abilities. In meetings with new individuals, she'd whisper in my ear what type of fae they were or what magic they held. Knowledge was power, and that was an extraordinary gift in my line of work.

"Thank you, Thara." I nodded and pushed open the door with a deep breath.

Castien lay in bed, IVs sticking out of his arms as bags of blood helped replenish his lost supply. The majority of his face was still black, shredded, and scalded.

My hand went to my mouth, my lids blinking frantically. He was alive, but the damage was so severe.

He was there because he was protecting you.

Lea is dead because of you.

"It looks a lot worse than it is. The principal healer said he will be fine," a voice broke the silence, drawing my attention to the person in the chair next to Castien. "In a few weeks."

"Ryan." I bounded for my best friend. He barely stood before my body collided into him, my arms wrapping around him so tight. Ryan was like a happy trigger for me. Having his arms around me and breathing in his familiar scent made me feel so comforted, like I was young again, safe in our tree fort when our lives consisted of playtime and warm afternoons.

Ryan exhaled in my ear, and his muscles relaxed into me.

"I am so sorry, Ry." I squeezed him firmly to me.

"It's not your fault, Ken. Do not blame yourself." He pulled away, hurriedly brushing under his eyes before I could see the tears. His eyes were bloodshot with bags, and worry weighed down his shoulders. But being typical Ryan, he waved away the vulnerable emotion. "I tried to get over to see you too, but your Nurse Hatchet pulled a Mr. Miyagi and practically used my ass to wax the floor."

I snorted, picturing Hazel doing just that. "Yeah. She's a *treasure*."

"Relic is more like it." He grinned, running his hand through his spiky brown hair.

I felt the first genuine smile tug at my mouth. Ryan was like ointment, soothing me with his presence. "I've missed you so much." I looked away, blinking back tears.

"I miss you more." He reached over, pulling my head to him and kissing my forehead. "I hate we can't see each other more."

"Me too." I had hoped Ryan and Castien would move into the castle since Castien had to be here a majority of his days now. But Ryan couldn't do it. The memories of this place, of his time being held captive here, kept him happily living with Lily and Mark in a large cabin near the dwellers. I understood especially because I think he related this place to Ian's murder. Even though he technically lived closer to the actual spot Ian died, this was where Ryan dealt with it, mourned him.

A soft groan came from the bed, and we both whirled toward Castien. Ryan moved to his side, taking his hand.

"Cas?" His free hand fingered through the dark mop of his boyfriend's hair. Castien didn't respond, seeming about to slip back into deeper sleep. Fae didn't need to be in infirmaries often, but when they did it usually kept them there for a month.

"He's going to be okay," I said more for myself than Ryan.

"Of course he is." Ryan's brows furrowed. "My man is made of everything stubborn and ornery. He'll be awake and doing sit-ups at five a.m., annoying the hell out of me. Batman forbid he'd miss a workout."

Another reason why Ryan and I got on, we were the "excuse queens" of getting out of gym class. He used to annoy the gym coach all the time, nudging me, always making me cover my face in embarrassment. *"I know I'm a boy, but they're sympathy cramps. It is too a real thing. You're in the health profession, so you of all people should know that."* or *"Why would I want to get sweaty running when I can get sweaty without even leaving a bed?"*

Now I understood the last one. Or I did a year ago…

A soft knock rattled the door before it opened. "My lady?" Torin stuck his head in.

Crap.

"Sorry to interrupt, but you are already late."

I sighed. "Okay, thank you, Torin." He nodded and shut the door again.

"The way that man looks at you." Ryan wiggled his eyebrows. "He definitely wants you to pour some *sugar* on him."

"Ugh. Ryan." I smacked his arm. When Ember joined our duo, Ryan took to calling me Sugar, the sweet one. Ember was Spice as she brought all the excitement to our lives. He was Salty, the sarcastic one.

"Except, I think my sweet one fell in the pepper jar. Got a bite now."

"Take care of your boy. I'll be back when I can." I kissed Ryan's cheek, ignoring his statement. I didn't want him to look too close, see too much...or ask something I couldn't answer. Lorcan was a taboo topic. I could never tell the details of my time with Lorcan to the friend I usually told everything to.

"Ken, it's time." His tone stopped me at the door. "He would want you to move on, to be happy."

Jared. I swallowed, grief coiling in my throat.

"Torin is a great guy. He's perfect for you. Don't let this slide by because you are trying to protect Jared's memory. He would not want you to stop living because of him."

My lashes fluttered; my chest clenched. No, he wouldn't. Jared would want me to be happy...and that was where the thorn lay. I didn't deserve to be happy, especially not when the precise person my heart longed for was the same one who would obliterate everything. Ryan would never accept it, and I would lose him.

"Listen to me. Ken?" Ryan asked. "After all you've been through. The loss and heartache. You only think about everyone else. Sometimes you need to think of yourself. If that hunk of a man out there will do that, then please don't walk...run. You deserve happiness too."

I couldn't hear any more. I flew out the door, my lungs struggling for oxygen.

If I thought of what I really wanted, it would end up destroying others and myself. Just like it had before.

✦✦✦

"Lea's memorial will be tomorrow; her family is traveling here now." Torin's voice was somber as he walked me down the hall, Thara on my other side.

"Let me know when they get here as I want to personally give them my condolences." It wouldn't bring her back, but it was the right thing to do.

"Dying in the line of duty, for us, is an honor. Her family will accept her Medal of Honor."

I nodded, my throat knotting up like a child's shoelaces.

"And Ember's called three times. She heard from Lily about the attack and is very worried about you."

"I'll call her after the meeting." What I really wanted was to have her home. Ryan, Ember, and me snuggled on a sofa, watching movies, and laughing like we used to. Talking about boys and dealing with our little dramas when we thought life was so difficult. We had no idea what complicated truly was. Now my reign was buckling under the foundation. One of my guards was dead, the other in intensive care. Yeah, I wanted to hide under my covers.

"What meeting am I going to?" I tugged at my hair, trying to fire up the engine to my brain. After yesterday's events, my head completely misfiled what was on the calendar for today. I thought I only had the visit to the orphanage scheduled and training with Torin later.

Torin's gaze went to Thara, then to me. "It's not on the books."

"O-kay." I waited for him to continue, but his hand went to my back, steering me down a rarely used hallway. "Are either of you going to tell me what is going on?" When I glanced back at Thara I saw her eyes move to where he touched me, her mouth tight. I had no reason to feel guilty, but I felt as though I was stealing his love from her. Her eyes lifted to mine, and whatever she saw reflected back at her made her frown more before her face turned up and went blank.

I had plenty of crushes on boys who never looked at me twice. It hurt, but I had always been aware they were a fantasy. I almost preferred them that way. Safe. But Thara's pain was real. Not some little crush. She deeply loved him.

Torin turned us down a few more corridors. When we reached a corner turret, we descended down the stairs.

"Okay, now I'm getting genuinely nervous." I tried to laugh, but legitimate nerves rubbed against my spine, prickling up the back of my neck. I had never ventured to this part of the castle. "Tell me where we are going."

"Somewhere no one but us knows about."

"That doesn't help at all," I teased, but my voice wobbled. "Are you going to kill me? Is that your plan this whole time?"

Torin smiled, rolling his eyes back. "Not even funny, my lady."

"Plus, if we were going to kill you, we wouldn't need to be this secretive. We could probably do it upstairs. Have a bonfire," Thara said dryly behind me. "Well, we'd have to see if you float first."

I twisted to look at her, my feet taking each step down carefully. A small smile hinted at her lips. "Witch. Got it." I snorted. "Now you decide to be funny, while you are taking me down into the abyss.

She shrugged.

"Plus, I'm not a witch," I huffed. It seemed to be bred in our bones to take offense at being compared to them. Witches were usually human and had no actual magic. They merely had the power of their mind, which they used in spells, only dancing on the edges of earth's energy. Druids were given the gift of true magic from the fae gods. Our favor with the gods was what started the hate, propaganda, and extermination of Druids. The fae, especially Aneira, did not like that our power not equaled, but in some ways overpowered, the fae's.

After another minute we came to the bottom, and Torin grabbed a lantern. Like the lights in the castle, it was a bulb, but the inside flickered with flames, giving off more light than any torch. The moment I hit the tunnel my lungs clenched together, and the blackness stayed thick and heavy a few steps ahead of us like a heavy drape. The smells…it took me right back to that night.

Tunnel. Darkness. War. Jared. Death. Lorcan.

"Breathe, my lady." Torin was suddenly in front of me, intertwining his hand in mine. I hadn't even realized I stopped walking, my lungs struggling to capture oxygen. He leaned in close, and it simply pushed me deeper into the memory of being in a similar space. The night the arrow burrowed into Jared's heart. Poetic, actually, as it symbolized what I had done to him: stabbed him through the heart, letting it bleed out on the ground.

The anger I felt at myself for what I did to him, for not being able to heal him, never went away, simply hibernated. Now the bear was awake and roaring.

Torin took both of my hands in his, pulling me into his chest, wrapping his arms around me. My inhales were jagged and shallow, and I couldn't seem to find my way out, the nightmare surrounding me.

"I am here," Torin whispered into my ear. "Everything will be all right."

My lids closed; Torin's words became someone else's. His warmth and body became another's. I hated myself, but I still let my imagination proceed. Let myself visualize the one thing I shouldn't.

I'm here, li'l bird. His voice strong in my mind, his arms muscular and comforting. *You're safe.* I sighed, my shoulders dropping, my heartbeat slowing.

I stepped back from Torin's hold, my head down.

"Thank you," I croaked. "I'm fine now."

Torin's finger went under my chin, lifting my head.

"Like I said, always, my lady." His gaze burned into mine.

My smile was strained as I stepped back. The feeling of Thara's gaze on me was like a fourth presence in the room.

"We need to go," Thara said, emotionless, stepping forward. "You know he does not like to be kept waiting."

Torin nodded and turned back around. I followed them down the passageway, blocking all my demons from attacking me again.

Little did I know an actual demon waited for me in the room down the hall.

SIX

I stepped into a brightly lit room, Torin shutting the door the moment the three of us entered. The Unseelie King sat at a table, leaning back in a high-back chair. He was dressed in his normal exquisite suit and tie. Goran and Travil, Lars's bodyguards, stood on either side of him.

"Lars?"

"Ms. Johnson." He dipped his head, his hands folded on his lap. I had tried over and over to get him to call me Kennedy, but he seemed inclined to call me by my last name.

"I didn't feel you." I looked around the room like I was expecting it to tell me why. Lars's magic was so profound it throbbed from yards away, letting you know exactly with whom you were dealing.

The room was set up with a long table and chairs set in the middle, several TVs and monitors on two walls, and a world map on the other, like some war room. *How did I not know about this place?*

"The walls here are lined to protect whatever is inside from magic, bombs, or chemical attack," Torin explained.

"Ah." I nodded. After September 11, the tragic time in the human world in which terrorists successfully attacked American soil, I'd researched what happened to a president if attacked. This was the fae version of the president's emergency operations center, PEOC. Guess mine would be QEOC.

"And why are we here?" I walked to the table.

"I felt it was necessary." Lars's chartreuse eyes met mine. "Your Knight heartily agreed with me when I contacted him this morning."

"Contacted Torin?" I spread out my arms. "Why not simply talk to me?"

"You were unconscious, Ms. Johnson, or I would have." Lars nodded to the bandages still around my arm. I was healed, but it still felt sore.

"Right."

"The last two days have been close calls for both of us." He tugged at his cuffs, an unconscious habit. "Once again, I want to express my gratitude for getting to us in time to prevent the attack…but also for saving Marguerite's life. I do not have to tell you what she means to me. To all of us at the compound."

"To me as well, Lars." I sat in the chair across from him. Torin and Thara leaned against the wall behind me. "I am so happy I was able to prevent it this time. If anything had happened to her…" I drifted off, my hand touching my heart. I didn't want to think about if I hadn't made it in time.

"Yes. Let's move on to why I am here."

Oh Lars. So in touch with his feelings. I smiled to myself. I would love to see the day someone challenged him and was able to find the passion he once held for Ember's mother, Aisling. It would turn his world upside down.

"After speaking with your Knight, I've grown more concerned about your safety."

"Mine? What about yours?"

"The assault from the strighoul is neither the first nor the last. They have found where I live somehow. Do not doubt I will find their benefactor, and be assured I will make them pay." He sat forward, his hands on the table. Did he suspect Luuk was behind it? His tone suggested he might. "The attack on you yesterday, how did they know you were there?"

"I was there for several hours. Someone must have noticed."

"No." Lars shook his head. "From what I've heard about it, the strike was well executed. It had been fully planned out. They were ready for you. Knew you were coming."

"What?" My mouth dipped open. "But I wasn't supposed to even go yesterday. It was scheduled for today, and it still was not on the public calendar."

"Exactly," Lars replied.

"What are you saying?" My stomach rolled, already knowing where he was going.

"You have a mole, Ms. Johnson. One closer than you think. One in your core team."

"A spy?" I glanced back at Torin, who nodded along with Lars.

"It is getting too dangerous for you. You cannot trust anyone besides the people in this room."

Castien and Olivia weren't in the room, but I completely trusted both of them. There were many who didn't like me, but I didn't sense any harm from those close; their auras were clean. Sturt, Georgia, Rowlands, Vander...I didn't want to think any of them hated me so much they wanted me dead. Torin trusted them and so did I.

"With a mole so close, it is far too dangerous. You can no longer stay here," Lars declared. "Torin is positive it's Luuk's men who went after you. He wants nothing more than to take you out of the equation."

"What do you mean? I can't just leave here. I am the Queen." I held out my arms. "I will not hide, Lars. You of all people should know that's not a possibility. I will not appear weak or let my enemy control me."

Lars pressed his mouth together, looking smug.

"You have a plan?" After the time working together, I was picking up on Lars's subtle expressions.

"I do."

"What is this scheme then?"

"My plan," Lars tugged on his sleeves, leaning back in the chair as if he was on a beach with a piña colada, "is for you to go to Europe."

"What?" Torin and I said in unison.

My Knight stepped forward. "This was not what we discussed."

"I changed my mind." Lars lifted an eyebrow. "And I do not need to clear *anything* with you."

"No. Absolutely not," Torin answered quickly, shaking his head. "It's too dangerous. Lars's glare leveled on him. Torin shut his mouth with a click.

"I will be joining you later. I have set a meeting with some powerful nobles. They could help *sway* those not in favor of us still ruling Europe to the correct side," Lars continued on, moving his gaze to me. "I normally would never travel for a few nobles. They come to me. However, circumstances are extreme at this time, and we need all the support we can get abroad." Lars frowned, tipping his arms forward on the desk. "Unfortunately we can't simply torture them into the right decision. Not with these fae. Their power and influence are too desirable to treat them like the scum they are."

"Do you think it will help?" I asked. I squeezed my hands into such tight fists the color drained from my knuckles. "And would it be all right for us to leave with how unstable it is here?"

"You are being threatened and attacked daily, and this last incident only signifies how strong they have grown. You need to be out of reach."

"As I said, I will not go into hiding. That simply proves my weakness to the enemy." I shoved back, rising out of the chair, and paced along the table like a cat locked behind bars. "I will not give them the satisfaction of seeing me cower or give them more proof I can't lead."

"I respect your sentiment, Ms. Johnson, but a dead Queen will certainly not be able to lead. And it will be only a matter of time before they get a clean shot." Lars glared at Torin. "No matter how prepared or trained the guards are. They are fighting against an invisible threat all the time from every direction, while the enemy only has to find one tiny fault and they win."

Torin's shoulders hitched back in defense, his jaw tensing.

"Tell me I'm wrong. Either one of you." Lars stared Torin down until the Knight shifted uncomfortably on his feet. Then Lars looked at Thara. Her head dropped forward in defeat.

"No. You are not," Torin gritted, sounding furious at his own declaration.

"Lars, I will appear weak. I can't hide." I gripped my fists together, pulling up my tiny frame with resolve.

An eyebrow curled the King's forehead up, like he knew some juicy secret I didn't.

"You won't appear to be hiding to the world. It's all about appearance, my dear Queen." His smugness nipped at my annoyance level.

"What does that mean?"

"We cancel any public events and meetings, but they will still see you from afar. Press releases... Reassuring people it is business as usual, you are not cowering. Even to the guards and staff." He clasped his hands together.

"You mean a stand-in." Torin's eyes widened, taking in Lars's meaning.

"No. It couldn't be pulled off," Thara exclaimed, her hands fisted.

"What?" My head whipped back and forth between the three. "You mean have some girl who looks like me pretend to be Queen while I go hide?"

Lars glanced up with a shrug.

"No!" My head swung vehemently. "No way. I will not put some innocent girl in danger because she happens to resemble me. I no longer hide in my locker when a bully is after me."

"Ms. Johnso—"

"No!" I shouted back.

Fists came down with a crash on the table as Lars soared to his feet, and his pupils sparked with black.

"Enough," he bellowed, causing my body to freeze like I was an animal caught in headlights. "This is not a choice. You have a spy in your castle. The enemy is knocking on the door. You are not safe. And I'm sorry if it upsets you that one person might get hurt, but there are millions who need you alive. There are too many elements against you…both of us. This trip will be a way you can still help, protect, and strengthen international relations. Do not let your ego get in the way, Ms. Johnson. People die for their country, for their leaders, in every war. It is a sacrifice you will have to get used to."

I rubbed my face. It wasn't something I could ever get used to, but I would have to find a way to accept it.

"Why can't I just say I'm going to Europe?"

Lars snorted. Even that sounded elegant and sexy coming from him. "Why don't you paint a target on your back? A leader away from their territory is even more vulnerable. Here the guards know their terrain, understand exactly what to look for or how to get you to safety the fastest. By stating you are leaving, you would merely be providing an easier target."

I saw Torin nod.

Crap squared.

"How will it work?" I sighed, lifting my head. "I mean with the staff. People see me all the time around here. They will know it's not me."

"No one, except Torin and Thara, will get really close." Lars motioned to the soldier. "Because of what happened here, no one will be surprised when you close the ranks tighter. Say it is mandatory while you figure out the infiltrator. Everything goes through them—food, people, gifts, requests.

"The girl has been watching and training since the moment you took the throne. She will also be glamoured to sound like you. No one from a hundred feet will see any difference."

"You've been training someone? This whole time?"

"Yes," Lars said impassively. "There is not a situation we are not ready for."

"Do you have one?"

"I did."

"Did?" My lids lifted higher.

Lars slanted his head to the side, telling me all I needed to know. The man was one of those sacrifices.

"What about all my meetings?"

"You will cancel them." He shoved one hand into his pocket. "If it's an emergency, I will step in for you, or we can set up a video chat from wherever you are. They will not know you are not here."

Wow. He had thought of everything.

"To sell this…" Lars's lashes flicked to Torin. "He must stay here."

Torin bolted forward, his thighs knocking into the table.

"No. I will not leave my Queen. Where she goes, I go."

"That will not be possible."

A growl vibrated Torin's chest, pressing farther over the table. "Where. She. Goes. I. Go." He seethed, leaning on his arms, challenging the King.

"Torin." I tugged on his sleeve. It took several times before he tore his gaze from Lars to me. His muscles flexed under my palms. "It has to be this way. People know you would never leave my side. Neither of you would." I glanced over at Thara. "It would raise too many questions if you weren't here. If you left with me, the façade would be blown."

"My lady—"

"It's an order, Torin," I said softy, knowing he would never go against me.

His blue eyes fixed on me, softening as they searched back and forth between mine. "I don't want to leave you," he replied hoarsely. "If anything ever happened to you…"

"I'm going to be fine." I squeezed his arm in reassurance. "I'm more afraid for those here. For that poor girl. I want you to protect her as fiercely as you protect me. More so. Your job is to keep her safe."

Torin continued to stare down at me while different emotions of fear, guilt, anger, and helplessness rolled behind his stone-like expression. His hand came up and brushed my cheek, moving into my hair and sending tingles where his fingers touched. The intimacy hitched my breath, warmth engulfing my body.

"You know there isn't anything I won't do for you. Whatever you ask, I will never be able to say no," he whispered. His intensity made my heart race. His aura was full of reds. I still couldn't decipher how I felt, but I couldn't deny my heart slammed against my ribs, and not completely in terror. Ryan's sentiment came back to me. Was it possible to find happiness again? With Torin?

"Sorry to interrupt this declaration of love…" Lars's voice was like a chainsaw cutting through blocks of ice. I jumped away from Torin, swinging back to Lars. "Other issues take precedence."

"Sorry. Continue." I cleared my throat, attempting to sound as "queenly" as possible as I tried to ignore Torin's heated gaze running along the entire side of me.

Finally Torin broke away, turning the penetrating energy on Lars. "Since I cannot be there, I still refuse to leave her unprotected. That is a no-go for me. Her safety is still my number one priority."

"I would not dream of leaving the Seelie Queen unprotected." Lars took his hand out of his pocket, tapping lightly on the table with one finger. "That was never in question. Her safety is the whole point. I took it upon myself to find her the best bodyguard possible.

Believe me, he will die without hesitation in the name of the Queen. Maybe even before you would."

Torin bristled, his arms folded, his mouth opened to counter Lars's statement.

"Who?" I cut in quickly, touching Torin's arm, my head shaking. He instantly shut his mouth, but his body still prickled.

Lars's head swiveled for the door, and energy vacuumed out of the room, like he was drawing something to him.

Or someone.

The doorknob twisted as a figure stepped into the room.

"You summoned?" the man said, his voice filled with snarky derision.

Oh. God.

The ground began to dissolve underneath my feet, wobbling my knees. Everything sounded and felt far away. Except for him.

No. No. No, my head said on repeat, not able to accept the person at the door.

"What's wrong, li'l Druid? Doesn't look like you're excited to see me." He lifted his lip with disdain, sounding about as happy as I was seeing him.

Lorcan. His name alone evoked a powerful reaction inside me, but seeing him standing there, the first time in over a year, I had to lock my knees to keep from falling to the floor. I didn't expect such an intense response, but emotions I'd kept buried for so long slipped from the tiny gaps, sizzling up my spine. He brought it all back. All the things I had grown used to shoving away to get through the day: anger, resentment, sorrow, guilt, shame, passion, love, happiness.

My head spun. I wanted to throw up. I tried to ignore the overwhelming urge to cry. Abhorrence and love pulled so strongly from either side it left me raw and bruised.

Commotion slowly turned my head to the figure next to me. Torin's mouth moved, his arms flailing as he shouted, face red, his muscles taut at his neck. I blinked a few times, then like being snapped back into the present, his voice zoomed into my ears with a roar.

"No! I will NOT have that dark dweller watching over her," Torin bellowed. "I'd rather a rat-shifter or a brownie be in charge of her protection. Not a fucking Dragen!"

"Fucking Dragen." Lorcan smirked, crossing his arms over each other. "Sounds about right. I'm full service with my charges."

Oh. No. It was barely a moment, but the silence which occupied the room shook with fury.

"Torin!" I reached for him but it was too late. He scrambled over the table, leaping for Lorcan, fists flying.

"Torin, don't!" Thara leaped for him, but the Knight slipped from her fingers.

"You son of a bitch!" His knuckles crashed into Lorcan's face, blood spurting out, specks splattering the table as red gushed from the dweller's nose.

They both moved so fast my eyes barely caught them. Lorcan lunged for Torin, tackling him on top of the table, their bodies rolling to the ground. The sounds of skin being struck, grunts, and vicious name-calling rebounded off the walls.

"Stop!" I darted to the end of the table where they were tangled on the floor. "Please stop this now!"

My glance went to Lars for help. He stared at the ceiling, annoyance twitching at the side of his mouth, like he had to wait for his dinner longer than he wanted.

"Lars?" I screamed at him.

"This was going to happen sooner or later. Maybe they'll get it out of their systems." He pulled at the bottom of his jacket, fixing it in place.

Lars didn't appear inclined to help. Thara tried to step in, but the two men were set on spilling each other's blood.

Frustration rumbled in my chest as I stared at them. Blood, cuts, and bruises covered their faces and hands as they tore into each other.

I lifted my hand, the chant coming easily to my lips. Like a hurricane, power flung the two bodies apart, smashing into opposite walls. Their breaths labored, their eyes still locked on each other.

"How old are you two?" I exclaimed, turning my head to talk to them both. "You're thousands of years old. Start acting like it. Especially when we have more important things to worry about."

"Believe me, Dragen guarding you is something to worry about." Torin wiped at the red liquid gushing from his nose and cheek with his sleeve. Both eyes were bruised, his lips cut, and his knuckles were shredded like he raked them over a cheese grater.

"If Kennedy almost getting killed last night is the bar you set, I think I'm overqualified." Lorcan dabbed at his bloody nose.

"She is called *Majesty*. How dare you speak so inform—"

"Shut up," I ordered with authority. "That is enough." Both men clenched their jaws, doing as I said, but they didn't stop glaring at each other.

"Torin, you have to stay here. There is no getting around that. None of the guards or staff here can know anything is different. All must be treated like suspects right now. We can't use anyone who would be noticed or missed, even if you trust them. It has to be someone on the outside to go." I moved to my Knight, squatting down next to him. He had become one of my best friends. I needed him to understand.

"I don't like this any more than you do, but if Lars is convinced Lorcan will be the best guard for me, then I have to accept it. We've got far more important things to deal with. This entire kingdom is holding on by a thread. People's lives... I need you here. Guard this girl like you would guard me. Can you do that?"

His head jolted to mine in shock I would even ask. Slowly, his fingers reached up, touching my jawbone. "You know I would do anything for you."

A low growl pulsated from the other side of the room, vibrating against my back as though a small child had smacked me. A stubborn, bullheaded one.

I moved away from Torin and stood up. "Thank you, Torin. You, Castien, and Thara are the only ones I can trust right now." Thara gave me a small nod and looked to Torin.

Torin pushed himself up the wall, standing at full height.

"I am at your service, my lady." He bowed his head. At a snort from over my shoulder I flipped around to the other problem child. I was being honest with Torin that I didn't want Lorcan around. There were too many things he stirred up; things I didn't even want in the pot. I was just starting to believe I could move on. To heal and be happy. Now, being this close, I could feel it all unraveling. Lorcan only reminded me why I should hate myself. And hate him.

I marched over to the dweller; a sneer edged the side of his split lip. The blood had stopped pouring from his nose, but a trail dried above his top lip, one eye at half-mast.

"This is the last thing I want." I put my hands on my hips, hating the way his smug grin easily tipped me off kilter. "But this is not about what I want. My people come first—"

"Always the giver, aren't you?" He winked. "Well, except with me...damn woman. You took and took, begging for more."

My cheeks flushed, anger easily coating the chagrin flooding my body. My foot jetted out, kicking his leg. "Dammit, Lorcan. Can't you for one moment be serious? Do you look at anything like it's not a joke?"

He stood up, his figure rising over mine, leaving only an inch between us. "You don't think I take shit seriously?" he rumbled, his mouth so close air halted in my lungs. His nose flared, and anger burned behind every word. "I know life is far from a fucking joke..."

It was instantaneous. The familiar scent, the warmth of him saturating me, twisting my mind in a pool of lust. That connection I loved to despise flamed back, like it had been simmering under the surface for over a year. And I hated it.

I squeezed my lids shut, my limbs trembling at his nearness. *No! You will not do this to yourself again. Keep this business. Only.*

The collection of hurt and fury I kept locked away was cracking open. I knew if it broke, wrath would rain down, burning all of us up. My lids flew open, and I inhaled deeply, stepping back. "We keep the past where it is. We deal with the situation and get home," I stated firmly.

"Sounds good to me," he snarled and turned for the door.

"Where are you going?"

"The abundance of memos and *lists* I am sure you will be sending my way will let me know all I need without wasting the next few hours regurgitating the same shit." He swung through the door, letting it slam shut behind him. The crackle of the fire in the glass bulbs above our heads was the only noise in the room for over a minute.

Lars let out a chuckle, and I jerked to look at him, wondering what in the world he could find amusing. He grabbed a chair, pulled it out, and sat down, his head shaking.

"What?"

His gaze lifted to mine. "I will be honest. I wasn't entirely sure I had made the right decision in calling on Mr. Dragen, but now I know."

"That you made a huge mistake." I nodded, waiting for him to join me. "We hate each other, and we'll probably kill each other before sundown?"

"Quite the opposite, Ms. Johnson." His eyebrow curved up with smugness. "I couldn't have picked any better."

SEVEN

"I don't like this, my lady." Torin stood in my room, watching me stuff some clothes in a bag. Lots of dark items with hoods.

"Torin, we've been over this." I brushed past him, heading into my closet, if that's what you wanted to call it. The former royalty had closets the size of my entire house growing up. It was a waste of space for me and most of it was empty now, cleared out of anything belonging to Aneira. The entire castle had been gutted of her, but I still felt the presence of the former Seelie Queen slithering in the walls, embedded in the precise stone of its foundations. Eventually I wanted to redesign the structure, put my own stamp on it, and banish everything reminding me of the war, of all the people's blood soaking the land. But that had to be low on my priority list.

"I still feel the need to say it again. I think this is a mistake." Torin trailed behind me like a puppy, emanating a mix of frustration and nervousness in me. I privately agreed with him, but the plan was set. There was no going back now.

Torin's hand touched my elbow, stopping me in my tracks. He never said how he felt, but the implications of his feelings were like spiderwebs, invisible, snaring me when I walked into them. "Lorcan Dragen has proven himself over and over to be a deceitful, narcissistic...and excuse my language, my Queen... asshole."

A dark laugh burst off my tongue. I couldn't argue with those descriptions. But there was so much more to Lorcan Dragen. Good and bad. The man's layers were secret and complex. He was an enigma I had attempted to solve, but each time I tried, I only discovered another level.

I was sure Torin sensed something had happened between us but wasn't privy to exactly what. He was better off not knowing. If he knew what actually went on, how Lorcan unlocked something inside me, challenged me, opened me up, and gave me so many orgasms my body couldn't be held by gravity—yeah, he was better off not knowing. And I was better not remembering.

Keep that door closed, Ken.

"I'm not kidding." Torin grabbed my arm, spinning me to face him, his expression a mosaic of worry and severity. "I don't trust him." He grabbed my other arm, drawing me closer to him, my body responding to his abruptness.

My heart climbed up the back of my throat, blocking my oxygen. "Torin…" It was meant as a warning but came out more a needy whisper.

"I don't want him near you." Torin's fingers clenched down firmer on my skin. "He only ruins everything he touches. He's dark. A killer. A beast. You are light. Pure." He moved his hands to my cheeks, cupping my face gently. "You should be respected and revered."

"I—" My mouth parted to speak, but nothing came out. Words were scrambled in my brain, not forming logical patterns.

"I want you to have this." Torin dropped his hands from my face, and with one hand he dipped into his pocket, pulling out a necklace. It was on a long silver chain, which was so light and thin it almost disappeared in the air. The pendant was a starburst with a blood-red stone anchored inside. It was the most beautiful thing I had ever seen. "I recently had it cleaned. It was my mother's."

Holy crap squared. His mother's? A family heirloom?

"I-I-I can't."

"Please, I want you to have it." He slipped it over my head, the pendant falling between my breasts, just below my bra line.

"Torin, I can't...this is…" I picked it up, looking at the light above sparkle off it. I lifted the necklace to take it back over my head.

"I know exactly what it is, what it means." His hand wrapped around mine, pushing my arm back down. "And I want you to wear it. I want you to know what you mean to me. After losing Lea yesterday and you about to leave...I'm not wasting another moment denying what I feel."

My mouth gaped, not finding words, but a heavy warmth hummed up my neck.

His hands slid back up my jaw, leaning forward. My mind went blank, but my body was telling me it wanted it, needed it. It had been sixteen months, and I was eager for someone's touch again. Still going through Druid "growing pains," I was always running hot. But my duty, my role as Queen, dampened the sex drive some. Death, Jared, the memories of every horror in this place also helped curb my appetite.

Right now it was done being restrained. My heart longed for someone to look at me the way he did.

Torin tipped my chin up, his lips brushing mine, waiting for my reaction, before his mouth came down firmer. His kiss was soft, nice, sparking enough heat to open my mouth and kiss back.

Torin was kissing me. Ember's once-betrothed and my First Knight. Why didn't I see this coming?

His hand drew deeper into my hair, pulling me closer.

"Wow, guess the same old policies still apply around here."

A deep voice collided into my ears, sinking into my gut like a grenade. I jerked back, wrenching from Torin's hold, the bomb freezing my insides with horror.

Oh. God. No.

Lorcan leaned against the doorframe, arms folded, his face neutral of any emotion.

"First Knights definitely seem to get a benefits package." His voice dropped, turning a tad icier, his lids narrowing on me. "Or is it the Queen who gets the package?"

"You do not speak to the Queen in that manner." Torin whirled around, his face flushing with anger.

Lorcan smirked. "Think I've spoken to *the Queen* in a lot dirtier manner."

Torin's shoulders rose to his ears, his fists rolled as he stepped in front of me, like a guard dog. "You are vulgar...filth. But what should I expect from a Dragen? You and your brother are cut from the same cloth."

"Thank you."

"That wasn't a compliment." Torin stepped toward Lorcan.

Irritation zipped through me, and I stepped around Torin. "Stop." I jumped in between. I wasn't about to have a repeat of earlier today. "What do you want, Lorcan?"

Lorcan glared at Torin for a few more beats before his gaze snapped to me. "I want *nothing*," he spat, twisting the knife already buried in my heart. "Lars wants us to leave tonight. He will fly over in a few days; his trip doesn't need to be so secret. But we will go through the doors."

"Through the doors?" I sputtered. The Otherworld doors were unpredictable since the war. You could get lost in them for years. A lot of human missing cases were because they stepped through one without knowing, never to be heard from again.

Ember was the only one I knew who seemed to understand them enough to get where she needed to. I shouldn't be surprised my friend's brain grasped the erratic system of the doors. That seemed to fit Ember's impulsive, passionate nature.

Lorcan's brows furrowed deeper, anger cracking his tongue. "You don't think I'm capable of getting us through?"

"No." I shook my head.

"No?" He growled.

"No. I mean yes." I floundered under the intensity of his stare. "Dammit, Lorcan. You know what I mean."

"Clearly I'm too stupid." He rolled his shoulders, stepping so close I had to jerk my head back. "You are going to have to talk slower. Use smaller words."

The numbness coating me earlier fully dissolved, waking the monster from its hibernation. Love. Hate. I felt them both. Kiss. Kill. I wanted to do both. My chest puffed up and down, fire raging up my spine, and I squeezed my hands into balls. He was the only one who invoked such an extreme response from me. And I had to deal with corrupt politicians and nobles on a daily basis.

"Back up." Torin's hand flattened against Lorcan's chest, shoving him back. The fury directed at me jumped to Torin, Lorcan's nose flaring.

"Get. Your. Hands. Off. Me." His voice was low and threatening.

Torin's jaw clenched. "Then I suggest you step away from her. Now." I felt Lorcan's hate consume his body, rush into his arms, and jerk his fist back to punch Torin.

"Stop!" I shoved force behind the word. It wasn't a spell, but I had learned in the last year how to throw my power behind words. But like everything else with me, it was still a work in progress. Nothing happened.

Lorcan's arm continued to go back, his expression locked on Torin. Prey.

Lorcan, stop! The scream built in my mind, never making it to my lips.

Lorcan's arm halted, his head snapping to me. His eyes widened for a moment before narrowing. Rage still bloomed around him, but he let his arm drop and stepped back.

What the hell? I hadn't actually spoken out loud, had I? I quickly shoved the thought away, knowing it would simply take me down a road I'd rather not be on.

"Be ready to go in an hour," he huffed, spun on his heels, and stormed out of the room.

I licked my lips, staring at the ground, hating that every time he left it felt like another tear into my gut.

"See?" Torin's voice was soft and sympathetic as he stepped in my direct line of Lorcan's exit. "He is unpredictable and unhinged. I cannot in good conscience leave you alone with him."

I had a feeling leaving me alone with Lorcan had little to do with his volatile trait.

"It is not your decision, Torin." I stared directly into his eyes, my chin up. "This is an order. If you don't think you can fulfill your duty and stay here to protect that innocent girl, then I need to know now."

Torin jerked like I had slapped him. "Are you serious, my lady?"

I knew I went too far, but I was tired of all the games.

"You know I will do anything for you. I cannot believe you would even question my allegiance." The hurt bleeding into his voice put guilt on my shoulders.

"I apologize, Torin." I sighed, pushing at my glasses. "I just need your attention here."

He stepped closer. My instant reaction was to retreat, but I held my position.

"My lady—"

"Please, your tongue was down my throat. I think you can call me Kennedy. Like you used to." I laughed, feeling a little punch drunk from the roller coaster ride my emotions had experienced in the last few hours.

His eyes bulged from his head, his mouth dropping. Shock. Even a trace of dismay.

"My lady…"

For all the horrors he had gone through, especially at the hands of Aneira, he still was this proper, innocent, old-fashioned gentleman. At least with me.

"You called Ember by her first name."

"She is not my Queen." He frowned slightly.

"But she was supposed to be. What would have happened if she was standing here instead?"

"I would call her by her proper title."

I thought I was a stickler for rules, but Torin lived and died by them. I wouldn't be surprised if he was the kind, even in the bedroom, to address me as "Your Majesty." The notion shot a giggle out of my nose, my hand covering my mouth.

He tilted his head in confusion, and I waved it off, letting the idea fade away.

"I will do as you request." He lowered his chin, inching near me. He reached out, taking my hand in his. "But it won't stop me from checking on you when I can. Nothing can stop me from keeping you safe."

The subtext was clear: Keep me guarded from Lorcan.

Could he protect me from myself, though?

~~~~

The dark latched on to the tree branches, spanning and weaving through the forest like a dreamcatcher. The brisk air clouded from my mouth as I took deep breaths, trying to keep up.

Our getaway from the castle had been simple. While the staff thought I was in bed, Lorcan slipped us through one of the escape passages in the castle, thanks to Grimmel's help. It was also how my doppelganger would get in. She'd climb into my bed and wake up as the Queen, ready to take on her role.

On Lars's order, Lorcan told me nothing about her, not even her name. He said it would be better if I was ignorant of the plan. If caught, I could honestly claim I had no part in it.

Lars would help get her situated and make sure everyone was accepting the new safety precautions and her as me. Olivia was one who had to be told of the plan to help pull it off, but I knew Lars would have someone watch her, check into her every move to make sure she was as faithful as I believed she was. Torin, Thara, and Olivia were the only ones who would know.

Castien had improved enough for Ryan to move him back to their house to continue healing, so I didn't have to worry about Ryan wondering why I didn't come down the hall to visit. The security would let him know of the enforcement crackdown. He would hate it, but if I called him every so often, hopefully I could keep him from getting suspicious. I wanted to tell him, but for his safety I couldn't. All had to believe I was at the castle.

My knee slammed into a rotting stump bringing me back to the present. "Owwwww!"

Lorcan didn't bother with a flashlight; with his predatory nature he could easily see into the night, letting me trip and stumble behind him through the woods.

"Jesus, Kennedy." He swung around, his green eyes blazing like tractor beams. "We are supposed to be fleeing 'undetected.' You're a tiny thing, so how the hell can you trample louder than an ogre?"

"Sorry, I don't have bionic night vision." I rubbed my knee then shoved my hands deeper into my jacket pockets.

"Follow my footsteps. That too hard?"

Breathe. In. Out. Keep calm.

I let my eyes close, trying to center myself instead of thinking of a spell I could use to maim him.

He chuckled derisively, causing my lashes to fling open again.

"What?" I demanded.

The side of his mouth curved in that annoyingly smug but hot-bad-boy smile. "Glad to see I haven't lost it."

I stared at him. Waiting.

"Pissing you off." He winked, spinning back around, taking off like a bullet, disappearing into the shadows.

"Dammit, Lorcan!" I clenched my fists, trying to catch up to him as a low chuckle haunted the forest ahead. In a matter of hours in his company I was swearing and fantasizing about murder. He was right; he hadn't lost his ability to piss me off. It actually was so highly tuned I fought my restraint, ready to snap.

~~~~~~

Lorcan slipped us through so many doors my brain felt like scrambled eggs. I had no idea if he meant to make sure our tracks couldn't be found, or if he was lost and didn't want to admit it. Finally, when I was about to sit down and refuse to budge, he tugged me through a final door.

"We're here," he declared, his voice low, his attention circling the area, making sure there were no unseen dangers.

I spun around. The late afternoon veneer of snow on the trees gave them a glittery glow. It didn't appear all that different from the forest we left from.

"And where's here?"

"Germany. The Black Forest." He took another deep breath, his shoulders relaxing, showing there was no sign of impending danger. "We're going to be moving to different locations until Lars updates us with the site of your meeting."

"You actually meant to get us here?"

Lorcan rubbed his head frantically. A sure sign he was irritated.

"That came out wrong. I meant…I didn't know you knew how to use the doors. I thought Ember was the only one who seemed to understand them."

"Tell her I'm vying for her job." He huffed, walking ahead, soggy leaves padding the muddy earth below his feet.

"I'm impressed." I caught up to him. "That's all I meant."

He glanced over at me, his head shaking with exasperation, a barely-there chuckle rushing out.

"Woman, I swear." He pinched between his eyes but let the sentence die off. His vexation with me generated familiarity. A sense I could touch him. Tease with him.

No! I folded my arms across my chest. I should be annoyed. Angry. Irritated.

"Where are we headed?" I cleared my throat with agitation, seeing a car through the trees whiz by. We were nearing civilization.

"Freiburg. A village close by." His boots stopped, mine automatically pausing with him. He spun to me, arms reaching around my head. The brush of his hands over my hair caused me to inhale sharply, air sticking in my throat. His eyes watched me as his fingers towed up my hood. "You need to keep this on and your head down while going through town." He tugged the fabric over me, pushing me deeper into my shield. "When we are out, I am in charge. There will be no hesitation or question. What I say, you do."

The rebuff formed on my mouth, my lids tapering.

He slipped his hand over my mouth, his expression stern.

"I'm not kidding, Kennedy. You may be Queen back at home, but here I am in command." He pressed closer to me, dropping his hand away. His mouth was only an inch from mine, his breath tickling against my skin, igniting a fire underneath. "Get used to me being on top again," he rumbled into my ear.

My lids closed, heat pooling between my thighs. I tried to swallow, my head dipping in accord. Daft hormones. They would have me agree to anything he said right then.

At his chuckle I eased my lids apart. Lorcan stood back, a smug grin glinting in his eyes. He knew he had me. And I hated my body could so easily betray me. Throw me to the wolves…or the beasts in this case.

"Let's go, li'l bird." He winked, self-satisfaction written all over his face.

Hearing the pet name was like being shot. It woke me up to reality. The meaning under the name, the way it pierced my chest, felt like a javelin.

"Don't. *Ever*. Call me that again." My lip went up in a snarl, and I shoved past him, heading for the street. I stomped several yards before I heard him yell.

"Wrong way, *li'l bird*."

I whirled around, ready to slam his body back into the earth with a simple spell.

He stood there, self-satisfied beyond words, tipping his head toward a road that cut down another side of the forest. He looked so unbelievably gorgeous, it almost bowled me over.

Earlier when I had first seen him, the shock of being in the same room with him again overloaded my senses.

But now in the frosty glow of the winter afternoon, every detail was emphasized. Clear. Crisp.

I could see dark circles under his eyes like he hadn't slept in weeks, and he looked thinner than he had, but that only highlighted the muscles straining along his T-shirt. He looked rugged and dangerous. His scruff was thicker, his dark brown hair on his head a little more grown out, but that mouth, which I recalled tasting every inch of my skin, were perfect.

He wore his usual dark jeans, black T-shirt, jacket, and boots. Somehow he wore it better than a suit. I wouldn't mind seeing him in a suit, but the way those jeans fit around his butt, and T-shirts…

Kennedy, get a grip!

I shook my head, bowing my neck to the ground. I watched the brown leaves pass underfoot as I walked to him.

Torin had been right…this had been a huge mistake. I should not be left alone with the likes of Lorcan Dragen.

He was bad for me…for my heart.

EIGHT

I stood at a huge window. It was night, and the moon glinted off the river below. Cobbled streets and bridges spanning over the water were outlined from the streetlights. A black silhouette flew by the window, squawking loudly.

"Grimmel?" I muttered.

"Kennedy."

I whipped around, taking in the large room, my heart pounding at the familiar voice. But no one stood there, only a huge empty room. It was decadent and expensively designed. A hotel room.

"KENNEDY!" My name screamed through the room, twisting my head back to the window. A reflection of Jared, his arm reaching for me. "Run!"

Before I could react an object smashed into the glass, tearing through the room. My scream echoed with a high-pitched squeal of glass and metal shredding the room.

Flash.

Bodies lay in pieces around me, blood and smoke drenching the room. I tripped over something, my knees crashing to the ground. I gasped. Lorcan's body lay covered with blood, and his eyes stared blankly at the ceiling.

Dead.

Flash.

I sprang up in bed, struggling for air. The early dawn wedged light along the edge of the curtains, leaking the unfamiliar room with shading. My heart pounded in my ears, my wheezes simply escalating.

Explosion.

Glass.

Blood.

Jared screaming my name.

"Hey, it's okay." A figure moved from the bed next to mine, the springs shrill and sharp. My gaze darted around. This was not familiar. Not my room.

Where was I?

"Breathe, li'l Druid." The man sat down on my bed, dipping the mattress. His hand curled around mine, placing it on his chest, his heartbeat firm under my palm. The rhythm was soothing and centered my attention on the bare chest. "This is real. You are in Germany. You are safe."

I gulped back the fear knotted in my throat, feeling awareness seeping in.

        1.) Lorcan.
        2.) Germany.
        3.) Hiding.
        4.) In a flat in the town of Freiburg.

Lorcan's thumb rubbed over the back of my hand, his heartbeat and slow inhales brought me back, giving me rope to hang on to. The speed of my recovery startled me.

For the last year, my visions had eased in frequency, but the aftermath was far worse. Many night guards would burst into my room finding me in the corner of the room shaking and crying, muttering nonsense, pinching my ear till it was bruised. Even when I finally came to understand I was back in my body, I felt like I was floating and any moment could drift off again. On genuinely bad days, it would take me a whole day to feel steady on earth.

"Tell me what you hear." His voice was low and calming, knowing the list I used even as a child, to center myself.

Scanning over the room, I took a deep breath. "I hear your voice. The sound of raindrops against the window. The cuckoo clock ticking in the kitchen."

"What do you smell?"

Taking another deep breath, I shut my lids. "I smell you. Woodsy, masculine, with a tiny bit of sweet." I wanted to roll in his scent. It was an aphrodisiac. "Also cheap laundry soap and dust."

"Feel?"

"Your skin. Warm. Your heartbeat. Scratchy bedsheet." I felt my shoulders starting to relax.

Without a word or needing a prompt, Lorcan's fingers trailed through my hair, over my ear, squeezing my earlobe, proving he was true. The slight sting was the final step I required. I slumped over, the top of my head leaning into Lorcan's chest.

He went rigid.

The moment I touched him, I realized what I did. The familiarity of our old routine had taken over effortlessly. I hadn't even thought about it.

Now it suffocated the air. Tension bowed between us like arches, and I scooted back, moving away from him.

"Can you tell me about it?" He cleared his throat, inching away from me as well, his voice void of emotion.

"Just bits and pieces. There was an explosion. I remember screaming, glass shattering...lots of blood and bodies."

"What else?"

I wagged my head, not wanting to talk about the constant elephant in the room. Jared.

"You forget, li'l Druid, I can tell when you're not telling me everything." His gaze met mine, burning through me. He didn't even have to touch me and every nerve came out of their coma, zapping to life with force.

He glanced away, his hand sliding over his head, rubbing furiously, like he sensed the change in me. He probably did. Another thing I could never hide from the dweller. He could hear my heartbeat, smell my arousal.

I missed him. So much. For the first time in months, I felt at peace. I wanted to bury myself in his arms and never come out again. Give over to the need and desire. But that was the problem. He made me weak, made me want things that could never be. I leaned in to the bed frame until it groaned under the pressure.

"Don't call me that either." I pinned my lips firmly together defiantly, like a child.

He stared at me, his eyes expressionless, before he stood and walked away from the bed. He padded over to the galley kitchenette in the attic-converted flat.

It was small, with one main room, and plain Ikea furniture, but it had lots of windows and skylights. A balcony overlooked the old village square. It was a good place to keep watch on the activity below.

"Go back to sleep. You need it."

"Me?" I shoved off the covers, my feet hitting the icy wood floors. "You look like you haven't slept in months."

"Try a year," he mumbled, flicking on the electric kettle. He reached for the coffee cups and instant grounds. The apartment was stocked with items that wouldn't go bad, which left mostly spices, sugar, tea, coffee, and one package of tea biscuits.

"A year?" I came up next to him, my chilled skin already seeking his warmth. The T-shirt I slept in scarcely covered the tops of my thighs.

Lorcan shot me a look before returning to making coffee, emptying three packets into one cup.

"Wait. Are you blaming me?" Ignoring me he poured hot water into his mug. His unspoken words were fire to the dried timber twisting around my spine for so long. "How is it my fault?"

He grunted, moving away from me, gulping the thick black liquid, and went out onto the veranda.

"Lorcan!" I exclaimed, my arms flailing as I trailed after him onto the sodden balcony. The brisk air and raindrops assaulted my exposed skin, goosebumps springing over my flesh. He only wore thin flannel bottoms, but his skin didn't react to the cold at all. It helped having an inner beast to keep you warm.

"Don't walk away from me." I folded my arms, disregarding the puddle I stepped in or the light drizzle sprinkling down.

He leaned his elbows on the rail, bending over until his head touched his arms, a low growl emanating from him.

"Is this how it's going to be for the unforeseeable future? One of us about to toss the other over the side?"

He slammed his cup down on the small round outdoor table, swinging around to me, his eyes flashing. "How do you want it to be, Kennedy?" he snarled. "What did you expect?"

"I-I..."

"The role of rug-under-your-feet or lapdog is already taken, *Majesty*."

I sucked in, stepping back, feeling the bitterness slap me harder than the chilly air. The shock of his words drenched my anger in gasoline.

"And what did *you* expect? I sit at home and mourn for you? I don't have the luxury." I regained my lost footing, folding my arms tight against my chest. "And why do you even care? I've heard enough rumors about you screwing every woman from here to Brazil!"

Red flared in his irises, his muscles coiling tight under his skin. "And why should you care who I fuck?"

"I don't."

"Liar." He strode to me, his toes barely brushing mine, water rolling in trails over his shoulders. I kinked back my neck, keeping my glare fixed on him. "Jealous, are we?"

I was. Completely. But he would never hear it from me. "No." I shook my head. Rain sputtered down until my hair clung to my face and my shirt adhered to my body.

"Really?" He inched closer to me. His nearness raised my fury, but the line to the flip side was thin as tissue paper. "Don't tell me the idea of my dick in someone else doesn't make you crazy. That it's not buried deep inside of you instead."

Oh. God. My mouth went dry. My body responded instantly to his words, need curling in my stomach. I despised he could make me feel this way.

"To know someone else was screaming my name while I was between their thighs?"

I turned my head to the side, not able to keep eye contact. My breath came short and choppy as I recalled exactly how it felt.

"What? Your Knight in shining armor doesn't fuck like I can?"

I shot my gaze back to him.

"At least with him, you can face your friends, right? Keep Jared's love in its untainted bubble?"

"Fuck you," I seethed.

"So there is still spunk underneath." He tilted his head. "Glad to see she's somewhere underneath that Disney façade."

"How dare you." My hand shoved at his chest, my wet hair swinging in clustered strands. "You have no idea what I have to do to get through each day. My feelings no longer matter. I can't mourn like everyone else. I have to keep going, provide everyone else support and strength, while every day I get threatened and attacked...verbally and physically. I'm not allowed to be scared or crawl in a ball and cry. Or fuck an entire country of men to feel better," I yelled as my hand continually smacked his chest. "Everything I do is up for judgment. Every move and decision. I'm no longer my own person...they own me."

"No one owns you." His chest pushed back against my hands. "Not unless you let them."

My brutal laugh echoed off the roof.

"Easy for you to say."

"They don't have all of you, li'l bird."

"Ahhhh!" I slammed into his chest with so much force he stumbled back. "Stop! Stop it! Don't call me that! You have no clue how hard this is for me."

Only two words and they felt like they could break me, shatter me into a million pieces no one could ever glue back together. I held on to myself by mere threads, trying to keep my feet in the real world, my mind sane, and my heart from fracturing.

He grabbed my swinging arms and pushed me against the wall. He pinned me against the rough surface, his entire frame flush with mine, forcing me to feel every inch of him. Every hard inch.

"You think I haven't a clue how hard this is?" he rumbled, his pupils elongating. "You think this is easy for me?"

I couldn't talk as my body absorbed the sensation of him. My hips opened, allowing him to get even closer. His nose flared; his eyes reddened. It would be so easy, a slight pull of his sweats, a tug of my underwear...

"I think of him every day." Lorcan pressed in, tipping his hips into me, spiraling logic out of my ears like curly fries. "The guilt consumes me, eats me alive."

My T-shirt soaked with water left nothing to the imagination. With each breath, my breasts rubbed his torso, pleasure tingling through my nerves. His grip on my wrists tightened, his hips moving into me.

Oh hell squared...

I wanted this. I wanted him.

"Half the time I can't even think about you without feeling sick...with myself, with what we did to him..." Lorcan licked his bottom lip, my gaze snapping to his mouth, my back arching in response.

"And the other half?" I whispered, my eyes locked on what I wanted, raindrops slipping off them. To know their taste again. He let out a staggered breath, angling closer to me. His answer swelled against my hip.

"The other half..." Lorcan's mouth barely a sliver from mine.

Somewhere in my lust-hazed head, a strange ringing arose from the house till it seeped outside into the early morning.

"Lorcan. Pick up." The Unseelie King's voice came from the phone inside, jolting us apart. An invisible guillotine cut between us, shredding the moment in pieces at our feet. Lars had his hand in many pots and one of them used magic to improve technology. Some things were a success, other things still needed work. I wasn't sure which this communication device fell under. It was like a long-distance walkie-talkie but had even more secure lines. Lately he had installed a feature which allowed him to talk without us answering it.

"Shit." Lorcan jerked his head toward the door leading inside. Running his hand over his head, a deep growl trembled over his lips before he started inside.

The moment he disappeared from sight, my head crashed back into the wall, my erratic breath trying to find a rhythm. The ringing and voice stopped the same time Lorcan spoke.

"What?" His curt tone boomed from inside.

"Excuse me?" The King responded with the same rudeness.

"Lars, it's early. I'm not exactly in the best mood right now. What do you want...*sir*?"

Lars paused like he was deciding either to allow Lorcan's insolence or ignore it. Eventually he cleared his throat.

"I have made contact with several of the nobles in the area. Two days hence, we will be meeting with them in Zurich. Be at the Hotel Baur au Lac at midnight. Penthouse."

Without ceremony, Lars clicked off.

"Asshole," Lorcan muttered.

I stared out at the rooflines of the old town; spires from the church vanished into the curling fog. The smell of baking bread from some local shop drifted up to me, my stomach gurgling. My body shivered in the crisp air, but my head cleared. Clarity of mind is a double-edged sword. Either way, I would get impaled. At least we hadn't gotten too far. This misstep could be taken back. The other...

I covered my face with my hands, scrubbing the images from my brain.

"I'm guessing you heard everything?" Lorcan said.

My neck craned to where he stood in the doorway. His demeanor had changed from what it was moments ago. Aloof. Emotionless. My eyes met his, and he glanced away, staring out on the village.

"It's freezing out here, and you're soaked. I'll go get us some breakfast while you shower."

I couldn't deny the hurt, but we both knew this was for the best. It would have only been worse later.

"And real coffee." I pushed off the wall, walking toward the patio doors. His gaze drifted down, the thin, wet shirt not hiding anything. I folded my arms, brushing by him haughtily. "It's cold."

"Sure." He snorted, not buying it either.

I grabbed my bag and headed for the bathroom.

"At least yours aren't blue," he mumbled as I closed the door between us. My hand moved to the doorknob with the desire to reopen it, invite him in. I twisted the lock and backed away, not trusting myself.

Being around him was like being a sober alcoholic working in a bar. The temptation was everywhere, constantly whispering in my ear to take a little sip, but I knew I would spiral out of control with one taste.

This was going to be the longest forty-eight hours ever.

NINE

My stomach ached, already stuffed with delicious cheeses, meats, and pretzel bread that cart after cart offered in abundance. But the sweet smell of pastries, cake, molasses cookies, apple cider, and hot chocolate hooked my nose, dragging me to the next booth. The vendors at the farmers market didn't care if I had to pop the top button of my jeans. The crisp, overcast day screamed for me to indulge in the warm tasty treats.

I wasn't going to sit around in a small apartment while the quaint old town of Freiburg called my name from below, asking me to come out and play. Going to Greece almost a year and a half ago to find the sword was the first time I had been to Europe. And that certainly hadn't been a vacation. I saw the inside of more caves than I cared to remember.

Lorcan could huff and puff all he wanted, but I was going to enjoy the tiny splinter of time away from my royal duties I was allotted here.

Tucked deep under my hood, it was freeing to be an ordinary tourist. No one knew who I was, which I'd come to yearn for in the last year. At home, my image was everywhere, on everything. What I wore, how I moved, the way I talked…all critiqued and written about. Humans and fae weren't much different when it came to gossip and dissecting their "royals." No matter what I did, some would find something wrong with it, while others held me up on this strange pedestal with no faults.

It felt nice simply being me.

"Jesus, I forgot how much you can eat." Lorcan snickered as I took the warm molasses cookies and hot chocolate from the vendor.

I shot him a look, shoving a small cookie into my mouth. Growing up, my parents had to force me to eat. I ate because I had to, never truly enjoying it like everyone else until I went through Druid "puberty" two years ago. Food became almost orgasmic, and the amount I inhaled tripled, my body quickly burning the energy as my magic demanded more. My hormones also raged out of control, emotions whiplashed, and my appetite for food and sex increased tenfold.

My emotions had since curbed, but the other two were still on high. And I was starting to think it wasn't a hormonal thing anymore. Just me.

"Don't they feed you at that castle of yours?" He nudged past me, speaking against my ear, his breath heating my neck. "Or is this covering what you are truly ravenous for?"

My fingers curled around my cup, knuckles turning white. My mouth thinned in a tight line.

He glanced over his shoulder at me, a side grin on his mouth, clearly enjoying he could still get a rise out of me.

If he only knew his mere presence was enough to get a rise from me. This afternoon was no different. In jeans, black puffy jacket, and beanie, he took me back to another time, when I was ankle deep in snow, working on my magic. Before the war...before...us.

I shook my head.

"Wow, someone lost her sense of humor. Lack of good sex can do that."

He was baiting me. I should be an adult and not let him get to me. *Should.*

"How do you know I'm not having extremely good sex?" I bumped his shoulder as I walked by, dodging a flailing child with sticky fingers as his mother trailed behind with a napkin. The market was full of locals and tourists, the on-and-off drizzle not dissuading the crowd from their shopping or tasting the local goods. The village felt like a movie set with its cobblestone roads and the mixture of curved and A-lined roofs and a gothic church with ornate steeples. Munsterplatz, the main plaza, was like stepping back into the 1400s or 1500s. I was in love.

Lorcan caught up with me. "Because you forget, li'l bird, I know what you are like after you've had *extremely* good sex." He winked, heat flushing into my veins. He turned to a cart, indicating to the vendor he wanted a beer. The man nodded, pouring him one from a wooden barrel.

Extremely good seemed a pathetic definition for what that time with Lorcan had been. My mind could barely graze over it without overheating and blushing so deeply people probably thought I had the flu.

"But I guess it's my fault. Your first time and you had the best...can't go back after that, huh? No one else will ever be as fulfilling."

He's baiting you, Ken. Don't fall for it.

"Believe me, it is better." I lifted my chin, trying to appear I wasn't lying so completely through my teeth. Not only did I doubt anything could be better, I hadn't had sex since Lorcan, which had left me restless and agitated for a good part of the year. If he wanted to assume Torin and I were doing it, why not let him?

"You are an awful liar." He laughed, taking a sip of his beer, the foam sticking to the tip of his nose. I stepped up to him. My fingers brushed over his nose, wiping away the froth before I realized what I was doing. The action felt so natural, so comfortable. I dropped my hand.

He hadn't moved a breath, the intensity of his gaze wrapping around us like vines, blocking out the rest of the world.

I stared up, his green eyes pulling me in like a reel. *Kiss me.* My body screamed over the objection in my mind.

Lorcan inhaled sharply through his nose, like he'd heard my plea, his pupils dilating. His mouth inched down.

I felt woozy, oxygen not quite reaching my lungs. As the heat from his mouth brushed mine an image slammed into my head. Usually it came with white light, pain, and loss of consciousness. But this one, similar to a few I had gotten recently, like the one with

Zoey, was more of a video playing in my head. It was fast, but it jolted me back.

Flash.

A woman and man walked quickly past vendor stalls. The Freiburg Munster, with its lacy spires and cheeky gargoyles, dominated the background. They were dressed in casual, dark clothes, but I knew they were anything but tourists. Both were extremely beautiful with violet-blue eyes. Fairies. The blonde woman walked ahead and held the power, her dark-haired partner all brawn.

They were coming for me.

That I knew with certainty.

Flash.

The image cleared as fast as it came, giving me a sharp headache, but not coming close to disabling, like they could. I jerked my head around.

"What? Did you *see* something?" Lorcan stiffened, sensing something wrong. Fae were everywhere here and with magic now a part of the combined world, I think it was harder for him to decipher the smells.

"Fairies. Here."

"Yes. There are a lot of them."

"No." I shook my head. "They're here for me."

"No one knows you're here."

My gaze landed on the top of a blonde ponytail and a man behind her heading our way. Lorcan followed my gaze to the couple. They spotted us at the same time, their faces darkening the moment they locked on us. They sped up.

"Shit." Lorcan grabbed my hand and yanked me hard to follow him. I stumbled, his grip on my hand clenching, the muscles along the slope of his shoulders rising as he slipped us quickly through the throng of people.

He glanced over his shoulder, and I did the same. My heart slammed in my chest, seeing they were gaining on us, with only a few shoppers separating us. Tourists frowned at them as they rushed through the throng.

"So much for staying under the radar." Lorcan pulled me, picking up his speed. "Time to run, li'l Druid."

My fingers fastened around his as we bolted into a full-out run. I heard the fairy woman yell something sounding German, but I had no idea what she said. Nor was I going to stop and ask.

"Bewegung!" Lorcan yelled as his shoulder rammed through the crowd like a linebacker, shoving people out of our way as we weaved through the market. Fear pumped into my veins, my legs kicking to keep pace.

In trying to lose them, he zigzagged around stands and clusters of market goers, his head constantly flipping back to keep an eye on them. My body knocked around like a ping-pong ball, bumping into people. I ignored the shouts tossed at us, the back of my neck prickling with the pursuer's magic.

"Faster!" Lorcan yanked on my arm, diving between two families with their kids talking and laughing. With a snap Lorcan tugged me to the side, slamming me into the toddler. The little boy fell onto his behind, a cry already ripping across the cold air.

"Oh no." I twisted automatically to help the child, dropping my hand away from Lorcan. "I'm so sorry."

"Ken!" Lorcan swiveled around and reached for me again. "Come on!"

My head lifted to see the blonde and her companion scarcely a few steps away from us. Terror kicked in, whirling me back around as we tore off again.

"Hallo!" I heard the father of the child yell at me angrily, tugging at my heart. I felt awful, but I was sure the child would be fine.

Lorcan curved us sharply around a cart, going in a circle, then pulling me into a booth.

"Geh raus!" The shop man waved us back toward the exit. Lorcan held his finger to his lips, his eyes flashing red. The man inhaled, his next words dying on his tongue as he stepped back, his eyes wide with fear.

Lorcan tilted his head, listening. He held me flat against his warm physique, our heartbeats pounding in unison. My lungs ached at the cold, sharp intakes. Even though every nerve was on high alert with the anxiety of being caught at any time, I felt safe. Content. The deep unrelenting restlessness I had felt for so long was quiet. I chewed on my inner cheek while looking to the side, shoving all thoughts from my head.

When Lorcan pulled away, I twisted my head to him. He crept toward the opening and peered out. "I think we might have lost them." He kept watch for another moment before his arm reached back for me. Lacing my fingers with his, I gave an apologetic nod to the vendor before sliding through the curtain with Lorcan.

"Where are we going?" I kept close, both of us still searching the area for any sign of the couple.

Lorcan didn't answer, his focus completely on the space around him. His nostrils kept wiggling as he took in the scents; his eyebrows furrowed. I could tell he was struggling to pick up any particular smell while the market swam with aromas.

He rushed us back the way we came, hopefully putting distance between the fairies and us. How did they find me? It shouldn't have been possible.

My mind reeled with questions when I felt Lorcan go rigid. At the same moment, a man jumped from around a booth, crashing into the dweller. The two large bodies slammed together, stumbling to the side, hitting a stall as they both fell. Ceramic souvenirs and trinkets smashed onto the ground and rained down on the two fighting men.

Movement in my periphery snapped my head to the side. The blonde woman barreled toward me. Instinct fired through me. The spell lashed off my tongue like a whip, striking out at my attacker, searching to cut deep.

My words exploded into her chest, her eyes widening as her body halted its forward movement, shoving it backward. She sailed back into a pastry stand, her spine hitting the wood display with a crack, sending the pastries into the air and slapping the pavement as they fell from the sky. Individuals around the booth also took the brunt of my spell, spreading out on the cement like a deck of cards.

"Ken!" Lorcan screamed behind me, and I whipped around. He got to his feet; the fae he had been fighting now lay out cold on the ground. Lorcan snatched my hand, not hesitating before he took off at a full sprint, leaving hordes of villagers screaming or staring at us with terror.

And this was only day one of being in hiding.

~~~~~

Lorcan didn't slow our pace as we weaved through town before ebbing a little when we reached a park, every few steps glancing over his shoulder.

"We're not going back to the flat, are we?" It wasn't a question. I already knew. My legs scissored double time to keep up with his strides. Lorcan's grip remained unyielding on my arm.

"Don't tell me you actually learned something from me last time?" he said humorless, scanning around.

"Not sure if *learned* is the right word. I merely know how you think."

He stopped dead, my body ramming into his then bouncing back.

"Believe me." He swung around, prowling up to me, his pupils vertical. "You don't have a clue what I'm thinking." He loomed over me.

Savage. Wild. Raw. Lorcan could scare and excite with the same magnitude. And I seemed to have no immunity to either.

"If I didn't think it would cause more attention, I'd strip you right here."

"What?" I breathed out.

He passed his hand roughly over his head, scrubbing the back of his neck. "I don't know how they know you're here, but they do. For all we know someone put a tracker on your bag or clothes." He motioned to my outfit. "Someone will be watching that place, it's not safe to return."

So the stripping wasn't for fun?

"But how would they even know to put it in my bag? Everyone still thinks I'm at the castle."

"Maybe it's been on an item of clothing of yours for a while now. What better way for your enemies to keep tabs on you than know the best time to attack."

That actually made sense. Maybe that was how they found me when I went to Honey House.

A constant parade of staff, visitors, and nobles had access to my rooms or me. At any time someone could have placed a tracker. Bumping into me. A brush of an arm. A staff member who secretly hated me put something on my clothes.

"My favorite T-shirt." I frowned, already missing my *Firefly* shirt, the worn, soft fabric.

"I'll buy you a new one." Lorcan rolled his eyes, curving back around. "Actually screw that, you're the fucking Queen, you buy me a shirt."

I laughed and nodded my head. "Fair enough."

"We can no longer use the doors either." He picked up his stride, following the sign to the train station. "And without Lars's phones, we're on our own till Monday." The way Lorcan said it, I knew he preferred it that way. He did not especially like to play with others. Unless he was in charge.

⁓⁓

Near the train station Lorcan got his wish, just not in the fun way. A clothing store provided me with a whole new outfit. Dark, stretchy jeans I could run in, new knee-length boots, a black sweater, and a black coat. This one came with faux fur trim around the hood. I also grabbed a daypack, telling the sales clerk to give all my old stuff to the homeless.

We grabbed some sandwiches and got on the next train heading southeast toward Zurich. Lorcan found us an empty compartment, shutting the door firmly. A few people opened it to join us, took one look at Lorcan, and backed out, their eyes wide with fright.

"What's sad is you're not even trying to scare people." I watched the latest commuter retreat out of the space, his Adam's apple bobbing nervously.

"If one more person opens the door, I won't be so nice."

"You growled at that man." I waved my hand toward the door.

"Yeah, and compared to what I wanted to do, that was very nice of me." Lorcan sat back in his seat, but his eyes stayed on the door. When the train departed from the platform, his shoulders barely inched down a hair. He was on guard, riled, his beast pawing at the edges of his human form.

My energy on the other hand was crashing after the high of the chase and the overindulgence of food. My lids lowered at the rocking of the train.

I heard rustling of fabric and cracked them open. He stood before me, taking off his jacket.

"Sleep, Ken." He eased my body down and stuffed the coat under my head. I sighed, taking in his familiar scent coating the fabric, snuggling into it. My eyes struggled to stay open. He sat back down across from me, his hand reaching over. "Rest. I got you." He slipped my glasses from my face and ran his hand over my head, my eyes shutting at his soft touch.

I was pretty sure I made a purring sound as sleep gripped my lids and pulled me down.

TEN

"Hey, li'l' Druid." A husky voice beckoned me from sleep with a smile. A finger brushed across my temple. My lashes lifted, and I almost forgot how to breathe. Even slightly blurry, he was unbelievable.

He was the exact type of man I had never worried or thought about before because I wasn't even a blimp on their radar. Not that I wanted to be. Most times, the extremely hot seemed to prove the cliché of being extremely shallow, boring, and self-absorbed. They were usually after women equivalent of themselves.

I was the nerd-boy type. Jared being the first who was equally a dork and hot. His naiveté and sweetness made it easier to overlook how stunning he was. With Lorcan you could never neglect to see his rugged sex appeal.

I sat up, brushing my long strands of hair off my face. "Are we there?" My hand went to my nose with the urge to touch my glasses, like they were a security blanket.

"We're in Basel." He put out his hand, helping me up. He pulled my glasses from his pocket and slipped them back on my face. I instantly relaxed. "We're gonna stay here tonight. Tomorrow head to Zurich."

I followed him out of the train station, not saying a word, taking in the city as we walked through. Based at the borders of Germany, France, and Switzerland, the influence of all the cultures blended cohesively in the city dabbling between its old culture and modern buildings. A dusting of snow coated the rooflines, crafting a storybook feel to it. I was in awe. Half-timber houses lined the cobbled streets, setting off the pillared, salmon-hued cathedral dominating the skyline. Walking through the old town of Basel, it was easy to imagine it centuries ago.

As we moved through the city, the more I saw pictures...of me. And for once they didn't seem to have big lines through them defacing me or the fact I was their Queen. I had to blink several times when I saw one store had a life-size cutout version of me in the window. It was from my coronation, the crown sitting proudly on my head. The first and last time I wore it.

"Yeah, they actually like you here." Lorcan nudged me playfully. "But to be fair, they don't know you."

"Shut up." I hit him back.

Up one of the narrow cobbled lanes, Lorcan found a small B&B-style hotel. It was a simple en-suite, with two pine framed beds and puffy down comforters and an electric teakettle with a variety of teas, hot chocolate, and coffee. The two windows overlooked a splinter of the Rhine River flowing by.

"You hungry?" Lorcan asked as he poked his head in any space someone could hide in, rechecking the windows were locked.

"No." Sitting on the bed closest to the windows, I watched him move. It felt strange to have no bags or personal items to busy yourself with unpacking.

"What do you want to do?" The tiny room only took a moment to examine, but he seemed restless, not wanting to sit. "We should stay away from public places as much as we can. As you saw, Switzerland is pro-Queen. We'd have a serious problem if anyone recognized you."

"So that's a no on the procession through the market?" I slanted my head, like I was actually asking. "Should probably cancel the trumpets, gymnasts, flags, and the cute little drummer boy."

"Not the gymnasts. They can stay."

"Of course." I laughed, rolling my eyes. The ease at which we could tease actually turned the room awkward and quiet. Both of us understood how simple it was to slip back into our old ways. Lorcan and me on the run? It was like stepping back in time. And the one thing we used to do together was the one thing I had longed for. For once I had no business meetings or people wanting anything from me.

"I know what I want to do." I peered up at him.

"What?" His forehead wrinkled with skepticism.

"Magic." I grinned.

His boyish, mischievous smile upped the side of his mouth. "I think that can be arranged."

~~~~~

Thirty minutes later we stood in a park, trees blocking us from the world. It was freezing in the middle of February and off the beaten tourist path, so we had no worry of encountering too many people. Magic and fae were well known and out in the world now, but Druid magic was still highly rare.

My first spell I set a protective circle around us, keeping people from getting near.

Having Lorcan next to me, even if I surpassed his teachings, was nice. He always pushed me to do better, not letting me get away with good enough.

"Again." His demand echoed off the frigid air, but sweat beaded at my hairline. Like stretching when you've been cramped in the same position for a long time, energy spread out of me, feeling the bliss of being used again. But I was also out of shape and tired easily.

"That was sloppy. Again." Lorcan came beside me. He had me working on my protection spells. I was getting better at isolating who I wanted to target, but not always. We worked till I could feel my limbs sagging with fatigue. It was also getting dark, the temperature dropping fast.

"You're slurring and are going to fall over." His "teacher" voice softened. "I think we need to get some food. Warm up."

"Fooood." I exhaled with relief. "And dessert. Something chocolatey and warm."

"We are in the land of fondue."

"Oh my god, yes."

"That's what I thought." He snickered and turned to head out of the park. I kept pace with him, the silence comfortable between us. But after a while I finally broke it.

"I stopped a vision from happening the other day."

"What?" His head jerked to me.

"Strighoul were going to attack Lars's compound. They had Marguerite." I gulped. "She was killed in my vision. I prevented it."

Lorcan stopped short, halting me, and turned to face me. "Ken, that's amazing." He clasped my face, a smile on his mouth. "*Very* rare."

"I know." His smile was contagious, my cold hands sliding over his, absorbing their heat. "I still can't believe I did it."

"Seriously, you are incredible. Most Druids can't do that even after decades of training." He pulled me in, his lips brushing my forehead. "Proud of you, little Druid." Warmth and joy fizzed beneath my skin, my heart thumping with utter contentment. I wanted to stay here in this moment forever. *Home. Mine.* The words buzzed my conscience.

All too soon Lorcan realized what he was doing. His form stiffened, and he dropped his hands, stepping back, clearing his throat. "Do you remember anything from what you saw?" he asked coolly, staring down the cobbled street.

"Hovek is their leader now."

"Seriously?" His head snapped back. "That fucker? He won't be there long if I can help it." Lorcan's lip hitched up. "How did they even get Marguerite?"

"I think they were going to nab her coming back from Sunday dinner with her family." The vision was like a puddle of water. It reflected back, but when I grabbed for it, it slipped through my fingers. Something bothered me though, the conversation between Hovek and Lars. It was blurry, but my idea that Luuk backed the strighoul didn't fully fit the bits of conversation I remembered.

"Marguerite's all right?"

"Yeah. Goran got her home safely."

Lorcan let out a breath. "Good. Anyone touched her, I'd kill them myself."

"I didn't know you knew her so well." My brows furrowed.

Lorcan leaned back on his heels and glanced at the string of Christmas lights still dripping down the lane, guiding us back to the square, his breath curling into the dark night. "I've spent a lot of time at the compound. She likes to cook for me and my boys. I'd protect her like my own." He glimpsed back at me, shoving his hands in his pockets. "Cole isn't the only entrepreneur. Working for the King is highly lucrative." I knew the relationship between the split groups, especially the three brothers, was healing, but they would never be one group again. Lorcan was alpha. He'd never go back to being beta.

"You work for Lars?" I couldn't imagine Lorcan taking orders from anyone. Or Lars letting the murderer of his true love work for him.

"We've learned to operate together. It's still touchy, but he understands putting away his emotions for the common good," Lorcan replied, like he had heard my thoughts. "He hires my pack to do what we do best. What we were meant to be."

"What does that mean?" A rope looped around my gut like a lasso, tightening.

Lorcan lifted his eyebrow, his expression saying *what do you think?*

I took a step back, and my stomach plummeted. "Assassins?"

"You are still trying to find the good man in me. I told you once he doesn't exist." A smirk twisted his mouth. "Cole's group does all the aboveboard and gray area transactions and dealings. My clan picks up the rest. We do what needs to be done."

"What do you mean? You murder people?"

"That's the last resort. But I do what I must." The muscles along his jaw strained. "What I do for him is my business, but don't think for one moment the people I'm dealing with are the pillars of society. Believe me."

"You don't have to. I know you, Lorcan; you're better than this."

"No, Ken. You just *want* me to be."

"What you did for Eli? For me?"

"Fuck!" he burst out, his hands running over his head. "Stop trying to make me into Jared or even your new boyfriend. I am a fucking dweller, Ken. If you can't accept me for who I truly am, then you were right to say goodbye to me in the tunnel."

"I'm not trying to make you Jared."

A sardonic laugh chuckled from him. "Please. Jared is right here." He motioned to the space between us. "He always will be. We can accept his ghost, deal with the pain and guilt, or we do what we always do. Ignore it." He started for me, forcing me to step back. His face loomed close to mine, his eyes coiling with red. "I've tried to fuck you out of my thoughts, out from under my skin. But nothing worked...until this exact moment."

Oxygen snapped into my lungs, burning my throat.

"All I needed was to see the truth in your eyes. The horror. The need to want to change me," he spit out. "Now I realize you could never have accepted me. Been with me. I'm a killer, Kennedy. It's who I am."

No. No. No. My mouth went dry, struggling to swallow. I hadn't even realized somewhere deep down hope had been flowering. For us to have a chance. Now it crumbled at my feet.

I was Queen. The Queen of Light. A Druid who believed in healing and protecting and opposed everything Lorcan stood for. Two opposing sides that could never meet up. With a final snap, I felt my heart tear apart. The truth set in, the ache sinking so deep my bones throbbed with grief.

I was a fool. We would *never* be. The conclusion was so clear. I squeezed my eyes shut. The tears I thought had dried stung the back of my lids.

We stood in tense silence.

"Yeah, that's what I thought," he whispered. He stared down the street. I couldn't respond, my teeth sawing into my bottom lip until I tasted the tang of blood.

"Let's go get dinner. I'm sure you're hungry." Detached, he started to walk down the street, his shoulders stiff, hands deep in his pockets.

Food was the last thing I wanted now. My stomach overflowed with sorrow. Whatever dream I had secretly been holding on to vanished. I thought I had said goodbye to him before, but I hadn't.

The impossibility of our situation truly settled in. Finally pushing out the last bits of hope.

~~~~~

The next morning, the frigid air in the room was not from the open window. Both of us said as little as possible to each other. Some wounds you can patch over, but others go too deep. Our chasm was too large to fill. Jared's death left a sharp canyon between Lorcan and me that tore my heart and ground my soul into dust, and I would never be able to get past what he did for a living.

I silently followed him out, tucking my hands and face deeper into my clothing to keep warm. We needed to eventually get more clothes besides the ones we bought at the train station yesterday, but Lorcan wanted to wait till after the meeting that night. I think he hoped deep down his shift would be over and he no longer had to be on Kennedy watch.

He sat us down at a café, a tiny table overlooking the Rhine River, the string of arched bridges connecting the two sides in procession. Thick fog hovered over the water as the large white swans glided along like they drifted on clouds.

The style of the buildings with their white facades and dark A-line roofs made you feel you were in some fairy tale, reminding me a little of the village around my own castle. A place I had never gotten to enjoy or explore. But here I felt a strange sense of freedom.

Even with my hood up, my back turned to the guests, under the constant threat of being discovered, I still felt more liberty.

A waitress came to our table—young, beautiful, blonde, and blue eyed. Exactly what you pictured coming out of Switzerland to be the next top model. She wore no makeup, but was stunning with her long silky hair and perfect skin.

Her eyes widened when they landed on Lorcan, pupils dilating, her aura flaring with red so bright she looked like a freaking Christmas tree.

"*Guete morge.*" A blush hinted at her pale complexion, her gaze focused on the dweller.

A huge bad-boy smile spread over Lorcan's face, quickly running his eyes over her, causing her blush to deepen.

"*Guete morge.*"

Let me say I had never, ever been a jealous person. It wasn't in my nature.

Until I met Lorcan.

Lorcan Dragen brought out every emotion with abundance. One smile or word and he could have me planning his death or wanting to tear his clothes off. Even after what he said last night, my urges had yet to catch up, causing a frustrating battle inside me. The goodbye last night was deafening, but still I sat here ready to jump over the table.

My teeth ground together as he spoke fluent Swiss-German to her and pointed at the menu. She leaned down, her long blonde hair tickling his arm as she looked at what he pointed at. Their faces were close.

A sensation gripped me like a vise. A growl from the depths of my being drew through the sludge, spiking the back of my brain with feral possessiveness.

Mine.

I shook my head, trying to dislodge the thought immediately.

Lorcan's eyes slid to me, his head still turned to the waitress. She didn't seem to hear me, but he certainly had.

Anger briefly coated the embarrassment heating my body. But I had no right. He could flirt or be with anyone he wanted. I had sent him away. He had merely confirmed what I had already destroyed. I looked down, hiding the flicker of pain pinching my forehead.

She nodded, touched his arm, then turned from the table. She glanced over one more time before heading to the back. She didn't look like a bitch or some boyfriend stealer, but I still wanted to punch her. Or did I want to punch him?

A smirk lifted his lip, along with an eyebrow.

Him. Definitely him.

I turned my head to the river, feeling his gaze burn my skin. But being as stubborn as me, he stayed silent. "What?" I spat, directing my irritation at him.

"Green. It's really your color." He sat back, the smugness on his expression blooming like a flower.

"Shut up."

"I'm not actually into you peeing on me, but if you want to wrestle her..." He shrugged. "I'm all for it."

"You *really* are despicable."

He sat up, leaning over the tiny table, his face a few inches from mine. "I thought we already established that." His voice was thick and heavy like the fog clinging to the water. "And you made it perfectly clear you didn't care what or *who* I did."

"I don't." I threw out the words, hoping they would stick. The solid goodbye I had felt last night seemed flimsy in the morning light. Like his *adieu* made me want him more. Declare my claim.

"Keep telling yourself that." He sat back as the waitress returned with two coffees, fried eggs, and *rösti*, one of the popular potato dishes around here.

I dug in while he and the server exchanged a few more words I didn't understand. His hand gripped her wrist with a squeeze. "*Merci.*"

"*Nut z'dangge.*" She exhaled, her cheeks spiking deep crimson.

Two bites and my breakfast already wanted to come back up.

Whether or not purposely trying to make me jealous, I couldn't deny it. I hated the sensation, this protectiveness that made me act like a cavewoman. And I almost used my knife as a club when he overtly watched her walk away, her hips swinging a little more than they had earlier.

His gaze came back to me, and I tried to school my expression into neutral, but by the glint in his eyes, I failed miserably.

"I didn't know you could speak Swiss-German." I changed the topic, seeking neutral ground to stand on again.

"I've been alive a long time and used to live in a world where all languages were spoken and intermixed."

"How many do you know?" I had gotten through conversational Spanish and French, but that was it.

The fingers curled around his fork, lifted up as he counted. "Ten fluently."

My mouth dropped open.

"Ten?"

"It would almost be eleven, but I'm a bit rusty in Mandarin."

"Now you're simply showing off."

"It was how I grew up. But since we've been on Earth, in the States, I barely use half of them."

I had to be honest with myself: my nerd girl just got totally turned on.

"You?"

"Spanish and French." I swallowed some of the warm potato *rösti* with eggs. "There were only three of us who took both all through school."

"Why am I not surprised?" He chuckled, scooping in another bite.

"I am an overachiever." I leaned forward. "I thought we already established that."

His irises flickered, the smile dropping from his mouth. His lips held a sheen of butter, and I had the urge to bite down on his bottom lip.

"*Exguusi?*" The waitress stood at our table, jerking us both back in our chairs. She stood there with a white piece of paper in her hand.

My brain thought it was our bill, until her hand reached toward me with the folded paper. "For you," she said in English.

I took it from her, and the moment I did, she swiveled around and walked to the kitchen. Lorcan's brows furrowed as I unfolded the note. Air caught, snaking like a weed around my lungs. The words came off the page and choked me.

Two false Queens, but the one who hides dies.

My heart thumped in my throat. Someone knew I was here. Watching me. Playing with me.

"What?" Lorcan snatched it, his eyes roaming over the words. "Shit." He was up, his chair tipping back, his head jerked all over the restaurant, pulling in deep breaths. I knew he wouldn't pick up anything. Magic was thick in Europe, and with the humans, fae, and food all in a large room, he had little chance to isolate the scent of one.

He tugged out his wallet, threw down some euros, and grabbed my arm. "Come on." He shoved me before him, his attention still scanning the room. Only a few looked up at our abrupt exit, but none seemed really interested in us.

I pushed through the door, the frigid air shocking my lungs and chilling my bones. Many questions hatched in my head, but I stayed quiet while he wormed us through the city. We rushed through the streets, taking random turns down alleyways, the feel of a ghost constantly on our tail.

How did they find me? I had nothing on me from the castle. We didn't even have the walkie-talkies. How would a spy find out about our whereabouts?

Lorcan got us to the train station quickly. Tickets in hand, he jogged us toward the train heading to Zurich. His physique was rigid and agitated, hunching over like a predator, scaring every person we passed. A woman tugged her child away from him, hiding the little boy behind her.

The knowledge of fae had created a palpable terror spreading across the nations. Fear brought out the worst in people: violence, ignorance, rage, and hate. A handful of fae deserved it, but most didn't. In general society, it didn't matter if you were innocent. If you were part of that race, you were guilty.

"How did they know where we were?" I asked as we neared the train.

Lorcan continued to scan the hundreds of people mulling around the station. "I don't know. But I'm starting to rethink your group of trusted confidants." He grabbed my arm, pulling me down the number ten platform. "Any reason any one of them would want you hurt?"

"No." I shook my head ardently. "I trust them all with my life."

"That's the problem," he responded. "And why you would be so easy to take out."

"Torin, Castien, and Thara have saved my life so many times, so why wouldn't they just let something happen to me one of those times? And Olivia could easily do something to me at any time. No. I trust them completely. Plus, none know my exact whereabouts now. Lars doesn't even know."

"He would be the one to benefit the most from your demise though." Lorcan glanced behind us again, his hand pushing on my back. "The one who rules everyone becomes exceedingly powerful."

"You think this is Lars's doing?" I gaped as we moved past the first couple of train cars. "Are you serious? Why would he do that? Doesn't make sense. He hired you to protect me."

"And what a good cover. Pretend to be protecting you at all cost, while you get taken out by a rebel group. He wouldn't be the first ruler to use that playbook."

I cringed. Aneira used Lorcan to secretly kill her sister while she played the devastated sister and Queen.

"No." I refused to accept it.

"I'm not saying he is. I'm simply suggesting he would have the most to gain. No Seelie Queen, he governs all."

I still couldn't imagine Lars going through this just to get rid of me, especially because I had grown to respect and care for him. I thought he felt the same about me. I did not want to believe he could be deceiving me. And because I was a seer, he would have to be excellent at hiding his true feelings.

Then again, he was the Unseelie King. He had the power to hide whatever he wanted from anyone. I couldn't deny the trickle of truth at Lorcan's idea. Lars would benefit from something happening to me. I shoved the idea away, not wanting to believe it.

"Here." Lorcan pointed to a compartment.

As I leaped for the steps, my mind seized. White light careened into my head, shoving my consciousness from my body.

Flash.

I sat up, drawing in gulps of air. My sight took in the small compartment, the gingerbread-like houses and vibrant green grass whizzing by the train window.

A hand touched my back, jerking me around.

"You're all right, Ken," the man next to me said. His jeans crumpled where I had laid my head on his leg.

I blinked, my lungs still heaving, but I knew he was my tether. My safety.

"I'm here." Lorcan's hands glided over my jaw. "This is real."

The door handle clicked, and the door slid open, spinning my gaze to the intruders. Two men stood on the other side, one with green hair, one white blond, their eyes bright violet.

Fairies.

The threat was instinctual. Instant. Fear scorched my muscles, locking them in place, my mouth open, but nothing came out.

Lorcan shoved me back, my shoulders ramming painfully into the wall next to the window. He jumped to his feet as the two large men, holding swords, crammed through and blocked our exit.

Lorcan sprang for them, a roar piercing the small compartment. I scrambled to my feet, my heart pounding in my ears, a spell opening my mouth.

The moment I opened my mouth to speak, the blond man shoved Lorcan back; the other with green hair lifted his sword and swung.

Time hazed around the edges as I watched the blade cut through the air. Aiming for Lorcan's neck.

"Noooo!" A scream shredded my throat as the edge sliced cleanly through, blood spraying over my face as his head detached from his body, knocking into the wall with a thud. His frame crumbled in a heap at my feet. His head had dropped onto the bench seat; green eyes stared up at me.

A guttural screech shook me as I fell to the ground, the cry booming around the room, bouncing off the walls, and crashing back on me in an echo of torture.

Flash.

I shot up, air fighting to get in and out of my lungs. The pounding of my heart strangled my throat. I blinked and looked around. The hum of the train rocked the compartment, and those gingerbread houses and green grass sped across the window.

Confused. Scared. But this also felt familiar.

A touch on my back whipped my neck around, oxygen lodged in my throat. A man sat there, his well-known green eyes looking into mine.

"You're all right, Ken," he said, his jeans creased from where my head lay.

Lorcan.

Train.

Safe.

But I still couldn't lose the tightness in my gut telling me something was wrong.

"I'm here." His fingers went to my face, cupping my cheek. "This is real."

I had been here before. Hearing these exact things.

My eyes danced around the room, my forehead lined with the strain from the sickness in my belly, like it was trying to tell me something.

The sound of the doorknob clicking was like a trigger. The door slid open. Suddenly every detail of my vision rushed back to me. One green-haired man. One blond. Violet eyes.

Oh god. It was happening.

I reacted with no thought. Protection over the man next to me engulfed me. I saw his blood spraying over my face, his head on the seat. I would not let them take him from me.

In the depths of my gut, I felt a strange dark spell coming up, ready to protect and kill. The words formed on my lips, pointed at the two figures about to enter the tiny space, blades in hands.

The incantation spit off my tongue, slamming into everything around me. The bodies flew back into the corridor. Deep gashes tore into their bodies like large invisible claws had ripped into their flesh. Lorcan sailed the opposite way, crashing into the wall. The safety glass on the large window cracked, splintering in a weblike pattern. The force of my magic punched out from me, and my anger was the eye of the hurricane. I got to my feet and walked to them like I was possessed. The men lay crumpled on the floor, stunned and bleeding from their wounds.

"Kennedy!" I heard Lorcan call behind me, but I ignored him and squatted down in front of the men.

"Know this." My words came out cold and foreign, having no control over the tone of the voice that came from the depths of my rage. "You hurt mine; I hurt you.

You *kill* mine? I will reign terror and destruction down upon your kind like you have never known. I am a descendant of Cathbad." I tilted my head, staring at the blond fairy, his face pinched in pain. "You think me weak? Not suitable to lead? Want to challenge my rule? Go ahead. I. Dare. You."

Unknown Latin invocations spilled from my lips, giddy to actually be let free. With a clink, the door to the outside wrenched open, wind whipping through the passage. The two men were lifted and thrown out of the train, the outside earth absorbing their bodies as they hit and rolled down the ravine. Another few words, the door shut.

The click of the lock was like someone punched my brain and gut with a battering ram. I snapped back to myself, gasping for air; my legs buckled, crashing me to the floor.

"Ken!" Lorcan moved in front of me, his eyes wide and roaming over me like I had two heads. "Shit. What is happening?" He clamped down on my form.

It was then I realized I wasn't just shaking, but seizing, jumping around like a fish. A pounding headache squeezed my lashes together. My body felt like it was battling between wanting to purge the blackness and wanting to hold on to it. Loving and hating it with the same breath.

"Stay with me, li'l bird."

I tried to lift my lids to Lorcan's voice, but I couldn't. The heavy magic sucked all my energy and sat down firmly on my brain. All I could do was let sleep take me, numb myself to the pain.

ELEVEN

My lashes lifted to darkness. A window across from me showed night had descended, shadowing the stone buildings and intricate spires across the river. The city lights twinkled off the water like a thousand lamprog, a mean, oversized ladybug with electric wings and sharp teeth. My experience with them had not been pleasant.

The room was small and neat. One bed. Table. Chairs. TV. Hotel room.

A hand ran over my stomach, a body tucking closer to me. I twisted my neck over my shoulder. Lorcan's head lay on the same pillow as mine, his eyes closed. His long, thick eyelashes fluttered, his cheekbones, jaw, and full bottom lip were like catnip. They made you want to roll around, high and happy in his features.

"Stop watching me, Ken," his deep voice rumbled, without one lid lifting.

"Shit." I flinched. "Sorry, I didn't think you were awake." I tried to roll over more, but his hands stopped me. Grunting, he pulled me in firmer against him. My frame fit into his perfectly.

"Just resting my eyes," he mumbled against my hair. "Can't fully fall asleep, but needed to power up after carrying your ass across the city."

I fought his hold and flipped around to face him. "I'm sorry."

His eyes opened, but almost in a glare. "Why are you apologizing?"

"Because...I..." I had no clue what had happened to me earlier.

"What happened on the train?" He put his head on his hand, looking down at me.

"I don't know." I had hurt those men. Darkness grew in me. I had felt it several times now, but it had never consolidated into something real or fused into magic that could truly harm. Deserved or not, I had hurt people.

"Try again."

I blew air out of my mouth. "I had a vision. Those men came in and killed you..." I crushed my lids together briefly, recalling the sickening image of Lorcan's head rolling around on the seat. "When I came out of it. I was confused, not sure what was reality. But when they walked in..." I waggled my head, still trying to decipher what happened, cold fear harboring in my stomach at what I said. "Something came over me. I mean, it happens a lot, saying stuff I have no control over, but this was different. It felt dark. No. It *was* dark. What I did and said. I tore into their skin like it was wrapping paper. And that spell to toss them out? I had never said it aloud before, but it rose out like it has been waiting this whole time."

"Wait. Have you experienced sensations like this before?"

"A couple times now." I gulped and slowly nodded my head. "It scares me. It feels dark."

Lorcan pressed his mouth together. "Maybe because your magic was held back for so long, it's coming out in violent ways. Doesn't mean the magic is dark. You come from an extremely powerful family. Your magic is stronger than any other Druid's."

"But Druids practice light magic. We do good things." I glanced up, wishing desperately I could believe his theory. "This was heavy and angry. I'm supposed to heal, protect, and help, but I swear in that moment I wanted to hurt them. Badly."

He adjusted his head on his palm, his green eyes watching me intently.

"The thought of them harming you…" I gulped, dropping my gaze from his. "It also scares me that part of me is capable of such violence and rage. It goes against who I am." I pinched the pillow between my fingers, my knuckles turning white. "I would have leveled this country. I would have killed and hurt anything in my path."

Lorcan's hands came to my face, turning my gaze to his. "That is what I feel on a daily basis for my family. For you?" he growled. "I would flatten the world."

Tears flooded the back of my lids. Yes, heat rocked my body because of his words, but also comfort. He made me feel normal, like I was okay for feeling what I did. No judgment or concern. Just acceptance. Something I did not give him the other night. Was I so righteous? Judgmental? Could I not accept him for what he was? The good and bad.

"Plus, I will not lie. What you did was so fucking hot." He tipped his forehead into mine.

"Hot?" I chuckled. "You didn't mind being pitched into the wall like a beanbag while I tossed two assassins from the train?"

"Mind?" He leaned back, an eyebrow curved. "Remember women in my culture are as strong and powerful as men. We never grew up with this damsel-in-distress idea. Our women are warriors, fighters, and leaders. Not that I don't enjoy being the dominant one, believe me…but I'm more than secure with being on bottom too."

Waves of lust crashed into me, stealing my oxygen. All the reasons we shouldn't be together just a night ago were now hazy. Not so black and white. And being in this bubble with him, away from the world, deflated any reasons I had. Outside this room, the reasons still were stacked against us. Five solid ones.

      1.) Jared.
      2.) Ryan.
      3.) Ember.
      4.) My role as Queen.
      5.) Who he was and what he did.

No one would ever accept us. Especially Ryan. My friends were my life; I had no choice when it came to them. Lorcan and I were too different. He would eventually move on to someone else. Someone way more his type. And my heart would break, again. Even now, being back with him like this was killing me. I had just gotten to be able to breathe through the day without him. Now I would have to start all over again. Each time more painful.

His fingers moved deeper through my hair; the stifling tension crackled between us. It would be so easy to forget for one night. Drown in the feel of him. I wanted him inside me, to lose myself in his touch. But it would kill me.

I pulled away, sitting up, and turned away from him. My glasses lay folded on the nightstand next to me. I slipped them on, my gaze landing on the clock next to the bed: 11:05 p.m.

"We should get going." I twisted my hands on my lap, my mind trying to set itself on my decision while my body ached for him, wanting nothing more than him to claim what was his. My need for him was on the cusp of winning. Merely one touch and I would have been done for.

But he didn't.

"Yeah. We should." He rolled off the bed and moved to the shower, his movement quick, his words blasé, like he felt nothing of what I did.

Even when he shut the door, my body stood to follow him. But I stopped myself at the door, falling against it, listening to the spray of water.

A part of me, the free Kennedy who had emerged before, intended to walk in and take what she wanted. But that part had gone to the wayside since becoming Queen. My needs were last on the list.

The other Kennedy liked comfort, lists, and safety. As usual, she won.

^^^^^^

After getting something to eat, Lorcan and I headed to the hotel where we were to meet Lars. We both stood out in grubby jeans, boots, and jackets. Hotel Baur au Lac was for clientele with high demands wearing expensive suits and dresses.

"What's funny is you're the only actual royalty in this place," Lorcan whispered in my ear after the door attendant scowled at us.

I had to wear dresses and evening gowns for engagements and events, but I could honestly say I preferred this version of Queen. Jeans and boots, the real me.

"May I help you?" a tall, lean man asked from behind the check-in desk in a thick accented voice.

Lorcan pushed me toward the elevators, ignoring the man. He strolled through like he belonged here, while I kept my head bowed deep into my hood.

"Sir?" the man spurted out from the desk, looking to stop us. "You're not allow—"

Lorcan turned his head slowly to the man. I couldn't see Lorcan's face, but I saw the clerk's. His eyes widened into dinner plates, all color rushing out of his features. His Adam's apple bobbed, and he took a step back.

Lorcan pushed me into the elevator, his attention on the man as he pushed the penthouse button. Petrified, the man didn't make another move to come for us, watching the doors close.

I snorted the moment we were alone.

"What?" A grin cracked Lorcan's mouth.

"You enjoyed that far too much."

"Hell yeah," he chuckled.

"And we wonder why there is so much prejudice against fae." I rubbed my forehead.

"Did I touch him? Did I even threaten that snobby prick?" Lorcan feigned innocence. "No."

"You don't need to do any of those things to make them pee their pants."

Lorcan's smile turned feral. "Sadly, I can't seem to inflict the same terror in you...maybe you'd do what I said then."

"Too bad." I shrugged, hiding my smile.

"I could inflict something else on you, which might make you obey—" He halted, gaze going cold as he locked down his jaw, stopping the rest of his sentence. We had made it clear it was over, but when we were together, neither one of us seemed able to stop the teasing and innuendos. It was unfair and torturous.

Still, his insinuation prickled warmth into my cheeks and my mind blanked on anything to say back. To my relief the elevator dinged. The doors opened on the top level. *Oh thank god.*

I stepped out, finding only two doors. Two penthouse suites took up the entire top floor. Lars didn't give us a room number, but my gut pulled me to the one on the left, feeling strong magic coming from the room.

"You ready?" Lorcan moved next to me. Whether I wanted to accept it or not, a possibility existed Lars wanted me dead. Once the thought was in my mind, it grew tendrils, strangling all my good memories of Lars. *What if this was a trap?*

I nodded.

Lorcan knocked on the door, and it swung open. An extremely short, chubby man stood on the other side. He had to be a fae dwarf. His dark brown hair was short, but his beard was long and in braids. The sleek suit he wore seemed odd in comparison. If he had opened the door dressed in an outfit from *The Lord of Rings*, I wouldn't have batted an eye.

"Your Majesty." The man bowed before me. I still was getting used to that. A man who was probably older than this country was bowing to me. "I am Demrik, high noble of the dwarfs. Please come in, Majesty."

"Thank you, Demrik." I bobbed my head back in respect. "Please call me Kennedy."

His eyes enlarged, and he shook his head. "No, I couldn't, my Queen. It would not be proper." He shut the door behind us.

He was old school, which was good and bad. It came with respect, loyalty, and I knew his word could still be trusted. But nobles of his ilk tended to be so formal and by the rules that nothing ever got done.

Demrik finally looked at my companion. "A d-dark dweller," Demrik stuttered, stepping back from Lorcan. The beast tilted his head, flashing his teeth.

I thought Demrik was going to faint. "Don't worry, Demrik. I'm pretty sure he's housebroken." I nudged Lorcan with my elbow and heard him chuckle to himself.

Demrik waved us to follow him from the entryway, his eyes still casting back to Lorcan every few steps.

Lorcan let out a whisper of a growl. The man jetted to the next room like Superman.

"Stop," I sighed.

"What? I'm not doing anything." I shot him a look before stepping into the large living room.

The penthouse was exquisite. Windows comprised one entire wall overlooking the river. The French doors led out onto a huge balcony. Crown molding, sleek lighting, and large pieces of art decorated the room. A gray velvet sofa faced a huge fireplace, the flames flickering in the hearth with a warm welcome. A seating area with silk-covered chairs and another sofa was set out facing the glistening water below on the other side of the room. Double doors on either side of the living space suggested two master suites behind the doors. Goran and Travil stood on either side of the hallway leading to the front door, on guard.

There seemed something familiar about all this, but my attention was quickly taken from the room to the company who were sitting in the seats facing the windows. Two other fae besides Demrik sat on the sofa.

Lars stood the moment I entered, his jaw twitching as he strolled to me.

"Lars," I greeted him.

He grabbed my elbow, towing me toward the fireplace, Lorcan following.

"Where in the hell have you two been?" His voice was low but sharp. "I tried several times to contact you."

"We had a little 'incident,'" Lorcan whispered hoarsely back. "We had to leave everything behind."

Lars jerked his head to Lorcan.

"What? Someone knows she is here?"

"Yes." Lorcan slanted his head, his eyes drilling into the King dubiously.

Lars sucked in, his hand dropping from my arm. "And you think I have something to do with it?"

"No," I replied.

"Maybe," Lorcan challenged.

"Don't forget to whom you are talking." Lars stepped up to Lorcan, his voice even.

"I'm only doing what you hired me to do. Protect her," Lorcan snapped back. "And if that is questioning everything, even you…I will do it to keep her safe."

Lars didn't move or respond. Thirty seconds is an incredibly long time when you wait for a demon to fling a beast across the room with his mind. Instead, Lars inched back, nodding in approval. "I knew I picked the right candidate to guard her."

"Guys, can we talk about this later?" I tipped my head toward the group staring at us with alarm. "Let's get to why we are here."

"I will hear about this *incident* after."

"Incident*s*." Lorcan stressed the *s* on the end.

Lars slid one hand in his pants pocket, his lips pinching. "Then I want to hear all. Later. Right now let us attend to business."

I followed Lars back to the gathering where he introduced me to the other two nobles: Sebille, a leggy, golden blonde fairy of the Hungarian territory, and Brokk, a fair-haired noble from Poland. Both held themselves with power, and I couldn't help but think insufferable egos. They gushed over me, but I could read in their auras their disgust at having a little Druid girl ruling them, especially one barely older than their shoes, and who was wearing dirty jeans. Demrik was the only genuine one, his aura bright and clear of any hidden agenda.

"We must stop Luuk. He is tearing us apart," Lars said to the gathered group, who went quiet as though in awe of his power. Or was it fear? I looked at Lars in a new light now that Lorcan had pointed out nefarious possibilities. "It is for the best interest of all our countries to stay together, united under one King and one Queen."

I watched the auras of both Sebille and Brokk flare green. Greed.

"If we come togeth—"

"What do you guys want?" I interrupted Lars, trying to rally the feeling I was his counterpart. It went against my nature, but I could not in front of anyone appear to be less than his equal. I felt Lars's glare on me, but I kept my focus on the two.

"I may be young and new to this, but you forget I am a seer. A very powerful one. I can see your truth." I pushed my shoulders back. "So let's get to the point. You are here purely because you want something for yourselves, not because you genuinely want to help our countries stay united."

Sebille mouth dropped open. "How dare you."

"I have never been spoken to in this manner," Brokk spat. "My liege, will you allow such accusations? After all we've done for you?"

Their words flew out of their mouths, only showing the truth to my claims. Demrik sat back in the sofa, arms crossed, and a smile growing on his face. Our eyes caught, and he winked at me. It seemed he agreed with me.

"I think this meeting is over." Sebille stood, swishing her hair off her shoulders. She must have been six feet in her heels, yet she didn't intimidate me.

"Sit down," Lars snapped.

Sebille halted, her lashes fluttering.

"Now." Lars didn't raise his voice, but the force behind it slammed into me like a truck.

She plopped down on the sofa like an obedient dog.

"You both have been nothing but a nuisance from the day I took the throne." Lars slid both hands in his pockets, staring at the two blonds. "I, however, dealt with it because of your families and your titles. You ask me if I will permit these accusations. I not only allow them but agree with the Queen. *Your* Queen. If I don't see you treat her with more respect, then I will make sure your families never know comfort again. You have grown fat, lazy, spoiled, and greedy. If your King and Queen call upon you, you act. Understand?" Inky black filled Lars's eyes, his demon threatening at the seams.

All three on the sofa nodded, gulping at the spiking magic in the room.

"Unfortunately, you two hold great power, so I am willing to look away this *once*. Demrik, I've never had to question where your loyalty lies, and I thank you." He dipped his head at the dwarf. Demrik's chest rose in pride, his eyes beaming with the compliment. I immediately adored him. There was something genuine about him; I liked his company already. "You three are our greatest hopes in stopping Luuk, shutting this uprising down before it gets any more legs. We need to become a united front. Are we all in agreement here?"

All three nodded their heads.

"Good. Now, let's have a drink to commemorate our *devoted* union." Lars moved to the tray of alcohol set out on a table behind the sofa.

I twisted toward the window. The figures in the glass softly reflected back, like a pond.

"Kennedy?" Lorcan called my name gently, my eyes lifting to the figure standing behind me in the reflection. I sucked in. For one brief moment I saw Jared's face looking back at me. When I blinked he was gone, but his image left me feeling hollow.

An eerie *déjà vu*.

Movement coming for the window cascaded horror over me. Oh. No. My mouth opened, and my head whipped back toward the people in the room.

"Run!" I screamed.

But I was too late.

An explosion filled the space with splintering wood and glass, flinging my body through the air. Fire scorched my skin; debris from the room pierced me. I tumbled in the air, my bones crunching as I hit the wall, knocking my senses from me. The last thing I heard was my name screamed in terror.

TWELVE

My lashes quivered, a groan clawing from my throat. I forced my lids to fully open, the haze and aching in my head blurring my vision. I knew my glasses were gone. I reached up anyway, which shot agony through my nerves. Pain covered me like a blanket. The smell of blood and smoke lay on my chest. I lifted my head, glancing down at my body. I looked like I'd been cooked with a blowtorch. Most of my clothes were melted or in tatters. Cuts swathed my blackened skin, fluid gushing out like tomato sauce.

A crackle of fire drew my attention to the room.

Holy shit!

The majority of the room was either demolished or on fire. Half the ceiling was gone, as though it had been peeled back by a giant can opener. Through the haze I saw the entire wall of windows was now open to elements, the balcony gone. The sofa near where we had stood was shredded, a heap of seared remains.

"Lorcan!" I screamed, ignoring the throbbing and bleeding wounds. I pushed myself up, my knees tearing more as I crawled over the debris to where I had last seen him. The thick fumes stung my eyes and burned holes in my lungs.

Oh. Please. Let him be okay. Acid seared my throat.

"Lorcan!"

I inched around what was left of the sofa, pockets of flames eating at remaining fabric and stuffing. I froze, vomit rising up the back of my throat. Three bodies, or parts of bodies, seared, bloody, and blackened lay there. Eyes and skin had melted to bone. I had to turn away. A strangled cry came from my mouth, and I gagged. The smell of burnt flesh filled my nose and coated my tongue. Fae were hard to kill, but not impossible. Not much remained of the three nobles.

Demrik. Tears pinched my tear ducts, already feeling his loss. He was good and kind. He did not deserve this.

At the thought of finding Lorcan in the same manner, I scanned the room.

"Lorcan!"

A groan whipped my head toward the fireplace where I spotted what appeared to be legs behind a pile of rubble. "Oh god." I scuttled toward the form, shoving the wreckage off him. I plucked and brushed glass and debris, my skin numb to the nicks tearing into my palms. Blood soaked his face and body, black soot singeing his scalp and face, lacerations carving huge fissures over his frame. But his chest moving up and down was all I cared about.

He's alive.

"Lorcan?" I grabbed his face, leaning over him. Large gashes sliced his forehead, cheeks, neck, and chest. A chunk of glass stuck out from both his torso and shoulder. "Be still. I'm going to heal you." I gripped the shard in his side and yanked it out. A slurping sound of flesh and matter followed. He groaned again, and his eyes rolled back when I did the same to his shoulder.

Trying to center myself when I'm freaking out is difficult, but with him bleeding out into my hands, I set my jaw tight. The memory of one other time I had to do this, save his life, wasn't far from the surface.

The spell came from me, plunging like a swan dive into Lorcan. *If I lose him...* The enchantment came out stronger and more determined, immediately healing his larger wounds. I kept chanting, rocking back and forth. My strength drained from me, and I stumbled over some words.

"Hey, li'l bird," Lorcan whispered hoarsely, his hand reaching to mine, pulling me out of my trance. "I'm fine. Don't use all your energy." He was not fine, he was trying to hide it, and the agony of his burns and wounds creased the corners of his eyes.

I couldn't talk; my eyes locked on the green of his irises, the terror in my gut still not unclasping from its iron grip. The deep undeniable truth of what I felt for him almost suffocated me. *I could have lost him.*

Sirens wailed in the distance. Police. Firefighters. EMTs. People we didn't want to deal with.

"Kennedy?" My name hurled through the smoke and cracking flames.

"Lars!" I yelled back, getting to my feet. "I'm here."

I helped lift Lorcan to his feet, his teeth sawing together as he put weight on one leg, pulling up the other. It was most likely broken, but I didn't have time to heal it now.

Three large outlines moved toward us. Relief washed over Lars's expression when he saw me. Or I think it was relief; half of his face was so bloody and charred it was hard to tell. Most of his suit was burnt or torn off, veins popping out of his lacerations.

Lars and Goran carried Travil, barely conscious, between them, his head flopping forward with every step, his dark hair streaked with red and black. All of them were caked in blood, covered in gashes, broken bones poking through skin, and clothing burned into their flesh.

My initial response was to heal, to help the wounded, but Lars shook his head.

"We don't have time; we have to get out of here. No one can know we were here."

"And how do you suggest we do that?" Lorcan looked around, the blast had torn through the room to the elevators.

"We have a helicopter on the other side of the hotel grounds. Let's hope the stairs are still functional. Let's go."

The men hobbled but moved as quickly as they could toward the stairs. Just as I was about to follow them into the stairway, I spotted a large chunk of metal on the tile. Normally I wouldn't have thought twice about it, but the symbol on it drew my attention. It appeared to be an Irish flag—to be exact, a Northern

Ireland flag—which I studied in school and knew to be the Irish Republican Army. The ones fighting against England as their sovereign leader. Next to the flag was another symbol. It had three bars with three dots at the top, the two outer ones tilting away from the middle one, almost like three upside-down exclamation points. Somewhere in my subconscious, I felt something stir, recognizing the symbol.

"Kennedy?" Lorcan waved me to the half-missing door. The top level of stairs was twisted and deformed from the heat of the explosion.

I reached over and picked it up. The palm-sized piece of thick metal was hot on my skin. I shoved it in my pocket, swiveled around, and trailed after my companions.

We were not unscathed, but at least we were escaping with our lives.

~~~~

Billows of smoke rose from the top of the hotel, a large hole blown out of the building where we stood only hours before. Lars hovered the helicopter to take in the damage; its red, blue, and white lights flickered, covering the streets around the building below. Emergency crews streamed in like ants.

We had scarcely made it out before an assembly of firefighters sprinted for the stairs, running into the danger as we ran away.

The helicopter barely fit us all. Lorcan and I sat like bookends keeping Travil in place, his huge limp form squeezing me against the door. Goran sat up front with his King. At first I was surprised Lars climbed into the pilot seat, but of course he knew how to do everything.

He was nothing if not prepared and skilled. He most likely could fly his own jet if he was inclined.

None of us spoke, but the air was heavy with our confusion about what had occurred. My limbs shook, blood still leaking from my head, neck, chest, and legs draining me of what was left of my energy.

The rhythmic beat of the propellers lulled me as the moon reflected off the clouds and dimly lit the cabin of the helicopter. Lars turned us away from the city, taking us to safety.

<center>~~~~</center>

"Hey. Wake up." I opened my eyes and looked around. The helicopter stood empty except for me. *When did I fall asleep?* Jolting up, I turned to see Lorcan standing outside, holding the door open for me.

"Where are we?" I rubbed my eyes, missing the feel of my glasses. Even if I didn't need them like I used to, I felt naked and unsure without them. It seemed with the gain of my Druid powers, my bad eyesight adjusted. It still wasn't perfect, but I found I needed the feel of them on my nose more than the prescription in the glass.

"Somewhere in France. Loire Valley, I think. One of Lars's properties." His critical wounds had mostly mended, but burns and grazes still covered him.

I climbed out, trying to breathe through the stabs of pain I could feel too potently now that my adrenaline wore off.

"Holy crap." I took notice of the "house" not too far from us. It was a castle, or what they would consider a château here, not a house. It had five stories of buttery limestone, not including the windows in the dormer

159

roof. A pushed-out entrance with a steeple roof stood in the middle, while two round turrets were placed asymmetrically on either side with steep pitched roofs. Toasty golden light spilled out from the windows; smoke billowed out of one of the chimneys.

"What a dump," Lorcan muttered to himself, his dry humor sounding flat, causing me to peer at him. He kept his head forward, slightly limping, with his expression harder than the stones forming the estate.

Lorcan and I walked silently across the vast lawn, the lights from the château guiding our way. So much was going on in my head, but I still caught the coolness coming off him like a fence I could not see through. He had his guard up, not letting me see his aura. This hurt, as all I wanted to do was hold him and forget all the strife between us. The thought of losing him had been like a slap, waking me up.

When we entered the house, he gave me a wide berth, as if he couldn't bear to touch me. I rubbed my temples, not understanding what had happened. My gut ached with the feeling that even though he lived, I had lost him anyway. Bile burned the back of my throat at the thought, panic fluttering my stomach.

"Ms. Johnson." Lars's voice turned my attention to the grand entrance. Despite tattered pants, all it took was a fresh shirt to restore him to his kingly demeanor.

The entry stood at least three stories high with sleek marble floors and the largest crystal chandelier I had ever seen. A large round table with white roses sat in the middle, welcoming visitors. It felt more like a hotel than a home.

As stunning as it was, I liked his "cozy" manor in

Washington better. "Excuse my rudeness for not showing you around, but I think we have much more pressing matters to discuss."

Oh yeah we did.

"How is Travil? Does he need me? Are you okay?" I stepped around the table.

"I am fine. Travil is sleeping; Goran is with him." Lars turned and led me down a corridor to the back of the house. "My powers numbed his pain. He will heal." I always forgot I wasn't the only one who could heal others. In Greece he had helped lessen my injuries.

He transported us to a large room toward the back of the château, looking to be a study or office. It had a pair of sofas perpendicular to the fireplace, books lining three walls, going up at least twenty feet, with two rolling ladders attached to the walls. It made me want to belt out a *Beauty and the Beast* song, and glide along the shelves, touching every book like a long-lost friend.

"Wow." I stared in awe. So much knowledge and facts...this could be my heaven.

A tall, skinny woman with long white hair bustled into the room, holding a tray of tea, coffee, and snacks. She was fae but must have been ancient, because her face bore actual wrinkles. Fae didn't age like humans. They could be hundreds of decades old and still look twenty. This woman looked to be in the same age group as Hazel. She was beautiful, with a long nose, blue eyes, and high cheekbones and appeared to be in her seventies.

"Sir." She bowed, setting the tray down.

"Thank you, Brynja. We'll take it from here." He nodded, and she quickly exited the room. I had to admit, it was strange seeing someone else besides Marguerite bringing life and love to any of Lars's homes. I missed Marguerite. And her cooking.

Lars motioned to the sofa for us to sit where the refreshments were placed. He continued to pace in front of the hearth, tension curling off him.

Lorcan sat opposite me, his elbows on his knees, hands clasped, his head bowed.

I felt like a raft bobbing around in the sea with no help in sight. "Soooo...?" I broke the silence. "Where do we start? How did someone find out I was there?"

Lars pinched the bridge of his nose. "I am not certain the bomb was meant for you. You being there may have been happenstance. I think its purpose was to take out the only nobles who could have stopped his progression."

"You think this was Luuk's doing?" My hand rubbed at the item in my pocket.

"Who else would it be? He gains from their deaths. It weakens us." Lars switched back between the sofas like a pinball.

"Does Luuk have connections to the Irish Republic?" Both men's heads jerked to me.

"No." Lars stopped, his chartreuse eyes worming into mine. "Never. The Irish are supporters of us. Not Luuk's cause. Why would you ask that?"

"Because..." I pulled the object from my pocket. "I found this next to the elevators. It looks like a piece of the bomb." I slid the metal across the coffee table for both to see.

They leaned over, eyeing the piece.

"Holy shit." Lorcan bounded up, while Lars went rigid, his lids blinking like he didn't believe what he saw.

"What?" I rose to my feet, feeling their anxiety.

Lorcan and Lars exchanged glances before Lars turned away, rubbing his hand over his chin.

"Tell me!" I whipped my head between them. "What does this symbol mean? The one below the flag."

"You don't know?" Lars swung around, an eyebrow curved.

I peered back down at the three lines, familiarity jogging my brain, but I was too tired to put it all together. "It feels familiar, but no. I don't know what it is."

"It means..." Lars cleared his throat, facing me. "We have a new player on the board."

"Who?" My throat tightened, sensing I was not ready for his answer.

Lars stared at me, his voice crisp.

"The Druids."

~~~~~

"I am sorry, what?" I sputtered. Did I hear him right?

Lars leaned over and snatched the chunk of metal, turning the symbol to face me.

"I'm impressed you recognized the Irish Republic Army flag. However, it merely suggests where they are getting the bombs from. The other mark is their calling card." His thumb rubbed over the dark lines and dots. "This symbol is the Awen. It means inspiration or spiritual illumination. It used to be like the yin-yang symbol. Harmony between feminine and masculine. But when the Druids were being prosecuted by Aneira, the rebellion adopted it as the covert symbol of their resistance against her. If you were caught with it on, you were killed on sight, but many continued to fight and this became the icon of their revolution. After most were executed, the emblem disappeared.

"This is no coincidence, and they are not trying to hide who did this," Lorcan said. "They want to be a known player in this battle."

"But…" I shook my head. "I thought most Druids were dead. You guys always act like I'm the only one left."

"You were the only one we could confirm alive, but now I have little doubt there are many out there, emerging from hiding now."

"Exactly. I am a Druid, so why would they want to kill me?"

"Again, I don't think this attack was meant for you."

"Okay, but what would they gain killing my allies?"

"Don't be naïve, Ms. Johnson." Lars slanted his head in disappointment. "See through their eyes, not yours."

I huffed, hating being chastised, but he was right; I needed to look at the facts and history.

"They're striking out at all fae," I acknowledged.

"Yes, especially anyone who was with Aneira during that time…those high-powered officials at her beck and call to destroy all Druids without reason or cause."

Not much different from what Hitler did to the Jewish. Except the Druids were now retaliating.

"This just feels wrong. Druids are healers; we don't murder."

"Anyone can if pushed too far." Lars leaned against the mantle.

My gaze darted to Lorcan, and a feeling of protectiveness clogged my chest. I would have killed those who set the bombs if they had killed him. Lorcan hadn't said a word, nor had he looked at me once. The wall between us grew thicker by the moment.

"We are at a great disadvantage, Ms. Johnson." *Would he ever get used to calling me by my first name?* "And I do not like any odds not in my favor. But tonight we lost three exceedingly powerful fae against our fight with Luuk. And now we have a whole new contender on the field, coming at us from the side."

"What do we do?" I felt like my entire kingdom was slipping through my fingers.

"I spoke to Torin right before you came in. He was very distraught and wanted to come here. His *dedication* to you is courageous. I had to threaten him to stay put."

Lars lifted an eyebrow, hinting at his underline meaning. "Everything is fine back home. Your double is doing an excellent job selling the story and playing you. So far Torin has received no word anyone has caught on. However, it will simply be a matter of time."

"I can't go back yet. We have to figure out what to do to save our kingdom."

"I agree completely with you." Lars nodded. "What would you do next? What would be the most logical step now?"

Lars loved to test me to see how worthy of my crown I was. I had no doubt he already had his answer but wanted to see if mine matched his.

I took a deep breath, letting my brain file the data in a coherent order.

What we didn't have:

    1.) Luuk's location and his next piece in the plot.

    2.) Support since losing the three nobles.

What we did have:

    1.) A lead on a new group against us.

    2.) A location of where they could be.

"We go to Ireland," I replied, standing behind my statement. "While we figure out what to do about Luuk and his militia, we follow the only lead we have. Find the leader of this Druid group and stop them from getting into the game."

A grin spread over Lars's mouth. "You are turning out to be an extraordinary Queen, Ms. Johnson."

Any kind of praise from Lars was few and far between, and I blushed with warm fuzzies. But with Lars, it always came with stipulations.

"I need you to go one step further, Ms. Johnson."

Finding them was such a general plan; he wanted a more concrete idea. Discovering a secret group, who probably took great care in not being discovered and had Druid powers to do it, was not an easy task.

I knew exactly what needed to be done. It was the only way to find this faction and get close enough to the kingpin. "I go undercover. Become the exact thing we seek."

Lars's eyes glinted with pride.

As a Druid, I was the only one. Lars was far too recognizable, and even in disguise they would not let a demon with power like his anywhere near the hive. He'd be killed in an instant. It had to be me—a Druid who had been in hiding, pursuing revenge like the others.

"What? Oh hell no." Lorcan flipped between Lars and me like a windshield wiper. "Are you serious? It's far too risky."

Lars spun toward Lorcan. "It's dangerous if we let them continue to grow in strength."

"No. Fuck. No." Lorcan's jaw set. "What if they find out who she is? They will kill her."

"That's why you will go with her. Protect her."

Lorcan's and my mouths dropped together.

"Wh-wh-a-t?" I stammered. "Lorcan can't come with me."

"Why the hell not?" Fury curled Lorcan's hands.

"Because you are fae." *Duh.* "You are the precise thing they want to kill."

A mechanical laugh sputtered from Lorcan. "And you think you can do this by yourself? *You?*"

"What is that supposed to mean?" I placed one hand on my hip, the other searching to adjust my nonexistent glasses, seeking the comfort of the action amidst a whirl of anger.

"Come on, Ken." He motioned up and down me. "You are honest, kind, and softhearted. You think you can walk up to the door and they will believe you're some Druid extremist? I know better than anyone you can't lie to save your life. It would be like a baby caribou walking into a lion's den drenched in its own blood."

Why did every supposedly nice word feel like an insult? "I am not that naïve," I exclaimed, feeling irritation burn my cheeks. "Maybe I was, but it was a long time ago. A lot has changed since then. I'm different."

"I don't doubt it, but your core hasn't changed. It's not a bad thing. You just weren't meant to deceive. That's what makes you, you." He was right. It was not in my nature, but it still upset me. I didn't like him "knowing" me so well.

"Don't underestimate me, *dweller*." My queenly tone flushed over my tongue. Yes, I had a certain tone which usually came out when dealing with obstinate nobles at meetings. "There isn't anything I won't do for the safety of my people."

Lorcan's shoulders rolled back, like I'd smacked his nose with a newspaper. "Fine." Lorcan rolled his jaw. "Suit yourself, *Majesty*," he sneered.

Lars watched us, his expression blank, but a hint of amusement remained in his eyes.

"I will head for Belfast tomorrow," I stated, staring at Lars.

"Both of you will."

"Lars—" I tried to interject, but he held up his hand, shutting my mouth.

"And *do not* underestimate me, Ms. Johnson. I am not foolish enough to send in a dark dweller with you if I thought it would put you in more danger."

"Then how—?" I touched my mouth, stopping myself.

"I have it on *extremely good* authority Druids are using their powers to control fae, to do their 'dirty' work."

Lorcan swung to Lars. "Are you serious?"

"Yes. The Druid who once practiced mind control had been taken care of, but I've heard rumors the method has continued on."

In the last year I had read a lot about fae history. The books actually told me their stories. The bonus of having fae books: it's like a fun audiotape. They loved to talk and tell you all that's written in the pages, plus bits of gossip that aren't.

One of them had been about the Druid genocide, which I was particularly interested in. Though Aneira had sown a great deal of hate, not all anti-Druid fears were unbiased.

A select group of "dark" Druids had started using fae as their puppets. Fae did not take well to being dominated. They could do it to others but did not want it done upon them.

My mind whirled with where Lars was going, the plan forming in my head. A slow smile crept on my face. "So Lorcan would go in as my marionette."

"Precisely." Lars rocked back and forth on his heels, a wicked grin pushing up his mouth. Lorcan's and Lars's past was rocky at best, as Lorcan was part of the reason the love of Lars's life was dead. Through the war they had become allies and now worked together, but the bond was precarious, and at any moment I sensed they could return to being enemies.

Lars seemed to be enjoying Lorcan's discomfort far too much.

"No." Lorcan's head began to move. "No. No. No. Absolutely not."

"You said you would protect her with your life, did you not, Mr. Dragen?" Lars's perfectly manicured eyebrow bowed up.

"Yes, but—"

"And you would do whatever it took to keep her safe?"

"Yeah, but—"

"There is no but. Her safety and well-being come first, and I thought you would agree with me." He wasn't forcing him, but the weight of Lars's power still bobbed like a buoy.

Lorcan ran his hand over his neck, his forehead crinkled with frustration. "Of course it is."

"Then we are at an agreement?" Lars clasped his hands in front of him.

Lorcan glared at Lars but nodded at long last.

"Good." Lars's smugness choked the room. He never had a doubt he would get his way. The King turned to me. "Don't be afraid to actually use your powers on him, Ms. Johnson...and make sure the collar is tight."

✦✦✦✦

Brynja showed us to our rooms upstairs, placing Lorcan and me across the hall from each other. He stayed stalwart in his silence, not even saying good night before he disappeared behind the door, shutting it firmly behind him.

I knew he was not happy about his role or going undercover, but the freeze had started prior to that. Now we had reached arctic levels of chill between us. Blinking back the hurt, I shut my door, my shoulders sagging with the weight of the night.

Lars told us we would set out for Ireland in the morning. He would head back to Seattle, encouraging the notion he'd been nowhere near this latest incident. The media was probably already hounding both our camps for a response to the death of the nobles. I knew Olivia could handle it. She was amazing, but I still hated putting this on her too.

I stepped farther into the large chamber. It reminded me of Ember's room at the compound. A mix of modern and old. Lush velvet and faux fur blankets and pillows, a modern chandelier hanging over the king-size, princess-style bed, designed in soft grays, creamy yellows, and icy blues. The lavish bathroom contained a claw-footed tub, walk-in shower, and heated floors.

It was gorgeous and luxurious, but lacked the homey feel I longed for. After the night we had, I craved a comfy couch, my friends, and a bowl of mac-n-cheese or pizza.

I stripped off what was left of my clothing and cringed when the melted fabric tore pieces of my skin from my body. But I was lucky. Very, very lucky.

Turning on the faucet I gritted my teeth as I stepped into the shower, my sensitive skin aching under the spray. I scrubbed away the blood, soot, and grime and tried not to think of the gruesome images of fragmented bodies and burnt flesh popping back into my head. But they wouldn't go away.

Neither would the overwhelming pressure of being Queen, along with all that had happened and what still lay ahead. The impossible feat of keeping the kingdom from crumbling. The family and friends I had lost but had no time to mourn. Now alone, sobs tore from my chest, my tears merging with the drops of water.

I wanted to give up. To step aside and let someone else take over. It was so tempting. I was a twenty-three-year-old girl who didn't even get to graduate high school before her life was turned upside down. I had dreamed of going to college, not ruling the fae nation. I had no clue what I was doing. Fighting against such extreme hatred, prejudice, constant threats, and attacks would cause anyone to buckle.

Unfortunately I was not the type to give up. I worked until I understood or figured it out. Being bad at something was never comfortable for me. And this was no different. I couldn't let down Lars, myself, or the people who counted on me. I turned my head up to the stream and washed away the last of my tears.

"Never give up. Never surrender," I mumbled to myself. It was a quote from one of my dad's favorite movies. When I had been picked on at school or had a bad day, he would come into my room, rub my back, and quote the line, never failing to make me smile. I could see him in my head, stroking my back and telling me to get up and to keep fighting.

"Okay, Dad," my voice cracked, feeling his ghost curl around my heart. "Never surrender. I promise."

Limp and exhausted, I dressed in a fluffy robe hanging behind the door and stumbled to the bed. Lars had promised fresh clothes would arrive in the morning.

I curled onto my side and let the huge bed engulf me, giving over to my exhaustion.

~~~~

I sat up, the scream shredding through my teeth into the pitch-black room, a drop of sweat trailing down the side of my temple.

Alone. Dark.

My heart thumped in my chest as I tried to swallow, shoving down the visual of the dead bodies, guts, blood, and bones spread over the hotel room. Lorcan's detached head in the middle.

"Shhh…" A voice surprised me as a figure crawled onto my bed next to me. "I'm here. You're safe." Lorcan's arms wrapped around me, pulling me into him, his hand stroking over my head and down my back. "This is real. I'm real."

It had merely been a nightmare, my soul's reaction to the horror I had seen tonight. I knew perfectly well where I was. Selfishly I still let him hold me as he went through our ritual. It felt so good snuggling into his chest. I blissed out at the sound of his heartbeat thumping against my ear. I could have so easily lost him tonight, finding him in pieces like I did Demrik.

And suddenly I was all too aware of his nudity, of the speed at which he'd run in here to console me without hesitation.

"What do you smell, hear, and feel?" He brushed my hair over my ear, tugging on it.

My body felt alive with need, his touch twisting my mind like a ball of twine.

"I smell you," I whispered, moving my head up toward his neck, allowing my impulse to override my brain, the night draping protectively over me, giving me confidence I wouldn't have in the light of day. "I hear the pounding of your heart..." My lips grazed his collarbone. He went still, his breath catching. The wall he had put up earlier re-formed.

I wanted to smash it to dust.

"Ken..." My name felt shrouded in cautionary tape. I ignored his tone, brushing my mouth over his Adam's apple. My fingers worked at the knot of my robe.

"And I want to feel you...deep inside." My bluntness would have embarrassed me at one time, but Lorcan had a way of smashing through my comfort zones and pushing me to the edge. Making me accept all aspects of myself.

He sucked in sharply, his throat bobbing as I nipped at his skin. My fingers loosened the robe tie as I climbed onto my knees, opened it, and let it slide off my body.

"Fuck," he muttered, red coating the green of his eyes. I could see every part of him was turned on.

Tonight I didn't want to think about the reasons I shouldn't be doing this or denying my attraction to him. I just wanted.

"Kennedy. Stop," he growled, barely clear enough to understand.

"No." I ran my hand down his torso, skimming the tip of him.

He grabbed my arms, tossing me back onto the bed, climbing over me, his expression fierce and angry.

"You think you want this, but you don't."

"Yes, I do." I exhaled, the ache growing into painful levels.

"No. You won't tomorrow." He growled. "I can't do this anymore...after what happened earlier..."

"*Please*," I pleaded. His lashes flattened together, a struggle clamping his features. "Just tonight."

"Exactly." He shook his head. "But it wouldn't be. You would hate me."

"I can't hate you." I pulled pointlessly against his hold on my wrists. "I tried."

He opened his eyes. Pinning both my arms with one hand, he palmed himself, skimming his length over me. I gasped, my hips bucking up.

"Jesus, I want to fuck you. So unbelievably hard," he spit out, fury rolling his muscles. "Until you shatter over and over… so filled with me, you can't breathe."

"Oh god. Yes." I heard myself begging, desperate for him to do exactly that.

My head spun at the friction of him sliding himself over me again and again. "You want this." A cruel smile twisted his mouth as he continued to rub against me.

I nodded feverishly.

"Say it," he demanded, low and gruff. His voice and movements fogged everything with lust.

"I want you. Now." I hissed, arching.

A smug smile grew on his mouth, flicking with rage. "You will hate yourself and me. Trust me," he rumbled, shoving back on his knees. He flicked the necklace lying between my breasts with disgust. "Stay with your fairy knight. Have him fuck you like the submissive dog he is."

Lorcan climbed off the bed, his feet heavy as he stomped through the room, slamming my door. A second later, the sound of his door banging rang down the hallway.

I propped myself on my elbows staring at the door with bewilderment. My chest crashed against my ribs at the same time I felt the sharp loss of near-gratification and extreme humiliation.

What the hell just happened? Why was he so mad?

Damn! He totally rejected me. A silent sob ricocheted in my chest. It was like he put my heart in an industrial-size shredder, tearing and slashing it into powder, covering me in utter mortification.

From the moment we got out of the helicopter I had felt his anger and coldness increase. All directed at me. I had no idea why, but now I had a taste of his cruel torment. My heart was hurt, my mind was furious, but my body still craved his like a junkie. An addict who never wanted to recover.

THIRTEEN

By morning the swirl of emotions condensed down to one. *Rage*. Hurt and embarrassment gave up the battle and produced one foul mood.

As Lars promised, I found clothes on the bed when I got out of the shower. A variation of what I had before: dark jeans, a black sweater, and this time black biker boots with steel toes. A thigh-length, faux fur jacket, beanie, and gloves were also included. Ireland at this time of year could be freezing.

I grabbed the jacket and clomped down the hallway, glaring at Lorcan's door before descending to the first level. Voices led me to the back of the house to the kitchen. This room held all the latest stainless steel appliances, with sleek white counters, and cupboards with glass insets. Glass penlights and a crystal lamp hung over the breakfast table. Hazy sun glinted through the windows, displaying the grand gardens in the back.

Lars sat at the table, reading a newspaper, drinking coffee, Goran beside him.

"Good morning." I forced a smile, but it came out as a grimace.

Lars looked up, his gaze trailing over me. "Good morning, Ms. Johnson. Did you not sleep well?"

Great. I looked like crap too. "Not really," I responded. "And *please*, call me Kennedy."

"Well, *Kennedy*, please help yourself to the coffee and breakfast on the counter."

"How is Travil?" I moved to the kitchen island, filled with fruit, croissants, cheese, meats, and coffee. It looked great, but what a difference from Marguerite. That woman would shriek at not having breakfast made from scratch and loaded with calories and love.

"He is healing. Might be a few more days till he is back to normal," Lars responded.

"I will go look in on him, then check in with the security on duty. See if the jet is ready." Goran stood, the chair grating over the gorgeous dark wood floors, and he walked out.

I poured coffee into a cup, the smell already lifting away some of my indignation. It didn't last long.

Lorcan stepped into the room looking like he just came from working out. Dressed in gym shorts and shoes, rubbing a towel over the back of his neck, his unclothed sweaty chest invoking lewd thoughts. My eyes wandered down the deep V-line at his hips damp with perspiration.

"Enjoy your workout, Mr. Dragen?" Lars folded his paper, standing up, strolling to the counter. "Hope you found the gym up to standard after your run."

Lorcan snorted. I didn't have to see this gym to know it was probably fully outfitted with the latest and greatest equipment. Probably better than any private health club in the world.

"Yeah. Thanks." Lorcan's gaze darted from Lars to me, then to the window.

"Mr. Dragen also had trouble sleeping last night." Lars poured himself another coffee, a hint of a smile on his mouth. "Needed to burn off some excess energy."

It always felt like Lars knew everything, as though his demon scurried into your soul for truths you didn't want anyone to know. Who knows? He probably was capable of doing just that. Not a pleasant thought, especially after last night.

"Is there a safe phone line? I'd like to call Torin and let him know I'm okay." I kept my head toward Lars but saw Lorcan's snap in my direction, the feel of his eyes burning into me.

I had stayed up almost all night. Thinking. Going over what happened. My conclusion: Lorcan probably did me a favor. We were all wrong, if not for each other, then our lives were. He would never be able to fit into mine, nor would I in his. Too many obstacles and objections. We had a powerful attraction, but it would have always ended badly.

I needed to move on, from Jared's memory and from any connection to him, especially Lorcan. Torin was smart, kind, and extremely good looking. He really was "perfect" for me, and our personalities were quite similar. He clearly wanted to progress our relationship. I liked he wasn't connected to my history. Before, I hadn't been ready...not sure how I truly felt about him. But now I felt more secure. I would at least give it a chance.

"Yes. You can call him from my office. There is a secure line there." Lars took a sip of coffee, then set the cup back down. "The jet will be taking you guys to Belfast in thirty minutes. You each have a backpack on board with clothes, walkie-talkies, and weapons. Information I could gather last night is also in a packet. It is up to you two to do some digging, locate the headquarters for this group."

Lorcan and I nodded, our glares crossing.

"Somehow you will have to find a way to contact me, without any suspicion." Lars tugged at his cuffs. "I wish I could go. However, my presence is a lot harder to keep a secret; too many people know who I am, and I am needed at home."

As Queen I had a lot of noticeability, but not like Lars, who had been King for decades. Centuries. After the fall of barrier between worlds, it took a while for Lars to get things like TVs, communications devices, and radios to function in this new world. My image was not embedded in people's brains like Lars's was.

I grabbed two croissants, cheese, and coffee and headed for the office, taking a breath once I got away from Lorcan's barely dressed physique.

Torin picked up after two rings. "My liege?"

"No, it's me." I resettled in the wingback chair, suddenly feeling anxious.

"My lady?" Torin's voice breathed out in a husky tone. "Thank the gods you are all right. I almost lost my mind with worry."

"I'm fine. Bruised and sore, but alive." My fingers peeled at the top layer of the croissant, my nerves taking out their energy on the poor pastry. Why was I so nervous? This was Torin. Someone who had become a very good friend. On numerous occasions we had been alone for hours, talking and at ease with each other.

Because never before did you think of him as a "possibility."

Now it was all I could think, and I kept trying to gauge my reaction to hearing his voice. It was nice to hear, and I had missed him....

Shit squared.

*As my friend...*my gut filled in the rest. It reminded me of how I felt about Jared at the end. I cared about him so much, confusing it for love, but deep down I knew it no longer was.

I bent over my lap, palming my face into my hands. *Damn that dark dweller. He messed everything up...he messed me up.*

"The thought of anything happening to you... I went insane thinking you might be hurt, and I couldn't do anything about it. All I wanted was to be by your side..." Torin trailed off, the airwaves crackling with anticipation, words he was building up to say. My throat clogged, wanting to stop him from saying more, to leave the unspoken in its box. "I don't want to be separated from you anymore."

My lids squeezed together. Thinking there was a high probability I would throw up on Lars's antique rugs.

"I was serious before. I want nothing more than to protect you forever. Be the man at your side, in and out of your bedroom."

Oh god, he said it.

Butterflies zoomed around my stomach, but these weren't the fluttery kind. They were petrified and trying to break out, or batter themselves against the lining until they killed themselves.

My eyes scanned the windows in front of me, contemplating using them as my escape hatch. This morning I had been sure I wanted this; now that it was being offered, all I wanted to do was run for my life.

"Uh..." My brain couldn't come up with one good response.

"Think about it, my lady. I know you are going through a lot right now. But I want to be clear how I feel about you. And when you return, I want to be the one you run to."

My fingers dug into my scalp before I raised my head, taking a deep breath. "I'll think about it," I responded. I was being honest. I *would* be thinking about his proposal, but I wasn't convinced my heart would alter. It would be so much easier if it would. We made sense. It would be so easy.

Easy and so incredibly boring.

I shoved the thought away. "I need to go, Torin. I will talk with you soon."

We said goodbye, and I clicked off the walkie-talkie with a stab of my finger. I groaned, folding over my lap, my forehead against my legs.

The flutter in my stomach tapped the back of my spine, broadcasting a warm tingle at the nape of my neck. My fists balled up, knowing without looking exactly why my skin sizzled with awareness. "It's rude to eavesdrop on another's conversation." I sat up, staring out at the manicured lawn. What appeared to be a maze designed with hedges lay beyond the large spouting fountain.

"Your thirty minutes are up, *Majesty*," Lorcan spat from the doorway. "Sorry, phone sex with your boyfriend is going to have to wait."

I rose to my feet, swiveling around to face him. He leaned against the doorjamb, dressed in jeans, T-shirt, boots, and jacket, fresh from the shower with water glistening off the scruff lining his jaw and the tips of his hair.

I did not swear much... But *fuck* Lorcan Dragen. Damn him for looking the way he did. For making me feel the way I did. For pushing me to be more...to *want* more. Anger had never threatened my sanity like it did until I met him. He took my serene personality and flipped her over till I wanted to claw and bite.

"Darn, because morning phone sex is always the best," I volleyed back at him. See what he did to me? The old Kennedy would have never said anything like that, never would have even thought of it.

Lorcan inhaled, his jaw crunching together.

I strolled past him, feeling quite proud I could silence the great Dragen. *Take that, almighty beast,* my thoughts shot at him.

He grabbed my arm, twisting me to face him, then pushed me back against the door, his form looming over mine. "You think this is a game?" He sneered, pressing closer to me; his fingers wrapped tightly around my biceps. "Fuck with this *almighty beast*...and he fucks back. Last warning, little Druid." He shoved off me and strode down the hall, leaving my heart pounding in my throat.

Confusion and fright kept me pinned against the door. *What the hell...? How did he know I called him that?*

It wasn't possible or logical. Only fae in the same species were able to link, and only some were powerful enough to do it. Ember and Eli had been a freak case, but now that she was part dark dweller herself, she could link to all of them.

Ember and Torin could because they were both noble fairies and had once been betrothed to each other. I knew they still could, but since she fell in love with Eli, Torin tried to sever the link as much as he could.

I was human. Okay, human plus. But still, there was no way—none—I should be able to link. Except I recalled the times in the past I felt we had to just look at each other and understand what the other one was thinking.

A coincidence, Ken. That's all it was.

Even my brain laughed at me.

Like so many other things, I filed it away. We had more pressing matters to deal with.

Like keeping a kingdom afloat.

FOURTEEN

The flight to Ireland was a little over an hour on Lars's private jet. Despite clouds and heavy rain, the plane landed smoothly on the tarmac in Belfast.

Lorcan and I had stayed on opposite sides of the jet. I tried to read over the material Lars left us, but all I heard were the giggles from the two obscenely hot stewardesses Lars employed. I recognized them from our flight to Greece. What a difference a year and half makes. Last time I'd flown in this jet, I'd been lying in Jared's lap on the seats across from me. Hands interlaced, kissing, laughing and talking the whole trip, our innocent love bubbling around protecting us in our own little world. Now, looking back, I saw the problems between us were already beginning, but I was far too enamored to see it then.

Tears sprang to my eyes, picturing his smile, his hand swiping back my hair, the love in his face as he looked down at me. Little did I know then what was to come.

God, I miss you, Jared. He was my first love. A best friend. No matter what that would never change. I would forever love him, and I now realized love comes in all different shapes and sizes.

Lorcan's laugh came from the back. Subtly, I looked between the seats.

"Whoa, there." He lifted the brunette's hand from the crotch of his pants. "Be careful there. That's not the beast you want to mess with right now."

"Oh I think I do," the other said. Both girls seemed eager to provide Lorcan with all the perks of riding this airline.

They had addressed me formally as Queen and made sure I was comfortable, then proceeded to fall over themselves to serve Lorcan. And it was not coffee they wanted to deliver.

My breakfast threatened to resurface at just the idea of him going to the back room with them. Every time I heard his jeans rub against the leather chair, my eyes darted over, making sure he hadn't gotten up to follow.

"Be careful what you ask for, sweetheart." He winked at the girl.

Lightning zapped through my bones, crackling with fury. I understood fae thought of sex differently than humans did. There were no sluts or manwhores. Sex to them was as natural as breathing. And they did it often, with many lovers. No judgment or shaming.

But I wanted to shove those girls out of the hatch...without parachutes.

Lorcan's gaze somehow found mine between the gap in the chairs, a smirk growing on his face.

Let's see if beasts can fly too. I growled to myself. He was converting me into a vindictive monster. I swiveled around, staring out the side window at the thick mist rolling over the wings of the plane.

He didn't move from his seat but ate up their attention like it was raw venison. Laughing louder than I had ever heard him, smiling bigger than his natural smile.

An hour flight felt longer than the entire nine hours to Greece. I was so happy to get off the plane and away from the swimsuit models, I almost knocked them over in my rush to get off. Too bad I couldn't leave him behind too. Then they could go at it like rabbits, and I wouldn't have to see or hear it.

"Hey, what's gotten up your ass this morning?" Lorcan caught up with me, tugging the pack Lars had provided us onto his back. "Phone sex with fairy boy had to be subpar...still far too tense there, li'l Druid."

I gritted my teeth, not responding to his jabs. Actually a part of me wanted to laugh. The brothers were so similar in ways. Eli had called Torin the same thing when he was pursuing Ember. Probably still did.

"Do I detect some jealousy?" He prodded at my temper.

"No."

"Really? Because you're looking awfully green."

"Because you make me ill."

Lorcan snorted and let it drop as we walked out to the front of the airport.

"Keep your head down." Lorcan flipped up my hood when we got near other people. "And stop touching your face like you have Tourette's. It pulls focus." He grabbed my hand from reaching to my nose, pushing at my imaginary glasses.

I hadn't even realized I was doing it. I had worn glasses from the time I was four; the habit to push them up my nose was ingrained in me. I hated not having them. Even if my vision had improved, I felt naked without them.

We caught a taxi to town. Lars didn't want to risk using any of his connections, just in case. They were people he employed and trusted with his life, but he was still afraid something might leak. Lorcan told the driver to drop us off at the train station. From there we weaved through the area like we were trying to lose a tail and came out the other side.

Lorcan found a hostel, which was the perfect place to get lost in a sea of young adults too drunk or busy to notice anything around them. We got the last private room with a sink but still had to share the bathroom with others.

"Head to the room. I'll be right back." Lorcan handed me the key.

"Where are you going?" I stopped my hand from rising to my face, not able to hide the slight concern in my voice.

"Go upstairs and *stay* there. I'll be back." He wagged his head, making for the door.

Yep, I should have tossed him out of the plane.

I proceeded to our room, opening the door on a single bed, nightstand, and sink in the corner. Simple.

Small. And trouble. I glared at the bed like it was taunting me. Guess a beast was going to get friendly with the floor tonight.

I took two steps into the room when my sight blanked out, my awareness ripped from the present, hurtling me to a different time and place.

Flash.

My body swayed to the beat of the music, the stickiness of a lot of bodies crammed into a small space all dancing around me. Only dim lights outlined the forms on the crowded dance floor. Lifting my head, I stared into a pair of brown eyes, glasses rimming the cute mysterious face of the guy I was dancing with. He smiled nervously down at me, his hands clenching my hips. He leaned in like he wanted to kiss me, but stopped, his Adam's apple bobbing.

I only hesitated a second before I raised on my toes, my mouth finding his.

Flash.

A jail cell surrounded me. I looked down feeling heaviness tugging at my wrists. Thick chains wrapped around my wrists.

"Ken..." I glanced to the left. Sitting against the same wall, another prisoner was shackled by the neck, ankles, and wrists.

"West!" I tried to yell his name, but nothing came out, something holding back my words. He stared straight ahead, his hands rolled in fists, body vibrating with tension, like he was ready to jump up.

"Whatever happens, I've got you," he whispered. "And I'm sorry. I had no choice."

Flash.

"Shit, Kennedy!" My name flung me out of the vision, opening my eyes to a pair of emerald ones, so deep and beautiful I wanted to go swimming in them, bask in their brilliance.

"Fuck." The man's hand went to my forehead, holding it against my skin. A sharp sting raced across my head and I sucked in. "I'm here. You're safe…I've got you." Worry creased his face, and I couldn't help but reach up, my fingers trying to smooth out the lines. In my core, I knew I was safe. He felt like home.

At my touch, he swallowed.

"What do you hear?" he asked me. The sentence was like a trigger, slamming me fully back into my body.

Lorcan.

Hostel.

"Tell me," he coaxed. "What do you smell? Feel?"

"I hear the buzz of fluorescent lights." My limbs shook as I tried to sit up. "I smell moldy, dirty carpet."

"Go slow." Lorcan's hand stayed at my forehead, his other hand helping me sit back against the bed. A trickle of liquid slid past my eye down my face. "You're bleeding pretty good." He leaned up, grabbed one of the towels left for us on the bed, and replaced his hold with the cloth, his hand drenched in blood. "What do you feel?"

"I feel like someone hit my head with a bat." I cringed when he adjusted the towel.

"No, but it looks like you tried to head-butt the bed railing. Is that how you Druids say hello?" He tried to smile, but instead reflected the pain flinching across my expression. "It was a close fight. Think I'm going have to give it to the bedframe this round."

"Shut up." I laughed before the sting on my forehead lit up.

His expression turned serious as he touched my jaw lightly, drifting to my ear. He barely pulled it, but it was more out of habit than me needing that dose of pain to clear my head. The gash on my forehead was doing it well enough.

"Another vision?"

"Yeah..." I tried to think back. "It didn't make sense. West was in one, I think. And I was..." I tapered off, not wanting to bring up I had been kissing someone else. A stranger. Who was that guy?

"West? What the hell was he doing in it?"

"We were locked in some underground dungeon or something..." I tapered off, the memories becoming soft and patchy.

"And I wasn't there?" He leaned back.

I shook my head.

He frowned, pulling the towel away from my head inspecting the cut. He stood, going to the sink, wetting the cotton before kneeling before me again. "Hold it there. It's still gushing."

I healed fast, but still a lot slower than fae.

Holding the towel in place, I finally looked around the room. A grocery bag lay by the door, tipped on its side, items spilling out, like it had been thrown down.

"What'd you get?" I nodded toward the bag as I leaned back against the mattress. The vision had been bad, but this was the second time I'd recovered so fast from one.

Actually they had been better since...

I swiped my mind clear of that thought. He made them better because he knew my ritual of getting out of them. He had been there when I had my first one and quickly learned what grounded me back to earth. That was all.

"Why don't you heal yourself then we can deal with what's in the bag."

"I'm intrigued." I used the bed to get to my feet. "Or scared."

"Nothing to be scared over." He swiped up the bag, bringing it over to the bed. "Go heal yourself."

I walked to the sink, staring into the mirror. Blood caked my hairline and leaked down my face.

The spell danced off my tongue, twirling up to my head in a variety of colors. The skin threaded itself back together, closing the wound right in front of my eyes. It still floored me I could do stuff like this. It really was badass. And now that I had a taste of magic, I never wanted to be without it. It was seductive and addictive. How I lived so long without it, I couldn't imagine anymore.

After I cleaned away the blood, I turned back to Lorcan. He had all the items from the bag out on the bed.

"I fought with Lars this morning. I don't want you here—"

"Dammit, Lorcan. I thought we already went over this?" I cut him off. The bullet of hurt embedded into my chest. "I am part of it. You cannot dictate what I do. It's *my* kingdom, *my* people. I will not sit out while it falls in ruins."

"Great. Can I finish my sentence?" Lorcan's mouth flattened, a glimpse of a warning in his gaze.

"Sorry." I folded my arms around my middle.

"Lars did agree with me on one thing: your appearance is still too noticeable. If we are to go undercover into the enemy's den, no one can recognize you." Lorcan sat on the bed. "He was firm you had to be here. Your being a Druid was our best bet to get close."

"I agree with Lars."

Lorcan squinted at the ceiling, inhaling deeply.

"Then what do you have in mind?" I moved closer to the bed, taking notice of the hair dye, scissors, fake tattoos, and what looked like a hoop earring. "A disguise?"

"We can't have anyone recognize you. Also, no one would believe, looking the way you do now, you could hurt anything, much less fight fae." He motioned to me.

"What does that mean?"

"Ken, you are beautiful." He tipped his head to the side. "Breathtaking…but too wholesome looking to be taken seriously in any kind of rebellion."

My fingers touched a box of hair dye. "And you think turning me 'raven black' is going to do that?" I smiled at the irony of the name of the dye.

"It's a start." He grinned, picking up the scissors.

"Oh. No." I shook my head at the sharp shears. My hair reached my lower back and had been my mother's pride and joy. I always had it long.

"Doesn't have to be up to your ears, but it needs to be different." He reached up brushing a line at my bicep. "Like to here. It will still be long. Believe me, I don't want to touch your hair, but you can't have hair the same as the Queen's."

I sucked in my bottom lip. He was right. I had to fit my part, and anything still resembling the Queen would put us in danger.

"Okay. But only to here." I tapped at the same spot he had indicated.

A wicked grin yanked at the side of his mouth. "You trust me to cut it?"

"Yes." I nodded. "Because you know I can take you down now if you mess with me."

"Sounds fun." Red flared at the rims of his gaze, our eyes meeting, driving a truck through my lungs. He snapped his head back toward the items on the bed, seizing the fake tattoos. "Also, no one would ever imagine the Queen having a raven tattooed behind her ear, or an Awen symbol on her shoulder."

"And how are earrings changing my image?" I motioned at the rings on the bed.

"Those don't go in your ears," he smirked.

"Did you actually get me nipple piercings?" I choked out.

He burst into laughter, grabbing the package, his head wagging. "Damn, I wish I had now." He stood up, standing in front of me, his laughter dying away. "That would be so fucking hot…but this is for your nose. Radicals are into piercings." He lifted an eyebrow.

He was so close, and his breath curled down my neck, heating my breasts. Torching desire drove from the tips of my hair to my feet, wanting nothing more than for him to seize me into his arms, not letting me think, or giving me a choice. Just taking…

"O-kay." I took a step back, needing space to clear my head. "I'll start with the dye."

He grabbed the box off the bed and tossed it to me.

Since I couldn't glamour like fae and there were no long-term spells I could use to change my appearance, there seemed to be no other option. The Druid part of me, the one longing to defy my sweet side, settled into the driver's seat, ready to take control of the wheel.

"*Goooodbye to Saaandra Dee.*" I hummed homage to *Grease* under my breath.

"What?"

"Nothing." I went to the sink, staring once again at the girl in the mirror.

I was sick of being scared and unsure. I was Queen. Looking the part was one thing. For once I wanted to feel it. I tore the hair dye box open.

Goodbye to Ken-ne-dy.

~~~~

"Wow." I stared wide-eyed at my reflection, shorter silky black tresses dangled to my shoulder blades, feeling like two pounds had been lifted from my head. I swung my head, loving the way it swished and tickled my arms. The simple color change and cut completely altered my appearance. My skin, already fair, looked even paler, in contrast. My brown eyes shone sharper and brighter, especially when I lined them with thick, black eyeliner.

I looked older. Tougher. A girl who was not afraid to fight.

"Very goth." Lorcan came behind me, watching me in the mirror.

Wrinkles formed at the bridge of my nose. "Goth?" In high school it was equivalent to being called a nerd. Unimaginative and derivative. Not really an insult.

"Sexy, dark, and mysterious." Lorcan flipped my hair to the side, his fingers sliding below my ear. My body went still, every nerve going numb except where he touched. "I think this is a good spot for your moniker."

"Moniker?"

He grabbed the fake tattoo and a wet cloth. "Raven."

"Raven," I repeated the name, looking at myself say it. It felt as natural to say as Kennedy, like it had always belonged to my Druid self. "I like it."

Lorcan wiped my skin, cleaning it before placing the tattoo on the spot, rubbing it with the cloth again. Holding it in place for several minutes, he then peeled the paper away, leaving a black raven in mid-flight stained on my neck.

"This one is infused with magic and should last for a month. Hopefully you won't need it past that."

His chest bumped my shoulder, his fingers grasping my chin and the back of my neck, tipping my head to the side. Leaning in, he blew on the tattoo, his breath running down my neck, sending shivers over my skin. I swallowed, feeling my body come to life.

What was it about us? We kept saying goodbye, set in our decision, only to find ourselves right back here. He was a force I could not fight, no matter if we were good for each other or not. Lorcan would forever be my weakness, the flame I could not help but fly into and burn up once I touched it.

Tugging my sweater up, he added another large tattoo to my shoulder blade. You couldn't just find the mark of Awen in a shop, so he drew the character himself with a magic-infused pen. It was huge, taking up most of my shoulder, but we had no time to be subtle. We had to get this group's attention.

Air softly stroked my skin like they were his fingers as he dried the tattoo, his mouth close to my shoulder. My lungs clenched, a tiny gasp escaping. Over my shoulder, green eyes met mine in the glass, the intensity parching my mind of lucid thoughts. Our connection pulled me under until I could no longer breathe.

He broke away first, curving back for the bed. With his back turned, I momentarily closed my eyes and took a deep breath, trying to regain my footing.

"Two more things." He ripped open another package, seizing a small hoop between his fingers, clipping it between my nostrils.

Raven, the Druid extremist, formed before my eyes.

Pulling out an item from his jacket pocket, he slid the dark red frames up my nose, hooking them on my ears.

"Lorcan…" I took in a deep breath, his gesture cutting deep across my heart.

"I know they aren't your normal prescription. But it's not like you really need them anyway." He turned his head away from my watery gaze. "I personally don't think Raven should have glasses at all, but watching you today absently touch your face repeatedly, people would notice."

"Thank you," I whispered. He nodded and moved farther away from me. I glanced back at the girl and took her in. I was already dressed in all black and with combat boots. Lorcan picked up a dark green army-style jacket with patches on it, fitting my new image better than the expensive stylish one Lars had given me. The differences were startling; I was a completely different girl. The Seelie Queen was nowhere in sight.

"You ready?" Lorcan pulled on his beanie and gloves. "Might as well start tonight."

One last glance in the mirror and I nodded. "Yes." Raven had emerged and was ready to play her part.

FIFTEEN

The bass thumped through the dark underground club, the air thick with lust, sweat, pot, and alcohol. The brick roof arched in shallow domes, stuffed with skulls and bones across the openings along the walls. I was pretty sure they were real. The tiny dance floor was packed with bodies bouncing along to the grunge band playing on stage. Dilapidated sofas and chairs grouped together filled most of the empty space between the bar and the dance floor. Disturbing art depicting death covered the walls, and the bar was designed out of coffins.

After the barrier between the worlds dropped, places like this made a huge comeback. While the masses claimed they were scared of fae and didn't like them, many were secretly fascinated with the monsters of the night. Succumbing to their darkest fantasies, people came to these kind of scenes hoping to encounter their desire. Clearly fae were no dummies. They were here in abundance, exploiting and fulfilling the curious humans' fancies and probably their own.

"Here." Lorcan handed me a bottle of beer. It had taken us two hours talking to some college students and fae to even find out about this place. It was still a long shot that anyone from the Irish Republican Army, the IRA, or Druid Liberal Republic, the DLR, would be here, but it was a start.

"Thanks." I grasped the chilled bottle, lifting it to him. I couldn't get over the impression I had been here before. "Cheers."

"Cheers." He tapped his against mine, taking a swig.

"What do we do now?" I yelled to him over the music as the band shifted to a haunting, sexy beat. Lorcan turned to me, grabbed the beer from my hand, and set it on the bar. He reached up, taking off my sweatshirt. His fingers slipped over my shoulders, peeling the fabric from me, tugging it off, leaving me in my thin racerback tank top.

"We dance." His mouth brushed against my ear.

Yearning flamed up my body. My veins pumped with it, cooking me from the inside out.

"You dance?"

"No, but I don't think what they're doing on the dance floor is called dancing."

From what I could see it was barely a half step above actually having sex.

"O-kay," I croaked.

Lorcan placed my beer back in my hand and took my free hand, tugging me to the packed floor. He kept to the edge but turned my back to the bar. "The more who see this..." His hand glided over my shoulder blade. "The more chances they will come to us. We only need one."

I nodded, a slight flicker of disappointment nicking my heart. I knew why we were here. We had a mission, but I still wanted Lorcan to dance with me without a motive.

Shut up, Ken. This is about the mission, which is the only thing that is important.

Lorcan kept his arms down, but pressed his physique into mine, slightly rolling his hips to the beat of the music.

Fuck. Yes, it was one of those times that called for swearing.

I let out a whimper, hoping it was absorbed by the music, my teeth digging into my bottom lip. I refused to look at his face. This was torture, my body intimately aware of how well he could move his hips and wanted nothing more than to be reacquainted again.

Slamming back a huge gulp of beer, I tried to fight back the overwhelming need for him as our bodies moved together in sync. Figures crowded around us, my neck and back growing damp with sweat, but I barely noticed anything beyond our bodies. The erotic beat of the music, his hand gliding up my arm, our chests moving in and out in shallow breaths, and his physique pressed into mine.

"Ken?" Lorcan whispered hoarsely in my ear, his mouth so close all I had to do was tilt my head to claim them with my own.

"Yes?"

I shifted a bit, making us even closer, and his mouth so near I could almost feel them on mine. *Kiss me. Now.*

"There is a man staring at you in the corner. His eyes haven't left you since we stepped out here."

"Oh." I jerked back. Not at all what I had imagined him to be saying. Or doing. I had lost focus, again, forgetting everything but Lorcan, and here he was eyeing the club, keeping on task. Acting the part.

"Don't look until I lead you back to the bar. Ginger in the corner, tall and skinny, with a beard."

"No. I lead you." I stepped back, folding my arms. "Time for the beast to be my plaything."

His mouth flattened, his lids narrowing.

"You need to look a little more vacant than that." I reached up and patted his chest. "I'm sure it won't be too hard."

He made a low rumble.

I was lashing out in hurt, once again becoming someone I never thought I could be. Before I met Lorcan I could relinquish my bad behavior. Now, I flipped around, heading back to the bar. I scanned the room, the man Lorcan described easy to find. He stood by himself, leaning against a corner pillar, his arms folded. He did not hide the fact he was staring at me intently. His face was expressionless, but I instantly picked up on magic rolling around him. Magic like mine.

A Druid.

It was like climbing back into your own bed after weeks or months away. My body recognized the familiarity. My heart leaped up my throat and excitement buzzed my spine. I had never encountered another Druid and hadn't expected the thrill of interacting with another one face to face. I felt an instant draw, a sensation of long-lost family, elation of not being completely alone. My legs itched with the longing to go over to him. I hadn't even realized I was complying till Lorcan hooked my belt loop, tugging me back.

"Let him come to us," he said.

I wiggled free of him, twirling around to look at the beast. "You have to stop being the dominant one here. I am in charge." I thrust my hands on my hips. Lorcan stared down at me, his eyes wandering over me. Hungry. Intense.

I had been a reluctant leader but quickly learned I could not let them see the deep fear and uncertainty I felt being Queen. With Lorcan those facades were hard to keep up. It scared me how willing I was to let him take the lead. Not in everything, but here and now I desired him to take what he wanted. I could easily shut down every excuse and denial on my lips.

He stepped back with a huff, ripping his gaze from mine, looking over my head. "Shit," he growled.

I whirled around. The spot where the man had been was empty. The Druid was gone.

"He left." My gaze drifted wildly over the club trying to see if I could find him. *No. We can't lose him.* Everything was based on us getting into this group. What were the chances we'd run into him or anyone else?

"By the door." Lorcan jerked his head at the exit.

My feet took off, not exactly sure of my plan yet.

    1.) Stop him.

    2.) Say what after that? I don't know.

I elbowed between the bottleneck of bodies near the door, pushing my way through, anxiety at losing our only lead spiking my adrenaline. I might be small, but I shoved at men twice my size, knocking them back with shock. My heart pummeled my throat, pulsating where my raven tattoo lay.

"Move!" I slipped through a couple, hitting the stairs up to the ground level, stumbling up the uneven stone steps. I practically fell out the door, knocking into the doorman.

"Watch it, lass." The six-foot bouncer frowned down at me. I ignored him, stepping out farther into the alley, the icy temperatures needling my bare arms.

Besides the line waiting to get into the club, the lane was empty. I twirled around, looking down the long row. "Where'd he go? He can't just disappear." Druids were good, but we couldn't just vanish into nothing. Right?

Lorcan came next to me, his nose flaring, taking in a deep breath. "I can't pick up anything. Too many people here."

Not ready to give up, I took off down the passage, heading for the main street. When I reached the end, I scanned the road. Couples and groups of people dotted down the sidewalks, cars zoomed by, but I didn't detect magic from anyone.

"Dammit!" I stomped my foot.

"Whoever he is, he's long gone," Lorcan nodded.

"Our one chance and I already blew it."

"It's only our first night. I have a feeling he will be back." He curved around to me, his fingers tugging at the sweatshirt tied around my waist, pulling it around my shoulders. "Think we should call it a night."

I rubbed my eyes, giving the street one last sweep. "Yeah."

"Come on. We need to get our jackets, then I'll get you a hot chocolate on the way back." His hands slid down my arms, warming them.

My gaze met Lorcan's and he dropped his hands away. It seemed so easy for us to fall into how we were before.

"Chocolate. Yes." I nodded with a small smile. "That always helps."

⚊⚊

When we reached our hostel after my stomach was full of sweet cocoa, exhaustion from the long day finally smacked me over the head. I took off my boots and jeans and climbed onto the bed, not bothering to change into the pajamas Lars had put in my bag. I was still sad about losing my favorite T-shirt in Freiburg.

Lorcan locked the door. Then the bed creaked and dipped as he sat on the edge. His boots hit the floor with a *thunk*. At the sound of fabric swishing against skin, my eyes popped open with a start.

He tossed his Henley onto his bag across the room and sat there, his scarred back facing me. Those scars were permanent memories donated by Aneira and his father. I longed to reach out and touch them, trail my fingers all the way down.

Suddenly I was no longer tired. The realization of our bed situation barreled into the room, scooping up my breath.

Earlier I was upset enough to think I'd make him sleep on the floor, but I couldn't do that.

> 1.) It was disgusting. I could see the dirt on it from here.
> 2.) He'd have to sleep halfway under the bed just to be able to lie down.
> 3.) There were no extra blankets.

My hand went to my chest, as though I could cover up its hammering. It was pointless as Lorcan could hear it from the next room. He didn't move, his elbows on his knees, just staring at the wall.

"I'll see if they have a double tomorrow," he said, standing up. "Get to sleep."

"Where are you going?" I propped myself on my arm, alarm swamping me.

"Nowhere, just going to sit here. Let you get some sleep." He still wouldn't face me, standing in the middle of the small room.

"You need sleep too."

"I'm fine."

"No. You're not." I sat all the way up. "When was the last time you got a good night's rest?"

A cankerous laugh crackled out of him. "Since meeting you?"

"How well can you protect me if you are about to fall over?" I spoke in desperation to keep him close, not with logic. "We're safe in here. Now get in this bed before I make you."

Lorcan swung around. "Make me?"

I lifted my eyebrows. "Remember I'm a Druid. I *can* make you if I want."

We both knew I was full of shit. I couldn't make him do anything.

"Are you talking about black magic?" His eyes twinkled with naughtiness. "My, my, li'l Druid. Walkin' on the dark side?"

"If I have to." I shrugged. Black magic had to be learned; it didn't just come to you, not that I heard of anyway. And I never planned on doing that.

Yes, you do. You crave to taste it. A voice trickled into my head, tightening my gut. Black magic was forbidden. Wrong. It went against pure Druid magic. But my darkest desire stirred like a witch's brew. Always there. I locked down on my jaw, shoving the thought far from my mind.

Lorcan returned to me and placed his palms on the bed, his face an inch from mine.

"Threatening me with black magic, just to get me in your bed?" He spoke low and husky. "You really are a Seelie Queen."

I inhaled sharply, my back slamming into the wall behind me. Hurt and embarrassment flooded my cheeks and eyes, and I turned away from him, my lids blinking.

"Ken…"

"No." I gritted my teeth, fighting back the tears. Suddenly so hot I couldn't stand the feeling of my sweater. I tore it off down to my tank, then turned my back on him, lying down.

"Ken, I didn't mean it." He huffed.

I tucked my arm under my head, digging farther into the pillow.

"Hey." The bed dipped with his weight, his hand resting on my shoulder.

I twisted away from his contact, almost rolling on my stomach. "Good night, Lorcan."

"Kennedy," he sighed, his voice soft. "I'm sorry. That was too far."

I squeezed my lids together, feeling one tear wedge through. I wasn't upset because a boy called me names. Hell, I was used to that. High school trained me for such things. I wasn't that weak or thin skinned. What upset me was this feeling of truth in his joke. I wasn't Aneira. I knew that, but I couldn't deny the darkness inside. And it frightened me.

"Kennedy, talk to me. You're not angry...you're scared...I can feel it."

I wrenched my neck to look at him over my shoulder. He reached up, wiping the single tear from my cheek, waiting for me to talk.

"I feel it," I whispered, gazing back at the wall.

"Feel what?"

"Darkness."

"What do you mean?"

"I can't explain it, but it's been happening for a few weeks now." I stared at the ceiling. "Maybe even before. I sense this power. And it's dark." I shifted higher on the pillow. "I know it shouldn't be possible, but that doesn't take away from what I feel."

He was quiet for a moment before speaking. "You can't have light without darkness."

"This is different."

"How?"

I didn't want to talk about it. I didn't want to think of what I could feel underneath. I understood the harmony of dark and light. Nature used balance. But black magic wasn't the yang to Druid magic. Our magic naturally already had good and bad intent. Black magic was its own entity. And it had no good in it.

I reached and grabbed his hand, tugging his arm into me. He didn't say a word, following my lead; he climbed in beside me, curving around my body.

The heat from his arms folding protectively over me gave me complete serenity. Briefly, the restless part of me, the one always searching for something, finally relented.

I drifted off to sleep, finally at peace.

SIXTEEN

Over the next three days, Lorcan and I spent our time researching and investigating leads to the Irish Republican Army or the DLR, not coming up with much. We spent our nights at the underground club, but my Druid guy never came back. Still, I couldn't lose the feeling of being watched.

With no results and an annoyed call from Lars about our progress, I was getting frustrated and losing hope on how we were going to proceed.

"One more night at the club, then we try a different lead." Lorcan rubbed his neck, prowling behind me in the small room. "I was sure he'd be back. He had to feel your power. It's too strong to ignore."

I hooked the fake ring into my nose and brushed out my shorter black hair in the mirror. My eyes were rimmed with black eyeliner under my glasses, my tank top showing off my tattoos. For once in my life I looked tough. And I liked it.

"I have an idea, but you're not going to be happy with it." He was going to *hate* it.

Lorcan's eyes met mine in the reflection, his lids narrowing. "No."

"You don't even know what I was going to say." I tossed my brush onto my bag, facing him.

"Yes, I do." He shook his head. "There is no way in hell I'm going to let you go by yourself."

Dammit.

"That's not what I was thinking."

Yes, it was.

Lorcan slanted his head, his gaze level with mine.

"Fine." I huffed. "But I wasn't thinking you'd stay here or anything. You could still be in the club. Just not near me. Maybe you're scaring him away."

Lorcan prowled up to me, his shoulders curved.

"Yeah, exactly like that." I motioned to him.

"I am not leaving you alone." He loomed over me. The feel of his beast prickled at the edges. "If anything happened and I couldn't get to you..."

"I can take care of myself, you know." I put my hands on my hips. "I've tossed your butt in the dirt a few times, dweller. Don't make me out as some helpless girl."

"Kenn—"

"I've done perfectly fine without you for sixteen months." I cut him off, hating I had let him know I had noticed. Noticed and counted. "I don't need you to protect me. I am a Druid. Not the weak human you first met."

"You were never weak." He snarled and pressed in closer.

"Then why are you treating me like I am?" I pushed at his chest, not buckling under his threatening form.

"You are by far smarter, stronger, and more capable than me." Anger rumbled in his voice. "I know you can handle it."

"Then what is this about?"

He peered at the ceiling.

"What?"

His face flickered, like he was struggling with something, but he swiftly locked his jaw, turning away from me. The moment vanished.

"Fine. But I will be there. I'll stay in the shadows." He grabbed his jacket, shoving his arms through the sleeves with irritation. "But if I get a whiff of anything off, the experiment is over."

It was the best I was going to get. And in reality, I wanted him close. I felt better with him near.

~~~~~

The rock band was in full swing by the time I entered the crypt. The bouncer, who recognized me on sight, flicked up his eyebrows in surprise. "Alone tonight, lass?" His thick Irish brogue hung on the air, his eyes wandering down my body.

"By myself, but never alone." A flirty smile pulled at my lips. Raven was blunt, confident, and comfortable in her own skin. Plus, it was true. I could feel the hooded dweller at the back of the line as potently as if he stood right next to me. I swear I could even hear a low grumble come from him.

The doorman eyed me, a salacious smile curving his mouth. "Well, if you get lonely down there, you can always come and keep me company."

I placed my hand on his arm and smiled, slipping by him with a wink. A thrill of my forwardness rushed up the back of my neck, pulling my shoulders back. I tossed my heavier jacket in coat check and headed for the bar.

I had never been to a bar by myself. Actually, I hadn't gone to any bars. I'd missed my twenty-first birthday while being held captive by Aneira. And when I returned, my life was no longer homework, movie nights, and boys. It became training, war, and death. Then when I became Queen, parties, clubbing, and whatever else people my age did were no longer options for me.

"Back again." The bartender smiled at me, already grabbing the beer I had been favoring all week. His eyes drifted over my shoulder searching for my partner, but he didn't comment about his absence.

"Thanks." I handed him my money and took a long gulp. I let my hips move to the beat of the music, drifting around the crowded club. I inspected every group, trying to get a feel of the crowd. The same as it had been since the Druid ran out. Knowing my Awen tattoo was on full display, I tried to spot for any reactions. Nothing.

Everything pointed to another disappointing night. The only shift in the space was when Lorcan entered. It was bizarre how I knew exactly where he was. He altered the molecules in the air, his gaze brushing me with the potency of fingers.

"Hi." A guy came up next to me at the bar, sparking a sense of familiarity. *Had I seen him here before?* He was around my age, lean, dark spiky hair, brown eyes, and wearing glasses. Cute and completely my type. Or what used to be my type. "My name's Adam, but everyone calls me Wizard."

"Wizard?"

"My computer skills. Not an actual one." He grinned, fidgeting and awkward.

"Of course."

"American?"

"Yeah. Starting at the Queen's University this semester." Raven's story rolled off my tongue, and I almost giggled. Queen's University. Funny. I guess in a way I was attending the Queen's University of Life.

"What? Have something against the *Queen*?" The way he said it made me feel he wasn't exactly talking about the university.

"Just not my top choice...of schools." I weaved around his question.

"Not mine either. But could have been worse." His Irish accent landed heavily on each word, his double meaning clear. "I graduated from Uni just before the war." He bobbed on his feet, shoving his hands into his pocket. "So what is your name?"

"Raven," I replied, finishing the last of my beer.

"Well, Raven, what do you do?"

"I am a supervisor of sorts."

"Sounds grueling."

"You have no idea."

He smiled at me, dipping his head, a silence growing between us.

"Dance with me?" Adam blurted. He was so awkward and adorable. He was everything I used to like in a guy. And I had *no* interest in him. *Damn you, dweller*. Suddenly I felt daggers of irritation prickle my back from the shadows, raising up on its hackles.

"Sure." I heard my response roll off my tongue, and I placed my hand in his, letting him lead me out to the dance floor. The song was in between slow and fast, and both of us struggled to find a beat.

"Sorry, I am genuinely bad at this." He laughed nervously.

Kennedy would continue to dance awkwardly, not confident enough to take control. Raven reached out, clutching his hips with my palms, moving them in sync with mine. He laughed again, but moved in closer, his legs brushing against mine.

My back felt on fire as eyes from behind me burned into my skin. Lorcan had turned me down. We were not together, nor would we be. He had screwed every girl in sight. I was free to dance with anyone whenever I liked. But an image of Lorcan grinding on the gorgeous fae girl I saw when I entered sent blistering rage down my spine. I tossed the picture out with all my other thoughts.

Adam's hand moved to my hip, and he pulled me close. His head bowed, his mouth close to mine. At high school parties, I saw people making out within minutes of meeting each other all the time, but it was never my style. I couldn't do that. I always knew the guy I crushed on, probably for years.

But I wasn't Kennedy tonight. I was Raven.

He shifted closer, his glasses hitting mine. "Sorry." He blushed, his cheeks flushed, brightening his eyes. I smiled, trying to cover up my nerves. He leaned in closer, but stopped, swallowing nervously.

A *déjà vu* feeling struck me hard, a memory floating to me like I had been here before. A vision. A boy. A kiss.

My visions didn't show me arbitrary moments in the future. They were important. Significant.

Before I could think of why I was doing it, my hands came to his face, pulling him down, my lips finding his. I had no idea why I was kissing this boy; I just knew I was supposed to. It was brief but filled with the angst Raven carried on her shoulders. Raven would do something like that. She was aggressive and angry. An extremist. She took what she wanted.

"Damn." Adam's eyes widened. "I'm glad I got to come here tonight."

"Thought we'd get it out of the way." I shrugged, Raven taking over my behavior.

"I hope there will be more...getting things out of the way." He grinned sheepishly.

I laughed, grabbing for his hand to go back to the bar. Raven needed liquor to stay dominant. My fingers slipped and pushed up his shirtsleeve, displaying a tattoo just above his wrist.

I froze, not believing what I saw. Three thick lines with three dots. "Awen," I whispered, and my gaze darted up to him. It was the Druid symbol, but I felt no magic coming from him. He was human.

"Shit." He jerked his hand back, pushing down his sleeve. His head turned toward the corner of the club. I followed his gaze. The bearded guy from the first night stood near the stairs. I whipped back to Adam, trying to understand what was going on.

He was gone. *Crap!* Then I saw Adam push through the throng, heading for the other man.

"Wait," I yelled, already in chase. No way was I going to lose them again. But the packed club conspired against me, hindering my progress as I swam upstream against the current of people on the dance floor.

Adam's spiky hair came into view as the pair jogged up the stairs near the exit. Adam's brown eyes looked back, catching mine, before they disappeared through the door.

No! I couldn't lose them.

My muscles snapped with energy, barreling me through bodies near the steps. I shoved them out of my way as my boots grazed the stone, and I leaped toward the door, my heart pounding in my chest. I slammed through the exit and curved around the large body blocking the door.

"Already lonely, eh?" The bouncer's chuckle stopped when I ran past him, my head swiveling up and down the alley. Panic dripped down the back of my throat, dread curling around my intestines. My eyes caught movement…two men turning down another backstreet.

"Hey?" The bouncer called after me, but I hardly took notice, sprinting down the alleyway in pursuit. A scuffle and holler came from the doorman behind me, and I knew Lorcan had reached the top. I didn't slow for a second. The shadows ate up the light the farther I went. I stretched my short legs, the lane they'd turned down only a few steps away.

Pivoting on my foot, I swung for the unlit passage, trying to make out shapes in the murk. I took ten paces, frantically searching for outlines or movement. Then an arm shot out of an entryway, fingers wrapping around my arm. I yelped, fear tangling around my lungs like weeds. A hand clamped over my mouth, dragging me into the doorway.

"Be quiet," a man's voice hissed into my ear, a knife at my throat. His magic slammed into my back, almost paralyzing me. Adam was next to him, pressing my body in the small space like a sandwich.

A growl echoed off the brick down the alley. Lorcan moved closer, his energy buzzing at my skin.

"Step back or I slice her throat," the Druid man yelled into the alley. He shoved me out, keeping the blade at my neck. Adam and the man moved behind me and faced us toward the beast. Red eyes glowed in the night, Lorcan's outline looming and hunched over like he was ready to attack.

"Call off your pet," the man demanded in my ear. The blade dug into my tender skin and caused my eyes to water. Panic colored my vision, hazing my mind. "And don't think about doing a spell. I can cut you faster than you can get any words out."

Don't lose it, Ken. Keep it together.

1.) He knows what you are. Senses your magic.
2.) He probably doesn't want to kill you. Not until he knows what you want.

I inhaled through my nose and nodded. He lifted his fingers just enough to uncover my lips. I knew what I had to do to survive. This was our only chance.

"Back down, beast." My command sailed through the air with complete authority.

Lorcan exhaled a rumble that shook the cobblestone, his shoulders riding up to his ears, his form growing in height and bulk.

"Now," I ordered, the condescension thick, smacking him in the face. He didn't move, and the air clotted with tension. *Please, Lorcan*. My eyes begged him.

He huffed, shaking his head, he took a step back. His irises stayed vertical but went back to green. A reddish-green, but I would take it.

"He is exceedingly protective of me." I swallowed, talking over the knife cutting at my skin. "But I still need to get better control of him. We're both a work in progress."

"Really?" the bearded man snipped. "Because the magic coming off you is extraordinary, so don't lie to me. I can feel your power."

"Look, I just found out what I was. Discovered my real parents were murdered in the war." All truths. "I don't even know who they were. I was raised by humans."

"Sounds like your story, Major," Adam said.

Major grunted at his partner, pulling me more firmly against him.

"If you're so new, then how can you already control a dark fae? He is powerful; I can tell."

"I know the important tricks to survive on the street. Alone." I forced a smile to curve my mouth. "Not like they are good for anything else."

"You seemed awfully cozy with it the other night." Major rewrapped his arm across my body. Lorcan's eyes shaded red.

"We can't play with our toys?" Raven had taken over, committed to her part.

Major snorted, twisted with derision. "Why are you here?"

"I heard about the cause. I want to be part of it."

"Don't know what you're talking about."

"Awen. I saw Adam's tattoo. I know what it means. I want to join the fight."

"I don't think so."

"I lost my family. They were butchered by the fae. I grew up not knowing what I was. But I could feel it, all my life, the fact I didn't belong…I always felt different." I swallowed, real anger sprouting in my gut. "I hate them. What they took from me. Since the barriers have fallen, I've been on the run because we are still being hunted. Killed. I want them to know how it feels to fear."

Major shifted behind me, the knife ebbing slightly from my throat.

"I believe her, Major," Adam muttered.

"Why, Wizard, because you think she's hot?" He huffed at his friend. "A few tattoos and claims of dead parents and you're all gooey. She's not one of us. We trust no one."

"But I am a Druid just like you, Major," I replied, knowing the power of simply using someone's moniker. "I've been searching for you guys. I don't want to run anymore. I want to fight. I want them to suffer like we have." My eyes landed on Lorcan, drilling into him. *Follow my lead.* I hoped he understood because my next words were against our plan. "Take me. Leave the fae behind. I don't care. But I want to be part of your cause. To *really* do something that counts."

A growl came from Lorcan, but I ignored him.

"You need me as much as I need you," I added quickly.

"What makes you think we need you?" Major sneered.

"Because I want the same thing you do." I twisted my head enough to peer at him. "Revenge. And I'm willing to do anything to get it."

SEVENTEEN

Outlines hinted at my vision from the pillowcase over my head. The only source of light came from flashes of streetlights and car headlights dimly glowing through the fabric. My arms ached from being tied behind me.

The van took a corner roughly, slamming my body against the wall, the metal bruising my spine. From what I could see before they put the pillowcase over my head was some kind of small delivery vehicle.

Lorcan's legs nudged mine, his frame cramped in the tiny space. They cuffed him, putting a bag over his head too, but we all knew it was for show. He could tear through both like they were tissue. Lorcan had to be seething, but he didn't say a word, following along like he was under my control. I knew this was torture for him, but he didn't try to fight when they put us in bonds. He simply looked at me, his eyes blazing with intensity before they slipped a black pillowcase over his head. It was the only way Major would take us to…well, I wasn't quite sure where yet.

"Tell Franklin we have someone." Major's voice bounced off the metal walls to the back. Franklin? Who was he or she? "Yeah, the Druid from the club." He huffed. "No, it was Wizard. He has more game than we thought. She came to us." A pause. "We'll be there soon. Be ready. She comes with a fae puppet."

Lorcan's knee dug into my hip. I could feel him shaking with rage, fighting to stay in control. Would he be able to contain the beast? What if he snapped? Everything we were working for would be lost, and I couldn't take the chance. I knew what I had to do. And he was going to hate it. "I'm sorry," I whispered to him.

"Don't." His voice was tight with warning, almost as if he knew what I intended to do.

Guilt gnawed at the back of my throat, but I shoved the spell through the tangled weeds of remorse. It was for the best. The invocation was an updated version of the calming spell I once used on Ember. This one was more powerful and would keep him placid, like he had taken a Valium. His form went stiff, then as my words trickled over him, he sat back, heaving out a sigh.

"I am so sorry." I rubbed his leg with my knee. Sluggishly he pulled away from me, and I nipped my bottom lip. He was an alpha where nothing was out of his control. Once the spell wore off, there was no doubt he was going to be livid.

We drove for what seemed like another fifteen minutes before the breaks squeaked and the car turned, hitting gravel. I bounced around the back, my rear taking bruising hits on the uneven floor.

Then just as quickly, the vehicle screeched to a stop and the engine turned off. The doors opened, then slammed shut. I counted five seconds before the doors at the rear of the van were yanked open, cold air sending goosebumps over my flesh. I had run out without my jacket, and my tank did little to fight against Northern Ireland's winter. Hands grabbed me, pulling me roughly out, and I was placed on my feet.

"Wizard, take her," Major's voice commanded. He certainly was in charge of these two, but I wondered where he sat on the DLR chain. How far were we from the top?

Adam's arm wrapped around me, leading me blindly forward. He was gentle. I could tell he was not the aggressive type. He seemed the kind that would bring down the government with a computer virus, not violence.

"Adam?" My words were muffled under the linen, my feet shifting from gravel to smooth pavement.

"Call me Wizard," he said into my ear. "No one goes by their real name here. I shouldn't even have told you. Not sure why I did…your eyes, lips. I couldn't stop myself," he babbled.

"Okay, *Wizard*, where are you taking us?" I cut him off.

"You'll see soon enough." He sighed. I was still confused he was human, but I didn't have time to consider it further before I heard footsteps moving over the gravel toward us.

"*This* is the powerful Druid you were talking about?" A woman's voice broke in, her British accent thick. Cockney. I could tell she wasn't the only one waiting for us as my seer picked up on three others besides her. "She's the size of a pea."

"Just because she's small doesn't mean she doesn't have a lot of magic." Major's voice emerged behind me. Heavy feet shuffled over the gravel to the pavement. Lorcan. "She controls him."

The girl's inhale sounded full of fear and awe. Even with his head covered, Lorcan's human form was enough to bring most girls to their knees. Average humans would be able to feel the magic of the beast siphoning off him. They wouldn't know or understand, but they would instantly feel his presence with terror, wonder, and most likely, lust.

"Fuck," she whispered. "He's like the oth—"

"I know." Major cut her off. "And she's powerful enough to control him."

The girl cleared her throat. "Franklin's waiting."

The way she said the name, I gathered Franklin was in charge here. Was this the leader we were looking for? The one who had almost killed us? I had so many questions, but I kept silent, letting Wizard lead me. My boots hit cement, our steps echoing off distant walls, and the brutal wind receded. The bag was ripped from my head.

I flinched from the glare of a flashlight someone held but quickly took in my surroundings. The building was massive, at least three stories high and several football fields long. It appeared to be an old, abandoned factory left in decay and ruins.

The four people leading us came into focus, all Druids, except one. Two of the women were in their early thirties. One woman of average height had short blonde hair pulled in a tiny ponytail and eyebrow piercings. The other girl was tall, dark-skinned, her hair braided, displaying a string of tattoos down her neck. Two men stood next to them. One was tall, slender, with a large, long nose, and wavy brown hair. The human among them was about five ten, built, with gray hair and beard. All wore dark clothes in greens, blacks, blues, and grays. They carried guns hooked to their belts and old-school walkie-talkies.

The blonde glanced at me over her shoulder, her eyebrows scrunching slightly as if to say she wasn't very impressed with what she saw.

Dripping water echoed through the vast space. I sensed no other life except for the rats. Where were they taking us?

The troop led us down corridors, through a door hidden behind some shelving and rubbish, before descending stairs. My stomach tightened as we entered the tunnel. Tunnels always took me back to Jared. To that night.

Only a few single hanging lights lit the path. The air turned slightly warmer the lower we went, my skin relishing this tiny bit of heat.

When we got to the bottom, I could see old curved brick ceilings and walls in the dimly lit passageway. It appeared to be an old aqueduct or military shaft.

I stayed alert, taking in everything we passed, but the scenery stayed the same. It was a good ten minutes before the group halted in front of a cement barrier covered in graffiti.

The blonde gave a cryptic-sounding knock. What I thought was a cement wall suddenly opened, the paint disguising the edges of the doorway. A large, thirty-something man, dressed like a member of a SWAT team, opened the door for us. He was armed with two semiautomatic rifles, a huge knife, and a handgun. They were not fooling around here.

He was also human.

"Thanks, Ghost." The blonde nodded at the guard. He grunted, narrowing his gaze on Lorcan, his finger rubbing the trigger.

"Loaded with 'special' bullets here," Ghost said, his glare on the beast. It wasn't a threat, but a warning. He wouldn't hesitate if Lorcan did anything he didn't like.

"He's fine," I said quickly, hating the truth of my words. He would be mad, but I hoped he'd understand why I had to do it. "He's my pet."

"Better stay that way, or your pet will be a dead one." Ghost removed his finger from the trigger but still kept his hand on the gun.

Ghost stepped aside, letting us pass. The room was small and dimly lit, and the troop made for another door straight ahead. This was the first line of defense. The blonde did another set of knocks on the wall. This time when it opened by another guard, light streamed through like daylight had just broken. This guard looked to be of Native American descent, just as big and just as loaded with weapons as Ghost. He nodded at our group, opening the door wider. They moved us through the door, and I gasped.

The brick gave way to aged cement and stone. Cords with hanging lights dotted the supermarket-size rectangular room. It looked like an old underground bunker. Life buzzed as people moved around the space.

On one side of the room dozens of mats were laid out where people were training to fight. Punching bags hung from the ceiling next to a small boxing ring in the center of the room. People training in sword fighting were toward the back. The other side of the space seemed to be the "magic zone"—a handful practicing charms and spells or blasting each other onto mats. I felt like I stepped into two movie sets: a dystopia and a magical wizard one.

My body hummed with the familiar magic. Druids. A lot of them… forty or so. In the scheme of things hardly a drop, but more than I had ever imagined. My mouth gaped, every sense and thought overwhelmed.

These were my people.

Hiding in a realm under the world.

☙❧

Wizard kept me close, his fingers latching onto my cuffed arms. My head swiveled around as I tried to take in everything. Excitement whirred through me at the sensation of being around other Druids. I wasn't completely alone. I wasn't the last of my kind.

We went down another hallway before turning and entering a smaller room. Computers, maps, and screens covered the walls, and a large table sat in the center of the room.

My gaze went to the man standing at the head of the table, bent over a map. He lifted his head, his crystal blue eyes curious. For a brief second he did a double take, his brows crinkling with puzzlement before his gaze dropped and became emotionless. He had a silvering brown beard and hair. Green khakis and a black wool sweater fit his lean, tall torso. Like the others, he wore combat boots. The similarities to Major were too obvious; they were related in some way.

"Franklin," the blonde addressed him, motioning to me.

"Thank you, Poppy." A gruff voice rolled out of him. "You and Ophelia get back to training. Those newbies need a lot of work."

Poppy and Ophelia nodded then left the room.

"The mysterious Druid girl." Franklin looked at Wizard. "Untie her. I think she understands there is no chance of getting out of here."

Wizard dug into his pants, pulled out a Swiss army knife, and sawed at the ties digging into my wrists. Relief flicked up my nerves when my arms fell to my sides.

"Sit." The leader motioned to one of the chairs around the table. I glanced back at Lorcan as I moved around to the chair. He stared off in the distance, his eyes vacant of any emotion or threat. However, Major kept him pressed against the wall while the two other men guarding his other side tensed as though ready to pull out their guns.

Lorcan being spelled was the glaring fault in my plan to keep us from being found out. If anything *did* happen, he would be inefficient in a fight. We would be screwed.

"He is under my influence. He will not attack anyone." I settled down in the chair with a commanding air, knowing if the leader had the ability to feel magic, he would see I told the truth. It was all up to me now to sell this.

"We aren't willing to take that chance yet." Franklin's blue eyes pinned me to my spot. "We don't know you. Nor do we trust you."

I pressed my lips together and nodded.

"You have to prove yourself. Just because you're a Druid doesn't mean you get an automatic club card here."

"Understand."

"Your name?"

"Raven."

He stared at me, assessing, poking my aura. I had learned early to build a wall to block anyone from seeing anything I didn't want them to. But to be faced with another powerful Druid, I hoped my talent was as good as I needed.

"You think me a fool?" He folded his arms.

I swallowed, struggling to keep Raven's blasé attitude on my face though fear crawled through my lungs like bugs.

"You parade around with an Awen tattoo for all to see, like a fuckin' idiot. Do you know what still happens to Druids who sport that symbol?" Franklin leaned on the table, his fingers white as he pressed down. "They murder them. But I think you know this. Now that I've met you…" He tilted his head, taking me in. "You aren't dimwitted like I thought. Far from it. So what the hell do you want?"

"I want to fight," I replied evenly.

He huffed out his nose. "Do better than that, girl."

"I lost my real parents in Aneira's genocide." I sat up tall, letting my real anger slip into my declaration.

"My adoptive family was killed in the war. I lost everything. I may sound like every other recruit out there, but I don't want to be in hiding anymore. I want revenge. I want to make a difference."

Franklin straightened up, his eyes narrowing as he watched me intently. "You remind me of someone."

Don't react, Ken. But what if they recognized me? What would happen if they found out I was the Queen?

"I can sense you are powerful." He rubbed his chin, his gaze sizzling through me. "How have you been hiding this whole time unnoticed? What family do you come from?"

"I don't know." I tried to keep myself calm and centered. I didn't want him to pick up on my lies. "I didn't even know I was a Druid until a couple years ago. They left no trail. But I know they're dead. I feel it."

Franklin was hard to read. He just watched me like an animal in the zoo. It was a good minute before he spoke again.

"What about your fae pet?" He flicked his chin toward Lorcan. "Only two people here know how to command a fae, and that was after extensive training in black magic. Not a newbie talent."

I shrugged with disinterest. "When you're a single female Druid on the run, you learn what you need. Fast."

Franklin pinched his mouth together like he wasn't buying my story. Terror sucked out the marrow in my bones, leaving them hollow. What would happen if he didn't believe me? I knew this was going to be risky, but being here with no easy escape, and Lorcan under a spell? So much was on the line, and I began to feel the severity of it.

He paced around the room, his head bowed in thought. My cool façade stayed strong, while my heart pounded and moisture dampened my palms.

"He stays in the fae pit." Franklin finally stopped, twisting to me. "And until you prove yourself here, you will be monitored. This isn't playtime. We are here to make a real difference. *Whatever* it entails. Your first test will be in three days. If you fail..." He let his sentence fade out.

It was clear. If I failed to show my dedication to the cause, I was finished. And that probably didn't mean just packing my bags.

"If you make it through, you will find a position here. Everyone has their place. Even if it's just building bombs."

"Bombs?"

I twisted my hands together in my lap, my voice even. The memory of the explosion crackled through my head. The smell of burnt flesh and smoke. The sight of bloody bodies in chunks. Lorcan impaled with glass. Had it been his order to murder the fae nobles, almost killing the King and Queen?

"This isn't the place for picket signs and protests. If you can't handle it, then you should walk away now."

"I can handle it," I replied firmly, pushing my glasses up my nose.

"I hope so. We can use your level of magic. The commander will be pleased if you work out."

"Commander?" I went rigid.

"While I'm touched you think so highly of me, do you sincerely think you could so easily meet with the leader of DLR?" Franklin tipped his head back with a snarky chuckle before it died in his throat. "You don't get anywhere near the commander. Not unless you prove yourself *completely indispensable* here."

I held my shoulders back, hiding the disappointment and apprehension. Deep down I knew it wouldn't be that easy to find the head of the snake. I had hoped, especially because I had no idea what they had planned for me and knowing at any moment someone might recognize me.

The line I walked was needle thin.

"I guess welcome, Raven." Franklin rubbed his hands together. "This is the war room, the core of our base." He held his arms out. "Where everything is planned."

"Where I live." Wizard snorted from behind my chair.

The first smile hinted at Franklin's face. "Yes. Wizard is our computer mastermind. This is his domain. He gets us all the intel we need. A true hacking genius."

I glanced at Wizard. He met my eyes, a shy smile creeping up his face.

"Have you heard anything about the attack in Switzerland?" Franklin asked.

I almost wanted to laugh, my teeth sawing together. "I saw it on the news."

Franklin smiled. "Three Seelie fae who had helped Aneira gather up and kill Druids, all dead," he stated proudly. "Rumor had it the King was supposed to be with them, but from my sources they only found the three. How powerful our attack would have been if he had killed the Unseelie King."

Fire flamed under my mask, along with rage and nausea. How easy it was for them to talk, sitting here a thousand miles away. I had seen the brutality myself. I had to take a steadying breath now to push away the image of Demrik's burnt body. He didn't deserve that. He had been faithful to Lars, not Aneira. He was good and kind. They just clumped them all together. Even Lars.

"The King, if I recall, was never for the genocide nor on the old Queen's side."

"He didn't stop it." Franklin frowned. "And he is certainly chummy with this new Queen."

"She's a Druid. Isn't that a good thing for us?"

"You'd think. But she's only a puppet, a figurehead to look like we are progressing. Out here nothing has changed. And most fae don't even respect her rule. There is a huge revolt happening on the mainland. It won't be long before she is assassinated."

My teeth crunched painfully, trying to stop any reaction from showing on my face. Thankfully, Lorcan was sedated. There was a good possibility he would not have responded well to that claim.

Franklin continued, "We may be mostly against the old Queen's followers, but all fae are our enemy. If taking out the Demon King unsettles the fae world, their dominance over humans, over us...then I will happily do it."

They wanted a change no matter the costs and clearly did not understand the difference. Lars and I had prevented total anarchy. But if they got rid of the King or me? Life for everyone, including humans, Druids, and fae would be worse. Humans and fae would call open hunting season on all, with no limits or consequences.

"Wizard, why don't you show Raven around? Get her settled." Franklin returned to the map he was looking over. "Mayhem, take the fae to the pit." He nodded at the older, muscular human man who had led us down here. "Go as well, Fox." He motioned to the young guy.

I took a peek at Lorcan. He wouldn't look at me, letting the two men shove him out of the room without a struggle.

It hurt to watch him like that. The beast so passive because of me, even though it probably saved both of us. My eyes tracked him until the door shut.

"Raven?" Wizard held out his hand, helping me stand. Major moved to the other side of the table, studying the map with Franklin.

I followed Wizard out of the room, feeling like I had just stepped into quicksand. I was *so* far out of my league and my comfort zone. And *any* little slip would bury me.

EIGHTEEN

"Don't worry about Franklin." Wizard swiped his hand in the air. "He's like that with everyone, especially if he doesn't know you."

"He was fine." I followed him down the hall. "Believe me, I've dealt with a lot worse. A lot. He should be protective of what you have here. I understand that."

"Yeah, all the burden of allowing someone in, doing what the commander tells us, keeping up to date on leads, it all comes down on him and Major. Mainly him."

"Are Major and Franklin related?"

"Would you believe they're father and son? Franklin was seventeen when Major was born. Bloody young. They act more like brothers though. That's probably because they just reunited in the last year."

"He didn't raise him? Was he with his mother?"

"Neither. Major was raised by humans to protect him. Mommy, Daddy, and son found each other after the war."

That was why Wizard said my story sounded like Major's. Giving up your child and the person you love to keep safe? No wonder they blamed and hated fae so much.

"Where's his mother now?"

"You'll meet her in a bit. They never married. They were so young, and with the threat on Druids, they went their separate ways, escaping death. What happened when they found each other again? Let's just say, they are making up for lost time. They say they aren't *together*." Wizard made air quotes with his fingers. "But they sure as hell act like it." Wizard turned around a corridor, one that opened up to a large room at the end. It was set up like a cafeteria. Empty tables and chairs for about seventy lined the middle of the room, and on the far side was the buffet.

"Breakfast is six to nine, lunch twelve to one, dinner five to seven. Otherwise they just leave water, fruit, and snacks to grab if we're hungry." Wizard took me back down the hall, speeding past another corridor.

"What's down there?" I pointed at the closed-door hallway down the lane.

"Uh. It's off limits." He rushed through his words. "For the top tier only."

I peered down the passage; nothing looked out of the ordinary. But it had me curious what was there. When I glanced back at Wizard, he was steps in front of me. I hurried to catch up. Then he took me back to the main area. It was quieter than it had been before. Barely a few people still wrestled on the mats and a handful worked on their spells.

"This is the hub, the heart of our base. Where we train, work, and hang out. Right now most are heading to bed or on a mission," Wizard said then pointed to the mats. "Ophelia and Poppy are two of the fight leaders. They used to be self-defense trainers. Fox and Mayhem do the advanced classes and also teach target practice in the empty factory above." He twisted to the magic half of the vast room. "Kenya oversees the Druids."

A pretty woman with wavy red hair and a curvy figure stood yelling at one of the practicing pupils. She had a heart-shaped face and blue eyes, a few inches taller than me, and looked to be in her early forties.

"That's mommy dearest," Wizard whispered in my ear. "She is a force. The kindest heart in the world but will take you down to your knees if you make her mad. We all love her, but I'm warning you, you don't want to be on her bad side."

"I'll remember that."

"Kenya?" Wizard called her over. She walked up, her magic slamming into me. "This is Raven, our newest recruit."

Her lids tapered, her brows furrowing as her eyes ran over me. She frowned and placed her hands on her hips. "Raven?" She continued to stare me up and down, her Irish accent weighty in my ear. "You remind me of someone…"

"You're getting that a lot today." Wizard nudged me playfully.

"I have that face." I tried to smile and shrug it off.

Kenya pursed her lips, then finally nodded. "Welcome, Raven. I look forward to seeing what you can do."

I nodded, not sure how to respond. Her critical gaze seemed to want to open me up and see right to my soul. I didn't back away, staring right back at her with the same intensity.

"Well. O-kay." Wizard clapped his hands together, trying to defuse the tension growing around us. "Let's finish our tour and get you settled." Wizard steered me away, curving us toward a hallway splintering off opposite the war room and kitchen.

"See you, Raven." Kenya's watchful eyes still probed, trying to figure me out. I could tell something bothered her. The fact my image was plastered everywhere didn't help. I hadn't realized how precarious this was until I was here. Just one movement or facial expression might be enough to trigger recognition.

What would they do if they found out I was the Seelie Queen? I didn't think they'd kill me immediately, but they would certainly use me. A bargaining chip? Lars would rightfully sacrifice me before giving in to their demands. Another outcome where he came out the lone leader. In every situation Lars was in the prime seat. I began to question whether this was by chance.

"Raven?" Wizard's voice snapped my head to the side.

"Sorry." I turned to follow him, looking one more time at Kenya. She furrowed her brow as she watched me. I would have to be careful around her. She would try to figure me out, so I'd have to be on guard all the time.

Wizard nervously jabbered as we walked, talking about people I didn't know, or just pointing out places to fill the silence. I was never good at small talk. It exhausted me. I tended to stay in my head. Watching. Observing. Only my close friends saw the talkative side of me.

"So this is where the bedrooms are located. We bunk two to a room, but I think you will get a room to yourself until someone new comes."

I let out an exhale. Thank goodness. One place I didn't have to keep up the pretense.

"It's all mixed here, even the loos. Druids are pretty free, so there are no rules about sex or dating each other." Wizard's gaze slid to mine at the last part, his cheeks flushing.

Oh, nerf herder.

It was my fault. I had kissed him, and I hadn't even known why except my vision told me to do it. If it led me here, it was for a reason, but now I had to deal with the aftermath. He was adorable. Only two years ago I would have had a crush on him. But I already had enough problems between a knight and a beast. I gave him a slight smile and looked away.

"This is going to be your room." He grabbed the doorknob and opened the door. "The loos and showers are around the corner." He flicked on the light and let me go into the room first. It was a box. Of course it had no windows being under ground and only filled with a single bed on each wall, a trunk at the end of each cot for storage, and one table with a lamp between the two.

On the end of one bed lay two pairs of dark gray sweats, two pairs of underwear, a sports bra, hoodie, bathroom kit, backpack, and two towels. I walked over and touched the items. I felt like I was being committed to prison or an institution. Both, probably.

"Once you do a few missions, you can upgrade clothes," Wizard said.

Ah. Until I proved myself I could not leave here, nor would they waste time or money getting clothes for someone who was not staying.

"There is also a laundry next to the bathrooms." He shoved his hands in his pockets. "But until your first mission, you're required to wear the tracksuits while you train."

"Is there a training schedule?"

"Yeah, they post it each morning after breakfast." He leaned against the doorjamb. "Everyone has different areas of concentration, but you are the fastest Franklin has had anyone do a mission. Normally the newbies are here for at least a couple of weeks before they have any kind of trial in the field."

Lucky me. I wasn't surprised. Franklin knew something was different about me, and he wanted to rub out his inkling to mistrust me and prove my faith to the cause. I wasn't some average Druid. If I pulled through, I would be a player and a huge asset to them.

"Well, I'll let you settle in. You missed dinner, but if you're hungry there are snacks in the café."

Right. I forgot it was probably nearing midnight by now.

"Show me the pit." I pushed my glasses up.

"Uh…" Wizard rocked between his feet.

"I need to have access to him, to make sure he stays under my control."

"The pit is not for someone like you."

"What does that mean?"

"No…I mean…you are..." He stumbled with his words, staring at his feet, then at the ceiling.

"Don't let my small size deceive you. I've been through a lot in my life. Seen a lot of bad shit." I let Raven's brisk attitude snap out. "I can handle a bunch of fae."

Wizard rubbed at his arm, then at his temples.

"*Wizard.*"

"Okay, but don't tell anyone." His shoulders fell in defeat. "I'm not supposed to take you there."

That didn't take much. It hit me with glaring clarity I could walk all over someone like him now. My inner strength as Queen had flourished. It made me realize in my personal life I needed someone who would challenge that.

Wizard grabbed my hand, slipping down the hallway right around the corner from my room. Going down another hallway, we hit a set of double doors. Wizard went to a box and typed in a code while I watched out of my peripheral vision. The door popped open.

"During the day, there is a guard to help retrieve your fae for you, but after eleven, they lock it for the night."

It took everything I had to keep my composure. They were treating them worse than animals. Zoo hours. Disgusting.

Funny how those claiming they had been treated so awful were now doing that exact thing. Two wrongs did not equal a right. I could relate to so much of the anger the Druids felt, but turning around and behaving just as badly was no way to end the hate and discrimination.

Stone steps led us down, barely lit by a few dim lights above. The smell was the first thing to hit me: pee, sweat, blood. With no windows and an inadequate air ventilation, it was stuffy, the air heavy with stench.

My gut screwed into a ball, my lungs taking in limited breaths. We reached the bottom, and I stopped, trying to take in what lay before me.

"Stay close to me." Wizard grabbed for my hand, but I walked past him, scanning the room with disbelief. I was the one who could protect him, not the other way around.

It was a large stone room with curved ceilings and pillars, dark and musky like a dungeon. My nose wrinkled with an even sharper stench of urine and body odor. Several hay beds with blankets dotted the wall. The space on the side looked like open showers and toilets. No doors or curtains.

Three figures were asleep on the straw beds. Each had a bucket filled with a towel, a basic bathroom kit, and they wore matching black sweats and hoodies. The fae uniform. My eyes danced over each form until it landed on the outline farthest away. My stomach wound up like a vortex.

Lorcan.

Dressed in the sweat ensemble, he sat with his back against the wall, his arms on his knees, his eyes closed. My hand went to my throat, trembling.

"We should get out of here." Wizard looked around frantically, ready for one of the unconscious fae to leap for him. All except Lorcan were sound asleep.

"Who controls these other fae?" I motioned to the three figures sleeping, their backs to me, but I saw all were male.

"Kenya is the only one able to control more than one. These are all hers." Property. I had heard fae talk about humans the same, like we circled back to the slave era. We talked like we progressed, but had we? We just seemed to be repeating history.

"Franklin dabbles in black magic, but he's not very good. His fae broke free and escaped. Black magic is being taught to only a few of the more skilled Druids here."

My knowledge of black magic was minimal. The little I read about said Druids weren't born with it like their normal magic. It was something you had to learn, to be taught because it wasn't natural for Druids to do harm. We were known to be one with nature, not against it. Hurting, control, power—it corrupted the soul. The book I had read was very firm that it was wrong and immoral.

Except you desire it, don't you? A voice tickled the back of my mind.

I wrapped a strand of hair around my finger, shoving the thought back. "Is there a reason they're all male?"

"The male fae minds are easier to control than the women's." Wizard shifted his weight back and forth. "Not much different from humans, huh?" He laughed, but when I didn't join in, it died away awkwardly. "So...um...there's another girl who dabbles in the black arts, Cali, who is also an American, but she's out on a mission with hers. They have a *special* relationship."

"What does that mean?"

"She sleeps with hers." He cringed. "I know fae are supposed to be great at sex and all, but…" He shook his head like he had a bad taste in his mouth.

"Really?" I kept my face blank.

"It's not against the rules here or anything, just frowned on."

My stomach clenched at the indignity. No, we had not progressed at all. Only the players on the field had changed.

"Kenya is one of the most powerful in the dark arts here and still struggles to keep them under a spell. That's why Major took notice of you in the club. You seemed to control yours with little effort or magic."

I should have been more guarded. There were so many times I could have slipped.

"Believe me, it takes more effort than you think to handle this one." I stared at the silhouette of Lorcan. "Could you give me a few moments?" I tried to hide my nervousness. "I actually wouldn't mind strengthening my spell."

Wizard shook his head. "No way am I leaving you here with *them*."

"I'll be fine. Go," I ordered, my jaw set.

He hesitated and gazed around the pit as if trying to imagine the worst that could happen but finally relented. "Okay, but come up soon. We shouldn't even be down here after hours." He headed for the stairs then stopped. "You might think because I'm human I don't really have a fight in this like the Druids, but my parents were killed for harboring a Druid family. I was scarcely five when fae murdered them in front of me. Everyone here has a reason to hate them. Don't pity these things; they'll turn on you in a moment. They're ruthless and malicious."

I bit my lip against the onslaught of grief he exuded. I understood his need to blame, but it never made the situation better. How was turning these men, who probably had nothing to do with the killings, into slaves going to help the situation? So easy to blame. If I thought this way, I'd also want all the fae murdered for killing my family. But not all fae, humans, or Druids are the same.

Wizard darted up the stairs. The moment I heard the sound of the door shutting behind him, my feet flew across the room.

"Lorcan," I cried out his name, falling to my knees on the hay. He didn't move or open his eyes. The spell was only temporary, it had to be mostly through his system by now. "Lorcan?" My hands slid over his stubble, cupping his face.

His mouth pressed together, letting me tilt his face down to me.

"Please, look at me," I whispered.

He lifted his lids, his irises were green, but his pupils were vertical. Absolutely no emotion seeped through them, gutting me like an ice cream scooper.

"I'm so sorry." I tipped my head into his, the apology feeling pathetic.

"You should go," his voice rumbled low, blank of sentiment.

"No. I can't leave you like this."

"What are you going to do?" He sneered. "I'm fae. This is where fae sleep. Where the pitiless and malicious belong."

"Lorcan…"

"Go." His eyes flared with red.

"No." I gritted out.

"Kennedy, I understand why you did it." His was voice hollow, not matching his statement. "But you shouldn't be here."

My heart felt like it had been tossed off a high-rise, splatting onto hard concrete. The pain of walking away from him, leaving him in this hell, was torture.

"Go now," he growled. "Before you're caught."

I choked back a whimper, letting my hands drop from his face. He was right. I couldn't do anything. We had to stay in character if we wanted this to work. We'd made it this far, and it couldn't be for nothing. "I'm sorry," I muttered, my head down.

He didn't respond in any way, staying still. I couldn't imagine how hard this was for him. A proud alpha, letting himself be caged and humiliated, all because he made a deal with a demon to protect me.

This is all because of you, Ken. He is only sitting here, pretending to be a zombie, because of you.

The knot in my throat bobbed back up, and I squeaked out a woeful noise as I stood. He stared straight ahead, like I wasn't even there, tearing my heart into tiny pieces.

I leaned over and brushed my lips across the spot between his eyebrows. Then I whirled around and ran back up the stairs before I completely lost my will.

I would get him—us—out of here as soon as I could, whatever it entailed. Whatever I had to do to prove myself, I would do it. Quickly.

The truth bubbled under the surface and rooted in my bones. There was nothing I wouldn't do for him.

NINETEEN

A hard pounding on the door bolted me awake with a cry. "Raven?" Wizard's voice came through the door. A strip of light glowed at the base of the doorway.

"Yeah?" I rubbed my head, feeling I had just shut my eyes. I probably had. My thoughts of Lorcan, of what I had to accomplish here, kept me up most of the night.

"It's six a.m. I thought you might want to have breakfast together before you start training."

"Oh, yeah…sure." I scrubbed my face, trying to wake up.

"Twenty minutes, I'll meet you in the hub?"

"Uh-huh." I yawned, sliding my feet to the floor. I was exhausted, but as Queen I was used to moving before my lids even opened. Normally I was okay with early mornings. Not today. "They better have coffee here. A lot of it," I mumbled to myself. Grabbing my bathroom bag, towel, and sweats, I hurried to the showers.

I walked into the shower stalls and yelped, a deep blush heating my face. Wizard warned me they were coed and Druids were free with their bodies. This early in the morning, I wasn't prepared for it. Several men and women walked around naked in front of me. I grew up in a household where we *never* saw each other naked.

Most of the humans ignored me, but the few Druids stared at me with interest, watching me carefully as I passed them. At least I was used to being stared at as Queen. I kept my chin up and moved to an empty stall at the end, closing the curtain behind me.

Loud groaning and grunts came from the stall next to mine. Great. Naked strangers and sex before I even had any coffee.

I turned on the water, drowning my head under the stream of water, hoping to block out the moans. My body reacted to the sounds of pleasure, craving its own. My thoughts put me in a similar situation, but the man joining me was not who I should be thinking of. The dweller had always been the one who breached my visions and took over my fantasies, even when I thought I loathed him. The first time I touched myself, it had been his image that pushed me over. Not my boyfriend.

Him. It always came back to him.

I let my hand slide down my body, pretending it was Lorcan's hand. My body woke up from a coma, coming to life with force. I squeezed my lids, gasping as I rubbed harder. Memories of how he felt inside, what he did to me, reached me to the edge faster than I thought.

"Har-der! Fuck…harder," a woman's thick Irish accent demanded, her voice instantly recognizable.

Kenya.

A man grunted, skin slapping together frantically. "Oh. Fuck…woman."

Franklin.

My hand dropped away, my head leaning against the cool tile. When it was anonymous, it was hot, but now that I had their faces in my head. Ugh.

I showered as fast as I could and got out. After brushing my teeth, I hurried back to my room, deciding to change there.

A few minutes after my scheduled meetup, I greeted Wizard in the hub. No one was training yet, most heading toward the cafeteria.

"Good shower? They can sometimes get cold if you're too late."

"Uh." I swept my wet hair over my shoulder, trying to air-dry it. "It was interesting. Little hotter than I expected."

A grin spread over Wizard's mouth. "I should have warned you. It's why I take showers before six."

I peered at him, wondering if he really understood my meaning.

"Every morning." He shook his head. "That's why everyone laughs when both say they are not together."

"Every morning?" I was going to have to go way earlier or later from now on.

"And sometimes at night. I caught them in the war room several times. I keep disinfectant close by."

"Wow." I chuckled. "Thanks for the warning."

"They are passionate. They fight and have sex at the same volume and intensity. I imagine it's what split them up, and keeps them coming back for more," Wizard said as we stepped into the cafeteria. About twenty already sat eating, though a line formed at the buffet area. "Coffee?"

I suddenly missed Torin, the way he took my hand the moment I walked out my bedroom door. I missed his smile, those bright blue-violet eyes glimmering as he bowed in greeting, saying, "My lady," and handed me my coffee. A flinch of sadness constricted my chest. I couldn't deny I missed talking to him, having him by my side. But not one time did his face come to me when I touched myself. Not one time did I think about him in my bed.

"It's not great." Wizard motioned over to a table. Hot water and coffee were in large orange thermoses, like those at football games. Dry creamer and sugar sat to the side. "But caffeine's caffeine, right?"

Not exactly, but I filled my cup, dumping in whatever processed products they had to improve it. I realized how spoiled I had become having the best natural ingredients. Fae weren't into processed food. It took me a lot of begging to even get flavored coffee creamers.

Eyes were on me from around the room as Wizard and I ate. Major, Poppy, and Ophelia sat with us. I noticed most of the newbies sat together, shooting me curious looks over their shoulders. I was already singled out, sitting with the instructors and leaders.

"Raven's already had the shower initiation." Wizard bumped Ophelia's arm.

"Ah." She grinned. "Har-der. Har-der!" Ophelia mimicked Kenya's voice perfectly, making me snort eggs up my nose.

"Please, I'm eating," Major choked. "Seriously. Stop."

"What's wrong, Major? Upset your parents get it on more than you do?" Poppy chuckled, shoving a bite into her mouth.

"Not like they're actually the parents who raised me." He frowned, annoyance curling his lip. "But no one wants to hear any mother and father having sex," he grumbled. It was the first time his stoic shield came down, and I actually saw someone besides the apathetic guy who held a knife to my throat.

"Told you, whenever you want to give them a run for their money, I'm in." Poppy shrugged then continued to eat, like she hadn't just bluntly propositioned him.

Major looked down at his food, muttering something, but a blush crawled up his neck.

"Will you two just screw and get it over with?" Ophelia rolled her eyes, but she quickly peered at Major.

"All him. I'm more than ready." Poppy wiped her hands on her napkin, grabbing her tray. "You ready, Lia? Time we get out there."

Ophelia rose with her. "See you on the mats, Raven."

I nodded, watching the two girls walk away. I liked her.

"Poor Major." Wizard snickered in his coffee. "What a troubled web we weave."

Major glared at him, tossing his fork on his plate.

"What?" I asked.

"Poppy wants Major. Major wants Ophelia."

"Shut up, wanker." Major's face became stone.

"And who does Ophelia like?" It was like being in high school.

"Oh, Ophelia secretly wants him so bad it's heartbreaking, but Poppy is her best friend. She'll never go there."

Major shoved back his chair, stood, and stomped away with aggravation.

Wizard laughed. "He's so screwed because if he gives in to Poppy, he ruins the deal with Ophelia, and he sincerely likes her. So the three dance around each other. No one will cave."

"And here I thought Druids were into *ménage a trois* and group sex. Problem solved."

Coffee sprayed from Wizard's mouth onto his breakfast tray. His eyes widened as he looked at me through his glasses with surprise.

A laugh buckled my stomach. I covered my mouth, heaving with giggles. The comment may have been a Raven thing to say, but I hadn't been *trying* to be her this morning. I felt the two sides of me rubbing against each other. Kennedy, the controlled Seelie Queen, and Raven, the outspoken Druid.

I was here to infiltrate these people. Betray them even. But I was also starting to like them.

Yeah, what a troubled web we weave.

⌁⌁⌁

I was signed up for a morning training session with Kenya, after lunch target practice with Mayhem, then after-dinner training with Poppy and Ophelia, finishing with another lesson from Kenya.

Wizard headed off for the war room, saying something about meeting for lunch, while I directed myself to the hub. A mix of humans and Druids tussled with each other. The trainees wore dark gray sweat outfits, while the leaders wore black military-type pants.

"Hey, you must be the new girl." An American accent reached my ears. A girl in her twenties with dark hair, dark eyes, and dark skin, possibly of Hispanic descent, walked boldly up to me. Her figure was curvy under her cargo pants and tank, her hair wrapped in a bun. She exuded confidence. Security in herself, her body, and her sexuality almost smacked you in the face. "I'm Cali." She held out her hand.

"Raven." I shook it.

"You are already the talk of the hub." She had a loud voice, drawing attention to us. "It's nice. For once it's not me this crew is talking about." I opened my mouth, but she continued. "We Yanks have to stick together, right?"

"Uh, yeah."

"I heard you also dabbled in black magic before coming here, and you have a fae too."

My very own pet fae.

"Another thing we have in common. Mine's been with me for over a year now. Started practicing the dark arts when I was a teenager." She brushed a loose hair from her face. "I'm sure you've already heard about us. This place is like high school. But the joke's on them. Sex with fae is incredible." She tilted her head back. She talked fast, but she was not bubbly. She had a hard, blunt edge to her, and I instantly liked her. I suspected she would say whatever was on her mind. And probably more. "And I swear, Wolf has trained in the sex Olympics or something like it."

"Wolf?"

"He's a shape-shifter. A wolf-snake." She folded her arm under her voluminous breasts. In contrast, mine felt flat as planks. "Slinking into places is his forte. Comes in handy when you're on a mission or need to get into tight places." She grinned.

Please say there was no double meaning there. "He's easy to control?"

"I only had to do one initial spell on him. Quite unusual." She shrugged. "I know Kenya has had to refresh her thrall a couple times. All her fae fight it tooth and nail."

"Wolf doesn't?"

"No. He just does what I say without me even having to ask. It's awesome." Her lashes flicked to the side, twisting her gaze from mine. My instincts told me there was more to the story.

"What about you?" She turned back, a naughty grin hinting on her mouth. "You ever taken yours for a ride?"

"Uh." More like he took me.

"Cali, can you shut your gob for a moment, luv?" Kenya yelled over at us. I turned, realizing she had been waiting for us with three other Druids I had yet to meet. They were all staring at us impatiently.

"What do you think?" Cali lifted a perfectly manicured eyebrow at Kenya.

"How you do missions without being caught is beyond me." Kenya rolled her eyes, but warmth hinted at her mouth.

"I'm good." Cali stepped up to the practice area.

"Not that good yet. You haven't been able to control more than one fae."

Cali rolled her eyes back. "One's all I need."

"Cali." Kenya frowned, shaking her head.

"Don't give me that look. You're the one missing out. You think sex with your baby daddy is good? You have *no* idea what good is until you've been with a fae."

"Think I'm just fine, luv." Kenya tilted her head, an eyebrow cocked. If the morning escapade told me anything, she was a very satisfied woman. "Now let's get to work." Kenya waved us over to the space dedicated to magic. The three other Druids introduced themselves as Auckland, a guy from New Zealand, Lotus, a girl from Egypt, and Wire, a guy who was excellent at hot-wiring and stealing cars. Seriously?

I was nervous, torn between showing too much of my power or too little. Being Queen had increased the amount of magic I exuded. Though I was nowhere as powerful as Lars, I'd been told I radiated royalty when I walked into a room. Thus my magic was still at a higher level than anyone here. None of them were fae, so they didn't sense it as much, but I still had to block it. I needed to keep my power from dominating the room, something I was taught by Owen and Cole, but learned to excel in my time with Lorcan. Being with him had shown me how to truly keep calm and find my inner peace.

This plan was so full of things that could go wrong. Even though my ruse kept fear constantly at the surface, burning holes in my esophagus, I had to stick to this façade.

Training with Kenya turned out to be almost fun. The brutal, guerilla-style training Lorcan had put me through made everything else seem easy.

"You are a natural healer." Kenya came up beside me.

"Aren't most Druids?"

"We don't all shine in it, no," she said. "Druids have multiple powers, but few are good at all of them. My family line was exceedingly strong in channeling our power with the weather. The stormier it is, the more I can draw from the electricity in the air."

I needed to remember never to let her near my best friend, Ember, a walking electrical charge.

"The top healers, the most powerful Druids, were also able to see the future. Visions." She peered at me. "But there hasn't been a Druid that powerful since Aneira's annihilation of them."

My eyes didn't waver from hers. I couldn't tell if she was testing me or just telling me a fact. Neither of us broke away but my breathing grew shallow in my chest.

"Kenya, are we done? I'm starving!" Cali turned back to us, a hand brushing the sweat from her forehead.

Kenya's head snapped to Cali's, then down to her watch. "Oh, yeah. Sorry. You guys can go."

I exhaled with relief, making for the hallway toward my room, thankful for Cali's interruption.

"I will see you later, Raven," Kenya said. I nodded and quickly returned to my exit.

"Hey, wait up." Cali caught up with me. "You know, the lunchroom is the other way."

"I know. I just need a moment to relax." I pinned a smile to face.

"Yeah, me too." A mischievous smile curved her mouth. "Plus, I'm starving."

"Then why are you coming this way?"

Her smile grew bigger.

"I didn't say I was hungry for food." She winked and headed down the hall toward the fae room. "See you later. You'll have fun in the later lessons with Kenya."

"Aren't they just more of the same?"

"Oh no." Cali faced me, walking backward. "At night our group trains in black magic. Controlling fae isn't the only thing we are doing. The fae think they have nothing to really fear with us because there are just a few of us. Little do they know we're building a black magic army here." She lifted her brows before turning back and disappearing around the corner.

A black magic army. The phrase halted me in place. I knew this group was dabbling in it, and at least a few were controlling fae. But this went way past that. The bomb that destroyed my hotel room was an electric zap compared to what the dark arts could do to fae. Another tyranny rising.

As Queen I was supposed to be bringing all the sides together, graying the extremes of each side. Yet the thought of dark magic caused a thrill to run through me and awakened a need in my bones.

How far undercover would I go before I became one of them?

TWENTY

I rubbed my hands together trying to heat them up. Not even the gloves were blocking out the freezing night air. The Pacific Northwest got chilly, but nothing like this. This kind of cold drilled into your bones, making everything ache, even your lungs.

Ophelia let me borrow one of her winter coats as mine was in the lost-and-found at the underground club. And some employee at the hostel was probably loving the designer jacket Lars had given me.

We were just behind the old factory, a plot of land with weeds and mud stretching out between the building and the river close by. The moonlight and a few handheld gas lamps were the only sources of light.

"Guys, gather around." Kenya waved a group of us over. Only about ten Druids were here for the special class. It wasn't much of an army, but with the dark arts, you didn't need many to do damage…if they were good. "Divide into the groups I put you in last time. Newbies, you're with me."

My throat was thick as I stepped up to Kenya, joined by two others. I was trying not to think of the huge hole in Lars's scheme. I could pretend I was controlling Lorcan with black magic, but put those words into practice? I didn't know black magic. Not even enough to pretend.

Yes, you do. My subconscious licked at my thoughts. *You can feel it deep down.* I gritted my teeth, feeling the truth float up. It wasn't something you had, but something you learned. *Then what happened on the train, Ken?* No doubt the energy coming from me then was dark, but how was it possible?

Everything might unravel tonight, and I couldn't escape the fallout. Lorcan was stories below my feet, and I would not leave him.

"Cali, can you work with these two?" Kenya motioned to the other two standing with me. "I'd like to work with Raven tonight."

"Of course." Cali transferred the two others to a different section of the empty lot.

Kenya shoved her hands in her jacket, her stare boring into me. "You aren't really at entry level because you can control a fae, but I still want to see what basics you know."

Crap divided. Truth was the one thing that might save me. "Honestly, I didn't even know what I was doing. It just kind of happened." My toe rubbed a dent into the murky ground.

"It *just* kind of happened?" Kenya folded her arms, her feet taking a wider stance.

"Yeah."

"Black magic doesn't 'just happen,' luv." She jutted out a hip, her head slanting. "It is something you train in. For years."

I fought against the knot in my throat, keeping my gaze steady on her. I wasn't lying. If what happened on the train was black magic, it had taken over me, not the other way around.

Kenya took a step to me, her critical gaze roaming over me.

"The only time I've heard of someone using black magic without training was a long, long time ago. They were burned…by fellow Druids."

A nerve in my jaw twitched, heat sizzling under the down jacket.

"Times have changed." She lifted her eyebrow. "But natural obscurers? They don't exist anymore."

My tongue licked at my frozen lips. "Natural obscurer?"

"It's when you are born with black magic already in your bones. While in your mother, she would have had to practice it extensively for it to seep into her pores, leak into you, while still a fetus."

Horror drove through my brain. My biological mother couldn't have been into black magic. Someone high in the Cathbad family? No way.

"I haven't heard about one for decades." She frowned. "Although the moment you entered, I could feel something was different about you," Kenya said. "I couldn't put my finger on it, but if you are a natural obscurer?"

"What? What if I am?" I whispered, all the denials couldn't change what I sensed in my gut. It was a tense, fearful moment before Kenya's mouth parted into a slow grin.

"The commander is going to be fuckin' delighted we found you. Like I said, times have changed."

A squeak of air escaped from the back of my throat, and the knotted fear in my chest loosened.

"You really don't know how to do any black magic?"

"No." There seemed to be no point in lying; she could find out way too easily.

She stared at me for what seemed a long time, then moved around me. "Major?" She called her son over. She met him halfway, speaking so low I couldn't hear what she said. He glanced over at me, his eyes narrowed on me before he nodded, then he grabbed Fox, the two of them walking back toward the factory.

"What's going on?" My nerves coiled up like a snake.

"I am sure you are telling the truth, but I still need to be sure you are truly a NO."

"And how do you do that?"

"A natural obscurer's magic, similar to a fae's, works off emotion." Puffs of condensation rolled out of her mouth as she talked. "You can train and become more skilled, but when it comes down to it, emotion will always instigate your power, at levels even the highly trained don't achieve. Druids who learn it are only as good as their practice. Emotions help them focus but don't help them be more powerful."

"And how do you plan on testing me?" I swallowed thickly. I could no longer sense the biting cold, as sweat glazed my skin inside my jacket, like another layer of insulation.

"The only way I can." Her gaze went to something behind me.

Oh. God. No. It was like I walked backward into a thick web, my skin prickling with awareness. My head swung around, knowing without looking who would be there.

Major and Fox walked back toward us, escorting someone between them.

Lorcan! My head screamed, his eyes jerked to mine for a moment, worry flooding them. Then he went vacant. He walked forward like a zombie, lifting his absent gaze over my head.

"If you did it once on him, you can do it again," Kenya said.

My neck snapped back to her.

"Good or bad, you have a connection to him. You were able to spell him without even knowing what you were doing. I'm going to have to see you do it again."

"If I don't?"

"Don't?" She tilted her head.

"Can't…" I exclaimed. "What if I can't do black magic again?"

Her brows crunched down. "Then we *can't* trust you. If we *don't* trust you…"

My lids squeezed together. I knew perfectly well what that meant. Most likely, Lorcan and I would be at the bottom of the river.

Crap, Ken. You have to do this. Find it in you somehow.

Both our lives depended on it.

~~~~~

Major and Fox placed Lorcan a few yards in front of me. I sensed every molecule of his body was on defense, but he blocked all other feelings from me.

"Now, I understand NOs need stimulation for their powers to work." Kenya walked around me, coming to my side.

"What are you suggesting?" My mouth felt like sandpaper, and I struggled to swallow over the knot in my throat.

"Order him to attack you."

"What?" My gut plummeted to my feet.

"It's instinct. Your body will protect you. And if you truly are a natural obscurer, it will kick in."

My mouth dropped. *Fuck.* Boy, did the time call for several of those words right now.

"Don't worry. If it doesn't, Major will shoot him." She nodded to where Fox and Major still bookended Lorcan.

"Shoot him?" My head whipped to Major, he tapped the gun at his waist, a hungry grin on his face, as if he wanted nothing more than to do it right now.

Kenya rubbed her red nose, taking a step away from me. "Whenever you're ready."

My heart thumped like a bird trying to escape out of a closed window, bashing against the barrier with the hope of fleeing.

My gaze lifted to Lorcan's and his met mine. My exterior showed none of the fear ripping me to shreds inside. They would notice if either one of us held back. Everything was on the line. We either proved ourselves, or all this was for nothing. We couldn't pretend or fake it.

"Don't hold back." I tried to communicate with my eyes.

"I won't." The words grazed through my mind, startling me. The thought didn't feel like my own. It felt like he had said it, but that was impossible.

I looked down at my feet, exhaling, pushing all superfluous notions away. I sensed everyone had stopped training. The field went quiet, and eyes sizzled into my skin from all angles.

I widened my stance, the pressure in the air encasing me as I centered myself. Lifting my head, my chin set with determination, my order came out strong and clear.

"Attack me."

Lorcan's nose flared, his lips parted, a snarl bounding into the frigid sky. I watched his muscles twitch, his shoulders roll forward, then he rushed for me. Everything in his manner told people he was more than ready to rip me apart. No one would notice his eyes stayed green, pupils round.

And in that exact second, as he lunged for me like a wild animal, I realized I had long stopped being afraid of him.

He was home.

Safety.

Happiness.

He collided into me, taking us both down, a gasp running through the crowd. "Spell me. Now," he growled in my ear.

"Shoot him!" Kenya yelled.

"No!" I screamed.

Boom!

The sound of a gun resounded, cracking across the space like a whip. Lorcan jerked, roaring back in pain as the bullet drove into his back, his body slipping to the side off mine.

Another gunshot rang in the air, and Lorcan's form twisted the opposite way with a garbled holler. Blood spurt from the wounds, pain flashing in his eyes.

Like someone hit a trigger inside me, everything in my mind shut off, and anger blasted through me, raising me from the ground. The memory of being in a forest with Lorcan flickered back in my mind—when I was trying to break the curse on him and I reached a new plane.

"I reached it. It's what Maya and Koke have been trying to get me to do but weren't able. It was brief, but it was amazing...I mean, I've never felt anything like that. It feared me."

"What feared you?"

"The magic. When I hit that level, it finally took notice of me. And it feared me."

I had thought it was because it felt my power. My Druid magic. Now I understood. It saw the darkness in me. The same sensation rushed through my veins now like lava. My arms shot out to my sides as a chant that I didn't remember learning hissed from the depths of my gut. It wanted to hurt, to kill. I felt myself slip to another plane, my rage directed on the man holding a gun.

"Raven? What are you doing?" Major took a step back, his eyes widening.

The spell flew to him, blackness slamming into his torso, bending him over. Then he flew in the air, and a gouge ripped through his clothes like the talon of a giant beast had swiped him. Major screamed in agony.

"Raven!" a woman shrieked.

"You do not hurt what is mine," I growled, taking a step toward Major, his body still suspended in the air. I wanted to harm him.

Then fingers wrapped around my ankle, drawing my attention down. Half-lidded green eyes stared up at me.

"Stop, li'l bird." The thought came into my head, halting me in place. Seeing him centered me again. I came hurtling back to earth.

Major yelled as he crashed to the ground. I fell to my knees, and my body shook and twitched with power so immense I couldn't handle it.

I turned to see everyone staring at me with fear and shock. I looked back down at Lorcan, darkness closing in. His eyes were closed, his physique still.

A whimper caught in my throat before my body gave out. Darkness swallowed me whole.

TWENTY-ONE

"I guess there's no doubt about her being a NO." A man's voice clawed into my eardrum, stirring me from a peaceful nothingness.

"Franklin, she almost killed our son." A woman spoke, flicking awareness deeper into my body.

"He's fine. Already back to work. He's a big boy, lass, stop babying him. Just because you missed those years, you can't continue to treat him like a child."

"I'm his mother. He will always be my boy," she huffed. "But I'm protective of all of them here. We're a family. And you know from day one I haven't trusted her. There is something about her…I can't figure it out. She's hiding something."

"We're all hiding something."

I kept still, letting them think I remained asleep.

"We have a natural obscurer. Do you get how rare it is? She could be a great asset." Franklin's voice bounced around the room as though he paced at the foot of my bed. "Or our gravest mistake."

"That's up to the commander."

My ears perked up. Would they finally take me to see him? Was I free or a prisoner here?

"This was kind of your fault." Franklin's boots clipped the floor. "You wanted to see if she was a NO. Your mistake was misjudging how that would manifest."

"She protected that fae."

A stone tugged my heart into a pit. Lorcan. Was he all right? Dead?

"Look, we might find it disgusting, but Cali is also emotionally attached to hers. He's like her pet. She's protected hers as well."

"She hurts one of her own to defend a fae? It's not right."

"Doesn't make her a traitor."

Kenya snorted but didn't respond.

"Let's see what she does tomorrow night. To prove herself to the cause."

"Fine."

Footsteps neared me, then a hand landed on my shoulder, shaking it. "Wake up." Franklin jostled me. I let him shake me a moment more before my lashes lifted up.

My tongue ran over my dry lips. I pushed myself up to sitting. I was in some kind of infirmary room. The rectangular room was chock full of cots with sheets draping off rope for dividers.

"How are you feeling?" Franklin stood on my left, peering at me with concern. Kenya stood back toward the end of my bed, her arms folded. She did not like me. Wanted me gone. That was clear.

"Okay." I settled higher in the bed.

"Do you remember what happened?"

Should I lie? Kenya's glare felt as though it burned away my skin.

"Yes." I nodded. "Is Major okay? I'm so sorry."

"He's fine. A little shaken up, but all right. He's tough." Franklin widened his stance, folding his arms.

I laced my hands in my lap, staring at them.

"I really am so sorry." I looked at Kenya. Her mouth tightened in a thin line, but she nodded, as though superficially accepting my apology.

"Is…is…?" I took a breath. I didn't know if I could handle the next answer. "Is my fae all right?" I felt appalled with myself. *My fae*…the sentiment stuck in my throat.

"They were normal bullets," Kenya spoke. She had purposely kept that little bit of information from me. Probably more of a test to see how I'd react. "He's already healed. He's down in the pit sleeping it off."

Relief washed over me, and I couldn't disguise the rush of air expelling from my lungs.

"We were never going to kill him. He is yours to deal with." Kenya moved closer, her expression tight. "But we found your trigger, and we saw you were telling the truth."

"I never wanted to hurt any of you."

"We believe you," Franklin responded, but it was obvious only one in the room actually believed that. It was the truth. I hadn't wanted to hurt anyone, but when it came to Lorcan, it seemed out of my control.

"Glad you're okay. Get some rest. Training starts early tomorrow." Franklin patted my arm, but it came with no comfort.

"You still want me to train?"

Franklin stopped at the door, rubbing his chin. "Yes. I think you're going to be a great addition here. You prove yourself on the mission tomorrow night, and I think the commander will be extremely interested in meeting you. You could be just what this fight needs."

Kenya's eyebrows furrowed, but she stayed quiet and followed Franklin out of the room. I flipped off the blanket the moment their footsteps disappeared down the hallway.

Lorcan was the only thing on my mind. I needed to see him. Despite being so drained that I had to drag my limbs down the hallway, I headed toward the pit. Two figures at the end of the hall caught my attention. A couple. Kissing.

I recognized the girl instantly. Cali. And the man she was with was no doubt a fae. Wolf. I could feel his energy. It was nowhere near as powerful as the dark dweller's, but he still could hold his own.

"You better go." She sighed, stepping back. He continued to watch her, but I felt no resentment from him. She went on her toes, her mouth finding his again. He grunted, slipping his hand through her black wavy hair, and pulling her into his chest, hungrily kissing her. I couldn't move, watching the scene before me. This felt like more than her using him for sex. And he certainly wasn't fighting it. Quite the opposite. Finally she broke away. "Maybe I should walk you down, make sure you're tucked in for the night."

She grabbed his hand, pulling him around the corner. Right before he disappeared, his gaze lifted to me, our eyes locking for a second before he was gone. In his yellow eyes, a spark of something shone through. Life. He wasn't entirely a zombie like the others in the pit.

He was in love with her. *Interesting*. My gut told me she was true to the Druid cause, but she cared for him just as much. My mind filled with so many questions. Was he doing this for her or had he given up, letting her break him? Along the way did they both fall for the enemy? I could certainly relate to that.

I wouldn't be able visit Lorcan if they were down there. It was torture, but I steered myself back to my room, promising to see him first thing in the morning. I undressed, putting on the issued black T-shirt, and crawled into bed.

The moment my head touched the pillow, white light shredded across my mind, blinding out everything else, kidnapping me from this world and plopping me into another.

Flash.

I stood over a body. All I could see was dark blond hair of a large man, his face hidden in the dirt, but something told me I knew him. Did I do this to him? Magic sparked under my skin, igniting me with life. It was dark. Black. The power welcomed and feared.

Reaching down, I needed to confirm what I knew in my gut. My fingers clutched the man's shoulder.

"Darkness surrounds Light," a voice squawked above me. I jerked my head up to see a black raven sitting on a fence.

"Grimmel!"

"That is my name."

As much as I loved that bird, I also wanted to kill him half the time.

"Return? False Queen had no light on inside."

A pained smile ghosted my mouth. "I wish. But I can't. Not yet."

Grimmel shook his head, ruffling his feathers all the way down his back. "Light. Home."

I actually got his meaning. Maybe I was starting to understand him. "I miss you too, Grimmel."

His feet shuffled along the fence. "Can't have one without the other. Part of you."

My understanding disappeared. "What is?"

"Beast forced. But one close. Betrayed."

"What?"

Grimmel clicked his beak like he was annoyed.

"Just tell me. No more riddles," I demanded.

"Life. Puzzle. Find pieces. Figure out before too late." Grimmel flapped into the sky. "Light. Dark. Good. Bad. All in you."

Damn that freakin' bird.

I looked down at my feet. The figure now faced me. But it was no longer the same one. Lorcan stared up at me, blackness oozing from a hole in his chest.

Flash.

I stared at myself. My brown eyes narrowed, pinned on something over my shoulder. Fury rippled the airwaves, magic coiling around me like a scarf. I tried to turn to focus on the object of my wrath, but I couldn't, as though I were only tuned into one channel, locked on my own image. Wearing the same clothes I had on the night I was taken from the club to DLR, my face was bruised and cut, a trail of blood drying down the side of my face.

My face twisted, words spitting from the mouth. An unseen wind swiped at my hair, twirling it away from my face. My other body jolted, a haze covering my doppelganger's gaze.

I didn't know the spell I was conjuring, but I felt its darkness.

Meant to hurt.

Black magic.

Metal shrieked behind me as screams flooded the room. I could feel their pain and fear bouncing off my skin, but no matter how hard I tried I couldn't see who I was hurting.

"Stop," I yelled at myself. I don't hurt. I heal. I protect. But my other version simply spoke faster, snarling out the black magic.

This was not me. But part of me couldn't deny the rush I felt even watching the darkness spill over me, the power and confidence filling my body.

I heard a pained roar next to me, a man's voice calling my name, then the sound of a body hitting the ground. My eyes lowered down to my feet. Blood pooled around them as if they were an island, waves breaking around my toes like a red sea. I caught a reflection in the pool. A face I knew.

"Darlin'…"

Flash.

My lids flew open, my body jackknifed, and sweat rolled down my temple. It was dark, only a green exit sign glowed from above the door, so I could scarcely make out shapes.

My heart thumped, the vision still coursing through my head. Where was I? Was this real? I tried to slow my breaths, taking in long, deep inhales, but my body still felt buoyant and confused. I felt a pull to leave the room and run down the hallway. Toward something. A feeling deep in my gut told me it was safer outside this room.

I rocked, grabbed my ear, and yanked it on. "What do you feel?" I muttered to myself, going through my three questions. The soothing words eased my thumping heart, bringing me back.

I knew I was in a room at DLR. Undercover. But even though I knew where I was, the urge to go down the hall grew stronger, setting my feet on the floor. The need for him, my anchor, the one thing keeping me tethered to this earth, was too great to ignore. In all this fear and uncertainty, I craved our routine: him asking me those three questions, tugging on my ear.

Trembling, I pulled on my sweatpants and snuck down the passage toward the pit. The corridor was silent, everyone asleep. I tapped the code in and the door released.

Glancing over my shoulder, I slipped into the dim stairway, the door clicking behind me. I padded softly on bare feet. My eyes were slow to adjust in the dim light. The earthy scent of fresh hay wiggled up my nose, and I fought a sneeze. Fae could move around during the day, especially with their "owner," but at night they were locked up.

All five forms appeared to be sound asleep, curled on their hay beds. Another wave of sickness rolled in my stomach. How could I do this to Lorcan? We had to stop the rogue Druids, but at what cost?

I made my way over to the last figure. His back was to me, and he did not flinch as I dropped next to him. I knew Lorcan; he was always on high alert. He was choosing to ignore me. I reached my hand out, trailing my finger softly through the stubble on his head. One muscle along his shoulder constricted.

"Lorcan." I moved closer, keeping my voice low. "I am so sorry. Are you okay?" He rolled closer to the wall, moving away from me. "Please..." Whatever was in my voice twisted his head back to look at me, his forehead wrinkled.

"What's wrong?"

"Everything." I gnawed on my inner cheek, hoping pain would keep back the tears. "I was so worried about you. I wanted to come earlier..."

"I'm fine. Completely healed." He sat up, the hay crinkling under his weight. "There's something else going on."

"I-I...vision."

He reached out, cupping my face, and drew me into him. I closed my eyes in bliss, his heart beating rhythmically in my ear. He ran his fingers down to my lobe, pinching it. The pain made me sigh, falling deeper into his embrace.

"What did you see?"

The vision had consisted more of sensations than images. "Me. I was working black magic. Hurting people." *You.* I rubbed my face into his soft T-shirt, remembering the feeling of power. The body lying at my feet. His and his brothers'. "I'm scared."

"We'll face whatever comes," he mumbled into my ear while his hands slid down my arms.

The "we" was what drew my head up to look at him. It eased the panic, the fear, and restlessness inside.

"I could have blown our cover tonight. But I couldn't stop myself," I muttered against his chest. "When you were shot I lost it."

He didn't respond but gripped me firmer. I tilted my head more to look at him. He was so close, his breath traced over my mouth, parting my lips. His gaze dropped down, a hitch catching his breath.

The draw was too much, and I was way too weak to fight it. Pushing off my heels, my mouth brushed at his, friction flaring between us. I could feel him lock up, but once again I continued, hoping to feel him respond in kind. My tongue grazed his mouth, tracing the fullness. He inhaled through his nose, his fingers digging into my skin.

"Ken…" he rumbled.

I nipped his bottom lip, disregarding his warning. I was so forward with him, going for what I wanted, instead of being insecure and shy.

"Stop," he stated, but his body still pressed against mine, his warmth blending my brain into jelly. The energy coming off both of us was intoxicating. I wanted nothing more than for it to take me under.

"Kiss me," I murmured into his ear.

His chest rose and fell, his muscles still locked, his grip on my biceps almost painful.

"*Please*," I begged. When did I become that girl? Oh right, the day I met Lorcan Dragen.

He dipped his chin, a groan rumbling in his chest. His mouth skimmed mine, leaving tingles behind. Sucking in sharply, the wall between us grew thin as tissue, our heavy breathing mixing together.

"No." A pained moan came from him. He pushed himself back, his spine hitting the wall, his hand scouring his face.

My body felt chilled and lost. I stayed on my knees, blinking back the rejection. Again. I swallowed, tears building behind my lids as I stared at the ground.

"You're vulnerable right now. This is not what you want."

I pinched my mouth together, my chest whirling with hurt and anger.

"We can't keep doing this. I think you know it…and I certainly do. We only cause pain. We've already made this *mistake*."

I flinched. His sentiment might be right but didn't take away the sting. I had thought the same thing and turned him away because of it. But hearing it from him planted utter agony in my stomach, the roots tunneling deep.

Silence engulfed us.

"You should go." His tone was hollow.

I met his eyes.

Vacant.

Empty.

Not one ounce of emotion. He had shut down and become the zombie again.

"Lorcan…" Anger I could handle. It was the absence of emotion I couldn't deal with.

"I'm here for one thing. My job. You need to focus on yours." He leaned his arms on his knees, turning to the side. "Go now. Please."

Cracks in my barricade splintered into gaping cavities. My vision blurred as I rose to my feet, my head held high. I headed for the stairs, not letting my wounds show. I had become good at putting on a front. But the moment I returned to the safety of my room, I let the tears flow.

I was the one to force him to walk away, but now that he had come back into my life, I could feel myself scrambling to hold on to anything. Any hope. My choice in the tunnel when I told Lorcan to leave felt so right at the time. Now all I wanted to do was take it back. Redo my mistake.

But life didn't let you go back. I could only look forward living with a decision that would haunt me the rest of my life.

TWENTY-TWO

Wizard was at my door first thing in the morning, his face full of worry and concern. He had heard the story from Franklin and Major but wanted to hear it again from me. I had to fudge a lot, altering my reasons for attacking Major. Stressing more my feelings of "ownership" than the actual truth. I could deny it all I want, but I knew now I had fallen in love with Lorcan long ago…and despite my rejection, I'd never stopped. If anything, it seemed to be growing.

My muscles itched with the desire to run down to him the moment I woke up. I was swimming upstream with every step I took with Wizard toward the café.

"Franklin told me to leave you alone till the morning, but I've been going crazy all night. I couldn't sleep; I wanted to talk to you so bad." Wizard shoved his hands in his pockets as we walked together. "I'm so sorry I wasn't there."

"Why?" My question came out a little harsher than I wanted. Coffee was still too far from my lips, and I had to admit I was terrified of facing everyone this morning. Would they hate me? Treat me like I had a disease? No matter what, I *was* the freak. A rare NO. And one who attacked one of the leaders.

Everyone staring at me like I had two heads should have been almost comforting. It was nothing new, after all. I was a freak in my own castle; why shouldn't I be one here?

Wizard and I came around the corner into the cafeteria. The low buzz of voices and clinking dishes instantly stopped and every head turned to me. My instinct was still to run and hide from the intense stares, but I rolled my shoulders back and held myself with pride.

Don't show fear.

Fingers laced with mine, clasping my hand tightly. Wizard pulled me against him, standing defiantly at my side. His statement was clear. The gesture was sweet, but positioning himself like a boyfriend irked me. He was declaring there was more to our relationship without even asking me.

I tried to let go, but he gripped harder, tugging me toward the food. Slowly murmurs and activity picked back up. People returned to their conversations, which were probably about me, but at least they weren't staring.

"They'll move on to something else soon." He flicked his head at the crowd. "But what you did…what you are…is going to produce some whispers for a bit."

"Sounds familiar," I mumbled to myself, filling my cup to the brim with coffee. My stomach growled, but the thought of food made me feel a little ill. I grabbed some oatmeal and a banana before following Wizard back to the table.

Ophelia, Poppy, and Fox were already there. Each turned as we walked up. The sickness in my belly was reminiscent of junior high, ready to have food or hurtful words flung at me.

"Hey." Wizard climbed over the bench, sitting down next to Fox. "We all good here?"

There was a moment of silence as acid burned my intestines. Then a soft smile curled Ophelia's mouth. "Yep." She motioned for me to sit. "Anyone who puts Major in his place is all right in my book."

"Oh my god." Poppy burst into laughter, bending over her plate of eggs. "I hadn't even thought of that." She lifted her head and waved the fork at me. "Girl, you are our hero. Sit your ass down."

A smile tugged at my lips. I moved to sit next to Wizard.

"We knew something was different about you, but a natural obscurer? It's like a bloody unicorn," Poppy exclaimed. "And one that shoved her horn up Major's ass. I think I'm in love."

Not everyone had that reaction to me. Others ranged from intrigue to fear, skepticism to awe. Kenya watched me at every turn. I knew she was being protective of the group, and probably the only one actually right about me, but it annoyed me. Her gaze never let up, like she was waiting for me to break.

"Ooooffffffffftt." Bones crunched as my body slammed back on the mat; muscles I didn't know were a part of me rose up in fury. They didn't understand why they were suddenly being punished. Torin had been tough but had been easing me into defensive fighting. Here you were thrown in head first.

"Get up, Raven." Ophelia's face came into view above me. "Again."

I groaned as I rolled over, getting back on my feet and counting the moments until lunch break.

The morning was spent mostly on my back in pain. Ophelia may have been sweet off the mats, but she was vicious on. The afternoon training with Kenya was no better. Her distrust of me was clear, and she was determined to find a way to break me.

The day dragged painfully on and on. But what tortured me the most was the one thing I needed to avoid, the only thing I wanted to do. Lorcan was my magnetic north, and several times I found myself headed for him without thinking. From the moment I attacked Major to protect him, something shifted deep in me. My connection to him grew even stronger. And denying it was like a thousand knives in my soul.

Finally, before the dinner break, I was able to slip away early from training on a path toward the pit. I needed to try to talk with Lorcan again.

"Raven?" Wizard's voice came from behind me.

I squeezed my lids, forcing back the spurt of anger. He had been on me like a shadow every chance he got, acting like we were a couple.

"Yes?" I swallowed, facing him.

"Franklin wants to see you." He pushed at his glasses. "To go over the plan for tonight."

"Right." I nodded and changed course. I had asked several times about my "mission" tonight, but no one gave me a straight answer. I sensed tonight was pass or fail on a test I couldn't study for.

Butterflies tumbled around my stomach. It wouldn't be easy.

〰〰

I stopped in the doorway, and Wizard bumped into me. "Major." My gaze wandered over him, but he looked unharmed. "I'm sorry." I stepped in, allowing Wizard to slip around me, where he took a seat at his computer. "I didn't—"

"Let's forget it, okay?" Major flicked through the files he was looking at, his mouth lined. His blue eyes turned to mine. "I don't blame you. I don't understand, but your personal life is not my concern."

My mouth pinched as I entered the room.

"Hey, girl." Cali patted the seat next to her. "Have a seat."

Wizard frowned when I settled in next to her but went back to what he was doing.

"I would have done the same." Cali leaned into my ear. "Anyone touched Wolf, I'd attack too. No one's gonna take mind-blowing sex away from me. Am I right?" she added flippantly, but I wasn't fooled. She was in love with him.

"It's not like that."

"Right." She let out a chuckle. "I can see you know. You're not fooling me. You have it baaadd."

My eyes widened, terror creeping up my throat.

"I have extra abilities in seeing auras. And you two? Holy shit. Red hot. Like fuckin' intense."

My head darted around to see if anyone was in earshot. Only Wizard, Major, and Cali, and myself were here, and neither of the men glanced over.

"Don't worry. No one else can see it." Cali nudged me and winked. "Your secret's safe with me."

Soon Poppy, Fox, Mayhem, Ophelia, and Kenya entered the room, followed by Franklin.

"All right, I just want to do a quick meetup." Franklin addressed the room, rounding to the far end of the table.

I was ready for a whole breakdown on events for the night and what he had planned for me, but he merely went through who was going, what to wear, and when to meet back in the war room.

"Aren't you going to tell me what I'm doing?" I sat up in my seat.

"We're working out a few more details." Franklin rubbed his chin. "Our target has been misplaced, but with Wizard on it, I have no doubt we'll be ready in time for tonight."

"Still, shouldn't I get an outline? A rundown of my part?"

"That's part of the test, Raven. We need you to react in unforeseen circumstances." Franklin leaned his hip on the table. "All new recruits go through the same exercise. You are no different."

But I was. We all knew it even if they didn't realize how much.

"Okay, everyone get some rest; we head out at midnight. Be back here at eleven thirty." Franklin flicked his head, dismissing us.

Sleep. Right. I hated not knowing what I had to do tonight. It bothered me. I wanted to plan and prepare. Sleep would be pointless. Everyone cleared the room, rushing to be first in line for dinner. Sleep and food would be lost on me.

"Did you want to grab a quick dinner first?" Wizard shoved his hands into his pockets, standing over me, looking sheepish.

"No. I think I'm gonna go get some rest." I stood from the conference table.

"Oh." Wizard bobbed his head. "Okay. I guess I'll see you back here later?"

"Yep," I said, waiting for Wizard to walk away, but he tipped forward and back on his feet, like he was waiting for something. "Well, then…I'll see you."

"Yeah. Later." He finally twisted to leave, but his feet still pointed toward me, bouncing. I could feel he wanted to ask me out, which up till now I had avoided or changed subjects before he could do it. I looked down, not wanting to meet his gaze as he asked the question I would have to refuse.

He sighed, turning and walking out the door, his head bowed. I felt awful but still couldn't deny the relief at dodging him one more time.

Once I saw him head down the hallway for the café, I ran full force to the pit, not slowing till my feet pounded down the steps where I found Lorcan sitting in the exact spot I left him. All the other fae sat or laid on their beds, staring off into space.

With Wolf and Lorcan I sensed annoyance, but nothing like the rest. Wrath, resentment, and loathing pumped off the others with a stench almost as literal as the one filling the room. If given the chance, the three fae would tear us into tiny bits and laugh the entire time. Death was what they desired for us. And I couldn't blame them for feeling that way.

"Hey." I walked up to Lorcan. Only his eyes moved to me, then snapped back to the far wall. "You want to go to the upper level and walk around a bit before the mission tonight?"

"No," he responded. Cold and aloof. I didn't think he was even acting anymore.

My lids fluttered, batting away the hurt. "I don't think I can sleep or eat. I'm too scared."

Lorcan's chin rose, and his gaze shifted side to side, a muscle along his jaw twitching. "No point worrying about it. You can't control it."

"You know that's not how I work." I absently grabbed for his arm, running my fingers down his skin, needing to touch him. He jerked under my touch, his head snapping toward the door.

"Ken, stop," he rasped out. It was the first inkling of emotion I had heard from him.

"Why?" Cali was not shy about touching Wolf in front of people. DLR didn't like it, but they didn't kick her out over it.

"Come on. You need to rest." Lorcan pushed off the wall, his hand skimming my lower back, pointing me for the stairs up to the exit. The feeling of his body next to mine invoked a sensually heightened awareness to collide over my skin.

Lorcan was silent as he walked me to my room. My heart spilled over with things I wanted to say, but none of them made it to the surface.

"Try to get some sleep." He paused at my door, rubbing the back of his neck. "With everything you've gone through, you'll handle whatever they throw at you," he said as if he had no doubt. He dropped his arm and walked away.

Seeing him disappear around the corner did something to me. Panic burst from my chest and moved me before I even realized it. Dread thumped my heart. Not because of the unknown ahead, but the known now.

I knew I didn't want to be without him. Cali was right; I had it bad. I was so deeply in love with him I couldn't think straight. And I could feel it...I was losing him, which scared me beyond anything else in the world. The last three days watching him become a shell killed me. He was doing it for me, but because of that, I was losing him.

"Lorcan. Wait," I called out, running around the corner. He was almost down the hall where the door to the pit was. "Stop!" I yelled again.

His feet halted, but he didn't turn around. "Yes, master?"

"Don't." I reached him, my toes knocking into his heels. "That's not fair."

"Fair." He snorted scornfully. "What does that have to do with anything?"

I took a deep breath, trying to ignore his tone, my fingers lightly touching his elbow. "Stay with me," I whispered.

His spine went rigid, every muscle contracting across his shoulder blades. He inhaled sharply, turning so abruptly I jumped back. Anger swelled in him, seeping out of his pores. "Now who's not being fair?" He growled through his teeth.

At one time I would have bowed my head and run away, scared and hurt. Not to say the tendency wasn't still there, but it was overshadowed. I had overcome too many threats, hateful words, and challenges in my life to cower and hide. Especially from him. I stared at him, challenging his anger with silence.

"Stop that." He inched closer, his growl deepening. I didn't move. He gritted his teeth, glancing to the side, his hand running over the back of his head. His eyes fell back on me. "Stop fuckin' looking at me like that. It seriously freaks me out." He pulled away from me, shaking his head.

"Stay with me tonight," I said softly.

His eyes snapped back to me, his expression full of warning. "Just tonight?" His fingers rolled into a fist. "I don't think so."

"Why?" I couldn't hide the hurt lacing my voice.

"I am right where I'm supposed to be." He nodded back toward the door where the fae slept. "With the depraved. Right at home there. My kind. So go, before anyone sees you."

"No." I shook my head. "It's not who you are."

"I'm worse." He stabbed a finger in his chest. "The only difference between me and them is I came here on my own. I wasn't forced, which makes me even more fucked up," he spit through his teeth. "You will always be out of my reach. Close enough to taunt me, but never to have. It's something I've known all along, especially after Jared died. But I kept denying it, thinking it could be different. But it's not. I don't fit in your world and you certainly don't fit in mine." He twisted to head for the door. "Go back to your kind. Leave me be."

"No!" I shoved at his arm, wrenching him to face me, fury cracking through me. "Stop being like this."

"Stop being like what?" He sneered, leaning in toward me, his arms out. "This is me, Kennedy. This is it."

"No. It's. Not!" I pushed him again. "I *know* you. You can pretend and hide behind all your masks, but I've seen you. The real you. So don't give me this cheap version and act like that's all there is."

He opened his mouth, but I kept going, anger spewing off my tongue.

"You can hate it. *Despise me* because I can see past all your layers of bullshit. But I won't settle for the guy you make everyone hate because you're afraid."

"Afraid?" He growled, slanting his head. "Do I fuckin' look scared of anything to you?"

"Yes." I nodded.

"And what is it I'm scared of?" he countered, his nose flaring and pupils elongating.

I dropped my hand, craning my neck to look directly into his eyes, challenging the beast for dominance. "Me."

Lorcan jerked back, his teeth cracking as they clenched. "You?" A derisive snort huffed from him, a cruel gaze running over me. "What the hell would I be afraid of from a pint-size girl like you?"

"Because I see *you*."

He folded his arms, taking another step away from me. His jaw muscles flexed and tension filled the space, our heavy breaths ping-ponging off the walls. He broke first, turning away from me. His hand ran from the back of his head to the front, scouring over his temples.

"Lorc—" I went to touch his arm, my fingertips barely grazing his skin before he whipped around, grabbing me and pushing me back against the wall.

"I can't do this anymore. I'm done, Kennedy," he rumbled, his eyes fully dark dweller.

"Can't do what?" I whispered.

"This. Us. It is killing me." His shoulders bunched around his neck, his hands pushing into the wall on either side of my head. "I told you once, I don't do maybes. Not with you." He shoved away.

My hand automatically grabbed for his. "No." The thought of him walking out on me sawed me in half. "Talk to me. Tell me why you are so mad at me."

His laugh was manic and twisted. "Mad at you?" He shook his head, his expression feral. "Fuck! I wish it was that simple. I don't even wish I could *hate* you. I want to feel *nothing* for you."

I sucked in, my head hitting the wall, my heart crushing under his words.

"Then I could walk away from this whole thing, from you, and never have you cross my mind again."

Pain stabbed right through my heart, my hand releasing his arm, my face scrunching with agony.

"What do you want from me?" His temper grew more agitated. "You don't want to be with me...so what the hell do you want? A quick fuck? Is that it?"

His harsh bluntness hit me in the stomach like a game of dodgeball.

"You can't keep doing this. Make up your fucking mind. It's not only me who's scared." Both hands rubbed his face. He took a deep breath, then he straightened up. "Actually, I'll make this easy for you. I'm out."

I could sense the resolve. The truth behind his declaration. This time when he turned for the door, I felt him truly walking away from me.

Whatever barrier I had been trying to keep up disintegrated at my feet. "No!"

He ignored me.

"Lorcan." I scrambled after him, my throat clogging with fear. "Lorcan, stop!" I grabbed him, blocking his progress, both of our breathing sounded ragged. "Do you know how hard this past year was?" The words I hadn't planned to say broke out. "It was hell. Alone, terrified, and heartbroken. You act like I didn't think of you once, when in truth, you haunted my every waking hour. Some days just breathing was an accomplishment. Jared killed me...but you...you obliterated me."

Lorcan reeled around, his eyes tapered with distrust.

"But I couldn't show any of that. Every day I'm threatened. I can't show one moment of weakness. I couldn't even mourn my own family's death. I am Queen. My role is to be there for my people. To be their pillar of strength." I gulped. "And it's not like you were around. You walked away from me."

"You told me to."

"I did." I nodded. "Jared's death. The guilt swallowed me whole. And I took it out on you. On myself."

"You don't think I feel guilty? Jesus, Kennedy. Every time I look at you I feel another shackle of blame wrapping around my neck."

"I-I thought it would be easier to cut you out. Having nothing to remind me of you." I laughed humorlessly. "What a joke. Everything reminds me of you. You are in everything...under my skin. In my head."

"Don't say that." He folded his arms.

"Don't speak the truth?" I bellowed in frustration. "I swear sometimes you can hear my thoughts…and I hear yours. It freaks me out."

"Shit." He palmed his face, rubbing fiercely. "I was hoping it would lessen for you."

"What would lessen?"

He bent over, his hands drumming his thighs before pulling to his full height.

"Do you know why I pushed you away that night at Lars's château? Why I continue to? I don't want this for you."

"What?" My chest squeezed, my intuition knowing, but my brain still was not ready.

Lorcan paced, his movements frantic.

"Tell me."

He swore under his breath, pacing faster.

"I said tell me!"

Lorcan swung to me, ire straining his muscles. "My beast fucking claimed you," he yelled, hurling it at me like an accusation. The word slammed into me like a bullet. "That's why you can hear me. Why I can hear you. There. Are you happy?"

"What?" I sucked in.

"You heard me."

I blinked, my mouth ajar.

"You're not stupid. You've known it somewhere inside you since the first night together," he snapped. "It began to claim you way before, but that night finalized it."

I was pretty sure I did, but to hear it out loud was like he opened a locked cabinet and let the truth fall out on the floor. So many things he'd said, especially the exchange in Lars's office, the morning after we were together, between Lorcan and Cole. Cole must have figured out then Lorcan had claimed me, all made sense now.

"Why didn't you tell me?"

"Honestly? At first I didn't want it to be true. But that's not how it works. Jared was another reason. Then the war..." He trailed off. When I told him I wanted nothing to do with him.

"And you didn't have sex with me—"

"Because each time it only increases the bond." He cut in. "You weren't and never could be a casual fuck." The word plummeted straight between my thighs, letting my own beast out, roaring to life. "I was already screwed, but I wanted you to be free. You didn't need this...or me."

Mine. I could hear the primal part of my brain loud and clear. Now my feelings were out there, my body clamored for his.

"What if I want it?"

"Really?" He took a step toward me. "Because this isn't just for a night, Ken. Who I am? What I do? I don't see you welcoming me into your life or with your friends."

"Some of those friends are your own family."

"Yeah." He snorted. "And you know how much they adore me."

"I didn't say it wouldn't be hard work."

His boots hit mine, his voice low. "You're not going to change me."

"I don't want to." I tipped my head back to look up, his body heat crashing into mine. "The beast, the monster, the man. I want all of you."

"So, you'll be all right with how Ryan and Ember will react? How your court will respond to you taking on a dark dweller for a lover?" He inched closer till there wasn't a sliver of space between us. "When I go to *work*?"

"For once I'm going to think about what I want."

"And what do you want?" His fingers brutally slid over my ear and down my neck, tangling in my hair. Desire zipped through my veins, heating my skin.

"You." I rolled my hand in his T-shirt, tugging him closer. "Always. You."

He paused a moment and stared into my eyes. *Mine.* The word came into my head and this time I knew it was from him.

A smile curved my mouth. *Mine*, I said back.

Lorcan's hands skated up my jaw, his mouth crashing down on mine, capturing my mouth hungrily with his. The kiss quickly turned crazed, his tongue parting my lips, demanding more. My fingers clawed under his shirt, ran over his abs to his back, and pulled him in closer.

Our passion was anything but sweet and slow. The year apart and the temptations we both struggled with daily on this crazy adventure had turned into unadulterated need. Desperate. Raw. Primal.

Lorcan's hands curved over my butt, lifting me up, my legs wrapping around his hips. I grasped the sides of his face, squeezing my thighs firmer around him, deepening the kiss, nipping at his bottom lip.

He growled, my spine colliding with the nearest wall, kissing my neck and working down to my chest. I tipped my head back, allowing him better access. Keeping me pinned to the wall, he leaned back, his fingers curling around the collar of my T-shirt. One pull, the fabric split down the middle. He dragged down my bra, exposing my breasts. His warm mouth claimed one. I groaned, grabbing the back of his head, raking my fingers roughly down the back of his neck.

He let out a noise I knew belonged to the beast. Our lust escalated so high, I thought I might explode right there.

I suddenly grew aware we were still in the HQ hallway. Most were at dinner, and this walkway was almost as untraveled as the pit, but at any moment any member could step around the corner and see us. Knowing what they seemed to believe of Lorcan and me, they'd think I had some kinky fetish, using a fae as my sex toy.

Or they would see through our façade.

Either way, it was really hard to care when Lorcan moved to the other breast, nipping and sucking.

"In public." My throat was so thick with desire, I could barely manage those few words. "My room."

Lorcan glanced up at me, a bad-boy smile tugging on his mouth.

Shit. I knew that look. He loved shoving me off my theoretical comfy couch.

He undid the top button of my jeans, zipping them down before I could even blink. Yanking them over my hips just enough to allow access. His fingers brushed over me, my breath hitching before he shoved my underwear to the side.

"Lorcan." Trying to fight the urge to give in, my eyes darted around. "Someone will cat—"

I cut off my own words with a hiss as his fingers plunged deep into me, curling. "Oh. God."

"If you want to be with me, you're gonna have to get extremely used to sex in public." He increased his movement, my eyes glazing over with pleasure. "Because I will be fucking you all the time. And I don't care who wants to watch."

I gulped, nodding, my hips moving against his fingers. He could do anything to me, with a stadium of viewers, and I wouldn't have cared. It actually increased the thrill.

What happened to the shy, quiet girl from school? I had no idea, but she was not shy or quiet now.

Especially when he hiked me up the wall, draping my legs over his shoulders, his mouth joining his fingers. His tongue created a high-pitched noise from my throat and proved once again he had full control over my body, turning me feral and wild. Bucking against him, I could feel the edge I teetered on, my moans turning into shrieks the more he sucked and licked. When it came to sex and pleasure...Lorcan was a gifted *genius*.

He nipped me, biting down just enough to inflict a thread of pain, sending pleasure smashing through my body. My orgasm detonated. I knew I cried out boisterously, but my body spiraled out into space, not caring how loud I was back on earth.

The sensation of Lorcan pulling away, the cool air against me, him kissing me softly once more, slowly, sank me back down, my chest trying to catch up with my rapid heart.

"Holy. Shit."

"I've wanted to do that for a *long* time." He smiled, sliding me back down.

"*Whenever* you want." I leaned all my weight into the wall to keep me upright, pulling back up my pants and repositioning my bra. "I won't stop you."

He chuckled, widening his stance; he cupped my face, tipping my head up.

"You might come to regret that, li'l bird." His eyes glinted with mischief.

"I highly doubt it."

"Wait until you're trying to have a business meeting and I'm the one under your desk, my head between your thighs, with my tongue."

Shit squared and multiplied.

A split second and my body went from sedated to aching again. Lorcan's nostrils flared, probably smelling the spike of lust rushing through me.

"Now, let's go back to your room before the guy at the end of the hall gets another show," Lorcan growled, his eyes completely red.

I turned against his hold, spotting a balding man at the far end. Dressed in a towel like he was heading to the shower, he stared at us with wide eyes. His room was the only one that had a view down this hallway. He was human and had no control over his feelings or thoughts, which poured into the atmosphere. His aura sparked red, gray, and green.

Turned on, lonely, and envious.

Ick. He let himself be an open book and my seer saw more than I wanted. What *he* wanted.

"Maybe if you had done that to your wife, instead of the *fae* guy at the massage spa, she wouldn't have left you," my seer declared honestly to the man before I had a chance to stop it. "Or at least asked her to join."

His mouth dropped open, his hand going to his chest, insulted, then he rushed away.

Lorcan snorted, turning me toward my room. "Come on, woman, before I have to spank you for being rude...that's my job."

"Do you mean I get to spank you every time you're offensive?" I grinned at him, rubbing my hands together.

"No." Lorcan hauled me down the passage, pushing me into my room, slamming the door behind us.

"You're right. I would have my hand in a cast within a few hours." I backed up, a coy grin teasing my mouth as he prowled up to me.

"You ever spank me…" Lorcan's humor went underground, the beast in full control, stalking its prey. "I will not be responsible for what I do to you."

It was a threat, but one I wanted to test. I lifted an eyebrow. "I'm sure I have the authority."

"You think you're embarrassed the old man saw us? I *promise* you…" he declared. My eyes darted to his; fae did *not* promise because promises were binds and fae *had* to fulfill the pledge. He grabbed my wrists, walking me back to the wall, pinning them above my head. "I will bend you over wherever you are and fuck you till you cannot take any more. In front of everyone. I don't care who is there. Got it?"

I stared up at him; my body shook with need, responding to his brutal furiousness. I liked it. A lot.

"I am not one of your servants, or a noble you can order around. I will not call you my lady or Majesty." He gripped my wrists with the free hand, the other sliding from my throat to my belly button, sparking electricity through me. "I will not be your doll to dress up and take to events, or sit by your side, like a housebroken mutt. I am a beast. That will not change. I am dark. You may be Queen, but you are not my queen. You're my mate. Equals. The one I will fuck every night, morning, and afternoon until you are sick of me. Does that scare you?"

I gulped for air, wanting so bad for him to start. "No."

I used to hate when Jared called me his mate or said he "claimed me." I had felt trapped, like I didn't have an option. I hadn't wanted it. Jared and I were never meant to be; I understood that clearly now. Because when Lorcan said it, heat consumed my body so powerfully it shocked me. I wanted to claim him as intensely in return, leaving no doubt he was mine.

"You can walk away now." His gaze dared me. "Before I sink *deep* into you and make your decision almost impossible."

"The more we have sex, the more the beast claims me?" My voice emerged low and raspy.

His fingers dug into my wrists. "It's already claimed you. But the more I come inside of you, the more I bond to you. You have a window right now; we've only been together a few times before spending a year apart. You can walk away. Free. Like you were before."

"You think I've been free?" I glared at him. "Did you not hear what I said earlier? You haunt me every moment in my own prison of hell. And even when I was too busy to think, I felt something was always missing. And funny enough, the moment I was with you again, it disappeared. I am tired of fighting you, Lorcan, fighting what I feel and want."

"And if you change your mind once we get back? When reality sinks in?"

"I won't."

"You sure?" He dropped my arms, the blood rushing back into them. "I'm not sure I can go through that again. I'd rather do it now." Something showed in his eyes, and his thoughts came to mine like words on a page. It was so natural. Not intrusive or scary at all.

"If I did, it would kill you," I stated. "What you said earlier, you meant it literally."

"Not entirely, but I'd continue to get weaker." His lips twisted. "Fun perks, I've learned, of claiming and being rejected."

My hand went to my mouth. "The weight loss and lack of sleep was actually because of me?"

"Don't take that on. It's not your fault." He shook his head. "This is your decision. You have full say in what you want."

"I know, but…" Pain and guilt burrowed into my gut.

"No buts. I will not have you choose me out of pity." He growled, spinning away from me. "Fuck that."

"It's not pity." I grabbed his arm firmly, needing him to understand. "It actually physically hurts me knowing I caused you pain. If I had known…"

"You still should have done the same thing. I hated it at the time. But seeing you now, the woman you've become, walking away from me was the best decision you could have made. For both of us."

He was right. I would never have grown if I had stayed with him, and maybe eventually resenting him because the pain over Jared would have never healed. I needed the time to develop as a person, as a queen, to rebuild my heart. Now I was ready to be with him.

I peered at him, still hating the agony that choice put him through.

"Don't look at me like that," he snarled. "I will lose my mind if I get another look of sympathy from you."

"Dammit, Lorcan!" I bellowed, getting fully in front of him. "I love you, you jerk! That means I'm going to care if you're in pain. I'm going to worry if you're sick or hurting. That's the way it works. *Especially* with me. So if *you* want to be with *me* you're going to have to deal with it."

He stood there frozen in place, then clamped his eyes shut.

"Did you hear me? I am in love with you. I want to be your mate; I want to be claimed. It might sound very anti-feminist, but I don't care. I don't give a damn what anyone else thinks. All that matters is you and me. And if your beast already claimed me, then I should be on even terrain here. I demand to stake my own claim. It's only fair. We're equals, right?"

Lorcan's lashes rose, flames scorching his irises. In an instant I was in his arms, crashing back onto the bed, the dweller moving between my legs. When his mouth found mine, I felt the fire burn through me. The kiss was as hungry as earlier but was filled with more intense emotion, like he finally unhinged the gate and let it flood into me, allowing me to feel and see it.

"There's only one thing I demand." He broke from my mouth.

"What?"

"This needs to come off. For good." He grabbed at the chain, knowing who put it there and the declaration it represented. I helped him pull it off, tossing it on the floor. "The moment I saw him put it on you, I wanted to crush it into powder." But he hadn't. He never said a word, letting me choose what I wanted.

Though the charm was light as a feather, the moment it came off I felt a weight lift off me. There was no doubt whom I wanted. My mouth captured Lorcan's, letting him know without words he was all I desired.

His hands tore the rest of the shirt from my body, unhooking my bra as I tugged at his shirt, our lips barely separating for him to yank it off before he was back, stealing my breath.

Our hands skated over every inch of skin, rediscovering each other. My fingers dragged up his back and through his hair. My legs hugged his torso, tugging him down on me. One hand moved down his frame and playfully swatted at his butt, an impish smile curling my mouth.

"Oh, you are so in trouble," Lorcan growled deeply.

Bring it, I thought.

He pulled back, a roguish grin on his mouth. *It's on, li'l bird,* his eyes said back to mine. He climbed off the bed, chucking off my shoes. My sweats and underwear soon followed. He stared down at my naked form, gazing at me like I was the most beautiful, sexy woman he had ever seen. His irises flared with need; he kicked out of his boots, then started on his pants. I climbed onto my knees, stopping his fingers.

"Let me," I said. My hands worked the buttons, quickly shoving the jeans to the floor. Lorcan didn't wear underwear, for which I was grateful. I had forgotten when he said he was a beast it wasn't simply the dark dweller he was talking about. "I think I still owe you." I grabbed his hips and gazed up at him through my lashes, reminding him of the promise I made him if we survived the war.

"And I'm collecting with a year of interest." He smirked, his lids hooded as I let my fingers run the length of him. He swore when I gripped him, moving my hand up and down. I remembered the first time I had held him like this. The memory of us in the bathtub had made appearances in many of my fantasies over the past year.

"Tell me how you like it." I licked the length of him.

"Do-ing good so far." He huffed, his head going back with a groan as my tongue wrapped around him.

I was nervous, but Lorcan had a way of making me feel comfortable with myself. And not embarrassed to ask. If I had to practice over and over, I would learn exactly what made him lose his mind. He knew how to make me.

It was only fair.

TWENTY-THREE

Kisses trailed across my shoulder blades, waking me from a brief but peaceful sleep. I grinned, snuggling into the pillow, my eyes not ready to open. I was exhausted and sore, but in the best way possible. I was pretty sure Lorcan was trying to make up for a year in a few hours. One orgasm rolled into the next throughout the evening, our need only increasing instead of diminishing. Finally my mind and body had given over to sleep.

Clearly my break was over.

Lorcan's mouth nipped behind my ear, his hand sweeping my hair off my neck. I hummed out a happy noise, stretching my limbs.

"What time is it?" The windowless room made it impossible to tell the time.

"Little before eleven."

"Really?" I yawned. We had to meet the group in about thirty minutes. "Did you even sleep?" Drowsily lifting my lashes, I looked over my shoulder. Only the dim green exit light by the door gave me enough to see his outline, his eyes glowing even brighter than the light in the darkness.

"Enough." He worked down my neck. "Too many things distracting me."

"Talking about me, being caught here, or the mission?"

"All the above." His tongue drifted along my jaw. Rolling me onto my back, he hovered over me. "But I think by far you were the most distracting." His hand glided up my inner thigh, brushing me. "Especially this." His mouth moved to my breast. "And this."

I swallowed, a moan already curling out of me.

A touch was all it took, and I was completely at his will, ready to challenge his fever with my own. I knew couples went through the honeymoon period where they couldn't get enough of each other but eventually petered out. What I knew of fae in general and particularly Ember and Eli or West and Rez, it didn't appear those mated to fae ever got over that period. I couldn't be more grateful. I'd never not want him, craving his touch till the end of time.

"What happens when I die?" The thought shot out my mouth before I could stop it. Lorcan's head jerked up, the corners of his eyes creasing.

"I don't think we have to worry about that for a long, long time."

"But eventually I will." My fingers ran over his stubble, my thumb tugging at his bottom lip.

"You're going to live for thousands of years." His teeth grazed my thumb, biting it. "Why are you thinking about this now?"

"Because you live pretty much forever. I'm just curious."

He grabbed both my wrists and pinned them back into the pillow by my head with one hand, red flaring through his gaze.

"From what I've seen we don't do well at the loss of our mate. We may not die, but we go a little insane."

My eyes widened, hating I would cause Lorcan to go crazy.

"Ken, I've lived a long, long time. I plan on living even longer...with you." His knees pushed my legs apart, his free hand hooking my thigh up on his hip. "But if you must know, I plan to follow wherever you go…and *when* you go."

His declaration fell on me, taking me a moment before the meaning soaked into my skin. I was the girl no boy ever looked at school; now I had a man, a sexy beast of a man, not wanting to live without me. My brain struggled to wrap around it.

We may have not started as a sweet love story, but I loved where the journey had brought me. Here, in this bed, with the man I loved. My head pitched up, my lips colliding with his with deep hunger. He was mine. And I was never going to take that for granted.

Our mouths grew hungry and desperate, his gaze flickering to mine.

What do you want, li'l bird? Tell me, his gaze said to me.

I want you deep in me. Hard, I said back, the blunt words no longer sounding foreign or embarrassing.

Whatever the Queen demands. His eyes glistened with mischief. He flipped me over on my knees, wrapping my fingers around the bed railing, his hands running up the back of my thighs, spreading my legs. He scraped the tip of himself against me.

"Oh god." I moaned, my back arching, wanting more. "Please. Now."

He tortured me instead. His mouth started at the base of my spine, licking all the way to the back, his tongue working in places I never thought I would want touched. Pleasure so unbearable consumed me that I made a noise I had never heard before.

"Like that, li'l bird?" It really wasn't a question, my whimpers displaying I did. His fingers and tongue continued to play with me, dipping farther until my legs shook. I couldn't get a full breath, ignoring my pleas, pushing my pleasure to the limit before backing off again.

"Please…" I reached around, grabbing his tight round butt, pulling him to me.

"Hands stay where they are." He chuckled and locked my fingers around the bar again.

"Then you better get inside me, now. I'm not kidding, Lorcan," I practically growled.

"Oh, someone is getting bossy in bed." He breathed into my ear, his voice low and husky. "I like it."

"Fuck me," I whispered hoarsely back, rubbing my butt against him. "Is that direct enough for you?"

"Shit," Lorcan rumbled as I leaned farther. His hand went to my back, pushing me forward. Then I felt him slide into me. We both let out loud groans, his fingers digging into my hips as he pushed all the way in.

"Jesus…" He choked, starting to move inside me. We already had sex a lot tonight, but each time felt more unbelievable than the time before, and my climaxes hit new levels till I was no longer in my body. I pushed against the railing, slamming back with as much force as he was giving.

Bundling my black locks in his fist, he tugged my head back. Fire flared up my veins, responding to the flick of pain, making me crazed. Our movements became deeper and faster.

Kennedy disappeared, letting Raven out. Forgetting about anything else except the feel of him, the sounds, and smell of us.

I bent over, which caused Lorcan to swear out a string of obscenities, pounding in deeper. His hand came around, rubbing me. When he hit the spot, sending me soaring over the cliff, I shrieked. The moment I tightened around him, I heard a roar shake the room. He slammed in so hard my eyes watered, my body only clamping down harder on him. He let out another roar, emptying himself in me, hot and claiming.

This time I felt it, the bond, heating me with warmth and love. It felt so good, like I'd been soaked in warm, silky chocolate. With chili pepper. Smooth, sensuous, and an explosion of passionate heat.

I panted, my head on my forearms, trying to draw in enough oxygen to not kill any more of my brain cells. My mind had already decided to take a vacation, leaving me with quivering limbs and clouds of bliss in my head.

It took us both a moment to come back, to regain any sense of reality.

"Jesus, Ken." Lorcan inhaled deeply, his hand gliding down my spine. "One of these times I'm actually going to black out."

"Me too." My heart still pounded against my ribs like a racehorse.

He pulled out, twisting my hips so I would face him, and I frowned.

"What?" He sank us down into the pillows, tugging me to him.

"I hate that."

"Hate what?" His eyebrows shot up, his arm curling around me.

I bent my head, embarrassed to admit it. Kennedy was back, but the black Raven was now a part of me too. "I hate when you pull out of me. I feel so empty."

A wicked grin grew on his face. "Believe me, I hate it too." He adjusted me in his arms, kissing my head. "If it was up to me, I never would."

A laugh barked out. "And how would that work? Meetings with nobles would be a bit awkward."

"Nah, I'd just carry you around...maybe get one of those Babybjörns…"

"Oh my god. A visual came with that. Stop, now." I laughed, covering his mouth with mine. He chuckled and turned to me, kissing me again deeply. He pulled back, my fingers clasping the side of his face, my gaze searching his.

Hell. I had told him I loved him, but in this moment I realized how deeply I did. I was so far gone it should have scared the crap out of me. It didn't.

No doubt everyone might have a huge problem with us, but I would fight for us. I felt so happy and content. Whatever came at us, we were in it together.

I brought him to me, my kisses showing him all I felt. He picked up on my emotions right away, rolling me on my back, returning my kisses. It was passionate and full of words we didn't need to say. This time when he entered me, it was slow and gentle, our hands, lips, and eyes never leaving each other. He rocked into me, taking his time. My climax was gradual, but when it blurred the edges of my vision, I knew the intensity was going to consume me in an obliterating grip.

"Raven?" A knock pounded the door.

Oh. God. Not right now.

Lorcan didn't stop, his hips pumping, ramming me into the bed frame.

My lips parted to talk, but a cry broke over my mouth, my lids shutting.

"Raven? You okay?" I knew the voice to be Wizard. And I knew Lorcan recognized it too, because his intensity dialed up, the possessiveness of the beast nailing into me.

"Y-y-yeahhh."

"It's almost eleven thirty; thought you might want to head over with me."

"I-I'll meet...oh god...there." My nails dug into Lorcan's back, my head tipping back as I felt myself about to hit the glass roof and shatter.

"So…ummm. I was wanting to ask you for a while. Do you want to grab dinner with me sometime? Or a coffee? Like a date. A real one. I mean, you don't have to…but if you want to…"

Lorcan snarled in my ear, his elbows set along my head, pinning me in place, moving more quickly, staking full claim. The edge was approaching and nothing was going to stop us, even if Wizard walked in. Again, I got a strange thrill at the possibility of being caught.

"Raven?"

"Y-y-es...I'm coming!" I cried out, not knowing to whom I was talking, my orgasm tearing through me. Wave after wave rolled within me as Lorcan left his mark, asserting his right to the territory. And I asserted mine right back. My hips continued to buck a few more times before I felt my body loosen around him. Lorcan's head fell against mine, my muscles going limp.

"Oh...well…okay...it's a date then. I'll see you in the war room?" Wizard's voice was odd, like he figured out I might not be alone.

I couldn't answer, my head and body still in the haze of ecstasy.

Lorcan's head tilted toward the door like he was listening, a smile growing on his mouth. "Thought that little fucker would never leave."

"That was incredibly risky."

"You wanted me to stop?" He lifted his head off mine, a smug grin tipping up the side of his mouth.

"Noooo."

"What I thought." He shifted some of his weight off me, but still hadn't broken from me. "Admit it, you liked it. And you *really* liked it earlier in the hallway...I can tell. Remember."

I didn't answer, but my silence spoke volumes.

"My dirty li'l bird." He chuckled, kissing my nose and rolling off me, once again making me feel hollow. He put his feet on the floor, switching the light on the table, gazing over his shoulder at me. "Like you said, it's frowned upon, but it's not against the rules to fuck a fae...the man in the hallway seemed overly keen to join us."

"Not sure he would have cared if I was there or not."

"That Druid girl and the snake shape-shifter are fucking every moment they have free. They did it next to me last night."

That was pretty brazen, just like her personality.

I sat up, scooting around him, grabbing my glasses and the newly cleaned clothes I'd arrived at DLR wearing. Heading for my bag, I snatched the discarded pendant off the floor, my fingers curling around it. The thought of hurting Torin hammered spikes in my heart. I cared about him so much. I simply wasn't in love with him. But after the same thing happened with Ember, my guilt swirled deep. He was my friend, and I didn't look forward to the conversation that would accompany my return of his mother's necklace.

With a sigh, I tucked it in the side pocket of the backpack they'd given me. I yanked on a sweatshirt long enough to cover me and snatched my toiletries. I didn't care if I was late; a shower was a must. Sweat, sex, and Lorcan covered me.

"Doesn't matter, Ken. I'm already there." He winked. "If I can't be in you, I love that I can smell myself all over you."

"Do I smell different?" My hand stopped on the doorknob.

"Any powerful fae would probably know you're mine."

My mouth opened. Now I kind of felt like I'd been peed on. And smelled like it too?

"Works in reverse too." Lorcan stood, grabbing his jeans on the floor. "We're bastards, but dwellers are nothing if not equal opportunists."

"Well. Good." I liked knowing any female fae, especially every fae he screwed, would be aware he was no longer theirs to play with. My eyes wandered down his physique, tilting my head. *No, we couldn't use the coed showers. No way. Nope.*

"Dirty bird." A salacious grin curved his mouth.

Dammit. I was going to have to be careful what I let him read in my eyes.

"Go, before I change my mind. You have to get to your meeting. And if I follow you to the showers, it will never happen. I can guarantee you that." Lorcan slipped on his jeans, hunger building behind his gaze. "I'll use the fae showers."

I nodded, darting out of the room, knowing if I hesitated a moment, I would be pulling him with me, damned the meeting and our mission.

Time to get your head back on straight, girl. Tonight was crucial. All our work to get here, to take this group down, relied on us being on our game. So many counted on me, but could I kill innocents to keep my kingdom? Could I eventually turn against my own kind? Betray and hurt them? I could see their side as well as the fae's. Both were wrong and right.

Whatever lay ahead, I was in too deep to stop it now. I shut off my emotions, the Queen reassuming her role, and focused on the task at hand.

~~~~~

Franklin, Wizard, Major, Cali, Kenya, and Mayhem were already in the room when I appeared. The fae slaves stood against the wall like statues.

"Where is your fae?" Franklin asked, taking a sip of his coffee.

Wizard shot me a look, his eyebrows furrowing before he turned back to the papers in front of him, a scowl pinching his lips.

"He will be here shortly." I swallowed nervously. I grabbed a chair and sat down, looking away from him. There was little doubt he suspected I had been with someone. Probably didn't take a genius to have Lorcan as the top candidate.

My entire body felt Lorcan's approach before he even came into the room. His hair was damp from the shower, like mine. His dark shirt was snug, clinging to his damp chest. He was like a match, heating me the moment he came near. He lined himself next to the other fae, staring off into nothing.

Cali lifted her eyebrow, her eyes darting between Lorcan and me, a smile inching the side of her mouth. Whatever she saw in our auras before, I didn't doubt it was even more intense now.

She wasn't the only one though. Kenya also glanced at us, a puzzlement crinkling her forehead.

Oh, nerf herder.

If powerful fae could see the bond, maybe it was strong enough for Druids to pick up. Sweat dotted the back of my neck as I tried to stay blank, not letting her read me. I had to keep my guard up at all times.

Her eyes stayed locked on me until the sound of other people entering the room pulled them away. I twisted to see Poppy, Fox, and Ophelia come into the room dressed in the same dark outfits as the others in the room. I had dressed in my jeans and black sweater with boots. It was clear I was not considered part of the group yet.

"All right. We're all here. I wanted to go through this one last time. Wizard was able to finally pinpoint the exact location of the fae we've been watching with the help of Mayhem and Fox. Thank you." Franklin nodded at the three men. "He's been sniffing too close to us, but because of our spells guarding the place, he couldn't enter." Franklin pulled out a map, circling a spot on a street map. "It's time the tables turned."

My hands twisted in my lap, feeling a sense of dread come over me.

"Your mission tonight is to capture him." Franklin stood to full height. "Let me warn you again. He is extremely powerful and dangerous. A shape-shifter."

"What kind?" I asked.

Franklin hesitated, a nerve flicking at his lids. "We're not sure. He hasn't shown his true form. Not that we were able to catch." He turned to Wizard and nodded.

Wizard pulled up an aerial view of a street in infrared vision. It looked run down and some of the buildings appeared to be destroyed, like they had been bombed or crumbled under a massive weight. Lots of areas over the world looked exactly like this. After the wall between worlds collapsed, magic gushed in like a tsunami, crushing many of the newer or weaker buildings.

My gaze locked on the heat signature in one of the buildings. In the other there were clusters, but nothing as bright as this one.

"This is where it is located." Franklin tapped at the map. "Raven, you will be at the back with your fae, while Mayhem and Fox attack from the front. Poppy, Cali, her fae, and Ophelia will be on the side exits. Major, Kenya, and I, along with their fae will be behind you. Disable him. Control him. Whatever you need to do. Do not go easy, as he will fight the spell. We want to question him, but do what you must in that moment. I'd rather take it dead than let it escape."

I nodded, feeling everyone's eyes drill into me.

"Do I get a gun?" I shifted in my seat, feeling a spike of anger from Lorcan.

"You already have your weapon," Franklin responded. "Don't worry, we will be behind you. Just worry about the spell you need to perform."

They were leaving me unarmed? A nagging sensation tugged at my gut, but I pushed it aside.

"Are you ready for your mission, Raven?" Franklin folded his arms, staring down at me. "Prove yourself to the cause? To become one of us?"

"Yes." My nerves almost strangled the word.

"No matter what it takes or what happens?" His intensity grew.

I swallowed.

"Remember how many lives they have taken, how many families they have ripped apart. They hunted us down, exterminating us like rats. It is your turn to avenge your family's death."

I nodded, not trusting my voice. I understood Franklin's anger, but I did not agree killing fae righted those wrongs. You can't blame an entire race for something a select group of them did a long time ago.

~~~~

Fifteen minutes later, I sat in back of a van with half of the group, the other half in a van behind us. I was not merely weaponless but also the only one without an ear mic. Franklin said it would distract me if I had voices in my ear while I did the spell. True, but it still left me even more vulnerable.

Lorcan sat on the opposite side of me, his eyes finding mine every so often, telling me he would not let anything hurt me. My hands trembled in my lap, but I forced my heartbeat to stay even.

Both vans drove with the headlights off, slipping through the empty streets. We had only been driving a short distance from the factory when Franklin halted the vehicle and nodded to Mayhem and Poppy. They jumped quietly out the back, opening the doors. The other van came to a stop behind us. I followed Cali and Wolf and climbed out.

From here on out we could not talk until the attack was in progress. I knew Wizard was watching from the war room, keeping them updated if the fae moved.

Hand signals combined the two groups in the direction of the house. Mayhem and Fox led the way, followed by Franklin, Major, and Kenya. I was in the middle with Lorcan, the rest of the group behind us.

The night was so completely still it left me with an unsettled feeling, anxiety spiking up and down my neck like blinking lights. Cold condensation puffed like clouds out of my mouth.

I eyed Lorcan in my peripheral vision a few paces behind me. He stared ahead with blankness, but I could feel him, his wariness, rippling around me protectively.

The unknown was the worst. The little preparation I had for the mission didn't sit right with me. And the more I let my mind drift over that fact, the greater the warning compressed my spine.

Franklin motioned for me to follow him through a side gate to the back of a row of derelict houses. Shingles from the roofs lay broken on the ground, the roofs sagging around the windows on the top level. Wood panels boarded the holes where the windows used to be. Dirt and soot from the city stained the chipping paint around the doors.

I could sense life inside all the houses. Humans. Probably homeless and staying where they could.

Franklin pointed at the house in the middle, gesturing for his team to get into their positions.

Terror pummeled my chest like someone played drums with my heart. Nothing about this felt right. The entire mission seemed a strange way to prove myself. I didn't have to kill the fae, just stun it. It felt too easy. That's all I had to do to establish myself with them?

Lorcan stirred behind me, and I turned to look at him over my shoulder. His neck was bunched, his nostrils flaring, taking in long slugs of air.

Can you smell anything? My eyes stared into his, the link coming more naturally to me than I thought it would.

Not clearly...too many human feces odors around...but something feels off.

*Yeah...*I turned back around, swallowing down the dread coating my insides.

"Copy," I heard Franklin mumble behind me into his earpiece, clicking off the safety of his gun.

The crack of a door being opened echoed through the vacant house. Loud voices and a gunshot jolted my nerves, filling me with trepidation. My fingers rolled into fists, fear sweeping in and out of my lungs. Anxiety grew so huge inside me my heart thumped in my ears, and sweat beaded at my hairline.

As a Druid and Queen I was supposed to protect, to keep this kind of attack from happening. It felt wrong. I didn't want to hurt this fae, but I couldn't afford not to. I felt trapped.

"He's coming. Get ready" Franklin yelled at me, the group closing in on the back door. Nausea filled my stomach, my head spinning with fear.

I heard a roar from inside, but it sounded so familiar I turned to Lorcan behind me. His mouth was shut, his eyes were wide, his expression flicking between disbelief and horror as he took in what was headed our way. Terror engulfed me, partly his, partly mine.

"Now, Raven!" Franklin's voice boomed from behind me. My head swung back, the spell sitting on my tongue as the back door splintered, spraying wood chunks. A man's form flew through the back door to the lawn.

The hex locked in my throat. *Oh my god. No.*

"Raven!" My name was screamed again, but I stared, locking eyes with the red-eyed fae.

Words sprang from over my shoulder when I faltered, Kenya's curse heading toward its victim.

Family. Protect. Instinct seized my body. I whirled around, the dark invocation spewing from my mouth, directed at the one I stood with scarcely a moment before.

Kenya's eyes widened, seeing the change. She slung the words of her spell at the same time my curse hit her. With a bounce, the black magic vaulted off her, heading back to the precise fae I was trying to protect.

Nooo! I screamed in my head at the same time Lorcan cried out, flinging himself forward. Both of us reached out for the person in front of us.

West.

Time both stopped and sped up as the curse flew for him. Then with a pop it hit a target, crashing into a dweller with a hiss.

"Lorcan!" I screamed, watching him leap ahead of his brother, trying to shield him from the dark magic. A pained howl tore from his throat as it broke over his chest, burning a hole through his sweater down to his skin. His body went still, landing with a crunch on the ground.

A cry tore deep from my lungs, ripping my heart in half. I moved to Lorcan's lifeless form. My knees skated on the frozen earth as I reached for Lorcan's face. I no longer cared about anything or anyone else around Lorcan and me. *Mine.*

"Lorcan," I cried, drawing his head onto my lap. Black goo leaked from the wound in his chest. "Oh my god." It took my fingers a few seconds to sense a low pulse tapping in his neck. I bowed my head with relief. He was alive but under a spell. I had no idea what curse I had done, nor how to take it off, but it was meant to hurt. To torture. "I am so sorry," I whispered, leaning over, kissing his forehead.

A figure moved over me, drawing my face up to West. He was in human form, but everything about him felt beast. Feral and ready to protect or kill, his vertical pupils locked on mine, breathing like he was in pain. Ember slipped one time, hinting West couldn't turn into his beast anymore. I knew now it was true. There would be no way a dark dweller would not turn and try to protect their family. It was their nature.

West's gaze was full of intense emotion, and I sensed a connection there now. One I understood immediately. I was a pack member.

He snarled so softly only I could hear it. I reached up, gripping his hand, trying to reassure him Lorcan would be okay. I would flip the world upside down if I had to.

West's eyes stayed locked on me, the red leaking out of them, but a noise from behind snapped them up. They went deep crimson, a growl vibrating the ground, his body moving forward. I bolted up, stepping in front of him. "Don't." I shook my head. "Let me handle this." He watched me for a bit then eased back. I turned to face my old allies. The "cat" was out of the bag. There was no way of coming back from this. Nor did I want to. I was done with this game.

All my former allies stood staring at me, guns raised. My head darted around toward the faces I had grown to know, their expressions twisted with utter shock. Not one was friendly or kind anymore. My gaze landed on Kenya and Franklin. Franklin's mouth twisted in fury. But Kenya almost looked smug. Neither seemed surprised by my actions. Like they had known.

Shit. "This was the test." It was not a question.

"And you failed horribly. It's a shame. You would have been useful to us," Franklin snarled. "I didn't want to believe it. Kenya kept telling me something was not right about you. To set this up." He kept his gun pointed at me. "You come out of the blue, overtly flaunting a tattoo of Awen, with the same type of shape-shifter that's been observing us for weeks, your connection to him unquestionable." Franklin pressured his lips. "The attack on Major instead of that fae sealed it for me. You chose the fae over your own kind.

"I knew you were awake the other night," he continued, motioning between him and Kenya. "Good cop, bad cop. You fell for it. I don't know how dumb you think we are, but we've learned over time to be diligent. Careful with even other Druids. They can be traitors and spies as well." Franklin took a step forward.

"Don't get any closer," West growled, moving until his chest bumped my back.

"Keep him back or I will do worse." Kenya snapped at me, her eyes blazing with hate. "And don't think about doing a spell. I promise, I am faster than you."

I didn't doubt it.

"These also have fae bullets in them." Franklin waved his gun at West. "Now move."

I peered down at Lorcan, his chest barely rising.

"Move. Now."

I leaned over and ran my thumb over his cheek one last time before standing back up. West moved closer to both of us.

"What are you going to do with us?" I asked. When should I pull out my Queen card? Would it even help or actually condemn us more? They would have the biggest bargaining chip ever. But I could not let Lars or my kingdom concede to keep me safe.

"You are going to tell us who you are working for," Franklin responded. "You don't have pets as powerful as them without having ties to something."

No way was I telling them. They would get nothing from me.

"Not talking?" Major spoke, inching toward me on the right. "For every minute you don't talk, your pets get a fae bullet embedded into their body."

"You even think about it, and I will gut you faster than you can even pop one off," West rumbled behind me, pawing the dirt like he wanted to charge. I could feel his anger. He wanted to attack, to take them all out.

"Then how about we start with her?" Major lowered the gun till it was directed at my gut, his finger curling down on the trigger.

Boom!

West's hand shoved me to the side, the bullet lodging into the dirt right where I had been standing. The dweller bellowed, tearing off for Major.

"West, no!" I reached out for him, but it was too late. I heard Kenya cry out, her chant filled the air with speed and precision as she struck him. He flew back, slamming into me with force. I rolled over the ground, my bones crunching, my head smacking on the back porch. I didn't feel any pain, my body numb. Darkness came from the outside of my vision, swallowing me up. I tried to swim toward the surface, but it flooded over me, drowning me beneath.

TWENTY-FOUR

My eyes opened, lids fluttering against the low voltage light in the room. My brain registered bars, and the cold, hard floor caused my bones to ache. My jaw pounded and I moved it to find a piece of cloth tied over my mouth. Twinges ran up my neck as I tried to lift my head, my skull throbbing.

"Kennedy?" a voice called my name softly, rolling my head to the side. In the corner, West sat against the wall, his neck, arms, legs, and neck chained to the wall.

Rising on my elbow with a moan, I tried to lift my hand to my aching head. At the sound of clanking metal I looked down to see I was also shackled. Only my arms were, but that was enough, especially because they had bound the only threat I was capable of: my mouth.

Magic.

I grunted to West, pushing my back against the wall. The haze slowly lifted from my mind.

Oh. God.

Lorcan!

My head whipped around, searching the space for him. It was a room I had never seen. I could tell we were deep under the earth, but this room was smaller and had one large holding cell against one wall. West and I were imprisoned, but otherwise it was empty.

"Lorcan?" My mouth choked over the gag, my eyes locking on West's brown ones. Dried blood crusted his hairline and a healing gash sliced his cheek. Dirt and blood covered his clothes.

"I don't know." He shook his head, grimacing. It was then I noticed the collar around his neck was lined with nails, draining him of blood. Weakening him.

My heart twisted in my chest. I had heard this was one of the ways Aneira had tortured him. I couldn't imagine what this was bringing back up for him. When I had first met him, after his return from being captive, I saw a dark soul underneath his cheeky humor, damaged and twisted with self-hate and demons. After mating with Rez, it had significantly lightened, but the darkness was still under his southern charm. Whatever happened to him there…I didn't want to even consider.

West was probably the most "charming" of the dark dwellers. And so utterly good looking it was hard to look at him without sighing. Actually, all the dwellers were drop-dead sexy. Yet whatever it was about Lorcan, he took my breath away. He had my heart, soul, and body.

"So, darlin'." West swallowed, dipping his head to look at me down the wall. "Should I say welcome to the family?" A smirk hinted on his lip.

He was the first one to know, and I couldn't stop my head from dropping, looking at my hands in my lap. I wasn't ashamed of Lorcan but still felt guilty about Jared, a fear of the others' reactions to this.

"Hey." He drew my attention back up, his gaze serious. "He would be happy for you two." He didn't have to say whom he was talking about. Jared was never far from any of us. "Believe me, you can't pick who you fall in love with. It picks you. I understand that the most." He had fallen for the Unseelie King's lover, the ultimate no-no. Probably lucky he was even still alive. "Lorc and I have had our differences, but I love him. And you are the *best* thing for him. I've seen such a huge change in him since meeting you. He is good for you too. Truly happy for both of you."

I bobbed my head, trying to keep the tears from my eyes. I could only wish Ryan, Ember, and the rest of my court would take it that well. But I knew it was not going to be so easy.

I was about to ask West why he was here when a door banged down the corridor on the other side of the cage.

"Ken...whatever happens, I've got you," West whispered. "And I'm sorry. I had no choice."

My forehead crinkled, the statement vaguely familiar. Like I had heard him say it before. What did he mean he had no choice?

A scuffle of shoes pounded the floor down the hallway, surrounding the sound of clipped heeled boots.

My seer could pick up the power, the energy coming down the hall toward us. In my gut I knew I was finally about to meet the head of the Druid Liberal Republic.

West pushed himself up, trying to get closer to me, his chest puffed up, ready to guard me. This whole mate thing came with built-in protection. They looked out for their own, and I was one of their family now.

A handful of DLR members, all of whom I recognized, walked to the cage grouped together. Fox, Poppy, Kenya, and Major stared at us like we were the scum of the galaxy, desiring nothing more than to see us hang. Ophelia and Wizard stared at me with pain and hurt, like I had killed their puppies on purpose. Their looks of betrayal were the worst. I noticed Cali stood all the way in the back, her expression pinched, but it didn't feel directed at me.

"Sorry, guys, petting time at the zoo is closed for the day." West smirked, malevolence lying underneath his sneer. Even with his legs, neck, and wrists cuffed, he still appeared menacing.

"Shut up, shifter." Mayhem snarled and stepped closer to the bars, hate spewing out of his gaze. "We should have muzzled you."

"Oh, then you'd miss all my witty charm." West feigned looking hurt. "Everything that comes out of my mouth is a pure gem. I'm *hilarious*."

"You like to *think* you are." A woman's voice spoke from the back of the group, her thick Irish accent fluttering the room with melody. She stepped forward, and the group parted on either side as her power pushed them back like flipped magnets. "Don't you, Mr. Moseley?"

West's entire body went rigid, invoking a panic I didn't understand.

The woman stepped to the bars, the light from the wall reflecting off her beautiful face.

"Holy crap." West crashed back against the wall, his eyes widening with disbelief. He kept trying to scramble back, staring at the woman like he'd seen a ghost.

"And here I thought you'd be happy to see me." She tilted her head, her high ponytail brushing over her shoulder. Not only could I sense she was a Druid, but the power and confidence coming off her was like a smack to the face. Her authority saturated the room. No doubt she was the commander.

"Fionna," he whispered her name, his head shaking. Then his eyes moved between us, a strange expression crimping his face, his mouth widening even farther.

They knew each other? How would West know the leader of the DLR? What is going on? Nerves coiled around my throat, constricting while fear pumped into my veins.

She was not what I expected. She couldn't have been more than a few years older than me. She stood taller than me but had the same petite bone structure. Her long silky brown hair matched her brown eyes, and a sprinkle of freckles dotted her nose and cheeks. If it wasn't for the tight black jeans, tight T-shirt, leather jacket, knee-length boots, knives hanging from her belt loops, and an unfailing self-confidence, you might want to call her cute. But her face and body language put her at intimidatingly beautiful despite her small size. Instinctually you knew not to mess with her.

"No..." West shook his head. "You-you're supposed..."

"To be dead?" She filled in, her gaze locked on West.

West gulped, nodding his head.

"Sorry, to disappoint, dweller. But I'm not that easy to kill either. You'll have to try harder next time." She cocked her eyebrow, taunting him.

My head boomeranged back and forth between the two, lost in the act playing live for me.

"I didn't want you dead."

"Really? So when you pushed me off the Cliffs of Moher it was to show you cared? How sweet."

"You went after mine. I only did what was in my nature. You were going to kill Rez."

Oh my god. What was happening? I knew West had gone to Ireland on a mission for Lars with Rez, where the two fell in love, but I didn't know anything else. It hadn't been my place to ask, and I had been too busy trying to get my feet underneath me.

I wiggled my chains, grunting through my gag, drawing the attention over to me.

Fionna curved her body, putting her weight on one hip. "Ah, yes...and how could I forget you?" She clicked her tongue. "The Druid *Queen*. Welcome, Majesty."

Oh. Shit. The entire assembly around her gasped, all eyes turning on me with disbelief, fear, and awe. Raven, the punk girl they had been fighting beside, the one covered in tattoos and piercings, was surely difficult to link to the Queen's image.

Wizard's gaze met mine, his former affection turning to hate in front of me.

"Didn't you think I would figure out who you were?" Fionna stepped down the row, closer to me. "Lars has greatly underestimated me. I know how he works. I've been waiting for someone to infiltrate us from your side for a while now. I have to admit, I didn't actually think it would be the Queen herself, as she's 'supposedly' safe in her castle right now." Fionna's eyebrows rose mockingly. "But it makes sense. A Druid is the only one you could send in."

"You kept this from us?" Franklin's fists punched his leg.

"Yes. I apologize. I couldn't let you guys in on it until I was sure." Fionna nodded at me. "How special we must be for the Queen to attend to us herself. We must have done something right."

I didn't flinch but held my chin up, ready to take on whatever was coming. Like a true Queen, I would not hide or cower.

"You should have been our greatest front-runner in this fight. A true leader seeking revenge for what the fae have done to us, but instead you took *their* side. A traitor to our kind is even worse than a fae."

I gurgled, my tongue shoving against the constraint, retaliation on my lips.

"I will untie you, but remember you are surrounded by Druids. Most are far quicker than you, *Queen*. And I promise you do not want to go up against me."

Fionna lifted her hands, a chant spilling from her mouth with ease. Her accent made the Latin sound more like an eerie song than a spell.

The knot behind my head loosened, and the tie dropped to the ground.

I worked my jaw, stretching it after being stuck in the same position for so long. I strolled out as far as the chains would allow me, my attention on her. "A true leader knows extremists in any cause destroy this world. You are no better than Aneira."

Fionna hissed, her head jerking back. "I am nothing like her. She took everything from my people. From me. I am simply going after those who harmed us. This is retribution."

"But by going after the handful, you are killing dozens of innocents and enslaving fae against their will. Exactly what Aneira wanted to do with humans. So don't tell me your cause is different. It only is because it happened to you. Druids are light; we help, heal, and protect. We do not hurt."

"God, you are so naïve," Fionna lashed back, her lids narrowing. "No one listens unless you force them. Do you think if I held weekend protests with cardboard signs anyone would care? No. You have to make them."

I understood her reasoning, misguided as it was. People didn't concern themselves unless it directly affected them. That didn't make it right, but I understood her, which scared me.

"Lars has the perfect playfellow. He can mold you exactly how he wants. He is not on your side. You know that, right? He is on his own side. The things he's been doing behind your back…like with this one."

"Fionna." West tugged against his manacles, his voice laced with warning.

Fionna glanced at him; a knowing smile curved up her mouth. A look transpired between them, spiking my curiosity.

"What?" I asked. "What are you talking about?"

West's eyes blazed into Fionna's, widening her smile.

"Still his puppet, huh?" She tapped at her lip. "You know I can help you with that. You no longer have to be his bitch."

"And what? Become yours? No, thank you," West scoffed. "I gave my word. I don't hide from that. Not anymore."

"So noble."

"Fionna, come on. You know you can't go against the Unseelie King. Stop before you get all your people killed."

A bubbly laugh rose so lightly I almost laughed along with her. "You think we're so easy to take down? He may have the object now, but my magic can still challenge his. He should be the one running scared."

I snorted at the idea of Lars ever running scared.

"Last chance." Fionna turned back to me. "Help us or your dark lover is the first to be sent back to the King in pieces."

West's growl sounded next to me as my own clogged my throat. The innate reaction to protect Lorcan, to fight for him, coursed through me like a rushing river, almost knocking me off my feet.

"Where is he?" I strained against the binds, anger filling me with darkness. Black magic simmered in my soul, ready to attack anything hurting Lorcan.

"He's alive." She shrugged. "Barely. Dark dwellers sure are resistant to extreme torture."

Bottomless rage rose from deep within like a wave about to crash, my vision growing hazy around the edges. My body hummed with the thought of tapping that dark magic I'd tasted in my vision. The craving was getting worse. It was alive and wanted to come out so bad it exploded to the surface. The sensation rose up and slipped over into a different plane where everything went dull except my target. My words came from depths unknown to my conscious mind, directed at Fionna.

The hex slashed through the space, ripped the door of the cage off its hinges, and slammed them to the floor. Like one large claw, the spell didn't isolate on one person, but sliced deep gouges into every person standing around me, sending them flying back.

Blood spilled onto the floor, pooling around my feet, his reflection staring at me from the liquid. *West!* My heart cried his name, feeling his pain. I didn't know if I was connected to him as a seer or through Lorcan's bond with me, but it tore at me to hurt one of my own. He was family now. I hurtled back to earth with a crunch.

"West!" I cried out, trying to reach him. He was on his side, his hand gripping at the deep gashes cut in his chest, bleeding out. "Oh god...I'm so sorry."

He gritted his teeth, curving his head to peer at me.

"I've had worse, darlin'."

Dammit. I did it again. What was happening to me? Why did I have this darkness inside? This black magic I had no control over?

A rustling of bodies outside the cage stirred. Some started to get up. I stared out in horror at the bloody wounds I caused. I couldn't regulate it, but that was no excuse. Harming people was not my strength and not the Queen or person I wanted to be. In the history of the world, violence against violence did not cure or help, it simply caused more hate and bloodshed.

Fionna looked down at the wounds I caused, shock widening her eyes, her shirt soaking with blood, a bone showing below the gash. She sucked in her pain, wrath flaming her face as she got to her feet. A low chant healed her instantly. She turned, walking toward me, magic boiling off her.

Terror dripped down my throat like bitter medicine, yet I swallowed, knowing I had just sealed my fate. Because I was Queen, I would be more difficult to kill, but I wasn't immortal like fae. Aneira had been so bulletproof it took the Sword of Light, a rare treasure of Tuatha De Danann thought to be a myth, to kill her. I was far more vulnerable.

Fionna's spell blasted into me before I could even think to protect myself. With the chains still holding me down, I only lifted a few inches before my head smacked against the stone with a sickening crack, and I crumbled to the ground.

"You're a natural obscurer," she seethed, a dash of fear in her tone. "How is it possible? You should not be. There are none left." She bent over me, grabbed my chin, and forced me to look at her.

Interesting. Franklin had not told her what I was. Maybe the trust between the leaders wasn't as strong as I thought.

Her brown eyes searched mine, looking for something, but I reinforced the walls I had kept locked in place since the moment I walked in here.

The more Fionna stared at me, the more she became unsettled, crazed. She huffed out another spell, gagging me from speaking, before unlocking my chains. Then she shoved me forward onto my hands and knees, my head still spinning and aching, blood dripping down my neck.

"I don't know how this is possible... *Shite*..." She trailed off. "You shouldn't exist anymore." She grabbed the back of my head, her eyes dancing between mine, like I was some puzzle to figure out. "You're far too dangerous to keep around. Especially if you are against us."

"Fionna, stop!" West yelled, trying to get to me. "You don't want to hurt her."

"Why? Because she is the Queen? One who plans to keep business as usual, letting fae secretly hunt and kill us."

"No." West shook his head, his eyes snapping between us.

"I don't *want* to kill anyone, but that's not how it works. You should know better than anyone, dweller. Isn't that what you did? How many of us did you slaughter for a price?" Fionna's voice sounded desperate and scared now. "It's not in a Druid's nature to harm, but I have no choice but to play by your cruel fae rules. If you want to stand on the big boys' playground, you have to compete at their level."

She tugged the knife from her belt, bringing it to my neck.

"NO! DON'T!" West roared, tugging so hard on the shackles cement crumbled around the embedded bolts. "Fionna, you don't want to do it... She's. Your. *Sister!*"

Time paused, the hand of the clock halting in place as his statement exploded at our feet. I felt like I had been backhanded, the shock of his declaration jerking me back on my knees, stinging my face, and evaporating the air in my lungs. Fionna went still, the knife dropping from her grip.

What? Sister? What was he talking about? My sister was dead.

"Wh-what?" Fionna stumbled away from me, her head snapping back and forth between West and me.

"You're sisters." West's shoulders sagged in relief, seeing the immediate threat to me suspended.

"My sister is dead." She repeated what I had just thought. "She was killed with my parents."

"No, they got her out before Aneira found them. She was adopted by a human couple."

I felt like throwing up. My head spun so hard I couldn't lock down one thought except he had to be lying. There was no way... I peered up at Fionna and had to put my hand on the floor to keep myself steady.

Holy shit squared, multiplied, and divided.

The leader of the Druid Liberal Republic fell away, and all I saw was a woman. Hair, eyes, freckles, mouth, frame...all like mine. Taller, yes, and her nose was different, but everything else was similar.

"The moment I met you, Fionna, you seemed so familiar to me, but I didn't make the connection. It wasn't till my search for a link to Kennedy's line led me here. A direct heir to Cathbad was leading the DLR. And then you walked up..." He rubbed at his head, the chains clacking. "Jesus, look at you two. There is no denying it."

This was why, even with my black hair, so many had given me double takes when I first came to the DLR, saying I reminded them of someone. I assumed they saw through my disguise, spotting the Queen under the tattoos. But by the "aha" expressions circling around the room, they had seen Fionna.

"No. It's impossible." Fionna's head shook, still trying to deny it, but when she gazed down on me, her hand went to her mouth, blinking tears in her eyes. "You survived?" She choked, turning away from me, taking in deep breaths.

Shakily, I rose to my feet, still feeling stunned, my head rolling and twisting to compute the revelation.

"My little sister has been alive this whole time," Fionna muttered to herself. Grabbing the bars, she curved over, looking like she was about to throw up.

The idea of having a biological sister had been a faraway notion. It was only in the last few years I even knew I once had one. But I had no memories of her or my parents, no connection. It never registered on a deeper level. Now that sister was flesh and blood and stood before me. My sister. My blood. My family.

I had no idea how I felt about any of those titles. Especially when she was also my enemy.

TWENTY-FIVE

"This changes nothing." Fionna rose to her full height, rotating toward me, rolling back her shoulders, undoing the spell around my throat. "It's probably not even true. More claims to try and disarm me."

"Changes nothing?" My voice broke free of its jail. It changed everything for me.

"You still are here to take down my faction. And no matter who you are, I will not let anyone stop me from my quest."

"From killing and enslaving fae? Don't you see what you are doing is wrong? This is not how to help your people."

"You think mind-numbing meetings, where nothing gets accomplished and no side is satisfied, is the way to go?" Fionna took a step to me. "You have to know nothing gets solved that way."

"Neither does violence." I balled my hands into fists.

"Sometimes it's the only way. You think Luuk will stop? He will keep coming till he destroys you. It's kill or be killed."

"And on your order you almost killed me. The attack on the fae in Switzerland? I was there. I barely survived."

Fionna's eyes widened. "You were supposed to be in America."

"It's okay if the fae are faceless. But in your desire for revenge you almost killed your sister, my friends, people I love and care about."

"I won't apologize for killing fae who have gladly murdered us for centuries."

I rubbed my sore head. Would I feel the same if I'd grown up differently? Everyone believed their point of view was the right one. But which actually was? My list of things I didn't know how to figure out grew longer. There was only one thing I could and desperately had to solve immediately.

"Where is Lorcan?" I countered her step, trying to inch my height up to hers. "Is he all right?"

"I broke the spell on him."

"That's not an answer," I growled.

She shrugged.

"You need to free him."

"I don't need to do anything. I am in charge here." Fionna's brown eyes narrowed as she thrust her hands to her hips. "But I will take you to him on one condition."

344

"What is that?"

"You and your fae pets will not hurt, attack, or try to escape."

"I can only promise we will not attack if you do not provoke first." I leveled my gaze on her. "If you do, all bets are off."

Fionna appeared to consider my counterproposal before she nodded. "Agreed." She swiveled around, walking out of the damaged cage. "Follow me."

"He comes with me." I pointed at West.

Fionna looked at both of us and nodded. "Free him, but the same rules apply."

Hate spilled from Mayhem's face, but he stepped up, unlocking West from his chains.

West winked at Mayhem. "I can tell you *like* me. It's okay; it will be our little secret." He bumped Mayhem's shoulder, heading for me. His hand touched my back protectively the moment he reached me.

As I stepped over the crumbled metal door, hostility radiated off every pair of eyes. Beneath the rage of Kenya, Franklin, and Major I felt almost burned.

I followed at Fionna's heels, eager to be led to Lorcan. We headed down the hallway they condemned as off limits to me when I first arrived and went to the last room. She unlocked the door, swinging it open.

My hand went to my mouth. The area was dimly lit and empty except for the rack in the middle of the room with wires coming off it. A shirtless man lay cuffed by his ankles, wrists, and neck.

"Lorcan!" I bolted to him.

His lids cracked open at my voice, a ghost of a smile on his face. "Li'l bird."

Vibrant purple, blue, yellow, and green bruising covered his body. A landscape of burn marks and cuts covered his torso like a gruesome version of connect the dots. My hands cupped his face, grief burrowing into my heart. I understood his body would be okay, as he healed quickly, but what about his heart, his pride?

I stared down into his eyes. "Are you okay?"

"Come on, this was like foreplay for me." He tried to smile, which split his healing lip, allowing blood to ooze out.

I pressed my mouth briefly to his to comfort him, tasting the sharp tang of blood on my tongue. It was quick but passionate.

"Damn. That was hot," Lorcan rumbled, his eyes sparking as his tongue swiped over my lips again. Blood was some kind of aphrodisiac. I recalled a time I saw Ember lick deer blood off Eli's mouth and got so thoroughly grossed out I thought I'd vomit. I didn't have an urge to eat raw carcass or drink blood from Bambi, but Lorcan's...tasting it...yeah, I liked it. Add that to the list of things I was discovering about myself.

I kissed him again, then whipped around to face Fionna. *My sister?* My head still couldn't wrap around it, but the more I looked at her, the more I saw the obvious family resemblance. It was a bit freaky.

"Release him. Now."

"You're not the Queen here." Fionna frowned, not hiding her aversion at seeing us together, and stepped farther into the room, motioning around. "This is my kingdom. I'm the one who gives orders."

Lorcan's head turned to the crowd at the door, his lids narrowing. It was a blink and he jerked, his mouth opening. "Holy shit." His head pitched between Fionna and me. "What the…?" Lorcan was faster at picking up the clear connection.

"Meet the DLR leader, Fionna…my sister."

Lorcan's mouth gaped. "Sister?"

"They have family reunions just like we do." West shoulder checked a few gawkers to get into the room. "Hey, brother."

"West? Jesus, I thought I made you up." Lorcan blinked, his eyes moving around the room, confused. "What the hell is going on? I'm dreaming, right? I've actually passed out and this is some twisted hallucination going on in my head?"

"I wish, brother," West scoffed, slapping his hand down on Lorcan's leg. At the contact, Lorcan groaned, shutting his lids and waggling his head back and forth.

"What are you doing here?"

"All for later, Lorc." West's mouth flattened.

"He's here on the King's request." Fionna tipped her head toward West.

"What?" I jerked to West. "What is she talking about?"

"Against my will, Ken." Regret tapered his eyes. "I never wanted anything to do with this."

"With what exactly?"

"For another time." Fionna swished her hand, moving farther into the room. "We'll get to all that later."

"How about now." I gritted my teeth.

"Later." Fionna clenched her own together, combatting my stubbornness.

There were so many secrets and accusations swirling in this room, and I wanted to demand to know what was going on. But I eased back, sensing the answers would fracture my already frazzled brain, which was crumbling like old chalk. I had to focus on what was in front of me. What I could change. First and foremost. Lorcan.

"Fionna, let him go. I promised you and I keep my word." I pinched Lorcan's arm, giving him a look. "We will not attack or harm anyone here."

Lorcan peered at me like he wanted to shove my promise up someone's ass, but gritted his teeth, nodding.

"*They* better stick to your pact." She strolled to the other side of Lorcan. "Or I will have no choice but to retaliate. This time I won't be so lenient. My magic can strike faster than they could reach one of us. I won't be afraid to kill."

"You're right." Lorcan flicked his chin at West. "Their family reunions sound *a lot* like ours."

West snorted, patting Lorcan's leg again.

At Fionna's beckoning, a man switched off a machine and unlocked Lorcan from the chains. Black marks circled his wrists, ankles, and neck like paint. My fingers went to his bruised neck when he sat up and touched the burnt flesh.

"You electrocuted him?" I screeched, anger billowing inside like a storm. "Are you kidding me?

You. Did. Not." I didn't even realize I was moving to Fionna until Lorcan grabbed my arm, pulling me back into him. Fionna bristled, her shoulders rising, ready to counter my attack.

"Calm down, li'l bird." He gripped my face, trying to turn me to look at him. It took a couple of tries before I broke my glare off her and turned to him. Oddly, a dash of humor showed in his eyes, like he enjoyed my fierce protectiveness. "I'm fine. Really. West and I used to do worse to each other growing up."

West laughed. "Remember the time when we first got to Earth, and I hooked you up to a car battery with jumper cables? Simply to see what would happen. Damn...you lit up like a Christmas tree."

"And if you remember, I got you back." A smug grin engulfed Lorcan's mouth.

"Right." West's humor faded, a snarl inching up his lips. Okay, I was curious, but now wasn't time to stroll down memory lane.

I squeezed Lorcan's fingers, which still cupped my face, and stepped away from him, toward Fionna.

"What now?" I asked. "Where do we go from here?"

She inhaled deeply, glancing around the room, before landing on me. "I think you and I should have a conversation. In private."

※※※

Settled in the war room across the table, both of us crossed arms and stared with hostile glares at each other. The tension mounted, neither of us speaking right away. This day was chalking up to be one of the strangest for me, which was saying a lot.

"You look like her." Fionna broke the silence, stiffly waving at my face. "Our mother. Same nose."

I touched my face.

"Kennedy..." She shook her mane of hair, the same shade as mine underneath the dye. "Gonna have to get used to that."

"Right." I frowned. "It wasn't my original name, was it?" It was a strange notion to think of myself other than Kennedy.

"No, it was Evelina...Evie...which means light."

My nose scrunched up, rejecting the name. No, I was Kennedy. But it was kind of ironic I'd become the Queen of Light.

Robust silence congested the room again, neither of us seemed to know what to say or do. Just because we might be sisters didn't make us automatically like or trust each other.

"I don't know how to feel about this." I huffed, waving my hand around. "I have no memory of you or my parents. All I knew of my birth parents were their names, Keela and Raghnall. I only found out a year or so ago I even had a sibling and I was a Druid." I clasped my hands together on the table. "How old were you when they were killed? How did you survive?"

"I was seven when you were born," she replied formally, like she was being interviewed for a job. "I was so enamored of you at first. Like my little doll...until I realized you weren't going away." A hint of humor zipped over her face, disappearing faster than it came. "It was the peak of the extermination of our people. Every day our parents stayed alive was like Russian roulette. Mom and Dad knew it wouldn't be long. They sent me away to live with this human witch, Olwyn. She kept me hidden, raised me. Daily I waited, knowing the news would come. Then one day it did. Olwyn heard they were killed. Aneira sent a special squad to 'take care' of them. I figured you were there since you were barely a few months old."

"Why didn't they run? Go into hiding?"

"They could never run from Aneira for long. Their magic was too strong…she would have found them."

"So they gave up both of us. To keep us safe." Emotion threatened to choke me. I cleared my throat.

"It was better to keep us separated. I was already exceptionally powerful for a Druid child and fully aware of my power. You were just a baby. They must have thought it better to tuck you away, unaware of what you really were. Together, we would have drawn attention."

"Why?"

"Um. Well. Besides being extremely powerful, especially together…" She rubbed her nose, sitting back in her chair. "We're not normal Druids."

"What do you mean?" I countered her movement, leaning in.

She peered at the ceiling, adding to the knots in my stomach. Again a notion simmered in my gut, knowing before she even said the words.

"Our family line possesses inherited 'extra' gifts. Strong ones not necessarily looked upon with respect by other Druids."

I let my lids shut briefly, the simmering pot boiling up. "Dark magic," I whispered.

"Ah, you're intuitive," she retorted. "Another strong family trait, along with the healing gift." She shifted in her seat. "Healing to the point we can raise people from the dead."

"What? Th-that's forbidden. Wrong!"

"Black magic is forbidden in most Druid circles, but our parents were so high up the ladder, most assumed it was gossip. It was far from rumor; they were deep in it."

My parents worked in black magic? I felt a piece of my heart twist, darkening my idealistic imaginings of them. "So it's something our whole family inherited? Not something we could help?"

"Oh, you are so gullible, little sister." Fionna clicked her tongue, the pet name held no sentiment. I was also struggling with feeling the leader of DLR was my flesh and blood, even though my gut knew it. "*We* inherited it; *they* did not. Magic seeps into you, your skin, your bloodstream, like nutrients straight to the baby you're carrying. They knew perfectly well what they were doing."

That was exactly what Kenya told me, but I hadn't wanted to believe a mother would do it on purpose.

"I was still young and absorbing everything around me like a sponge; it comes easily to me, but you are a true natural obscurer."

"You're saying our parents deliberately passed on their dark magic to us?"

"Yes."

Tears pricked my lids. I had put my parents on a pedestal, these beautiful, kind, loving Druids. Being murdered by Aneira, I turned them into martyrs. Now it was hard to let them stumble off, full of faults and blemishes.

"They were good people, Kennedy. Loving parents. But probably not as virtuous as you thought them to be. They weren't perfect, but they were doing their best in a horrible time. Day-to-day life was merely about survival. You have never had to live through the constant fear that any day could be the day we were caught and killed. You have no idea what it was like for them. For me."

Fionna sat up in her seat, the resentment and horror of those years pinching her face and clouding her eyes with tears. It was the first glimpse of emotion I saw from her. She quickly schooled her expression back to stone. "At five, I became aware of secret meetings they held. There were just a dozen members at first, but the more Aneira's reign came down on us, the larger the number grew, and they started to strike back at the fae."

"You mean control them," I added. "Use them as puppets."

"That and they started bombing fae hangouts. Mom was the leader. She was obsessed with practicing black magic, showing me how to use it. Dad and she fought about it all the time. I remember them getting into the biggest fight after he found Mom trying to teach me the spell to control the fae. He said she was endangering us, that she was going too far. He didn't know until it was too late what she was doing with you."

"Me?"

"She was pregnant with you while she taught me black magic, knowing it would absorb into you. She was also always at the frontline when they bombed or attacked fae." Fionna ran a hand down her ponytail. "I can see now how fanatical Mom was, crazed almost, like the dark magic had taken her over. But she had a vision and saw something she didn't want to tell Father. She would mumble things about how it needed to be done, it was the only way *we* would survive. She didn't do it because she was a bad mother; she did it to keep us protected. To fight for ourselves. I think she saw they weren't going to be around for us." Fionna gestured between us.

It was strange to hear about two people I only held in my mind as my biological parents, and now know they had flaws and personalities. They were coming to life. Being made real.

"I can kind of understand the desperation they must have felt when all their friends were being murdered around them." Fionna gripped the chair arms, anger flashing over her features.

"But when I read the history, some scrolls said Aneira started the war on Druids *because* of the black magic." I ran my fingers through my tangled ends, blood and dirt still coating me. "So did Aneira start the propaganda because of the rumors, or did they pick up the black magic because Aneira started the gossip against the Druids?"

Fionna's mouth pulled down at the edges.

"You are doing the same. Don't you see that?" I dropped my hands on the table, motioning around the war room.

"I learned from Mother you do what you need to survive." She stiffly lifted her chin in defiance. It was something I did all the time, and the resemblance between us went beyond looks. I felt a small flicker of warmth toward her. The first stirring of a connection between us.

"And *I* learned from *my* father, the man who raised me, that you fight back with intellect, love, and cleverness. Not with more hate."

"That's why your kingdom is failing."

"Never miscalculate the underdog." I lifted my brows, a plan forming in my head.

"What does that mean?" She quirked her eyebrows in return.

A smile grew over my face.

"What do you have in mind?"

I clasped my hands together on the table. "Enemies of an enemy make great allies."

TWENTY-SIX

"Hell. No!" Lorcan threw out his arms, pacing the length of the room and back. "No. *Fuck that!* There is no way, Kennedy. None."

My mouth stayed closed, my gaze staring right into him.

"Stop." His nose flared. "Stop looking at me. I said no."

I slanted my head the other way, remaining silent.

"No! Did you hear me?"

No response from me.

"Uhhh!" He curled his fingers in his scalp. "Don't do that." He pointed at me. "It's too dangerous, and I don't trust them to not stab us in the back when given the chance."

"Like you might do to us." Fionna folded her arms, almost snarling at him.

Lorcan's head continued wagging back and forth, but his arms slumped to his sides. At last, my unbending calm affected him and he stopped pacing. I realized then he did the same for me when I got upset. We were each other's counterpart to return to serenity.

"Damn you, woman," he grumbled under his breath and rubbed the back of his neck. He peered at me through narrowed lids and rubbed his neck harder. "Fuck. I'm never gonna win an argument ever again, am I?"

"Nope." West sighed deeply, looking wistful. "Get used to it, man."

"You might." I curled my hand in a fist, punching it up in encouragement. "Don't give up hope. It could happen again."

He glared at me.

I grinned, reaching over and stroking his shoulder. "Just not this one."

"I swear, li'l Druid," he muttered to himself. "You really are going to be the death of me."

"That's the spirit." I patted his arm, turning back to Fionna.

"We have a deal?" Fionna stepped closer to me. Her people stood behind her, while Lorcan and West hovered by me. I felt like I had stepped back into high school and was about to be pounded in dodgeball.

"We help you find Luuk. Bring him down." Fionna paused. It wasn't too hard to convince her to help us go against the same person she wanted dead as well. He was one who had faithfully, probably willingly, helped in Aneira's crusade to slaughter all the Druids. Fionna had been after him for months, and her vengeance was bloodthirsty.

I had some guilt because I didn't feel the same retribution for the parents we lost, but she had a life with them, memories. I had none. They were not real people to me, but stories told to me by others. My "real" parents were killed when the wall came down. My retaliation for my dead parents and little sister had no face or name.

"And *we* get to deal with him...and…"

"And? There was no 'and,'" I countered.

Fionna glanced at West, another strange look passing between them.

"What?" I swung to West then back to my sister. "What aren't you telling me?"

"West understands me. Don't you?" she responded.

"You know I have no control over that, darlin'. I just work here. Unwillingly."

"Control over what?" Lorcan faced West. "What the hell are you into?"

West ignored Lorcan, snapping at Fionna, his fists clenched. "You mess with the devil, you have to pay the price."

"You mean the devil's mistress." Fionna quirked her mouth. "Being the Unseelie King's bitch is an enormously tricky job, especially when you have to go after one of your brothers' lovers."

Lorcan swung around, his hand clamping down on West's throat, ramming him back into the wall, forcing a yelp from my lips. West didn't even put up a fight, taking Lorcan's rage with an acceptance.

"Are you here for Kennedy?" Lorcan snarled, slamming him harder into the concrete. "Are you the one who betrayed us?"

"No. I would *never* hurt her. Especially now. She's family," West replied, locking gazes with Lorcan. "You *know* that, brother. I'm here for her now." West flicked his head to Fionna but kept his attention locked on Lorcan. Whatever Lorcan saw in West's eyes, he stepped back with a huff.

"I won't allow you to get it. You know that, right?" Fionna's boots clipped on the floor as she moved closer to West. "I will not let him have this one too. No matter what I have to do to keep it away from him. And I know you agree with me."

West's silence implied so much it twitched Fionna's lips with smugness.

"Even though he pledged to help you get the thing you want most." She tilted her neck to the side, like she was reading a menu.

"Get out of my head, Druid." West growled.

"Get what? What are you talking ab—?" My question died in my throat. Blinding white light once again slammed into my head like a crowbar, yanking me away from the war room.

Flash.

I was standing outside, a sliver of moonlight shimmering off the river running next to me. The lapping of the lazy water slapped against the shore. The night to others might appear calm, but a chill crept up my spine, icing my skin. It wasn't from the cold air. A pause held in the atmosphere, like the earth was holding its breath. Something was wrong. I turned toward the old brick factory.

I was outside the Druid Liberal Republic headquarters.

A banging sounded behind me, causing me to swing around. A man dressed in a long black duster coat stood there like he had stepped out of *The Matrix*. The darkness around him only sharpened the whiteness of his skin and hair. He stood on the hood of one of the cars, his pale eyes rolled past me, his arms open like he was on stage, drawing in the crowds. The field behind him was walled in silhouettes silently moving closer, metal from their weapons glinting.

Oh god. Luuk. Luuk was here. To kill us.

"Need to wake, Light," a robotic voice squawked above my head. "Snow is here. And it kills."

"Then help me wake up," I pleaded to the raven. "Shove me back. Whatever you are able to do, so I can warn everyone."

"Grimmel does everything."

"Please, Grimmel."

He tilted his head. "Light must use the darkness to see again."

"Dammit, Grimmel! Help me."

He shook his body, ruffling his feathers with a birdlike sigh.

Then Luuk yelled out into the frosty night. "Attack!" And his army roared to life, running straight for us.

In my bones all I felt was death.

Flash.

I blinked and the scene changed.

I stood in the same field. Bodies covered the earth. I could not see their faces, but I knew by their clothes they were Druids and humans. The DLR. Some of my friends. The people who stepped up to fight next to me watered the ground with their sacrifice.

I peered down at my hands, blood dripping off them. It wasn't mine but from those at my feet.

More lives lost.

Flash.

Like someone stabbed my heart with adrenaline, I jumped up, gasping for air.

"I'm right here." A man kneeled on the floor next to me, a hand rubbing my back. "This is real."

"Shit. That was fuckin' freaky." Another huge man stood by my feet, peering down at me, his brown eyes crunched up with concern.

My gaze darted around the room, taking in the computers, screens, maps, and a group of people staring down at me. I turned back to the pair of green eyes next to me, my moor.

"You're okay, li'l bird." He brushed my hair back in soothing strokes, calming my racing heart.

Lorcan.

DLR.

War room.

Luuk.

My lips parted, the words not finding their way out.

"It's okay. Breathe deeply." Lorcan grabbed my face, forcing me to see just him. "You and me. Now tell me what you see."

"You." I relaxed in his hold. "I hear the buzzing of computers, and I smell watermelon gum." The overly sweet stench of Wizard's gum irritated my nose. Lorcan pinched my ear, then ran his fingers over my temples.

"Does she always get them this bad?" Fionna stepped to West and peered down at me with irritation. "Why hasn't she learned to control them? She can't let them cripple her or she's a sitting duck. She has to learn how to handle them."

"She's still pretty new at this, Fionna." Lorcan snarled at her. "Back off."

"I was ten when I got my first one and discovered how to control them by twelve," Fionna countered.

"Aren't you lucky?" I glowered, finding my voice. Lorcan helped me to my feet. "You had the luxury of growing up knowing you were a Druid, being taught by our parents. I didn't. I got my first vision last year. And I've had no other Druid to help me understand how to regulate them. I've been completely on my own."

Fionna pursed her lips, guilt furrowing her brow. "We'll have to change that," she added stiffly and strolled back to the table.

What did that mean? Did she want a relationship with me? I couldn't deny I'd like that. To get to know my sister. And I liked the idea of learning from someone who truly understood what I was going through as a Druid. Time would tell if Fionna and I had any chance at some kind of relationship, but right now, my vision took precedence.

"I saw Luuk." The entire room turned to look at me. "He's here. In Belfast. And he didn't come alone."

"What?" Dozens of voices shouted.

"Are you sure?" Franklin stepped from the mass. "There should be no way he can find us. We spelled this area."

"I don't know how, but I know what I saw. He's here. Right now."

Fionna walked up beside me, staring back at her DLR members.

"It doesn't matter. We want this fight, and he brought it straight to us." She tipped her chin at Franklin. "Get everyone ready. The war they've been training for is here."

There were only about sixty people here. Even if eighty percent of those contained magic, it still was feeble against the numbers I saw Luuk surround himself with.

"Fionna…"

"We're greatly outnumbered, right?" she whispered, rounding to me. "That's what you were going to tell me."

"Did you read my mind? Can you do that?"

"No." She shook her head. "It's written all over your face."

"What do we do?" I surveyed the buzz of activity around me, people preparing to step into a fight they weren't quite ready for.

"The one thing we can do: fight." She met my gaze, steady and defiant. "Together."

I stared at my sister, taking in her strength and determination. How would it have been growing up with her to look up to? I was sad over what we lost, but I didn't regret how my life went. I loved my little sister and adoptive parents so much. With all our problems.

I hoped I'd come to love Fionna with all of hers and she mine.

I put my hand on hers. "Together."

TWENTY-SEVEN

"How many can you control?" I mumbled. This was a question I never thought I would be asking, but our options were slim.

"The most I've done was ten." Fionna swallowed, her head locked on the scene before us. She tried to hide her dread, but I could feel it emanating off her.

"Fuck." The word rushed over my lips, unfiltered and raw.

"Took the sentiment right from my mouth."

Just like in my vision, hundreds of fae stood before us outside the rundown factory, on the other side of the protective barrier, ready for battle. The sickle of the moon glinted off the variety of weapons each one held: blades, guns, arrows, metal spikes, clubs. They greeted us with a menacing gleam.

Anxiety sank like a boat in my stomach as our group stepped past the spell boundary lines and faced the enemy. Fionna seemed to understand as I had the sacrifice would be tremendous, but this fight was necessary. Both our fates had been leading us to face Luuk once and for all.

Fionna could control a handful, Kenya even fewer. Cali said she could only do one. I couldn't do any, not on cue anyway. Even if we each did a dozen, the odds were against us at least three to one. In other words, we were screwed.

I touched the handle of the gun strapped to my belt, for reassurance. My magic would be my weapon, but it made me feel better to know I had backup. Just in case.

"I still want to know how they found us." Franklin approached Fionna with Kenya next to him. The factory was guarded with spells. No one, including West, had been able to get close or find the true location of DLR.

"Doesn't matter. He has," Lorcan replied next to me, his presence giving me even more strength.

"Where's West?" I peered behind us. We needed every capable fighter we could.

"He'll be here. Just doing a last-minute errand." Lorcan kept his face forward. He wore only sweatpants, knowing he'd soon be in beast form, resilient to the freezing temperatures.

"Errand?"

"I'm here, darlin'." West came to the other side of Lorcan. He was still wearing his jeans, boots, and sweater. It was clear he would not be shifting into a beast. West was a strong man, but I couldn't imagine how excruciating that must be for him. Being a dark dweller was their entire identity. To take that away? I couldn't even contemplate how Lorcan would react to that happening to him.

The dwellers looked at each other, something passing between them. West's head dipped, nodding at the unsaid question Lorcan asked.

"Hope it's in time," Lorcan mumbled.

"What?"

"Nothing, darlin'." West winked at me, then looked forward.

Unfortunately being a mate didn't give you access to their private link.

Major, Mayhem, Cali, Wolf, Poppy, Fox, and Ophelia stood right behind us. The rest of the DLR and the few fae stood behind them. Humans and Druids were dressed and ready to fight back, scared and untrained in the true art of war against fae.

From the shadows a man stepped forward, his colorless skin shining in the dark like a nightlight. His dark clothes gave him the ghostly appearance of a head and hands floating in the air.

Oxygen sucked sharply in my lungs, burning with terror. In person, Luuk was even more unusual and eerie, like a marbled statue come to life. His tall, lean body stood proudly, his light blue eyes narrowed on me.

"Queen," Luuk snarled, jumping onto the hood of one of the vans. A couple of guards fortified the area around him.

"Luuk." I moved forward, not showing his physical dominance affected me. Fionna stepped with me, and I shot her a look, shaking my head. Her brow furrowed. I could see she did not like ceding control. But I was Queen. My authority surpassed hers, and she would simply weaken me.

Lorcan grabbed for her arm, tugging her back. He understood more than anyone the importance of a leader showing strength and power. She wiggled against his hold but didn't return to my side.

"Aren't you adorable in person?" Luuk's slight Scandinavian accent filled the air, his gaze running over my black hair, tattooed neck, and nose ring. "Not exactly the girl playing dress up at your coronation, but still so lovely. Like a little doll."

"You keep telling people not to judge things that come in small sizes." I lifted my hand, motioning to his lower half, the insult coming easily. *Ember and Ryan would be so proud.*

Luuk's jaw strained, his lids narrowing as he moved a foot closer. "You think it's smart to insult me?" He lifted his arms, glancing to his sides. "Look around, we outnumber you by far. It will be a slaughter. Do you really want all their deaths on you, *Queenie?*"

"Don't underestimate us. Druids have magic you fae only dream of." I rolled my wrists, like I was warming them up. "And do *you* think it is smart to challenge the Seelie Queen? To commit treason?"

Luuk's laugh filled the freezing air with a menacing cloud. "You should be looking closer to home for treasonous acts among those you trust. People in your own circle don't even want you as their Queen."

My throat went dry as the desert.

Luuk barked, his white lips spreading to show his pink gums.

"How do you think it was so easy to find you, *Majesty*? I've been tracking you this whole time. Every moment I knew exactly where you were," he taunted, rubbing his hands together. "Only a tiny token of affection, a symbol of love draped around your neck, was all it took to fool you."

My hand reached for my throat. The necklace. The one Torin gave me. I knew it wasn't there anymore but stuffed inside my backpack below the earth we stood on.

Like someone put my heart in a blender, the betrayal of someone I cared about ground my trust into dust. Pain punctured my entire body. My heart felt pierced by millions of tiny needles, like tiny holes behind my eyes and across my heart. I thought of him as a good friend. He *was* my friend. He said he wanted to be my lover. Someone who cared about me.

All lies?

My mind couldn't absorb the idea Torin could so cruelly deceive me. It seemed to go against his character and everything I thought I knew about him. I heard a growl behind me. I could feel Lorcan's anger buzzing like bees trapped in a jar.

"Sorry to be the bearer of bad news, but someone needed to tell you that even those in your castle do not respect you as their Queen. A Druid should *serve* royalty, like it used to be, not the other way around. It is disgusting. And I will not stand for it. Tonight, your short reign ends."

My spine snapped straight while the force of Lorcan's fury exploded over me like fireworks, crackling at my nerves.

"You don't have the King to hide behind. It's just you, Druid. Even being Queen, you are no match for me."

I felt the grip on my throat, my tongue taking over, my body going still. *What you seek will be the end and a beginning. Each side's victory is their own defeat. Death is approaching.* I jolted from the hold, feeling the power of my statement, but not knowing whether it was good or bad for either side.

Luuk stared at me, his bleached eyebrows drawing down, his eye glinting with hate. "Death happens in conflict. I will just make sure it is yours." He held up an arm, dropping it down. "Attack!" He leaped off the car as his army barreled toward us, screaming into the night like harbingers of death.

Terror ran in my veins, spilling adrenaline into my muscles. But this was what we wanted. We needed to fight. Roars reverberated behind me as Lorcan's beast zoomed past me, and spikes cresting his back strobed in the moonlight. West wasn't far behind him, a large dagger in one hand. Even in human form he was deadly. Both jumped for Luuk, but he slipped back behind his sentinels. The guards shifted into monsters, meeting Lorcan and West.

Creatures I had never seen before formed from the first three of Luuk's soldiers. Two seemed like a cross between a bear and a lion, with teeth and claws bigger than my head. The other was a Pegasus-like creature but with the head of a giant rodent and daggered teeth.

The dark dwellers, one beast, one human, collided into the other shifters, the sound of teeth crunching and nails tearing through flesh hinted at the edges of the sound of the Druids muttering spells behind me.

Luuk's warriors came running at us, weapons slicing into a few before spells could form in their mouths. Gunshots rang like cannons in the air, the humans advancing past the Druids, spilling their fae bullets into the other side.

The second time Fionna moved to my side, I welcomed it. She searched for Luuk, words forming on her lips. I recognized it as a revealing spell. Magic swirled around her, whipping the ends of my ponytail in my face.

The energy raced through the fighting beasts, parting them and exposing Luuk, his arm pointed at us. His gun was aimed right for Fionna.

The firearm went off.

"Fionna!" I screamed, my body ramming into hers, taking both of us down, the bullet whizzing past us.

We had hit the frozen dirt with a thud, my body rolling off hers. I didn't hesitate. My invocation shot for Luuk, bursting over him like fireworks, scattering a dozen fighters around him to the ground. The energy caused him to stumble back a step, but it didn't pick him up and throw him like it had everyone else.

What the hell?

Fionna climbed to her feet and directed an invocation at him. The instant she spoke I could feel the darkness in her spell. My bones recognized the black magic. Like fog it slid around Luuk's ankles, climbing up his legs.

"Let's see how long your fight lasts when their leader is *my* bitch." Fionna smirked, watching the mist swirl over him. She chanted another Latin phrase, the vapor bursting away from the pale leader like someone blowing out a chain of smoke.

Luuk stood there, his face expressionless. Was Fionna controlling him now? Would the fight be over? How come I saw so much death in my vision?

"Come here, fae," Fionna demanded. Luuk moved until he was only feet away from us then stopped. "You fight for us now. Drop the gun and tell your people to stop."

Luuk blinked, his pale eyes staring into Fionna. The gun stayed in his grip.

My blood turned icy as I watched the corner of his mouth tug up, his gaze filling with menacing glee.

"Someone didn't study albinos." He leaned toward Fionna, his voice going low. "We're impervious to magic, Druid or fae. That's why Aneira chose me as her commander in the fight against Druids. You can't do *shit* to me." He started to lift his weapon.

My hand went straight for my belt, whipping the gun from the halter, pointing at his temple, bending down on the trigger.

"Don't move or this goblin bullet will find a new home in your brain."

His eyes shifted to me, a smile slowly curling his mouth.

Crunch! With the force of a car, a creature slammed into my body, sailing me back into the wall of the factory, the side of my head cracking against the brick.

Sliding down the side, I watched the rhinoceros-looking creature spin back for Fionna.

"Fionna," I grunted, trying to call out for her, my shoulder crashed back into the wall, my head spinning.

Figures moved around me, blocking the view to my sister. Magic streaked the sky, weapons clanked in conflict, guns firing, screams of death echoed. Bodies already dotted the ground, ones I knew. Like dominoes, I could foresee our fall, our magic simply not strong enough to overpower the numbers of fae striking.

So much death. All for nothing.

A cry tugged my head to the side. Cali bent forward on her knees over a man, his side lined with deep gashes.

Wolf.

A pained roar from the depths of the fight pulled my neck the opposite way like a chain had been yanked at my neck.

Lorcan.

Hearing him, my mate, was like setting off a bomb inside me, exploding my fear and confusion into tiny bits, leaving only a blistering cloud of rage.

Get up. Something from the depths of my soul pushed me to my feet. I moved forward, tripping over an object. I peered down, a cry breaking from my mouth. "No!" Falling to my knees, my fingers touched his face.

Wizard's empty eyes stared at the sky. A slash cut across his neck, and his intestines spilled through the gaping, gory wound in his gut. I felt no life from him, nothing I could use to heal or bring back.

"I'm so sorry." I cupped his face, feeling the memory of Jared return in burning bile.

After losing Jared, I would have given up if it wasn't for Ember, Ryan, and my family, the heartache breaking me. But recalling Jared's face now invoked fury that snapped up my spine. I was so blinded by pain I could not see what I was capable of.

Light must use the darkness to see again.

I would fight for Jared. For Wizard. Their sacrifices.

I kissed his forehead and stood up. A calmness descended over me as I stepped forward. I knew what slithered up my throat, swirling my backbone like a tornado.

And I *welcomed* it.

Stepping through the fighting groups, no one touched me, like I was in my own bubble, the black magic cascading off me. My tongue lashed phrases I didn't recall knowing. I could feel my mother and the spells she spoke into her womb now passing out of me.

Save my people.

My family.

My kingdom

My heart.

The words formed without my control, my ponytail whipping around as energy billowed up and out of me. I was overtaken by a sensation of slipping into another plane that was thicker, denser than this one, like diving into a pool of syrup.

I couldn't recognize any details, only the notion of moving forms. My spell moved over the ones closest to me, consuming them before rolling on to the next. Their bodies went rigid, weapons dropping to their sides. Five. Ten. The spell took over groups at a time. With each person it felt like nails being jabbed into my brain. Gritting my teeth, I shoved to the next individual.

"Kennedy! Stop!" a man's voice bellowed, turning my head to the side. "You're killing yourself." Lorcan's naked body moved to me, his green eyes locking on mine. "Stop. Please."

"No."

"This is not an argument I'm losing, li'l bird." Lorcan reached for my hand, but the magic circling me shoved it back. "I will not lose you to black magic. Not tonight. Not ever."

I turned my head back to the throng of fighters under my spell, only seeing my control over them. "You fight for me now…your Queen." My voice rang clear and sharp, forcing my will on the fae.

Some tried to fight, but none could break my hold, switching sides and attacking their comrades next to them, doing my bidding like puppets. Somewhere deep down I sensed the twist in my soul. I was doing the identical thing I vilified and condemned. I tried to push my magic further, pain drilling into my brain, bending me over.

"Fuck!" Lorcan bellowed, throwing himself against the shield surrounding me. He roared in agony, but I felt claws wrap around my wrist, digging into my skin, snapping my gaze down.

His hand was the beast's. The stabbing of my magic against the intruder forced his body to defend itself. I glanced at his face, stitched with agony, but he didn't let go. His green eyes drilled into me.

I love you. Don't leave me, li'l bird.

With a burst, I slipped out of the shield of magic, crashing to the ground on my knees. Breath sucked back into my lungs, my bones feeling like gelatin as I twitched and shook. Throbbing in my head heightened every sound around me, flinching me lower. Blood oozed from my nose, hot tears leaking down my face. Pain stabbed at every nerve, exploding like a bomb in my brain.

Arms drew me into a warm bare chest, Lorcan kissing the top of my head.

"I'm sorry," I whispered against his skin.

He gripped my cheeks, turning my face to his. My body still trembled and rocked under his embrace. His thumbs wiped at the liquid coming from my eyes, coming away crimson.

Holy fractions. My eyes were leaking blood.

"Don't ever scare me like that."

I nodded, inhaling deeply. My body was weak, but the fight was still going on around us. I had to keep fighting. Saving. Protecting.

"Where is my sister?" I pulled away from Lorcan.

"I don't know." Lorcan rose, pulling me with him, my legs wobbly.

A man's cry jerked Lorcan's head to the side, his lips parting. I knew in my gut it came from West. "Go. Help him." I shoved at him.

"No fucking way I'm leaving you." He shook his head.

"I'll be fine. Please. I need you out there fighting, not protecting me."

Lorcan tilted his head, his jaw working fiercely.

"Now! Don't force me to order you." I moved away from him. "I need you to do what you do best. Be a dark dweller." Our eyes connected. No words even crossed through our gazes, but I could feel it. His fear for me. His unbridled love.

"I love you too," I said before turning and running back into the fight, my gun ready, searching the faces for my sister.

It only took me several steps before I saw her. She lay on the ground, Luuk straddling her body, his hands wrapped around her throat. Her life slipped away with each claw at his arm. Then her form went limp.

"No!" I screamed, pulling at the trigger, again and again. He glanced up, the slugs sailing in the air heading for his face.

He dropped down on Fionna, the bullets grazing the top of his head, one clipping his temple. He rolled off her and jumped to his feet.

"Here's the other Druid I want to kill." He stalked toward me, ignoring the pistol pointed at him and the blood running down the side of his face.

"You think I won't shoot you?" I growled, aiming the barrel at his heart. "They're fae bullets."

"No magic affects me. Not even goblin metal." He used up the distance between us.

"But bullets still hurt." I pressed the trigger, a hollow clicking sound rolled around in the chamber.

Empty.

A smile split Luuk's face. The blood smearing his face made him look like the Joker from Batman. I gulped, stumbling back out of his reach. Without a gun that worked, I was helpless against him, but I held on to it like a security blanket.

"Look around you, *Majesty*. You are losing. All your people are dead or soon will be." He waved around the night as the sounds of agony twisted in my heart. "Don't you want to save them? I will stop right now. Let the rest live. All you have to do it say the word." He inched to me, his height towering over me. "Step aside and save the exact people you claim you want to protect. Your refusal is just going to cause more death, more innocent lives lost. Everywhere."

"You think I will let you win? Bow down and give up so easily?"

"I think you will do what's best for all the people who will die under your rule." His lids narrowed, the top lip hitching up. "Because this is just a warm-up to what I will do. The revolution has started. It will continue to grow. And it will only get bloodier."

"You actually hate Druids so much you will slaughter people, fae, simply to bring me down?" The bones in my hand ached, but I clutched the handle harder, my palm sweaty.

"Druids aren't natural," he spit out. "You aren't meant for this world."

"Your gods thought we were even better than you."

His nose wrinkled up, hate blazing from his gaze. "Mistake. You little human witches should never have been given the gifts of magic and life from the gods. An embarrassing time in our history. But I'm here to set it right."

"You think yourself a god? Egotistical enough to believe *you* have the right to judge? To question the gods?" I moved closer, my neck aching, but I would not back down. "You who are magicless…oh…" I nodded, realization smacking into me. "That's it, isn't it?"

"Shut up, you stupid bitch." He bared his teeth, looming over me.

"It is." I held my chin high, calm. "You resent that you, a fae, were born with no magic. And here I am, someone who shouldn't have magic, and I am far more powerful than you will ever be."

"I said to shut up!" Before I could react he struck. My eye socket burst with fire as I was knocked off my feet. My back smacked into the ground with a thud, ripping the air from my lungs.

He had punched me and pounced the moment I hit the earth, straddling me, his expression like a rabid dog. Crazed eyes looked down at me, the composure I had seen on the video gone. "You fucking witch!" He grabbed for my throat, pushing down on my esophagus.

My voice was my Achilles's heel. Even if my magic didn't affect him, the pressure from the spell would still push him back. I had seen him stumble against it earlier. But he blocked my weapon.

I gurgled out a scream, kicking and scratching the skin at his wrists. I scraped till I felt blood, but he did not seem to notice.

"I want every one of you dead. You should not exist!" His thumbs sank in deeper, blurring my eyesight. "And to be our Queen? What a fucking insult! I should be the one with magic. Not you. Like being a fucking albino wasn't hard enough, I had to be a total outcast and freak. Aneira saw my potential, but even she turned on me in the end. Sent me back to obscurity in Estonia."

He lifted my head off the ground, slamming it back down, till the world spun around me. I tried to fight, but my arms grew heavier, not able to shove against him.

Lorcan, my mind said his name. *I'm so sorry for wasting so much time we could have been together. I love you.*

My lids drifted closed, lungs burning for want of air. Everything hurt except the blackness creeping over me. It promised peace and relief. I wanted that.

Then a guttural scream sounded from far away.

Hands dropped from my throat, allowing air back in. I gasped, inhaling oxygen as it unfolded down my throat, filling my lungs. Hacking coughs tore through me, fighting with the air pouring in. My eyes popped open, my mind hazy.

Still sitting on me, Luuk's head was tilted, his lips parted in a silent scream. The end of a blade poked out the side of his neck, blood gushing down his torso and splattering on me.

Beside him stood Fionna, the moonlight glinting off the fury in her bright eyes, holding on to the handle of the blade. She was caked in dirt, blood, and cuts, but she looked like a fierce warrior striking down with revenge.

"That's for touching my little sister." Her foot came up and shoved him off me. "We might be small, but I promise you, you will regret ever picking a fight with us."

Luuk tried to gasp around the knife in his throat, red saliva bubbling from his lips, hate twisting his face into a wrinkled dog.

Fionna stepped over him, again gripping the blade handle. "This is for all the lives and families you destroyed." Fionna twisted the knife deeper into Luuk's neck, his eyes bugging as gurgling noises lobbied up his throat in strangled coughs. "You slaughtered my mother and father thinking you ended the Cathbad line." Fionna leaned over, clutching his chin with one hand. "Well, guess what? Cathbad's line is stronger than ever. Die knowing you failed everything you've ever strived for." Putting the force of her entire body into it, she drove the knife all the way through Luuk's esophagus, chanting a spell. Oily, thick magic descended down on us, crawling over my skin. Saliva spit from Fionna's mouth, hate raging her face.

"Fionna, stop! Magic doesn't work on him." My voice broke and stumbled painfully over each syllable.

"Magic has energy. Density," she seethed, getting closer to his face, speaking to him, turning as feral as he had. "Especially black magic. The spell may not kill you, but what do you think the residual of my spell will do when it goes off?"

I froze and stared at them, my horror dancing between the two. Whatever spell she was talking about wasn't a fluffy one.

Luuk snarled, lunging from the ground for Fionna. Latin curled angrily from her mouth, her body shaking. With a pop, his eyes widened, his body going still, red liquid spurted from his mouth, eyes, and neck, spraying over my face. Blood oozed from his lips, painting the white canvas of his face with the sharp contrasting color. It was horrific and creepily striking in some twisted way.

Fionna fell back, a cry erupting from her mouth, her head hitting the gravel.

"Fionna!" I crawled for her, leaning over her limp body. Black blood leaked from her nose, her eyes. She blinked, dazed. Grabbing my hand, she tried to sit but bounced back on the concrete, coughing up thick inky blood.

Nothing came without a price.

A fierce protectiveness came over me, my hands skimming from her head to her stomach, healing her with my words. She stilled under my spell, her pupils clearing, the hacking subsiding. I sat back when I felt she was healed, bowing my head. I could hear people still fighting around us, but the revolutionaries had just lost their leader. Soon the tables would turn.

Fionna curled herself up, mumbling something like a thank you. Silence stretched between us, both staring at the almost decapitated man at our feet.

"We should make sure it's completely separated," I said numbly. Sadly, decapitating fae was not new to me. It was how I won my place as Queen. Aneira's head had been the price.

Fionna only let one sob break through, reeling in whatever emotion wanted to leak through her tough exterior. She wiped her face with the back of her hand. "Yeah, but I doubt he will be returning anyway. I basically exploded his brain."

I jerked to look at Fionna, my mouth agape. She craned her neck slowly to me, her face emotionless.

She knew how to burst people's brains like a watermelon?

"Shit squared…" I muttered. Fionna was not solely a dominant Druid, but extremely formidable in black magic, a frightening combination.

While she finished the job, I stood searching for Lorcan. Seeing the fight was shifting, I felt a haze come over me, my control of my mouth lost.

"Your leader has fallen. You shall fall too. Depart. The Queen has spoken; her words as strong as her will," I boomed, my voice carrying through the throng of people, eclipsing the night.

Everyone halted around me as though someone pushed a pause button. Luuk's militia peered around, finally noticing their chief was dead.

"Leave now if you want your life spared," I yelled out.

"They will only come back. We must end them all here," Fionna said behind me.

"No." I turned my head, staring her down. "We will not kill freely like Luuk did. I will not be that Queen." I faced the group again. "But hear my words, if you ever come for me again or try to rise against me or my kingdom, I will not hesitate. Go. Now."

After a short pause, the dozens remaining took off, running for their lives.

"That was a mistake," Fionna said

"Maybe," I responded. "But I will not rule with fear and hate."

"*Shite*," Fionna snorted. "Guess who the good one is in our family?"

"I have to be." I rubbed my temples, feeling the tension starting. "I feel the darkness inside. It is there, wanting to be used, but that's why every other monarch has fallen. It has to be countered with empathy and kindness."

"You're going to be annoying." Fionna shook her head, but a small smile hinted at her lips.

"Aren't little sisters supposed to be?" I flashed a look at her.

"Good job so far." She patted my arm. The humor left us as we looked around, seeing the loss. My hand went to my mouth when I saw Kenya, Fox, and Poppy lying dead, painting the icy ground red, their twisted bodies like abstract art.

I felt dizzy. Guilt battled up my throat, making me gag. How many others were there? All the lives lost in my company, or for my cause, weighed heavily on my soul, pulling me down into trenches.

Franklin hobbled over to Kenya, silent and stricken as he stared down at her. He let out a chilling yowl, bending over her he placed his head on hers. Major joined him, agony twisting his face at the sight of his mother. Ophelia wailed next to him, crumpled over Poppy's dead form, her hand over her heart, like it was going to fall out. Major grabbed her, pulling her into his body, rocking. She fell into his embrace like she was boneless. Sobbing. The two held on to each other for dear life, lost in their pain.

I scanned the crowd...what was left. Some I recognized but didn't know their names, until my regard fell on Cali, her sobs echoing off the buildings around us, still next to Wolf's form. My heart wrenched, feeling her despair. But then I saw Wolf's hand reach for her face, wiping the tears from her cheeks, his arms wrapping around her. They were happy tears. Relieved.

In the horrors of tonight, my shoulders dropped, letting their love have a happy ending, appeasing a piece of my heart. Wizard, Kenya, Poppy, Fox. I would carry their ghosts for life, along with the others who already haunted me.

"Kennedy!" Lorcan parted the group, running to me, covered in gore and wounds, dressed once again in his sweatpants. A light in the dark. My anchor. My heart twisted with happiness at seeing him. Our bodies collided as I jumped into his arms, his fingers digging into the back of my head and lower spine, gripping me to him. He hugged me briefly before his mouth found mine, hungrily kissing me. I didn't care who was watching, or what they thought, or the fact dead bodies lay at our feet. I returned his demand with even more of mine, deepening our kiss till nothing was left in the world except us.

He growled, setting me back down on my feet as his irises smeared with fire. *We need to stop or everyone is going to watch me fuck you against this car*, his eyes said, producing a deep blush to flood my cheeks.

I licked my bottom lip, shrugging my shoulders slightly. Lorcan's eyes went crimson, his hands clutching at his side. I played with a live bomb, knew it could explode, and yet I still batted it around. He did this to me. Created this need to push my limits, to test him and myself.

Not nice, li'l bird.

Spank me later.

Lorcan groaned, bowing his head, he scoured fiercely at the back of his neck. "Don't worry, I plan on it."

TWENTY-EIGHT

"Majesty?" A voice came out of the darkness, spinning me around, my stomach hurtling to the ground. I knew that voice. *It couldn't be...*

A figure ran out of the shadows, his face twisted with worry, but his clothes and face looked perfect, as if he stepped out of the pages of *GQ*.

"Torin?" I gaped, not ready to believe my eyes. My First Knight reached me, wrapping me in his arms, lifting me off my feet.

"Oh thank the gods, my lady. You are all right," he mumbled into my hair. His grip squeezed the breath from me. My head was so confused. Torin looked out of place in the scene around me.

A warning growl vibrated from behind. I could feel Lorcan's entire body going rigid, wrath smoldering underneath.

"Torin, what are you doing here?" I dropped away from him, taking a slight step back. The moment I did, Lorcan was on him, grabbing him by the collar, tossing him against the van hood.

The few dozen of DLR who remained turned toward the ruckus, their eyes wide.

"How dare you show your face, you traitor."

"What?" Torin's eyes widened, glancing around with confusion. "What the hell are you talking about, dweller? You guys were the ones to call us here."

Ah. West's "last-minute" errand.

"We just learned... The necklace..." Lorcan banged Torin's head against the metal, claws growing from his hands. "Leading the enemy right to the Queen you swore to protect?"

At first I didn't stop Lorcan. The betrayal I had felt after Luuk's claim surged anew, but with one stunned expression I could sense Torin's confusion, his intention...his innocence.

"Lorcan, stop." I tried to tug on his arm, but it didn't budge. "He didn't do it." But neither one seemed to hear me.

Torin shoved against Lorcan, fury sliding of his expression. "I would never harm her! She is my Queen! The one who saved my life... I am in love with her."

Oh. No.

Every muscle locked in Lorcan's body, his pupils elongating into slits. Tension pounded between us like a heartbeat. I could feel that moment, that second, before Lorcan would slip into his beast and shred Torin into cheese.

"No!" I leaped forward, diving over Torin, looking up at Lorcan. "Do not hurt him," I snarled, needing to protect Torin as much as protecting Lorcan from doing something I would hate him for. "He is innocent. I can see it." I reached up, my hand cupping Lorcan's face. He flinched but took a deep breath. He closed his eyes, inhaling, releasing his grip of Torin. This time when he looked up, his eyes were back to normal.

"No," Torin strangled out a whisper, and I twisted my head to see him taking in Lorcan and me. He stared at me, his eyes almost pleading. "Please. Tell me it's not true. Not him."

"I'm sorry." The suffering in his voice ensnared mine in a twisted knot. "I never meant to hurt you."

"Don't." Standing up, he looked at the ground, agony lining his forehead. "Please don't say anything more, Majesty."

Once again I was the cause of someone's pain. All because I couldn't control who I fell in love with.

Torin took a step away from me, and Lorcan countered his movement, like he was keeping him corralled.

"Lorcan, stop. He's blameless in this."

"Not that innocent," Lorcan mumbled, his lip hitching up, but he took a step back.

Torin snapped to Lorcan, fury lighting his eyes. "What the hell was that for? *You* have her…why attack me?"

"It has nothing to do with that." I waited to get his full attention. "The necklace you gave me. There's a tracker in it. It was how Luuk kept finding me."

"What?" Torin's mouth dropped open, his eyes bugging, head shaking in disbelief. "H-how is that possible?"

"Was there anyone else who touched it besides you?"

"No..." He quickly answered, but then horror flashed over his face. "Wait, yes. I wanted it cleaned before I gave it to you."

"Who?" Lorcan barked.

Torin's mouth opened to answer, but a wave of magic capsized the air, punching against my skin. I whirled around, knowing without seeing, who had just arrived. It could be only one person.

Could he sincerely want me dead? How naïve. Of course he would; I was nothing but a pawn.

"It looks like you handled things here, Ms. Johnson." The Unseelie King strolled up in one of his gorgeously tailored suits, one hand in his pocket, his two guards flanking him. Thara and Castien stood behind them.

My instinct was to run and hug Castien. Seeing him healed and back to normal was a cool salve to my bruised soul. My hand went to my heart, and he mimicked me, giving me a wink.

"I assured your knight here you can handle yourself, but he insisted on coming. Actually, he ran far ahead of us, not able to wait." Lars's gaze revolved methodically over the scene.

"You," Fionna hissed at Lars, causing my head to snap to my sister. Her shoulders rolled back, and her frame twitched, going on defense. The few DLR members around her clutched their weapons tighter. Lars's chartreuse gaze slid to her, like a snake tongue tasting the air, before returning to me.

The energy in the air crackled with fumes, ready to ignite. I just wasn't ready for the person who lit the match.

"How *could* you?" Torin shouted, fury coating his tone, leaping at the newly arrived group. "I trusted you!"

Lars's men reacted in an instant, ready to defend their King, but Torin skated past them, hurtling himself at his comrade, his best friend, taking her to the ground with a thump.

Holy shit!

"You took an oath. Have you no honor?" He grabbed for her wrists, pinning them against the gravel.

I stood dumbfounded, watching Torin wrestle Thara, her expression turning defiant, almost angry. Her aura sparked with fury, hurt, and love.

"Oh my god." I clutched my stomach, the betrayal and hurt folding my stomach in on itself. "Thara, how could you?" I asked, even though I was fully aware of the answer.

Torin.

It was written all over her. Her absolute devotion and love for him was shaded heavily with jealousy and heartache. She clamped her lips together as Torin hauled her to her feet, his fingers strangling her wrists.

"Speak when the Queen addresses you." Torin shook her, causing her lids to change into narrow slits.

"She is not my Queen."

Torin's mouth gaped.

"We are fae. We should be ruled by a fae leader." She held up her chin, her tone stoic as ever.

I took a step toward her. Lorcan reached out for me, but I continued up to her, assessing her feelings. For once she didn't hide her aura from me.

"I see you do feel that way, but it's not why you did it." Sorrow burned like acid in my heart. I had truly thought of her as a friend. Someone I could trust.

Thara's mouth twisted at my words, glancing away from me.

"I'm sorry, Thara." Her head snapped back to me, anger rising into her cheeks.

"Why are you apologizing to her?" Torin exclaimed. "She betrayed you! Put the tracker in the necklace so you would be killed."

"No." I let my seer dive deeper into her. "She didn't want me dead."

"Get out of my head," she snarled.

"Then tell us, Thara. Why did you go against the crown?" Torin bristled, shaking her violently.

"She did not deserve you," Thara spat back at Torin. "None of them did. How blind you are. She was no more in love with you than Ember was. But like a puppy, you keep taking the punishment."

Torin reared his head back, taking in Thara. Her long chocolate hair was pulled in a tight braid trailing down her back. Dressed in leather pants and a long-sleeved shirt with my insignia on it, she stood proud, her head held high. She did not cower or shy away from the fury raining down on her from Torin. She challenged it.

"I've been there for you, centuries being at your side. I was the one you came crying to when Aneira hurt you, when Ember broke your heart. It was me. Always me." She tugged at his grip, pulling him in closer to her. "I loved you. Even when you threw it back in my face, shredded my heart, I stayed loyal you. I thought maybe you'd see me. Finally realize how good we are together. But she came along and by simply giving you back your role, you think the sun rises and sets on her.

"Do you know how badly it hurt when you say *she* saved your life? Who was the one who got you through the darkest times of your life? Me. And when you asked me to get the necklace of your mother's cleaned, to give to *her*…I'm the one who knows how special that is. What it means." She blinked away her tears. Years of pent-up emotion flooded out of Thara, rushing out of the dam. "*Everyone* could see it. She called *his* name. Not yours! How could you be so blind? She would *never* love you."

Torin dropped her arms and rubbed his temples. With all the people around her, she had nowhere to go. And she was not the type to flee. She remained strong, ready to take her punishment. I hated what she did, but I couldn't help respect her a little. She was not one who ran. She believed in something and stood by it. And for decades that had been Torin.

"You thought getting rid of the Queen would make me fall in love with you?" Torin pulled himself to full height, speaking low, but it sounded full of disgust. "That shows how little you understand me. How right I was to never look upon you."

Ouch. Even I flinched.

"Castien?" Torin nodded at his soldier. Castien stepped up to Thara, understanding what his knight wanted. "I can't look at this turncoat for another moment."

It was so fast I barely saw it, but grief and hurt flashed over Thara's face before she instructed her expression back to stone.

Castien pulled on gloves, unhooking the iron cuffs he always kept on him and latched them over Thara's wrists. She cried out, her knees buckling, but kept upright, huffing through her nose.

Castien gave me a small nod before tugging Thara away. She looked back once, pain rooted in her eyes, but turned away, following Castien to her fate.

Torin's words said one thing, but watching him track her, the hurt and duplicity he felt was clear on his face. She had also been his friend and partner for a long time.

"Torin, go with Castien. Make certain she gets there." She would be heading to the dungeons. I detested I had no choice but to lock her away. I could not be weak against traitors, even if I cared about her. But watching the fierce woman I thought of as a friend chained in iron tore my heart in half.

Torin's mouth parted to oppose my order, lines crisscrossing his forehead as he struggled between wanting to stay next to me and going after her. I sensed duty and concern tugging him in different directions. I could see he wanted to be strong, be the soldier, and stand by my side. But the man was hurt by Thara's confession and Lorcan's and my bond.

I did not want to be the cause of additional grief for him, because tonight of all nights, I would not censure my need to be by my mate. "Please. I need you to do this for me," I said soft but firm.

He swallowed, then nodded, almost like he was relieved I gave him this order. He bowed, accepting my command. His attention drifted between Lorcan and me, pain flinching his cheeks. He then turned and dissolved into the night along with the others.

In grief, I turned away rubbing my chest as though it could ease the agony. Without a word Lorcan strode to me, engulfing me in his arms, kissing my head.

Lars tugged on his cuffs. "I'm sure this could make fascinating TV, but honestly I couldn't care less about hurt feelings and broken hearts. We need to attend to business."

"That's because you don't have a heart," Fionna retaliated, her snarl returning to her face. "Nor do you have any common sense."

Everyone's mouth fell open. No one addressed the King that way. No. One.

Lars was in front of her face in a blink, gripping her chin, his fingers turning white. "You want to say that again, little girl?" He leaned down, an inch away from her face. "I've killed people for less."

Fionna's chest drew in and out rapidly, but her gaze stayed firmly on Lars, not backing away from his challenge.

It was a standoff I didn't want to see the ending of. "Lars." I grabbed his arm. "Please. Don't," I begged. "Sh-she's my sister."

He did not react, not even a blink, his gaze still burning into her. It was another few moments before he dropped his hand from her face, stepping back. "Sister?" A strange smirk pursed his mouth, like an idea came to him. A dangerous idea.

"Do you think defiance is showing strength?" He lifted one eyebrow. "Do it again and we will see how eager you are to keep at it when your mind is bending to *my* will."

"I promise you the same in return." A malicious grin formed on Fionna. I had just seen what she was capable of. These two would explode each other's heads in two minutes of being left alone together.

"Oh, really?" Lars stepped right into her, trying to intimidate. "You sure you are ready to make promises you cannot keep?"

She shoved right back into him, her head drawn back to look up. "Try me, demon."

In a blink Lars's eyes went completely black, his skin thinning along his cheekbones.

Oh. Holy. Crap.

"Stop!" I pulled at them, trying to tear them away from each other. "Please! Back off, both of you."

"You would not be saying that if you knew the truth. What you knew he wanted...and already had." Fionna remained locked on Lars, anger honing her voice to a deadly point.

"I would silence that mouth of yours." A chilling noise came from him, the King losing himself to the demon.

"Shouldn't she know what you have been doing behind her back?" Fionna put her hands on her hips. "Typical fae…deceitful liars."

Lars lurched forward, grabbing her by the throat. "You want to die?"

She wheezed, a derivative snort coming from her. "You won't kill me, Lars. We both know that." She swallowed against his hand. "I'm the only one who knows where it is."

Where what is? What are they talking about?

"If I die so does your chance of finding it. I know the game, demon." Fionna struggled with each word, her eyes watering. "I'm no *little* girl."

Lars's shoulders shrugged up, wrath billowing off him, choking the air around us. His fingers gripped down tighter, forcing Fionna's mouth to gape, her chest thrashing for a breath.

"Stop! Please stop!" I clawed at Lars's hand, trying to break his hold on her. Fionna was my sister. My only family, the link to my true past. I couldn't let Lars take it away.

The invocation spewed off from me in reaction, my heart overtaking my mind. Lars and Fionna ripped away from each other, their bodies flinging through the air, hitting the earth with a thud. Silence deafened like a piercing dog whistle. We all stood in shock at what I had done.

What did I just do? Did I really take the Unseelie Demon King to the ground like he was a pin at a bowling lane?

Fuuuuuck.

Goran was the first to run to Lars, but the King shoved him off, rising to his feet like a mountain. One about to send an avalanche my way. His skin was almost translucent, bones sticking out, with black eyes staring me down as he prowled to me. I held my place, defensive and trembling with fear.

"You dare spell me?" he spoke, deep and hissing with fury.

"You left me no choice, Lars." My heart thwacked against my ribs. I could feel Lorcan's presence behind me, a growl rumbling over my shoulder.

The dweller didn't intimidate Lars. Invisible hands circled my neck, and my fingers went to my throat trying to release his as he stalked toward me. Someday my powers could rival Lars's, but not without my voice. I choked. I gagged. I bent forward in agony, desperate for air. I heard Lorcan roar, but he too slammed to the ground by my feet, grappling at his own throat.

"Let her go," Fionna screamed.

Lars clenched down harder, and I writhed near his feet. I heard mumbling from behind me, and in an instant, the pressure on my throat was gone. Lars grunted, grabbing for his head.

"Fuck with my sister, you fuck with me," Fionna said, then went back to her chant.

Lars pressed his hands against his head with a snarl.

Before any of us could act, Travil slipped in behind Fionna, grabbing her and shoving a gag into her mouth. She thrashed against him with a screech. The DLR started to advance, but Travil pinned a knife to her throat, moving her back toward Lars.

"I will gut any one of you who advances on me or even hints at a spell." Lars boomed at the DLR group. They all halted, feeling the power and truth of his threat. No one had the power to fight a fae like him.

This was never going to stop, round and round until one of us actually killed the other. "ENOUGH!" I screamed, climbing to my feet, my hand at my neck, still feeling the impression of fingers.

Lars went to his full height, tugging at the bottom of his jacket, straightening it. "She has attacked a King. She must be dealt with," Lars said, emotionless.

"No." I took a step but halted when Travil poked the blade to her throat farther. She squirmed against him, but without her magic it was pointless. Travil's one hand was bigger than her entire neck.

"You know the law, Ms. Johnson." He leered down at me. "Just a moment ago, your own guard was hauled off for treason. She is no different. It was she who ordered the deaths of your noble. She almost killed us. Attempt on a monarch's life is death."

"Lars, I beg you, please don't hurt her."

"Were you aware she is behind the attacks on my compound? She is the benefactor behind the strighoul."

"What?" My mouth dropped, my gaze pinging between my sister and the King.

"Marguerite would be dead right now because of your *sister*." His yellow-green eyes darkened, rage bubbling up. "If you hadn't stopped it, Marguerite would have been killed, and my house would have fallen."

I struggled to swallow. Fionna was the one behind

those attacks? She had worked with strighoul? She didn't care that the woman she set up for sacrifice, merely as a statement, was the kindest, most beloved woman I had ever known.

I clutched my stomach. It made sense now why the strighoul were able to crack Lars's barriers. Druid magic was the only kind powerful enough to challenge his own. I shook my head, staring at Fionna. It didn't matter if she didn't know who I was then, or how important these people were to my life. The aching disloyalty I felt still seethed and festered like an open sore.

"Her crimes are extensive. All punishable by death."

My neck jerked to Lars. No matter how hurt I was, I still didn't want her dead. "Please, Lars. I will do anything."

"Anything?" His brows arched.

Fionna squeaked through the rag, eyes wide, shaking her head fiercely back and forth, her limbs thrashing. Lars nodded back at Travil. The dark-haired fae tipped the blade until blood rained down her neck. What did she want me to do? I couldn't let her be tortured or die. I wouldn't. I transferred my gaze from her, not able to see her pleading for me to do the opposite. My head bobbed. "Anything."

"Your word, Ms. Johnson?"

My lashes smashed onto my cheekbones, my head bowing. I knew exactly what would happen if I said yes. An oath. A bind.

Fionna went crazy, flapping and grunting. I couldn't look at her, the response whispered over my tongue.

"Yes." The bind jumped down on me, folding my knees.

A smug, I-got-my-way smile appeared on his face. This was how the fae did business. Especially dark demon kings. "I want something she has hidden; now it is up to you to retrieve it for me."

"What? What does she have?"

Lars ignored my question, strolling back and forth in front of me. "Every week you don't find it, the more severe her punishment becomes."

My stomach rolled. I knew what Lars was capable of.

Lars flicked his hand, and Travil shoved Fionna forward, Goran following as they exited. Fionna glanced back at me, animosity fired from her eyes into mine, like I had betrayed her. It stabbed right through my heart, and I jerked my head away, blinking back unshed tears.

"You know this is not personal, Ms. Johnson. You might hate me. That is fine, but know I am always thinking of the kingdom first. And believe me, she is no victim in this. Far from it. She is exceptionally lucky to have someone I value in her corner." Lars dipped his head in respect to me and started to drift away.

"Wait!" I moved forward. "Tell me what I am supposed to be getting for you. I need to know what I am looking for."

"A family heirloom of yours, Ms. Johnson," Lars said over his shoulder. "The Cauldron of the Dagda."

Every muscle in my body locked up, fear and disbelief fighting for room in my weary head. My tongue locked in place as I watched the King disappear into the night.

When Lars had taken the Sword of Nuada from Ember, I knew in my soul the danger of a powerful demon obtaining one of the treasures of Tuatha De Danann. But I had pushed it away, ignoring what I knew was coming. Lars wasn't going to stop at one. He was going to try and acquire them all. They were lethal on their own, but together? He could control everything.

No one person, especially fae, was ever meant to possess so much power. I had always trusted Lars. He was ruthless, but I believed deep down he was extremely intelligent in understanding what danger existed in holding too much power. He could no longer see clearly.

"Fuck." Lorcan strode up beside me.

I nodded with a gulp. "What am I going to do? I'm bound to help him find it." I could feel the panic attack ripping up my spine. Lorcan's hand rubbed at my back, trying to calm me. "What will happen when he gets two of them?"

"Uh." West moved to my other side. "Hate to be the one to break it to you." Lorcan and I glanced at West.

West continued to stare forward. "He *already* has two. That's what my mission with Rez was. How I met Fionna. She was the one guarding the Spear of Lugh. This will be the third. The stone is the only one left...and…"

"And what?" I clutched my stomach, feeling I already knew what he was going to say.

"There were rumors…before the war. Talk that it had been *found*." West rubbed his chin, his insinuation clear.

I blinked, staring out into the night.

All three of us stayed silent, gazing into the shadowy void, death scattered around our feet like leaves. Luuk was dead, the DLR no longer functioning, so my role as Queen was on more stable ground.

Then why did I feel the world crumbling under my feet? This time it wouldn't be by a stranger. This fight would be close to home.

EPILOGUE

"I want to thank you for your service, for putting your life on the line." I sat in the chair, clasping the girl's fingers in my own. "I hope you are comfortable in your new home."

"Oh, yes, my lady. It's wonderful. You don't know what this means to my family and me."

"They are unaware of how you actually obtained it, right?"

The girl's eyes rounded, as though horrified I would even ask. "Besides being bound to secrecy, I would never betray you. Ever."

"Thank you, Gemma." I gave her hand one last squeeze before standing and drifting around to my desk. "I know you are highly aware the delicacy of this matter. It must never be discovered."

"Completely, Majesty." Gemma bowed her head, her long brown hair tumbling down her shoulders. From afar I could see the similarity. She was my height and coloring, but glamour had helped with the rest, diluting her bright violet-blue eyes to brown and heart-shaped face to oval.

She could definitely pass for a relation of mine...

~~~~

Fionna.

From the moment I returned, I demanded to see my sister. Lars accepted my request. Fionna would not. Either she did not want to see me because she knew what I wanted, or she truly hated me for letting Lars take her.

I could not stop his ruling, no matter how much I wanted to. Fionna had threatened and attacked the King. Actually, she had attacked both of us. Opposing the crown was treason, punishable by death. And let's be honest, considering she almost squeezed his brains out of his head, she was lucky to be alive. She was his to seek justice upon. But that didn't mean I would stop fighting for her.

"Harm will come to her if she continues to disobey me," Lars said on my visit there. "For what she did, Ms. Johnson, you know my full rights to sentence her."

I bolted out of the chair, rebuttals flying to my tongue.

"I won't. Yet." Lars held up his hand. "I assure you she is being treated *quite* fairly here."

"Because of what you want." I glowered at him. "Always out for yourself. No matter who you hurt."

"And you, Ms. Johnson, are too inexperienced to see the bigger picture as I can. You think Luuk was our biggest enemy? Not even close." He placed his palms on the desk, leaning over. "What I want the item for is my business, but as you can see, I've been King for an extraordinarily long time, and I plan to keep it that way. It is up to you if you want to remain the Queen beside me."

I folded my arms and gritted my teeth together, torn between wanting to trust him and believing he was deceiving me. Had he finally gotten too hungry for power he'd lost his way, or was he right that I simply couldn't see the bigger picture yet?

"You didn't give me much of a choice, did you?" I hissed.

His mouth twitched, but he didn't grow angry. "No, but I usually get what I want in the end. I took the shortcut."

"Lars, no one should have the treasures of Tuatha De Danann. Haven't you learned from the past? These magic items hold too much power. They only cause destruction and death when they are together in one place; that's why they were separated and hidden."

"Trust me." He stood, peering coolly down on me. "I know what I have to do to save our kingdom."

It was probably going to come up and bite me in the butt later, but for some reason I did trust him enough to not destroy his reign. Past that I wasn't quite sure.

Lars and I had a complicated relationship, and even though he held my sister prisoner and bound me to a promise to seek an object that could destroy the world, we still held a united front in public. After the chaos Luuk stirred up in Europe, our outward appearance of unity was more crucial than ever.

And Lars had a maddening way of making me respect him no matter what he did.

~~~~~

"Majesty?" A voice jarred me back to the present.

"Yes, I apologize, Gemma. I've gotten little sleep since my return." I wagged my head, trying to clear it.

When we returned, Gemma's exit went as smoothly as her entrance. No one seemed the wiser. Against my Knight's approval, I asked to visit with the woman who had played me for so many weeks. It might be foolish and probably better if I had never met her, but it didn't stop me from setting up a meeting.

In payment for dedication to the crown, we provided her with a new home, money, and job. She was to tell her family her cushy new benefits came with her new employment. Having grown up enamored of Aneira's gorgeous chic dresses, she told me she eventually wanted to design dresses for me for events and parties.

Maybe I should ask for sweats with ruffles. That's stylish, right? At least Ember and I thought so long ago for the school dance. I grinned at the thought, knowing Ember would love my idea. *I'll have to tell her when we talk next*. She and Eli were in Peru hunting down a radical pack of strighoul.

"Thank you, Gemma." I nodded at her, giving Torin my "I'm done" look. He stepped up instantly. Things had been tense between us, especially after I returned his mother's necklace. I hoped time would lessen the stress, and we would be able to be friends again. I missed our ease with each other.

"Ms. Gemma? May I escort you to the car?" He held out his hand for her.

Her eyes lit up, a blush reddening her cheeks as she stood, taking his arm. "Thank you, Torin." A flustered smile twitched her mouth. "I would like that very much."

"It would be my honor." He grinned back, but the smile was empty. His opposite hand covered hers as they walked to the door, letting her step out first. He gave me one last nod before closing the door behind him.

I wanted so badly for someone to come along and steal Torin's heart. He was an amazing man, and he deserved someone as wonderful.

He would get over me, but not Thara. He mourned the loss of his best friend every day. He had yet to go see her, but I found him by the dungeon doors several times. Sitting or standing near the entrance, his feet never took him down the steps. The agony on his face looked like a war battled inside him. He lived by rules, and she had broken them. If she was anyone else, she would be forever a traitor in his eyes. But this was Thara. I don't think he realized until she wasn't there how much he counted on her and liked having her by his side. I could feel how much he missed her. Mourned and ached the loss in his life. It far overshadowed what he ever felt for me.

When I had visited her one time, all the anger and hate she had held for me once was gone. Only sorrow and shame remained. A husk of the woman sat before me. Her eyes only met mine when I told her I forgave her. I saw emotion flicker in her eyes before she returned to staring at the ceiling. It broke my heart to keep her there. I knew she was no longer a threat, but I could not show favoritism to a traitor. She asked one time to do the honorable thing and kill her. Maybe it was crueler, but I would never do that. I still cared about her.

"Dimwit gone. Room brighter." A voice rose from my open window, and I spun around. "Infuriate Grimmel."

"Missed me, huh?" I walked over to the window. He had mentioned several times he thought very little of the fake Queen.

"Infuriate less." He took off, gliding back down toward the dungeons.

"Wow, high compliment." I snorted, heading for my desk. Since my return, he had taken to hanging out on my window a lot, till his "Grimmel-isms" would force me to slam the window shut. I could only take so much.

Before I had a chance to sit, the door reopened and a figure slipped through. I pressed my lips together, fighting the biggest grin from engulfing my face.

"What can I do for you, Mr. Dragen?" I spoke in my professional "Queen" voice. "Do you have an appointment scheduled? I'm especially busy today with meetings back to back."

He prowled up to me, his eyes churning red, grabbed me by the hips, and tossed me on the desk. "I have a *standing* appointment," he growled, pressing himself between my legs and sliding my dress up my thighs. Heat fired through every nerve in my body, desire pumping louder than the blood in my veins. This morning he'd sent me off to my royal duties with buttery limbs and noodle bones, but the moment he appeared, I was ready for more.

Lorcan's presence at the castle had been anything but smooth. The Seelie had not happily accepted a dweller in the kingdom, especially one who slept with their Queen. It had been tense and the media had a field day. The scandal did not help my struggling reputation, but I knew eventually it would ebb.

They weren't the ones I spent restless nights caring about. The night I told Ryan still gutted me. We had a major fight. The first one ever. It killed me I was hurting him, but Lorcan was part of me, my life, and I wasn't going to deny it anymore.

"No." Ryan *shook his head, his gaze darting between Ember and me, hoping to see one of us crack into a fit of giggles.*

Except this was no joke.

"Ry?" I reached out for him. He jerked away from my touch, his gaze running over me like I was a stranger. "Believe me, it wasn't something I planned on. I fought it for so long. I didn't want to hurt you."

"Hurt me?" Ryan's mouth gaped, his voice rising. "Hurt me! Telling me my clothes look bad is hurtful. This? This goes way past hurt." He threw his arms in the air, pain etched deep in his eyes. "He fucking had my cousin killed! Ian is dead because of him. Did you miss Ian's throat being torn open in front of us?"

"Ryan—"

"No!" He cut me off, rage and hurt boiled under every word. "How could you, Kennedy? This isn't some guy who made fun of me in high school. He is a murderer. You are honestly all right with sleeping with someone who took my family away from me? From

Ember?" Ryan whirled around to Em. "And you are okay with this?"

"I can't say I'm happy about it." Ember took a tentative step to Ryan. "But spending time with Lorcan, I've come to understand him better. But more than anything I recognize their bond. That is a connection nobody in the world can fight. Believe me. Good or bad, he is her mate for life."

"Well, I can't." His shoulders slumped, the heartache replacing his anger. "I can't sit at a dinner or share holidays with someone who slaughtered Ian, kidnapped us, and worked with Aneira." He turned to me, tears running down his face. He didn't even bother to brush them away. Knowing Ryan, this only twisted the blade deeper in my gut. A sob broke from my soul, sorrow falling down my face.

"I understand an apology is not good enough, but I am sorry." A deep voice sounded behind me, and I twisted to see Lorcan in the doorway. "I know it probably won't mean anything to you. And I don't blame you. But I am truly sorry. I did not intend for him to be killed. And I do not want to be the reason to destroy your friendship with Kennedy."

Lorcan had said he wanted to apologize to Ryan in person. Most of me thought it was a bad idea. But if we had any hope to move forward, Lorcan needed to stand up and hold himself accountable. He did it for me. For my friendship with Ryan.

"You're right. It means nothing," Ryan spit out, rubbing the evidence of his tears from his face, fury rolling back in. "Your intent or not…Ian is still dead. We were there that night because of you. We were held

prisoners by Aneira because of you. I don't know how I can ever see past that." A hiccup of emotion turned Ryan's head away from the dweller. "I'm sorry, Kennedy. I can't." He turned for the exit, rushing out of the room.

"Ryan!" I cried, leaping after him.

"Let him go." Ember grabbed my hand. "I will talk to him later. Maybe coming from me will help." Ember embraced me, squeezing tight. "He'll come around, Ken."

I nodded, my throat clogged with agony. Ryan was my world. My heart.

She dropped back and slipped out of the room.

Lorcan's arms replaced hers, and he held me as my heart shattered into a million pieces.

~~~~~

Ember's support became my lifeline. She actually tried harder with Lorcan, teasing with him a few times when she and Eli visited the castle, or when Lorcan went to the dweller ranch. I knew she had spoken to Ryan after our fight, and since then, he had been making an obvious effort at civility. We would find our way back. Ryan was my soulmate, but it would take some time.

Now Lorcan brought his mouth to mine, claiming me hungrily, parting my mouth with his tongue. I tasted a tang on his lips.

"You went on a hunt, didn't you?" I mumbled against his mouth, my arms pulling him closer to me. At one time I would have found that gross, but nothing about Lorcan turned me off anymore. Especially when the beast came out.

"Your fault." He nipped at my bottom lip, tugging it, stirring the fire deeper in me.

"My fault?"

"You left me horny and wanting you." His fingers wrapped around my hair, tugging my head back. It was back to its natural color, but the new layers I had my stylist cut gave it more volume and shape, which he loved. He liked more to hold on to.

"Four times this morning wasn't enough?" My knees clamped at his waist, needing him closer.

"With you?" he rumbled, biting at the real tattoo inked below my ear. Raven had become a real part of me after the DLR, and I felt the need to honor her. I also, to Lorcan's delight, got my nipple pierced. Our little joke. People would have to get used to the idea their new Queen had a little punk in her. He slid his hands under my dress and hooked them around my underwear. With one yank he tore them from me. "Never."

My hands went to his pants, tearing at the buttons. Thoughts about the outside world disappeared; my one desire was Lorcan inside me.

We had only been back a month and this desk had already seen its fair share of sex. So had a few hall closets, the throne, the banquet table, along with a number of other places. But that's not surprising when you're with a dark dweller. Though I had initiated at least half those occasions. Guess that comes with being mated to a Druid.

My fingers grazed him, wrapping around. He sucked in, his mouth become more frantic, kissing me so deeply I felt like an electric wire sinking in melted chocolate. I shoved his jeans over his hips, my palms running over his pert ass, already aching for him.

"Your Majesty?" A knock thumped at my door, the voice of my assistant on the other side. "The nobles are here for your three o'clock."

"Fuck." I jumped, breaking away from Lorcan.

He snorted, cupping my face, kissing along my jaw. "Love when you talk dirty."

I had been swearing a lot lately. Stress did that to me. Hence, the abundance of late-night sex in my office and swear words. Lorcan made me very comfortable saying that word behind closed doors.

"Thank you, Olivia," I yelled back at the door. "Give me a moment." I tilted my head, hearing a noise from her.

"She's laughing, isn't she?" I sighed. Poor Olivia had actually walked in on us a few weeks ago. She didn't seem to mind as Lorcan's ass had been her primary view. Olivia was one of the few who had been taken with the dweller instead of disgusted. He could easily slide past her with a wink.

"Oh yeah." Lorcan's mouth skimmed at my throat.

"Sorry, this is extremely important. We can pick this up later." I shoved him back, shimmying off the desk, looking for my underwear. "Don't you have to meet with Lars for a job soon anyway?"

It was still a sore spot with us, but I no longer fought to change his nature. I had to love and accept him for who he was. That didn't mean I was happy with it, though when he reminded me the men of his clan were "handling" the lowest scum of the world—rapists, drug lords, murders, pedophiles—I felt a little better about it. And who was I to judge? I had killed people. Darkness swirled in me. My black magic had been quiet since I got home, but it was there and it was something I would live with and learn to control.

"Not till tonight." He tugged up his pants; a mischievous smile curled his mouth, one eyebrow crooking up as he grabbed my underwear first, shoving it into his pocket.

"No." I shook my head, brushing my dress down, trying to nudge him toward the side door.

"Stop me." He leaned over, whispering in my ear. "I want you saying words like *treaty* and *international agreements* while you're coming on my tongue."

My breath hitched, flames burning up my legs.

"Majesty?" Olivia knocked again.

"Uh." My head whipped to the door. When I looked back at Lorcan, he was gone. "Um. Yeah, let them in, Olivia."

A meeting with the nobles sans underwear. I couldn't deny the thrill of being bare beneath my short dress in a formal meeting.

The door swung open and I greeted the five nobles, shaking their hands. This was the final meeting on the Eastern European agreement. Luuk may be dead, but the ball was already rolling, encouraging more countries to revolt. Western Europe wanted to stay under our reign, but the Eastern bloc, like Hungry, the Czech Republic, and Ukraine threatened a bigger uprising under our rule. They no longer wanted two rulers who were across the world to govern them.

For the past month, Lars and I worked a deal with the nobles there. Lars and I had come to an accord. We would still be the overall leaders, but they would govern their own country. In essence, Lars and I were federal, and they were states, and we would leave them mostly to their own laws and regulations but impose important overarching decrees.

"Will the King not attend?" a noble woman from Romania asked.

"No. He apologizes for not being able to make it. Something exceedingly important came up," I lied. It *was* strange he wasn't at the meeting, and I had no idea where he was. Not like him at all. Lars was probably too busy tormenting my sister to remember to come. "But please have a seat. We should be able to get through this quickly." I motioned to the chairs around my desk, and they all obediently sat.

I turned for my seat, hesitating before grabbing my chair and settling myself down, divided between my serious mode and the spikes of lust still thrilling through me.

"Okay, let's get started on the…" Crap, I had to say it. "International agreement."

My seat yanked deeper into the desk, causing me to yelp.

"Are you all right, Majesty?"

"Fine. Thanks." I forced a smooth smile over my mouth. Hands pushed at my dress, the feel of hot breath drifting up my thigh, his tongue trailing along.

I cleared my throat, opening the folder to go over the last few documents. I could feel my legs being pushed open, his lips blowing hot air onto me. I gulped as I felt fingers slide into me. "Oh. God. So, this um…this en-tit-les… each Euuuuroppean country." His mouth joined in, his hands pushing my thighs farther apart to let him in deeper. Intense pleasure beat like a drum at the base of my spine. Sweat dampened my chest and back, my vision blurring a bit.

The five nobles stared at me like I was insane, but it was nothing new. I'd become known for getting visions and talking randomly in strange tones.

"Please. Sign." I shoved the folder at them, briefly closing my eyes. I had planned to go through each segment to reconfirm the deal. Screw that. He was not holding back, making sure I would climax in front of these people.

They all took turns signing their name to the contract.

"I-I-I…oh." I swallowed, my hands gripping the arms on my chair, not able to fight my hips from bucking against this passionate mouth. "I think that's all."

"I'm sorry?" The delegate from the Czech Republic peered at me with shock. "Weren't we going to go over the treaty again?"

"Noooooo." I shook my head frantically. His lips sucked, his tongue going in deeper as his thumb rubbed against me. I could feel my climax coming. "We've. Already... Been through it. Waste of. Time." I waved to the door. "You are excused."

With furrowed brows and insulted glances, they got up, heading out of the room. Before the door fully shut, Lorcan gently bit down, just enough to send a slice of pain and overwhelming bliss through me.

My head fell back, clutching the chair for life, a silent scream bouncing off my ribs, breath ripped from me. My frame shuddered as firecrackers danced across my vision. Then my pleasure blasted out of me, parting me from reality. I cried out. My awareness spiraled out into space.

White covered my vision, pulling me away from my body.

Flash.

A man stood before me, his back facing me. He stood on an empty street, parts of houses and buildings crumbling, as though a wrecking ball had smashed through them. A car was on fire, and debris spread out on the road.

I took a step, trying to get a better view of the man, his back bent forward, his shoulders rising and falling with every ragged breath he took.

"Hey?" I reached for him.

The man swung around, and I stumbled back.

"Lars!" But this was not the man I knew. His suit was rumpled, torn, and singed, his hair wild and streaked with red. Blood covered his face, his black eyes empty of any emotion.

My feet moved me back a few more paces. "Lars?" But I knew Lars was not there. I didn't even feel his demon inside of him, which sent terror pumping through my veins. He snarled, turning toward me. My gaze darted around. Then I saw the lumps on the ground were bodies. What had happened? Did he do this?

In the distance I noticed a girl…one I recognized. Zoey stood over a figure of a man. This was the vision of her I had before. Her face displayed the same blankness of spirit as Lars.

Wait your turn, Druid, a strange, familiar voice said into my head. *The King and the Wanderer are mine first. You and the Dae are next.*

Lars thrust out his arms, tipped his head back, and let out a deafening cry, chilling me to the core. Like an atomic blast, energy burst off him with a force I had never felt nor could fathom. It ripped through my body, igniting my vision with darkness.

Flash.

"Ken?"

I blinked. A face hovered over me. Handsome. Familiar. I twisted my head, taking in the room.

"Hey, focus on me," he said, turning my chin back to him. "This is real. You're here with me, li'l bird."

My nickname was a trigger.

Lorcan.

My office.

Vision.

I sat up; his hand stayed on my lower back, the other cupping my cheek. "Damn, I wasn't expecting to make you truly black out." He smirked. "I know I'm amazing, but…"

I tried to smile, but the images were raw in my head. Lorcan's forehead pinched, and he took my face in his hands.

"What do you hear?"

"You. Talking."

He snorted, his head bobbing. "Fair enough. What do you smell?"

"Disinfectant...and you." I leaned my head into his chest. He skated his fingers through my hair, pinching my ear.

"And what do you feel?"

My vision ran further away from me with every second, becoming more of a feeling than anything substantial. All I knew was the streets were again going to run red with blood, and I had no way of knowing what was truly coming or how to stop it from happening.

I leaned back, my gaze meeting his, my voice low and quivering.

"I feel scared."

Lightness was buckling underneath the darkness and soon both would fall.

Thank you to all my readers. Your opinion really matters to me and helps others decide if they want to purchase my book. If you enjoyed this book, please consider leaving a review on the site where you purchased it. It would mean a lot. Thank you.

Want to find out about my next series, *The Fall of the King*? Sign up for my newsletter on my website and keep updated on the latest news.

www.staceymariebrown.com

The Fall of the King
(Lightness Saga #3)
Fall 2017

Kennedy's story has ended, but like West, her journey in this tale has not. Continue on with Lars's story next, *The Fall of the King*.

There is nothing the Unseelie King can't acquire.

That is until he meets Fionna Cathbad, a fierce Druid who won't bow to anyone. Especially Lars.

The Demon King has every right to kill her. Her treasonous acts against the crown are undisputable. But she is the key to the one thing he wants more than anything: the Cauldron of Dagda. A powerful treasure that no fae, even the King, should possess.

To get what he wants, Lars discovers the very thing that forces Fionna to help him. This leads them down a treacherous path because it's not only Fionna who is deceiving him. His own mind is starting to turn on him, twisting his sanity, and releasing the demon he keeps pinned up.

As old ghosts and new foes step into this game, Lars needs to find the cauldron before all is lost, including his kingdom and himself.

Acknowledgements

With each book release, I am still floored that you all love these characters and their stories so much you won't let them end. Kennedy's story is turning out to be one of my favorites, and it only happened because of you guys. Thank you again for wanting me to bring her tale to light!

I am so lucky I get to work with the best of the best in this business!

A HUGE thanks to:

Kiki at Next Step P.R - For jumping on this crazy journey with me. Thank you for all your hard work! https://thenextsteppr.org/

Jordan - You make everything better. Even me. Thank you. http://jordanrosenfeld.net/

Hollie "the editor" - Don't ever, ever leave me. I will wander the streets in my slippers, mumbling your name. Love you lady! http://www.hollietheeditor.com/.

Dane at Ebook Launch! - Thank you for doing your thing and designing such beautiful covers. https://ebooklaunch.com/ebook-cover-design/

To Judi at http://www.formatting4u.com/ - You always have my back.

As always Mom, for being the best employee, sounding board, and mom.

To all the readers who have supported me - My gratitude is for all you do and how much you help indie authors out of the pure love of reading.

To all the indie/hybrid authors out there who inspire, challenge, support, and push me to be better. I love you!

And to anyone who has picked up an indie book and given an unknown author a chance. THANK YOU!

About The Author

Stacey Marie Brown is a lover of hot fictional bad boys and sarcastic heroines who kick butt. She also enjoys books, travel, TV shows, hiking, writing, design, and archery. Stacey swears she is part gypsy, being lucky enough to live and travel all over the world.

She grew up in Northern California, where she ran around on her family's farm, raising animals, riding horses, playing flashlight tag, and turning hay bales into cool forts.

When she's not writing she's out hiking, spending time with friends, and traveling. She also volunteers helping animals and is eco-friendly. She feels all animals, people, and environment should be treated kindly.

To learn more about Stacey or her books, visit her at:

Author website
www.staceymariebrown.com

Facebook Author page
https://www.facebook.com/staceymarie.brown.5

Pinterest
www.pinterest.com/s.mariebrown

Twitter @S_MarieBrown

Instagram Instagram.com/staceymariebrown

Crown of Light

CPSIA information can be obtained
at www.ICGtesting.com
Printed in the USA
LVHW080353210322
713971LV00022B/710

9 781546 972495